STORIES OF THE
DREAMLANDS

STORIES OF THE
DREAMLANDS

H. P. LOVECRAFT

This edition published in 2022 by Arcturus Publishing Limited
26/27 Bickels Yard, 151–153 Bermondsey Street,
London SE1 3HA

Cover design: Peter Ridley
Cover illustration: Peter Gray

AD005728US

Printed in the UK

Contents

Contents

Introduction

Howard Philips Lovecraft was the pioneer of modern horror fiction. Born in Rhode Island in 1890, his childhood was a troubling one. When he was just three years old, his father was placed in the psychiatric department at Butler Hospital. As a child, Howard was often ill and did not attend school regularly until he was eight years old. But this did not prevent Lovecraft from developing a voracious reading habit.

The death of his grandfather in 1904 profoundly affected Lovecraft. His family fell into poverty, and four years later he suffered a nervous breakdown that prevented him from obtaining his high school diploma. As a young adult, Lovecraft took on an isolated existence, living with his mother and turning his attention to writing. In 1916, he published his first story, "The Alchemist" in the *United Amateur Press Association*, but this brought him no income. He had to wait until 1922 before he received commercial remuneration for his work. For the next decade, he wrote prolifically. Despite his admiration for Edgar Allan Poe, Lovecraft broke away from earlier traditions of Gothic horror to create something entirely new – the primal gods and the eldritch powers of the mythology of Cthulhu.

During his own lifetime, Lovecraft was virtually unknown, forced to publish his stories in the humble pulp magazines of the era, such as *Weird Tales*. He lived in poverty and his imaginative genius would only be recognized by a later generation.

The *Dream Cycle* is a series of stories and novellas written between 1918 and 1932 and set in the "Dreamlands", an alternate dimension that could be entered through dreams. In this realm, Lovecraft's imagination was given full reign as he created an entire world full of wonder and terror. A group of "weak gods" stalk the Dreamlands, protected by the mysterious Nyarlathotep, as Lovecraft's protagonists navigate the alien landscape.

Lovecraft's influence on the horror genre has been immense. His writing made possible the careers of writers such as Stephen King, Clive Barker, Neil Gaiman and China Miéville. The Cthulhu Mythos he began was continued by a series of writers and several of his stories have been adapted into films, radio productions and videogames.

POLARIS

I nto the north window of my chamber glows the Pole Star with uncanny light. All through the long hellish hours of blackness it shines there. And in the autumn of the year, when the winds from the north curse and whine, and the red-leaved trees of the swamp mutter things to one another in the small hours of the morning under the horned waning moon, I sit by the casement and watch that star. Down from the heights reels the glittering Cassiopeia as the hours wear on, while Charles' Wain lumbers up from behind the vapor-soaked swamp trees that sway in the night-wind. Just before dawn Arcturus winks ruddily from above the cemetery on the low hillock, and Coma Berenices shimmers weirdly afar off in the mysterious east; but still the Pole Star leers down from the same place in the black vault, winking hideously like an insane watching eye which strives to convey some strange message, yet recalls nothing save that it once had a message to convey. Sometimes, when it is cloudy, I can sleep.

Well do I remember the night of the great Aurora, when over the swamp played the shocking coruscations of the daemon-light. After the beams came clouds, and then I slept.

And it was under a horned waning moon that I saw the city for the first time. Still and somnolent did it lie, on a strange plateau in a hollow betwixt strange peaks. Of ghastly marble were its walls and its towers, its columns, domes, and pavements. In the marble streets were marble pillars, the upper parts of which were carven into the images of grave bearded men. The air was warm and stirred not. And overhead, scarce ten degrees from the zenith, glowed that watching Pole Star. Long did I gaze on the city, but the day came not. When the red Aldebaran, which blinked low in the sky but never set, had crawled a quarter of the way around the horizon, I saw light and motion in the houses and the streets. Forms strangely robed, but at once noble and familiar, walked abroad, and under the horned waning moon men talked wisdom in a tongue which I understood, though it was unlike any language I had ever known. And when the red Aldebaran had crawled more than half way around the horizon, there were again darkness and silence.

When I awaked, I was not as I had been. Upon my memory was graven the vision of the city, and within my soul had arisen another and vaguer recollection, of whose nature I was not then certain. Thereafter, on the cloudy nights when I could sleep, I saw the city often; sometimes under that horned waning moon, and sometimes under the hot yellow rays of a sun which did not set, but which wheeled low around the horizon. And on the clear nights the Pole Star leered as never before.

Gradually I came to wonder what might be my place in that city on the strange plateau betwixt strange peaks. At first content to view the scene as an all-observant uncorporeal presence, I now desired to define my relation to it, and to speak my mind amongst the grave men who conversed each day in the public squares. I said to myself, "This is no dream, for by what means can I prove the greater reality of that other life in the house of stone and brick south of the sinister swamp and the cemetery on the low hillock, where the Pole Star peers into my north window each night?"

One night as I listened to the discourse in the large square containing many statues, I felt a change; and perceived that I had at last a bodily form. Nor was I a stranger in the streets of Olathoë, which lies on the plateau of Sarkis, betwixt the peaks Noton and Kadiphonek. It was my friend Alos who spoke, and his speech was one that pleased my soul, for it was the speech of a true man and patriot. That night had the news come of Daikos' fall, and of the advance of the Inutos; squat, hellish, yellow fiends who five years ago had appeared out of the unknown west to ravage the confines of our kingdom, and finally to besiege our towns. Having taken the fortified places at the foot of the mountains, their way now lay open to the plateau, unless every citizen could resist with the strength of ten men. For the squat creatures were mighty in the arts of war, and knew not the scruples of honor which held back our tall, gray-eyed men of Lomar from ruthless conquest.

Alos, my friend, was commander of all the forces on the plateau, and in him lay the last hope of our country. On this occasion he spoke of the perils to be faced, and exhorted the men of Olathoë, bravest of the Lomarians, to sustain the traditions of their ancestors, who when forced to move southward from Zobna before the advance of the great ice-sheet (even as our descendants must some day flee from the land of Lomar), valiantly and victoriously swept aside the hairy, long-armed, cannibal Gnophkehs that stood in their way. To me Alos denied a warrior's part, for I was feeble and given to strange faintings when subjected to stress and hardships. But my eyes were the keenest in the city, despite the long hours I gave each day to the study of the Pnakotic manuscripts and the wisdom of the Zobnarian Fathers; so my friend, desiring not to doom me to inaction, rewarded me with that duty which was second to nothing in importance. To the watch-tower of Thapnen he sent me, there to serve as the eyes of our army. Should the Inutos attempt to gain the citadel by the narrow pass behind the peak Noton, and thereby surprise the garrison, I was to give the signal of fire which would warn the waiting soldiers and save the town from immediate disaster.

Alone I mounted the tower, for every man of stout body was needed in the passes below. My brain was sore dazed with excitement and fatigue, for I had not slept in many days; yet was my purpose firm, for I loved my native land of Lomar, and the marble city of Olathoë that lies betwixt the peaks of Noton and Kadiphonek.

But as I stood in the tower's topmost chamber, I beheld the horned waning moon, red and sinister, quivering through the vapors that hovered over the distant valley of Banof. And through an opening in the roof glittered the pale Pole Star, fluttering as if alive, and leering like a fiend and tempter. Methought its spirit whispered

evil counsel, soothing me to traitorous somnolence with a damnable
rhythmical promise which it repeated over and over:

> Slumber, watcher, till the spheres
> Six and twenty thousand years
> Have revolv'd, and I return
> To the spot where now I burn.
> Other stars anon shall rise
> To the axis of the skies;
> Stars that soothe and stars that bless
> With a sweet forgetfulness:
> Only when my round is o'er
> Shall the past disturb thy door.

Vainly did I struggle with my drowsiness, seeking to connect these
strange words with some lore of the skies which I had learnt from
the Pnakotic manuscripts. My head, heavy and reeling, drooped
to my breast, and when next I looked up it was in a dream; with
the Pole Star grinning at me through a window from over the
horrible swaying trees of a dream-swamp. And I am still dreaming.

In my shame and despair I sometimes scream frantically,
begging the dream-creatures around me to waken me ere the
Inutos steal up the pass behind the peak Noton and take the
citadel by surprise; but these creatures are daemons, for they
laugh at me and tell me I am not dreaming. They mock me
whilst I sleep, and whilst the squat yellow foe may be creeping
silently upon us. I have failed in my duty and betrayed the
marble city of Olathoë; I have proven false to Alos, my friend
and commander. But still these shadows of my dream deride
me. They say there is no land of Lomar, save in my nocturnal
imaginings; that in those realms where the Pole Star shines high
and red Aldebaran crawls low around the horizon, there has
been naught save ice and snow for thousands of years, and
never a man save squat yellow creatures, blighted by the cold,
whom they call "Esquimaux."

And as I writhe in my guilty agony, frantic to save the city whose peril every moment grows, and vainly striving to shake off this unnatural dream of a house of stone and brick south of a sinister swamp and a cemetery on a low hillock; the Pole Star, evil and monstrous, leers down from the black vault, winking hideously like an insane watching eye which strives to convey some strange message, yet recalls nothing save that it once had a message to convey.

BEYOND THE WALL OF SLEEP

I have an exposition of sleep come upon me.
—Shakespeare

I have frequently wondered if the majority of mankind ever pause to reflect upon the occasionally titanic significance of dreams, and of the obscure world to which they belong. Whilst the greater number of our nocturnal visions are perhaps no more than faint and fantastic reflections of our waking experiences—Freud to the contrary with his puerile symbolism—there are still a certain remainder whose immundane and ethereal character permits of no ordinary interpretation, and whose vaguely exciting and disquieting effect suggests possible minute glimpses into a sphere of mental existence no less important than physical life, yet separated from that life by an all but impassable barrier. From my experience I cannot doubt but that man, when lost to terrestrial consciousness, is indeed sojourning in another and uncorporeal life of far different nature from the life we know; and of which only the slightest and most indistinct memories linger after waking. From those blurred and fragmentary memories we may infer much, yet prove little. We may guess that in dreams life, matter, and vitality, as the earth knows such things, are not necessarily constant; and that time and space do not exist as our waking selves comprehend them. Sometimes I believe that this less material life is our truer life, and that our vain presence on the terraqueous globe is itself the secondary or merely virtual phenomenon.

It was from a youthful reverie filled with speculations of this sort that I arose one afternoon in the winter of 1900-1901, when to the state psychopathic institution in which I served as an intern was brought the man whose case has ever since haunted me so unceasingly. His name, as given on the records, was Joe

Slater, or Slaader, and his appearance was that of the typical denizen of the Catskill Mountain region; one of those strange, repellent scions of a primitive colonial peasant stock whose isolation for nearly three centuries in the hilly fastnesses of a little-traveled countryside has caused them to sink to a kind of barbaric degeneracy, rather than advance with their more fortunately placed brethren of the thickly settled districts. Among these odd folk, who correspond exactly to the decadent element of "white trash" in the South, law and morals are non-existent; and their general mental status is probably below that of any other section of the native American people.

Joe Slater, who came to the institution in the vigilant custody of four state policemen, and who was described as a highly dangerous character, certainly presented no evidence of his perilous disposition when first I beheld him. Though well above the middle stature, and of somewhat brawny frame, he was given an absurd appearance of harmless stupidity by the pale, sleepy blueness of his small watery eyes, the scantiness of his neglected and never-shaven growth of yellow beard, and the listless drooping of his heavy nether lip. His age was unknown, since among his kind neither family records nor permanent family ties exist; but from the baldness of his head in front, and from the decayed condition of his teeth, the head surgeon wrote him down as a man of about forty.

From the medical and court documents we learned all that could be gathered of his case. This man, a vagabond, hunter, and trapper, had always been strange in the eyes of his primitive associates. He had habitually slept at night beyond the ordinary time, and upon waking would often talk of unknown things in a manner so bizarre as to inspire fear even in the hearts of an unimaginative populace. Not that his form of language was at all unusual, for he never spoke save in the debased patois of his environment; but the tone and tenor of his utterances were of such mysterious wildness, that none might listen without apprehension. He himself was generally as terrified and baffled as his auditors, and within an hour after awakening would forget all that he had said, or at least all that had caused him to say what he did; relapsing into a bovine, half-amiable normality like that of the other hill-dwellers.

As Slater grew older, it appeared, his matutinal aberrations had gradually increased in frequency and violence; till about a month before his arrival at the institution had occurred the shocking tragedy which caused his arrest by the authorities. One day near noon, after a profound sleep begun in a whiskey debauch at about five of the previous afternoon, the man had roused himself most suddenly; with ululations so horrible and unearthly that they brought several neighbors to his cabin—a filthy sty where he dwelt with a family as indescribable as himself. Rushing out into the snow, he had flung his arms aloft and commenced a series of leaps directly upward in the air; the while shouting his determination to reach some "big, big cabin with brightness in the roof and walls and floor, and the loud queer music far away." As two men of moderate size sought to restrain him, he had struggled with maniacal force and fury, screaming of his desire and need to find and kill a certain "thing that shines and shakes and laughs." At length, after temporarily felling one of his detainers with a sudden blow, he had flung himself upon the other in a daemoniac ecstasy of bloodthirstiness, shrieking fiendishly that he would "jump high in the air and burn his way through anything that stopped him." Family and neighbors had now fled in a panic, and when the more courageous of them returned, Slater was gone, leaving behind an unrecognizable pulp-like thing that had been a living man but an hour before. None of the mountaineers had dared to pursue him, and it is likely that they would have welcomed his death from the cold; but when several mornings later they heard his screams from a distant ravine, they realized that he had somehow managed to survive, and that his removal in one way or another would be necessary. Then had followed an armed searching party, whose purpose (whatever it may have been originally) became that of a sheriff's posse after one of the seldom popular state troopers had by accident observed, then questioned, and finally joined the seekers.

On the third day Slater was found unconscious in the hollow of a tree, and taken to the nearest jail; where alienists from Albany examined him as soon as his senses returned. To them he told a simple story. He had, he said, gone to sleep one afternoon about sundown after drinking much liquor. He had awaked to find himself standing bloody-handed in the snow before his cabin, the mangled corpse of his neighbor Peter Slader at his feet. Horrified, he had taken to the woods in a vague effort to escape from the scene of what must have been his crime. Beyond these things he seemed to know nothing, nor could the expert questioning of his interrogators bring out a single additional fact. That night Slater slept quietly, and the next morning he wakened with no singular feature save a certain alteration of expression. Dr. Barnard, who had been watching the patient, thought he noticed in the pale blue eyes a certain gleam of peculiar quality; and in the flaccid lips an all but imperceptible tightening, as if of intelligent determination. But when questioned, Slater relapsed into the habitual vacancy of the mountaineer, and only reiterated what he had said on the preceding day.

On the third morning occurred the first of the man's mental attacks. After some show of uneasiness in sleep, he burst forth into a frenzy so powerful that the combined efforts of four men were needed to bind him in a strait-jacket. The alienists listened with keen attention to his words, since their curiosity had been aroused to a high pitch by the suggestive yet mostly conflicting and incoherent stories of his family and neighbors. Slater raved for upward of fifteen minutes, babbling in his backwoods dialect of great edifices of light, oceans of space, strange music, and shadowy mountains and valleys. But most of all did he dwell upon some mysterious blazing entity that shook and laughed and mocked at him. This vast, vague personality seemed to have done him a terrible wrong, and to kill it in triumphant revenge was his paramount desire. In order to reach it, he said, he would soar through abysses of emptiness, *burning* every obstacle that stood in his way. Thus ran his discourse, until with the greatest suddenness he ceased. The fire of madness died from his eyes, and in dull wonder he looked at his questioners and asked why he was bound. Dr. Barnard unbuckled the leathern harness and did not restore it till night, when he succeeded in persuading Slater to don it of his own volition, for his own good. The man had now admitted that he sometimes talked queerly, though he knew not why.

Within a week two more attacks appeared, but from them the doctors learned little. On the *source* of Slater's visions they speculated at length, for since he could neither read nor write, and had apparently never heard a legend or fairy tale, his gorgeous imagery was quite inexplicable. That it could not come from any known myth or romance was made especially clear by the fact that the unfortunate lunatic expressed himself only in his own simple manner. He raved of things he did not understand and could not interpret; things which he claimed to have experienced, but which he could not have learned through any normal or connected narration. The alienists soon agreed that abnormal dreams were the foundation of the trouble; dreams whose vividness could for a time completely dominate the waking mind of this basically inferior man. With due formality Slater was tried for murder, acquitted on the ground of insanity, and committed to the institution wherein I held so humble a post.

I have said that I am a constant speculator concerning dream life, and from this you may judge of the eagerness with which I applied myself to the study of the new patient as soon as I had fully ascertained the facts of his case. He seemed to sense a certain friendliness in me; born no doubt of the interest I could not conceal, and the gentle manner in which I questioned him. Not that he ever recognized me during his attacks, when I hung breathlessly upon his chaotic but cosmic word-pictures; but he knew me in his quiet hours, when he would sit by his barred window weaving baskets of straw and willow, and perhaps pining for the mountain freedom he could never enjoy again. His family never called to see him; probably it had found another temporary head, after the manner of decadent mountain folk.

By degrees I commenced to feel an overwhelming wonder at the mad and fantastic conceptions of Joe Slater. The man himself was pitiably inferior in mentality and language alike; but his glowing, titanic visions, though described in a barbarous and disjointed jargon, were assuredly things which only a superior or even exceptional brain could conceive. How, I often asked myself, could the stolid imagination of a Catskill degenerate conjure up sights whose very possession argued a lurking spark of genius? How could any backwoods dullard have gained so much as an idea of those glittering realms of supernal radiance and space about which Slater ranted in his furious delirium? More and more I inclined to the belief that in the pitiful personality who cringed before me lay the disordered nucleus of something beyond my comprehension; something infinitely beyond the comprehension of my more experienced but less imaginative medical and scientific colleagues.

And yet I could extract nothing definite from the man. The sum of all my investigation was, that in a kind of semi-uncorporeal dream life Slater wandered or floated through resplendent and prodigious valleys, meadows, gardens, cities, and palaces of light; in a region unbounded and unknown to man. That there he was no peasant or degenerate, but a creature of importance and vivid life; moving proudly and dominantly, and checked only by a certain deadly enemy, who seemed to be a being of visible yet ethereal structure, and who did not appear to be of human shape, since Slater never referred to it as a *man,* or as aught save a *thing.* This *thing* had done Slater some hideous but unnamed wrong, which the maniac (if maniac he were) yearned to avenge. From the manner in which Slater alluded to their dealings, I judged that he and the luminous *thing* had met on equal terms; that in his dream existence the man was himself a luminous *thing* of the same race as his enemy. This impression was sustained by his frequent references to *flying through space* and *burning* all that impeded his progress. Yet these conceptions were formulated in rustic words wholly inadequate to convey them, a circumstance which drove me to the conclusion that if a true dream-world indeed existed, oral language was not its medium for the transmission of thought. Could it be that the dream-soul inhabiting this inferior body was desperately struggling to speak things which the simple and halting tongue of dulness could not utter? Could it be that I was face to face with intellectual emanations which would explain the mystery if I could but learn to discover and read them? I did not tell the older physicians of these things, for middle age is skeptical, cynical, and disinclined to accept new ideas. Besides, the head of the institution had but lately warned me in his paternal way that I was overworking; that my mind needed a rest.

It had long been my belief that human thought consists basically of atomic or molecular motion, convertible into ether waves of radiant energy like heat, light, and electricity. This belief had early led me to contemplate the possibility of telepathy or mental communication by means of suitable apparatus, and I had in my college days prepared a set of transmitting and receiving instruments somewhat similar to the cumbrous devices employed in wireless telegraphy at that crude, pre-radio period. These I had tested with a fellow-student; but achieving no result, had soon packed them away with other scientific odds and ends for possible future use. Now, in my intense desire to probe into the dream life of Joe Slater, I sought these instruments again; and spent several days in repairing them for action. When they were complete once more I missed no opportunity for their trial. At each outburst of Slater's violence, I would fit the transmitter to his forehead and the receiver to my own; constantly making delicate adjustments for various hypothetical wave-lengths of intellectual energy. I had but little notion of how the thought-impressions would, if successfully conveyed, arouse an intelligent response in my brain; but I felt certain that I could detect and interpret them. Accordingly I continued my experiments, though informing no one of their nature.

It was on the twenty-first of February, 1901, that the thing finally occurred. As I look back across the years I realize how unreal it seems; and sometimes half wonder if old Dr. Fenton was not right when he charged it all to my excited imagination. I recall that he listened with great kindness and patience when I told him, but afterward gave me a nerve-powder and arranged for the half-year's vacation on which I departed the next week. That fateful night I was wildly agitated and perturbed, for despite the excellent care he had received, Joe Slater was unmistakably dying. Perhaps it was his mountain freedom that he missed, or perhaps the turmoil in his brain had grown too acute for his rather sluggish physique; but at all events the flame of vitality flickered low in the decadent body. He was drowsy near the end, and as darkness fell he dropped off into a troubled sleep. I did not strap on the strait-jacket as was customary when he slept, since I saw that he was too feeble to be dangerous, even if he woke in mental disorder once more before passing away. But I did place upon his head and mine the two ends of my cosmic "radio"; hoping against hope for a first and last message from the dreamworld in the brief time remaining. In the cell with us was one nurse, a mediocre fellow who did not understand the purpose of the apparatus, or think to inquire into my course. As the hours wore on I saw his head droop awkwardly in sleep, but I did not disturb him. I myself, lulled by the rhythmical breathing of the healthy and the dying man, must have nodded a little later.

The sound of weird lyric melody was what aroused me. Chords, vibrations, and harmonic ecstasies echoed passionately on every hand; while on my ravished sight burst the stupendous spectacle of ultimate beauty. Walls, columns, and architraves of living fire blazed effulgently around the spot where I seemed to float in air; extending upward to an infinitely high vaulted dome of indescribable splendor. Blending with this display of palatial magnificence, or rather, supplanting it at times in kaleidoscopic rotation, were glimpses of wide plains and graceful valleys, high mountains and inviting grottoes; covered with every lovely attribute of scenery which my delighted eye could conceive of, yet formed wholly of some glowing, ethereal, plastic entity, which in consistency partook as much of spirit as of matter. As I gazed, I perceived that my own brain held the key to these enchanting metamorphoses; for each vista which appeared to me, was the one my changing mind most wished to behold. Amidst this Elysian realm I dwelt not as a stranger, for each sight and sound was familiar to me; just as it had been for uncounted eons of eternity before, and would be for like eternities to come.

Then the resplendent aura of my brother of light drew near and held colloquy with me, soul to soul, with silent and perfect interchange of thought. The hour was one of approaching triumph, for was not my fellow-being escaping at last from a degrading periodic bondage; escaping forever, and preparing to follow the accursed oppressor even unto the uttermost fields of ether, that upon it might be wrought a flaming cosmic vengeance which would shake the spheres? We floated thus for a little time, when I perceived a slight blurring and fading of the objects around us, as though some force were recalling me to earth—where I least wished to go. The form near me seemed to feel a change also, for it gradually brought its discourse toward a conclusion, and itself prepared to quit the scene; fading from my sight at a rate somewhat less rapid than that of the other objects. A few more thoughts were exchanged, and I knew that the luminous one and I were being recalled to bondage, though for my brother of light it would be the last time. The sorry planet-shell being well-nigh spent, in less than an hour my fellow would be free to pursue the oppressor along the Milky Way and past the hither stars to the very confines of infinity.

A well-defined shock separates my final impression of the fading scene of light from my sudden and somewhat shamefaced awakening and straightening up in my chair as I saw the dying figure on the couch move hesitantly. Joe Slater was indeed awaking, though probably for the last time. As I looked more closely, I saw that in the sallow cheeks shone spots of color which had never before been present. The lips, too, seemed unusual; being tightly compressed, as if by the force of a stronger character than had been Slater's. The whole face finally began to grow tense, and the head turned restlessly with closed eyes. I did not arouse the sleeping nurse, but readjusted the slightly disarranged head-bands of my telepathic "radio," intent to catch any parting message the dreamer might have to deliver. All at once the head turned sharply in my direction and the eyes fell open, causing me to stare in blank amazement at what I beheld. The man who had been Joe Slater, the Catskill decadent, was now gazing at me with a pair of luminous, expanded eyes whose blue seemed subtly to have deepened. Neither mania nor degeneracy was visible in that gaze, and I felt beyond a doubt that I was viewing a face behind which lay an active mind of high order.

At this juncture my brain became aware of a steady external influence operating upon it. I closed my eyes to concentrate my thoughts more profoundly, and was rewarded by the positive knowledge that *my long-sought mental message had come at last.* Each transmitted idea formed rapidly in my mind, and though no actual language was employed, my habitual association of conception and expression was so great that I seemed to be receiving the message in ordinary English.

"Joe Slater is dead," came the soul-petrifying voice or agency from beyond the wall of sleep. My opened eyes sought the couch of pain in curious horror, but the blue eyes were still calmly gazing, and the countenance was still intelligently animated. "He is better dead, for he was unfit to bear the active intellect of cosmic entity. His gross body could not undergo the needed adjustments between ethereal life and planet life. He was too much of an animal, too little a man; yet it is through his deficiency that you have come to discover me, for the cosmic and planet

souls rightly should never meet. He has been my torment and diurnal prison for forty-two of your terrestrial years. I am an entity like that which you yourself become in the freedom of dreamless sleep. I am your brother of light, and have floated with you in the effulgent valleys. It is not permitted me to tell your waking earth-self of your real self, but we are all roamers of vast spaces and travelers in many ages. Next year I may be dwelling in the dark Egypt which you call ancient, or in the cruel empire of Tsan-Chan which is to come three thousand years hence. You and I have drifted to the worlds that reel about the red Arcturus, and dwelt in the bodies of the insect-philosophers that crawl proudly over the fourth moon of Jupiter. How little does the earth-self know of life and its extent! How little, indeed, ought it to know for its own tranquility! Of the oppressor I cannot speak. You on earth have unwittingly felt its distant presence— you who without knowing idly gave to its blinking beacon the name of *Algol, the Daemon-Star.* It is to meet and conquer the oppressor that I have vainly striven for eons, held back by bodily encumbrances. Tonight I go as a Nemesis bearing just and blazingly cataclysmic vengeance. *Watch me in the sky close by the Daemon-Star.* I cannot speak longer, for the body of Joe Slater grows cold and rigid, and the coarse brains are ceasing to vibrate as I wish. You have been my friend in the cosmos; you have been my only friend on this planet—the only soul to sense and seek for me within the repellent form which lies on this couch. We shall meet again—perhaps in the shining mists of Orion's Sword, perhaps on a bleak plateau in prehistoric Asia. Perhaps in unremembered dreams tonight; perhaps in some other form an eon hence, when the solar system shall have been swept away."

At this point the thought-waves abruptly ceased, and the pale eyes of the dreamer—or can I say dead man?—commenced to glaze fishily. In a half-stupor I crossed over to the couch and felt of his wrist, but found it cold, stiff, and pulseless. The sallow cheeks paled again, and the thick lips fell open, disclosing the repulsively rotten fangs of the degenerate Joe Slater. I shivered, pulled a blanket over the hideous face, and awakened the nurse. Then I left the cell and went silently to my room. I had an insistent and unaccountable craving for a sleep whose dreams I should not remember.

The climax? What plain tale of science can boast of such a rhetorical effect? I have merely set down certain things appealing to me as facts, allowing you to construe them as you will. As I have already admitted, my superior, old Dr. Fenton, denies the reality of everything I have related. He vows that I was broken down with nervous strain, and badly in need of the long vacation on full pay which he so generously gave me. He assures me on his professional honor that Joe Slater was but a low-grade paranoiac, whose fantastic notions must have come from the crude hereditary folk-tales which circulate in even the most decadent of communities. All this he tells me—yet I cannot forget what I saw in the sky on the night after Slater died. Lest you think me a biassed witness, another's pen must add this final testimony, which may perhaps supply the climax you expect. I will quote the following account of the star *Nova Persei* verbatim from the pages of that eminent astronomical authority, Prof. Garrett P. Serviss:

> On February 22, 1901, a marvelous new star was discovered by Dr. Anderson, of Edinburgh, *not very far from Algol.* No star had been visible at that point before. Within twenty-four hours the stranger had become so bright that it outshone Capella. In a week or two it had visibly faded, and in the course of a few months it was hardly discernible with the naked eye.

THE WHITE SHIP

I am Basil Elton, keeper of the North Point light that my father and grandfather kept before me. Far from the shore stands the gray lighthouse, above sunken slimy rocks that are seen when the tide is low, but unseen when the tide is high. Past that beacon for a century have swept the majestic barques of the seven seas. In the days of my grandfather there were many; in the days of my father not so many; and now there are so few that I sometimes feel strangely alone, as though I were the last man on our planet.

From far shores came those white-sailed argosies of old; from far Eastern shores where warm suns shine and sweet odors linger about strange gardens and gay temples. The old captains of the sea came often to my grandfather and told him of these things, which in turn he told to my father, and my father told to me in the long autumn evenings when the wind howled eerily from the East. And I have read more of these things, and of many things besides, in the books men gave me when I was young and filled with wonder.

But more wonderful than the lore of old men and the lore of books is the secret lore of ocean. Blue, green, gray, white, or black; smooth, ruffled, or mountainous; that ocean is not silent. All my days have I watched it and listened to it, and I know it well. At first it told to me only the plain little tales of calm beaches and near ports, but with the years it grew more friendly and spoke of other things; of things more strange and more distant in space and in time. Sometimes at twilight the gray vapors of the horizon have parted to grant me glimpses of the ways beyond; and sometimes at night the deep waters of the sea have grown clear and phosphorescent, to grant me glimpses of the ways beneath. And these glimpses have been as often of the ways that were and the ways that might be, as of the ways that are; for

ocean is more ancient than the mountains, and freighted with
the memories and the dreams of Time.

Out of the South it was that the White Ship used to come
when the moon was full and high in the heavens. Out of the
South it would glide very smoothly and silently over the sea. And
whether the sea was rough or calm, and whether the wind was
friendly or adverse, it would always glide smoothly and silently,
its sails distant and its long strange tiers of oars moving rhythmically. One night I espied upon the deck a man, bearded and
robed, and he seemed to beckon me to embark for fair unknown
shores. Many times afterward I saw him under the full moon,
and ever did he beckon me.

Very brightly did the moon shine on the night I answered
the call, and I walked out over the waters to the White Ship on
a bridge of moonbeams. The man who had beckoned now spoke
a welcome to me in a soft language I seemed to know well, and
the hours were filled with soft songs of the oarsmen as we glided
away into a mysterious South, golden with the glow of that full,
mellow moon.

And when the day dawned, rosy and effulgent, I beheld the
green shore of far lands, bright and beautiful, and to me unknown.
Up from the sea rose lordly terraces of verdure, tree-studded, and
shewing here and there the gleaming white roofs and colonnades
of strange temples. As we drew nearer the green shore the bearded
man told me of that land, the Land of Zar, where dwell all the
dreams and thoughts of beauty that come to men once and then
are forgotten. And when I looked upon the terraces again I saw
that what he said was true, for among the sights before me were
many things I had once seen through the mists beyond the horizon
and in the phosphorescent depths of ocean. There too were forms
and fantasies more splendid than any I had ever known; the visions
of young poets who died in want before the world could learn
of what they had seen and dreamed. But we did not set foot upon
the sloping meadows of Zar, for it is told that he who treads them
may nevermore return to his native shore.

As the White Ship sailed silently away from the templed terraces of Zar, we beheld on the distant horizon ahead the spires of a mighty city; and the bearded man said to me: "This is Thalarion, the City of a Thousand Wonders, wherein reside all those mysteries that man has striven in vain to fathom." And I looked again, at closer range, and saw that the city was greater than any city I had known or dreamed of before. Into the sky the spires of its temples reached, so that no man might behold their peaks; and far back beyond the horizon stretched the grim, gray walls, over which one might spy only a few roofs, weird and ominous, yet adorned with rich friezes and alluring sculptures. I yearned mightily to enter this fascinating yet repellent city, and besought the bearded man to land me at the stone pier by the huge carven gate Akariel; but he gently denied my wish, saying: "Into Thalarion, the City of a Thousand Wonders, many have passed but none returned. Therein walk only daemons and mad things that are no longer men, and the streets are white with the unburied bones of those who have looked upon the eidolon Lathi, that reigns over the city." So the White Ship sailed on past the walls of Thalarion, and followed for many days a southward-flying bird, whose glossy plumage matched the sky out of which it had appeared.

Then came we to a pleasant coast gay with blossoms of every hue, where as far inland as we could see basked lovely groves and radiant arbors beneath a meridian sun. From bowers beyond our view came bursts of song and snatches of lyric harmony, interspersed with faint laughter so delicious that I urged the rowers onward in my eagerness to reach the scene. And the bearded man spoke no word, but watched me as we approached the lily-lined shore. Suddenly a wind blowing from over the flowery meadows and leafy woods brought a scent at which I trembled. The wind grew stronger, and the air was filled with the lethal, charnel odor of plague-stricken towns and uncovered cemeteries. And as we sailed madly away from that damnable coast the bearded man spoke at last, saying: "This is Xura, the Land of Pleasures Unattained."

So once more the White Ship followed the bird of heaven, over warm blessed seas fanned by caressing, aromatic breezes. Day after day and night after night did we sail, and when the moon was full we would listen to soft songs of the oarsmen, sweet as on that distant night when we sailed away from my far native land. And it was by moonlight that we anchored at last in the harbor of Sona-Nyl, which is guarded by twin headlands of crystal that rise from the sea and meet in a resplendent arch. This is the Land of Fancy, and we walked to the verdant shore upon a golden bridge of moonbeams.

In the Land of Sona-Nyl there is neither time nor space, neither suffering nor death; and there I dwelt for many eons. Green are the groves and pastures, bright and fragrant the flowers, blue and musical the streams, clear and cool the fountains, and stately and gorgeous the temples, castles, and cities of Sona-Nyl. Of that land there is no bound, for beyond each vista of beauty rises another more beautiful. Over the countryside and amidst the splendor of cities rove at will the happy folk, of whom all are gifted with unmarred grace and unalloyed happiness. For the eons that I dwelt there I wandered blissfully through gardens where quaint pagodas peep from pleasing clumps of bushes, and where the white walks are bordered with delicate blossoms. I climbed gentle hills from whose summits I could see entrancing panoramas of loveliness, with steepled towns nestling in verdant valleys, and with the golden domes of gigantic cities glittering on the infinitely distant horizon. And I viewed by moonlight the sparkling sea, the crystal headlands, and the placid harbor wherein lay anchored the White Ship.

It was against the full moon one night in the immemorial year of Tharp that I saw outlined the beckoning form of the celestial bird, and felt the first stirrings of unrest. Then I spoke with the bearded man, and told him of my new yearnings to depart for remote Cathuria, which no man hath seen, but which all believe to lie beyond the basalt pillars of the West. It is the Land of Hope, and in it shine the perfect ideals of all that we know elsewhere; or at least so men relate. But the bearded man said to me: "Beware of those perilous seas wherein men say Cathuria lies. In Sona-Nyl there is no pain nor death, but who can tell what lies beyond the basalt pillars of the West?" Nonetheless at the next full moon I boarded the White Ship, and with the reluctant bearded man left the happy harbor for untraveled seas.

And the bird of heaven flew before, and led us toward the basalt pillars of the West, but this time the oarsmen sang no soft songs under the full moon. In my mind I would often picture the unknown Land of Cathuria with its splendid groves and palaces, and would wonder what new delights there awaited me. "Cathuria," I would say to myself, "is the abode of gods and the land of unnumbered cities of gold. Its forests are of aloe and sandalwood, even as the fragrant groves of Camorin, and among the trees flutter gay birds sweet with song. On the green and flowery mountains of Cathuria stand temples of pink marble, rich with carven and painted glories, and having in their court-yards cool fountains of silver, where purl with ravishing music the scented waters that come from the grotto-born river Narg. And the cities of Cathuria are cinctured with golden walls, and their pavements also are of gold. In the gardens of these cities are strange orchids, and perfumed lakes whose beds are of coral and amber. At night the streets and the gardens are lit with gay lanthorns fashioned from the three-colored shell of the tortoise, and here resound the soft notes of the singer and the lutanist. And the houses of the cities of Cathuria are all palaces, each built over a fragrant canal bearing the waters of the sacred Narg. Of marble and porphyry are the houses, and roofed with glittering gold that reflects the rays of the sun and enhances the splendor of the cities as blissful gods view them from the distant peaks. Fairest of all is the palace of the great monarch Dorieb, whom some say to be a demigod and others a god. High is the palace of Dorieb, and many are the turrets of marble upon its walls. In its wide halls many multitudes assemble, and here hang the trophies of the ages. And the roof is of pure gold, set upon tall pillars of ruby and azure, and having such carven figures of gods and heroes that he who looks up to those heights seems to gaze upon the living Olympus. And the floor of the palace is of glass, under which flow the cunningly lighted waters of the Narg, gay with gaudy fish not known beyond the bounds of lovely Cathuria."

Thus would I speak to myself of Cathuria, but ever would the bearded man warn me to turn back to the happy shores of Sona-Nyl; for Sona-Nyl is known of men, while none hath ever beheld Cathuria.

And on the thirty-first day that we followed the bird, we beheld the basalt pillars of the West. Shrouded in mist they were, so that no man might peer beyond them or see their summits— which indeed some say reach even to the heavens. And the bearded man again implored me to turn back, but I heeded him not; for from the mists beyond the basalt pillars I fancied there came the notes of singer and lutanist; sweeter than the sweetest songs of Sona-Nyl, and sounding mine own praises; the praises of me, who had voyaged far under the full moon and dwelt in the Land of Fancy.

So to the sound of melody the White Ship sailed into the mist betwixt the basalt pillars of the West. And when the music ceased and the mist lifted, we beheld not the Land of Cathuria, but a swift-rushing resistless sea, over which our helpless barque was borne toward some unknown goal. Soon to our ears came the distant thunder of falling waters, and to our eyes appeared on the far horizon ahead the titanic spray of a monstrous cataract, wherein the oceans of the world drop down to abysmal nothingness. Then did the bearded man say to me with tears on his cheek: "We have rejected the beautiful Land of Sona-Nyl, which we may never behold again. The gods are greater than men, and they have conquered." And I closed my eyes before the crash that I knew would come, shutting out the sight of the celestial bird which flapped its mocking blue wings over the brink of the torrent.

Out of that crash came darkness, and I heard the shrieking of men and of things which were not men. From the East tempestuous winds arose, and chilled me as I crouched on the slab of damp stone which had risen beneath my feet. Then as I heard another crash I opened my eyes and beheld myself upon the platform of that lighthouse from whence I had sailed so many eons ago. In the darkness below there loomed the vast blurred outlines of a vessel breaking up on the cruel rocks, and as I glanced out over the waste I saw that the light had failed for the first time since my grandfather had assumed its care.

And in the later watches of the night, when I went within the tower, I saw on the wall a calendar which still remained as when I had left it at the hour I sailed away. With the dawn I descended the tower and looked for wreckage upon the rocks, but what I found was only this: a strange dead bird whose hue was as of the azure sky, and a single shattered spar, of a whiteness greater than that of the wave-tips or of the mountain snow.

And thereafter the ocean told me its secrets no more; and though many times since has the moon shone full and high in the heavens, the White Ship from the South came never again.

THE DOOM THAT
CAME TO SARNATH

There is in the land of Mnar a vast still lake that is fed by no stream and out of which no stream flows. Ten thousand years ago there stood by its shore the mighty city of Sarnath, but Sarnath stands there no more.

It is told that in the immemorial years when the world was young, before ever the men of Sarnath came to the land of Mnar, another city stood beside the lake; the gray stone city of Ib, which was old as the lake itself, and peopled with beings not pleasing to behold. Very odd and ugly were these beings, as indeed are most beings of a world yet inchoate and rudely fashioned. It is written on the brick cylinders of Kadatheron that the beings of Ib were in hue as green as the lake and the mists that rise above it; that they had bulging eyes, pouting, flabby lips, and curious ears, and were without voice. It is also written that they descended one night from the moon in a mist; they and the vast still lake and gray stone city Ib. However this may be, it is certain that they worshiped a sea-green stone idol chiseled in the likeness of Bokrug, the great water-lizard; before which they danced horribly when the moon was gibbous. And it is written in the papyrus of Ilarnek, that they one day discovered fire, and thereafter kindled flames on many ceremonial occasions. But not much is written of these beings, because they lived in very ancient times, and man is young, and knows little of the very ancient living things.

After many eons men came to the land of Mnar; dark shepherd folk with their fleecy flocks, who built Thraa, Ilarnek, and Kadatheron on the winding river Ai. And certain tribes, more hardy than the rest, pushed on to the border of the lake and built Sarnath at a spot where precious metals were found in the earth.

Not far from the gray city of Ib did the wandering tribes lay the first stones of Sarnath, and at the beings of Ib they marveled greatly. But with their marveling was mixed hate, for they thought it not meet that beings of such aspect should walk about the world of men at dusk. Nor did they like the strange sculptures upon the gray monoliths of Ib, for those sculptures were terrible with great antiquity. Why the beings and the sculptures lingered so late in the world, even until the coming of men, none can tell; unless it was because the land of Mnar is very still, and remote from most other lands both of waking and of dream.

As the men of Sarnath beheld more of the beings of Ib their hate grew, and it was not less because they found the beings weak, and soft as jelly to the touch of stones and spears and arrows. So one day the young warriors, the slingers and the spearmen and the bowmen, marched against Ib and slew all the inhabitants thereof, pushing the queer bodies into the lake with long spears, because they did not wish to touch them. And because they did not like the gray sculptured monoliths of Ib they cast these also into the lake; wondering from the greatness of the labor how ever the stones were brought from afar, as they must have been, since there is naught like them in all the land of Mnar or in the lands adjacent.

Thus of the very ancient city of Ib was nothing spared save the sea-green stone idol chiseled in the likeness of Bokrug, the water-lizard. This the young warriors took back with them to Sarnath as a symbol of conquest over the old gods and beings of Ib, and a sign of leadership in Mnar. But on the night after it was set up in the temple a terrible thing must have happened, for weird lights were seen over the lake, and in the morning the people found the idol gone, and the high-priest Taran-Ish lying dead, as from some fear unspeakable. And before he died, Taran-Ish had scrawled upon the altar of chrysolite with coarse shaky strokes the sign of DOOM.

After Taran-Ish there were many high-priests in Sarnath, but never was the sea-green stone idol found. And many centuries came and went, wherein Sarnath prospered exceedingly, so that only priests and old women remembered what Taran-Ish had scrawled upon the altar of chrysolite. Betwixt Sarnath and the city of Ilarnek arose a caravan route, and the precious metals from the earth were exchanged for other metals and rare cloths and jewels and books and tools for artificers and all things of luxury that are known to the people who dwell along the winding river Ai and beyond. So Sarnath waxed mighty and learned and beautiful, and sent forth conquering armies to subdue the neighboring cities; and in time there sat upon a throne in Sarnath the kings of all the land of Mnar and of many lands adjacent.

The wonder of the world and the pride of all mankind was Sarnath the magnificent. Of polished desert-quarried marble were its walls, in height 300 cubits and in breadth 75, so that chariots might pass each other as men drove them along the top. For full 500 stadia did they run, being open only on the side toward the lake; where a green stone sea-wall kept back the waves that rose oddly once a year at the festival of the destroying of Ib. In Sarnath were fifty streets from the lake to the gates of the caravans, and fifty more intersecting them. With onyx were they paved, save those whereon the horses and camels and elephants trod, which were paved with granite. And the gates of Sarnath were as many as the landward ends of the streets, each of bronze, and flanked by the figures of lions and elephants carven from some stone no longer known among men. The houses of Sarnath were of glazed brick and chalcedony, each having its walled garden and crystal lakelet. With strange art were they builded, for no other city had houses like them; and travelers from Thraa and Ilarnek and Kadatheron marveled at the shining domes wherewith they were surmounted.

But more marvelous still were the palaces and the temples, and the gardens made by Zokkar the olden king. There were many palaces, the least of which were mightier than any in Thraa or Ilarnek or Kadatheron. So high were they that one within might sometimes fancy himself beneath only the sky; yet when lighted with torches dipt in the oil of Dothur their walls shewed vast paintings of kings and armies, of a splendor at once inspiring and stupefying to the beholder. Many were the pillars of the palaces, all of tinted marble, and carven into designs of surpassing beauty. And in most of the palaces the floors were mosaics of beryl and lapis-lazuli and sardonyx and carbuncle and other choice materials, so disposed that the beholder might fancy himself walking over beds of the rarest flowers. And there were likewise fountains, which cast scented waters about in pleasing jets arranged with cunning art. Outshining all others was the palace of the kings of Mnar and of the lands adjacent. On a pair of golden crouching lions rested the throne, many steps above the gleaming floor. And it was wrought of one piece of ivory, though no man lives who knows whence so vast a piece could have come. In that palace there were also many galleries, and many amphitheaters where lions and men and elephants battled at the pleasure of the kings. Sometimes the amphitheaters were flooded with water conveyed from the lake in mighty aqueducts, and then were enacted stirring sea-fights, or combats betwixt swimmers and deadly marine things.

Lofty and amazing were the seventeen tower-like temples of Sarnath, fashioned of a bright multi-colored stone not known elsewhere. A full thousand cubits high stood the greatest among them, wherein the high-priests dwelt with a magnificence scarce less than that of the kings. On the ground were halls as vast and splendid as those of the palaces; where gathered throngs in worship of Zo-Kalar and Tamash and Lobon, the chief gods of Sarnath, whose incense-enveloped shrines were as the thrones of monarchs. Not like the eikons of other gods were those of Zo-Kalar and Tamash and Lobon, for so close to life were they that one might swear the graceful bearded gods themselves sat on the ivory thrones. And up unending steps of shining zircon was the tower-chamber, wherefrom the high-priests looked out over the city and the plains and the lake by day; and at the cryptic moon and significant stars and planets, and their reflec-

tions in the lake, by night. Here was done the very secret and
ancient rite in detestation of Bokrug, the water-lizard, and here
rested the altar of chrysolite which bore the DOOM-scrawl of
Taran-Ish.

Wonderful likewise were the gardens made by Zokkar the
olden king. In the center of Sarnath they lay, covering a great
space and encircled by a high wall. And they were surmounted
by a mighty dome of glass, through which shone the sun and
moon and stars and planets when it was clear, and from which
were hung fulgent images of the sun and moon and stars and
planets when it was not clear. In summer the gardens were
cooled with fresh odorous breezes skillfully wafted by fans, and
in winter they were heated with concealed fires, so that in those
gardens it was always spring. There ran little streams over bright
pebbles, dividing meadows of green and gardens of many hues,
and spanned by a multitude of bridges. Many were the waterfalls
in their courses, and many were the lilied lakelets into which
they expanded. Over the streams and lakelets rode white swans,
whilst the music of rare birds chimed in with the melody of the
waters. In ordered terraces rose the green banks, adorned here
and there with bowers of vines and sweet blossoms, and seats
and benches of marble and porphyry. And there were many small
shrines and temples where one might rest or pray to small gods.

Each year there was celebrated in Sarnath the feast of the
destroying of Ib, at which time wine, song, dancing, and merri-
ment of every kind abounded. Great honors were then paid to
the shades of those who had annihilated the odd ancient beings,
and the memory of those beings and of their elder gods was
derided by dancers and lutanists crowned with roses from the
gardens of Zokkar. And the kings would look out over the lake
and curse the bones of the dead that lay beneath it. At first the
high-priests liked not these festivals, for there had descended
amongst them queer tales of how the sea-green eikon had
vanished, and how Taran-Ish had died from fear and left a warning.
And they said that from their high tower they sometimes saw

lights beneath the waters of the lake. But as many years passed without calamity even the priests laughed and cursed and joined in the orgies of the feasters. Indeed, had they not themselves, in their high tower, often performed the very ancient and secret rite in detestation of Bokrug, the water-lizard? And a thousand years of riches and delight passed over Sarnath, wonder of the world and pride of all mankind.

Gorgeous beyond thought was the feast of the thousandth year of the destroying of Ib. For a decade had it been talked of in the land of Mnar, and as it drew nigh there came to Sarnath on horses and camels and elephants men from Thraa, Ilarnek, and Kadatheron, and all the cities of Mnar and the lands beyond. Before the marble walls on the appointed night were pitched the pavilions of princes and the tents of travelers, and all the shore resounded with the song of happy revelers. Within his banquet-hall reclined Nargis-Hei, the king, drunken with ancient wine from the vaults of conquered Pnath, and surrounded by feasting nobles and hurrying slaves. There were eaten many strange delicacies at that feast; peacocks from the isles of Nariel in the Middle Ocean, young goats from the distant hills of Implan, heels of camels from the Bnazic desert, nuts and spices from Cydathrian groves, and pearls from wave-washed Mtal dissolved in the vinegar of Thraa. Of sauces there were an untold number, prepared by the subtlest cooks in all Mnar, and suited to the palate of every feaster. But most prized of all the viands were the great fishes from the lake, each of vast size, and served up on golden platters set with rubies and diamonds.

Whilst the king and his nobles feasted within the palace, and viewed the crowning dish as it awaited them on golden platters, others feasted elsewhere. In the tower of the great temple the priests held revels, and in pavilions without the walls the princes of neighboring lands made merry. And it was the high-priest Gnai-Kah who first saw the shadows that descended from the gibbous moon into the lake, and the damnable green mists that arose from the lake to meet the moon and to shroud in a sinister haze the towers and the domes of fated Sarnath. Thereafter those in the towers and without the walls beheld strange lights on the water, and saw that the gray rock Akurion, which was wont to rear high above it near the shore, was almost submerged. And fear grew vaguely yet swiftly, so that the princes of Ilarnek and of far Rokol took down and folded their tents and pavilions and departed for the river Ai, though they scarce knew the reason for their departing.

Then, close to the hour of midnight, all the bronze gates of Sarnath burst open and emptied forth a frenzied throng that blackened the plain, so that all the visiting princes and travelers fled away in fright. For on the faces of this throng was writ a madness born of horror unendurable, and on their tongues were words so terrible that no hearer paused for proof. Men whose eyes were wild with fear shrieked aloud of the sight within the king's banquet-hall, where through the windows were seen no longer the forms of Nargis-Hei and his nobles and slaves, but a horde of indescribable green voiceless things with bulging eyes, pouting, flabby lips, and curious ears; things which danced horribly, bearing in their paws golden platters set with rubies and diamonds containing uncouth flames. And the princes and travelers, as they fled from the doomed city of Sarnath on horses and camels and elephants, looked again upon the mist-begetting lake and saw the gray rock Akurion was quite submerged.

Through all the land of Mnar and the lands adjacent spread the tales of those who had fled from Sarnath, and caravans sought that accursed city and its precious metals no more. It was long ere any traveler went thither, and even then only the brave and adventurous young men of distant Falona dared make the journey; adventurous young men of yellow hair and blue eyes, who are no kin to the men of Mnar. These men indeed went to the lake to view Sarnath; but though they found the vast still lake itself, and the gray rock Akurion which rears high above it near the shore, they beheld not the wonder of the world and pride of all mankind. Where once had risen walls of 300 cubits and towers yet higher, now stretched only the marshy shore, and where once had dwelt fifty millions of men now crawled only the detestable green water-lizard. Not even the mines of precious metal remained, for DOOM had come to Sarnath.

But half buried in the rushes was spied a curious green idol of stone; an exceedingly ancient idol coated with seaweed and chiseled in the likeness of Bokrug, the great water-lizard. That idol, enshrined in the high temple at Ilarnek, was subsequently worshiped beneath the gibbous moon throughout the land of Mnar.

THE CATS OF ULTHAR

It is said that in Ulthar, which lies beyond the river Skai, no man may kill a cat; and this I can verily believe as I gaze upon him who sitteth purring before the fire. For the cat is cryptic, and close to strange things which men cannot see. He is the soul of antique Aegyptus, and bearer of tales from forgotten cities in Meroë and Ophir. He is the kin of the jungle's lords, and heir to the secrets of hoary and sinister Africa. The Sphinx is his cousin, and he speaks her language; but he is more ancient than the Sphinx, and remembers that which she hath forgotten.

In Ulthar, before ever the burgesses forbade the killing of cats, there dwelt an old cotter and his wife who delighted to trap and slay the cats of their neighbors. Why they did this I know not; save that many hate the voice of the cat in the night, and take it ill that cats should run stealthily about yards and gardens at twilight. But whatever the reason, this old man and woman took pleasure in trapping and slaying every cat which came near to their hovel; and from some of the sounds heard after dark, many villagers fancied that the manner of slaying was exceedingly peculiar. But the villagers did not discuss such things with the old man and his wife; because of the habitual expression on the withered faces of the two, and because their cottage was so small and so darkly hidden under spreading oaks at the back of a neglected yard. In truth, much as the owners of cats hated these odd folk, they feared them more; and instead of berating them as brutal assassins, merely took care that no cherished pet or mouser should stray toward the remote hovel under the dark trees. When through some unavoidable oversight a cat was missed, and sounds heard after dark, the loser would lament impotently; or console himself by thanking Fate that it was not one of his children who had thus vanished. For the people of Ulthar were simple, and knew not whence it is all cats first came.

One day a caravan of strange wanderers from the South entered the narrow cobbled streets of Ulthar. Dark wanderers they were, and unlike the other roving folk who passed through the village twice every year. In the market-place they told fortunes for silver, and bought gay beads from the merchants. What was the land of these wanderers none could tell; but it was seen that they were given to strange prayers, and that they had painted on the sides of their wagons strange figures with human bodies and the heads of cats, hawks, rams, and lions. And the leader of the caravan wore a head-dress with two horns and a curious disc betwixt the horns.

There was in this singular caravan a little boy with no father or mother, but only a tiny black kitten to cherish. The plague had not been kind to him, yet had left him this small furry thing to mitigate his sorrow; and when one is very young, one can find great relief in the lively antics of a black kitten. So the boy whom the dark people called Menes smiled more often than he wept as he sat playing with his graceful kitten on the steps of an oddly painted wagon.

On the third morning of the wanderers' stay in Ulthar, Menes could not find his kitten; and as he sobbed aloud in the market-place certain villagers told him of the old man and his wife, and of sounds heard in the night. And when he heard these things his sobbing gave place to meditation, and finally to prayer. He stretched out his arms toward the sun and prayed in a tongue no villager could understand; though indeed the villagers did not try very hard to understand, since their attention was mostly taken up by the sky and the odd shapes the clouds were assuming. It was very peculiar, but as the little boy uttered his petition there seemed to form overhead the shadowy, nebulous figures of exotic things; of hybrid creatures crowned with horn-flanked discs. Nature is full of such illusions to impress the imaginative.

That night the wanderers left Ulthar, and were never seen again. And the householders were troubled when they noticed that in all the village there was not a cat to be found. From each hearth the familiar cat had vanished; cats large and small, black, gray, striped, yellow, and white. Old Kranon, the burgomaster, swore that the dark folk had taken the cats away in revenge for the killing of Menes' kitten; and cursed the caravan and the little boy. But Nith, the lean notary, declared that the old cotter and his wife were more likely persons to suspect; for their hatred of cats was notorious and increasingly bold. Still, no one durst complain to the sinister couple; even when little Atal, the inn-keeper's son, vowed that he had at twilight seen all the cats of Ulthar in that accursed yard under the trees, pacing very slowly and solemnly in a circle around the cottage, two abreast, as if in performance of some unheard-of rite of beasts. The villagers did not know how much to believe from so small a boy; and though they feared that the evil pair had charmed the cats to their death, they preferred not to chide the old cotter till they met him outside his dark and repellent yard.

So Ulthar went to sleep in vain anger; and when the people awaked at dawn—behold! Every cat was back at his accustomed hearth! Large and small, black, gray, striped, yellow, and white, none was missing. Very sleek and fat did the cats appear, and sonorous with purring content. The citizens talked with one another of the affair, and marveled not a little. Old Kranon again insisted that it was the dark folk who had taken them, since cats did not return alive from the cottage of the ancient man and his wife. But all agreed on one thing: that the refusal of all the cats to eat their portions of meat or drink their saucers of milk was exceedingly curious. And for two whole days the sleek, lazy cats of Ulthar would touch no food, but only doze by the fire or in the sun.

It was fully a week before the villagers noticed that no lights were appearing at dusk in the windows of the cottage under the trees. Then the lean Nith remarked that no one had seen the old man or his wife since the night the cats were away. In another week the burgomaster decided to overcome his fears and call at the strangely silent dwelling as a matter of duty, though in so doing he was careful to take with him Shang the blacksmith and

Thul the cutter of stone as witnesses. And when they had broken down the frail door they found only this: two cleanly picked human skeletons on the earthen floor, and a number of singular beetles crawling in the shadowy corners.

There was subsequently much talk among the burgesses of Ulthar. Zath, the coroner, disputed at length with Nith, the lean notary; and Kranon and Shang and Thul were overwhelmed with questions. Even little Atal, the innkeeper's son, was closely questioned and given a sweetmeat as reward. They talked of the old cotter and his wife, of the caravan of dark wanderers, of small Menes and his black kitten, of the prayer of Menes and of the sky during that prayer, of the doings of the cats on the night the caravan left, and of what was later found in the cottage under the dark trees in the repellent yard.

And in the end the burgesses passed that remarkable law which is told of by traders in Hatheg and discussed by travelers in Nir; namely, that in Ulthar no man may kill a cat.

CELEPHAÏS

In a dream Kuranes saw the city in the valley, and the sea-coast beyond, and the snowy peak overlooking the sea, and the gaily painted galleys that sail out of the harbor toward the distant regions where the sea meets the sky. In a dream it was also that he came by his name of Kuranes, for when awake he was called by another name. Perhaps it was natural for him to dream a new name; for he was the last of his family, and alone among the indifferent millions of London, so there were not many to speak to him and remind him who he had been. His money and lands were gone, and he did not care for the ways of people about him, but preferred to dream and write of his dreams. What he wrote was laughed at by those to whom he shewed it, so that after a time he kept his writings to himself, and finally ceased to write. The more he withdrew from the world about him, the more wonderful became his dreams; and it would have been quite futile to try to describe them on paper. Kuranes was not modern, and did not think like others who wrote. Whilst they strove to strip from life its embroidered robes of myth, and to shew in naked ugliness the foul thing that is reality, Kuranes sought for beauty alone. When truth and experience failed to reveal it, he sought it in fancy and illusion, and found it on his very doorstep, amid the nebulous memories of childhood tales and dreams.

There are not many persons who know what wonders are opened to them in the stories and visions of their youth; for when as children we listen and dream, we think but half-formed thoughts, and when as men we try to remember, we are dulled and prosaic with the poison of life. But some of us awake in the night with strange phantasms of enchanted hills and gardens, of fountains that sing in the sun, of golden cliffs overhanging murmuring seas, of plains that stretch down to sleeping cities of bronze and stone, and of shadowy companies of heroes that ride caparisoned white horses along the edges of thick forests; and then we know that we have looked back through the ivory gates into that world of wonder which was ours before we were wise and unhappy.

Kuranes came very suddenly upon his old world of childhood. He had been dreaming of the house where he was born; the great stone house covered with ivy, where thirteen generations of his ancestors had lived, and where he had hoped to die. It was moonlight, and he had stolen out into the fragrant summer night, through the gardens, down the terraces, past the great oaks of the park, and along the long white road to the village. The village seemed very old, eaten away at the edge like the moon which had commenced to wane, and Kuranes wondered whether the peaked roofs of the small houses hid sleep or death. In the streets were spears of long grass, and the window-panes on either side were either broken or filmily staring. Kuranes had not lingered, but had plodded on as though summoned toward some goal. He dared not disobey the summons for fear it might prove an illusion like the urges and aspirations of waking life, which do not lead to any goal. Then he had been drawn down a lane that led off from the village street toward the channel cliffs, and had come to the end of things—to the precipice and the abyss where all the village and all the world fell abruptly into the unechoing emptiness of infinity, and where even the sky ahead was empty and unlit by the crumbling moon and the peering stars. Faith had urged him on, over the precipice and into the gulf, where he had floated down, down, down; past dark, shapeless, undreamed dreams, faintly glowing spheres that may have been partly dreamed dreams, and laughing winged things that seemed to mock the dreamers of all the worlds. Then a rift seemed to open in the darkness before him, and he saw the city of the valley, glistening radiantly far, far below, with a background of sea and sky, and a snow-capped mountain near the shore.

Kuranes had awaked the very moment he beheld the city, yet

he knew from his brief glance that it was none other than Celephaïs, in the Valley of Ooth-Nargai beyond the Tanarian Hills, where his spirit had dwelt all the eternity of an hour one summer afternoon very long ago, when he had slipt away from his nurse and let the warm sea-breeze lull him to sleep as he watched the clouds from the cliff near the village. He had protested then, when they had found him, waked him, and carried him home, for just as he was aroused he had been about to sail in a golden galley for those alluring regions where the sea meets the sky. And now he was equally resentful of awaking, for he had found his fabulous city after forty weary years.

But three nights afterward Kuranes came again to Celephaïs. As before, he dreamed first of the village that was asleep or dead, and of the abyss down which one must float silently; then the rift appeared again, and he beheld the glittering minarets of the city, and saw the graceful galleys riding at anchor in the blue harbor, and watched the gingko trees of Mount Aran swaying in the sea-breeze. But this time he was not snatched away, and like a winged being settled gradually over a grassy hillside till finally his feet rested gently on the turf. He had indeed come back to the Valley of Ooth-Nargai and the splendid city of Celephaïs.

Down the hill amid scented grasses and brilliant flowers walked Kuranes, over the bubbling Naraxa on the small wooden bridge where he had carved his name so many years ago, and through the whispering grove to the great stone bridge by the city gate. All was as of old, nor were the marble walls discolored, nor the polished bronze statues upon them tarnished. And Kuranes saw that he need not tremble lest the things he knew be vanished; for even the sentries on the ramparts were the same, and still as young as he remembered them. When he entered the city, past the bronze gates and over the onyx pavements, the merchants and camel-drivers greeted him as if he had never been away; and it was the same at the turquoise temple of Nath-Horthath, where the orchid-wreathed priests told him that there is no time in Ooth-Nargai, but only perpetual youth. Then Kuranes walked through the Street of Pillars to the seaward wall, where gathered the traders and sailors, and strange men from the regions where the sea meets the sky. There he stayed long, gazing out over the bright harbor where the ripples sparkled beneath an unknown sun, and where rode lightly the galleys from far places over the water. And he gazed also upon Mount Aran rising regally from the shore, its lower slopes green with swaying trees and its white summit touching the sky.

More than ever Kuranes wished to sail in a galley to the far places of which he had heard so many strange tales, and he sought again the captain who had agreed to carry him so long ago. He found the man, Athib, sitting on the same chest of spices he had sat upon before, and Athib seemed not to realize that any time had passed. Then the two rowed to a galley in the harbor, and giving orders to the oarsmen, commenced to sail out into the billowy Cerenerian Sea that leads to the sky. For several days they glided undulatingly over the water, till finally they came to the horizon, where the sea meets the sky. Here the galley paused not at all, but floated easily in the blue of the sky among fleecy clouds tinted with rose. And far beneath the keel Kuranes could see strange lands and rivers and cities of surpassing beauty, spread indolently in the sunshine which seemed never to lessen or disappear. At length Athib told him that their journey was near its end, and that they would soon enter the harbor of Serannian, the pink marble city of the clouds, which is built on that ethereal coast where the west wind flows into the sky; but as the highest of the city's carven towers came into sight there was a sound somewhere in space, and Kuranes awaked in his London garret.

For many months after that Kuranes sought the marvelous city of Celephaïs and its sky-bound galleys in vain; and though his dreams carried him to many gorgeous and unheard-of places, no one whom he met could tell him how to find Ooth-Nargai, beyond the Tanarian Hills. One night he went flying over dark mountains where there were faint, lone campfires at great distances apart, and strange, shaggy herds with tinkling bells on the leaders; and in the wildest part of this hilly country, so remote that few men could ever have seen it, he found a hideously ancient wall or causeway of stone zigzagging along the ridges and valleys; too gigantic ever to have risen by human hands, and of such a length that neither end of it could be seen. Beyond that wall in the gray dawn he came to a land of quaint gardens and cherry trees, and when the sun rose he beheld such beauty of red and white flowers, green foliage and lawns, white paths, diamond brooks, blue lakelets, carven bridges, and red-roofed pagodas, that he for a moment forgot Celephaïs in sheer delight. But he remembered it again when he walked down a white path toward a red-roofed pagoda, and would have questioned the people of that land about it, had he not found that there were no people there, but only birds and bees and butterflies. On another night Kuranes walked up a damp stone spiral stairway endlessly, and came to a tower window overlooking a mighty plain and river lit by the full moon; and in the silent city that spread away from the river-bank he thought he beheld some feature or arrangement which he had known before. He would have descended and asked the way to Ooth-Nargai had not a fearsome aurora sputtered up from some remote place beyond the horizon, shewing the ruin and antiquity of the city, and the stagnation of the reedy river, and the death lying upon that land, as it had lain since King Kynaratholis came home from his conquests to find the vengeance of the gods.

So Kuranes sought fruitlessly for the marvelous city of Celephaïs and its galleys that sail to Serannian in the sky, meanwhile seeing many wonders and once barely escaping from the high-priest not to be described, which wears a yellow silken mask over its face and dwells all alone in a prehistoric stone monastery on the cold desert plateau of Leng. In time he grew so impatient of the bleak intervals of day that he began buying drugs in order to increase his periods of sleep. Hasheesh helped a great deal, and once sent him to a part of space where form does not exist, but where glowing gases study the secrets of existence. And a violet-colored gas told him that this part of space was outside what he had called infinity. The gas had not heard of planets and organisms before, but identified Kuranes merely as one from the infinity where matter, energy, and gravitation exist. Kuranes was now very anxious to return to minaret-studded Celephaïs, and increased his doses of drugs; but eventually he had no more money left, and could buy no drugs. Then one summer day he was turned out of his garret, and wandered aimlessly through the streets, drifting over a bridge to a place where the houses grew thinner and thinner. And it was there that fulfillment came, and he met the cortege of knights come from Celephaïs to bear him thither forever.

Handsome knights they were, astride roan horses and clad in shining armor with tabards of cloth-of-gold curiously emblazoned. So numerous were they, that Kuranes almost mistook them for an army, but their leader told him they were sent in his honor; since it was he who had created Ooth-Nargai in his dreams, on which account he was now to be appointed its chief god for evermore. Then they gave Kuranes a horse and placed him at the head of the cavalcade, and all rode majestically through the downs of Surrey and onward toward the region where Kuranes and his ancestors were born. It was very strange, but as the riders went on they seemed to gallop back through Time; for whenever they passed through a village in the twilight they saw only such houses and villages as Chaucer or men before him might have seen, and sometimes they saw knights on horseback with small companies of retainers. When it grew dark they traveled more swiftly, till soon they were flying uncannily as if in the air. In the dim dawn they came upon the village which Kuranes had seen alive in his childhood, and asleep or dead in his dreams. It was alive now, and early villagers curtsied as the horsemen clattered down the street and turned off into the lane that ends in the abyss of dream. Kuranes had previously entered that abyss only at night, and wondered what it would look like by day; so he watched anxiously as the column approached its brink. Just as they galloped up the rising ground to the precipice a golden glare came somewhere out of the east and hid all the landscape in its effulgent draperies. The abyss was now a seething chaos of roseate and cerulean splendor, and invisible voices sang exultantly as the knightly entourage plunged over the edge and floated gracefully down past glittering clouds and silvery coruscations. Endlessly down the horsemen floated, their chargers pawing the ether as if galloping over golden sands; and then the luminous vapors spread apart to reveal a greater brightness, the brightness of the city Celephaïs, and the sea-coast beyond, and the snowy peak overlooking the sea, and the gaily painted galleys that sail out of the harbor toward distant regions where the sea meets the sky.

And Kuranes reigned thereafter over Ooth-Nargai and all the neighboring regions of dream, and held his court alternately in Celephaïs and in the cloud-fashioned Serannian. He reigns there still, and will reign happily forever, though below the cliffs at Innsmouth the channel tides played mockingly with the body of a tramp who had stumbled through the half-deserted village at dawn; played mockingly, and cast it upon the rocks by ivy-covered Trevor Towers, where a notably fat and especially offensive millionaire brewer enjoys the purchased atmosphere of extinct nobility.

FROM BEYOND

Horrible beyond conception was the change which had taken place in my best friend, Crawford Tillinghast. I had not seen him since that day, two months and a half before, when he had told me toward what goal his physical and metaphysical researches were leading; when he had answered my awed and almost frightened remonstrances by driving me from his laboratory and his house in a burst of fanatical rage. I had known that he now remained mostly shut in the attic laboratory with that accursed electrical machine, eating little and excluding even the servants, but I had not thought that a brief period of ten weeks could so alter and disfigure any human creature. It is not pleasant to see a stout man suddenly grown thin, and it is even worse when the baggy skin becomes yellowed or grayed, the eyes sunken, circled, and uncannily glowing, the forehead veined and corrugated, and the hands tremulous and twitching. And if added to this there be a repellent unkemptness; a wild disorder of dress, a bushiness of dark hair white at the roots, and an unchecked growth of pure white beard on a face once clean-shaven, the cumulative effect is quite shocking. But such was the aspect of Crawford Tillinghast on the night his half-coherent message brought me to his door after my weeks of exile; such the specter that trembled as it admitted me, candle in hand, and glanced furtively over its shoulder as if fearful of unseen things in the ancient, lonely house set back from Benevolent Street.

That Crawford Tillinghast should ever have studied science and philosophy was a mistake. These things should be left to the frigid and impersonal investigator, for they offer two equally tragic alternatives to the man of feeling and action; despair if he fail in his quest, and terrors unutterable and unimaginable if he succeed. Tillinghast had once been the prey of failure, solitary and melancholy; but now I knew, with nauseating fears of my own, that he

was the prey of success. I had indeed warned him ten weeks
before, when he burst forth with his tale of what he felt himself
about to discover. He had been flushed and excited then, talking
in a high and unnatural, though always pedantic, voice.

"What do we know," he had said, "of the world and the universe
about us? Our means of receiving impressions are absurdly few,
and our notions of surrounding objects infinitely narrow. We see
things only as we are constructed to see them, and can gain no
idea of their absolute nature. With five feeble senses we pretend
to comprehend the boundlessly complex cosmos, yet other
beings with a wider, stronger, or different range of senses might
not only see very differently the things we see, but might see
and study whole worlds of matter, energy, and life which lie close
at hand yet can never be detected with the senses we have. I
have always believed that such strange, inaccessible worlds exist
at our very elbows, *and now I believe I have found a way to
break down the barriers.* I am not joking. Within twenty-four
hours that machine near the table will generate waves acting on
unrecognized sense-organs that exist in us as atrophied or rudi-
mentary vestiges. Those waves will open up to us many vistas
unknown to man, and several unknown to anything we consider
organic life. We shall see that at which dogs howl in the dark,
and that at which cats prick up their ears after midnight. We
shall see these things, and other things which no breathing
creature has yet seen. We shall overleap time, space, and dimensions, and without bodily motion peer to the bottom of creation."

When Tillinghast said these things I remonstrated, for I knew
him well enough to be frightened rather than amused; but he
was a fanatic, and drove me from the house. Now he was no
less a fanatic, but his desire to speak had conquered his resentment, and he had written me imperatively in a hand I could
scarcely recognize. As I entered the abode of the friend so
suddenly metamorphosed to a shivering gargoyle, I became
infected with the terror which seemed stalking in all the shadows.
The words and beliefs expressed ten weeks before seemed bodied

forth in the darkness beyond the small circle of candle light, and I sickened at the hollow, altered voice of my host. I wished the servants were about, and did not like it when he said they had all left three days previously. It seemed strange that old Gregory, at least, should desert his master without telling as tried a friend as I. It was he who had given me all the information I had of Tillinghast after I was repulsed in rage.

Yet I soon subordinated all my fears to my growing curiosity and fascination. Just what Crawford Tillinghast now wished of me I could only guess, but that he had some stupendous secret or discovery to impart, I could not doubt. Before I had protested at his unnatural pryings into the unthinkable; now that he had evidently succeeded to some degree I almost shared his spirit, terrible though the cost of victory appeared. Up through the dark emptiness of the house I followed the bobbing candle in the hand of this shaking parody on man. The electricity seemed to be turned off, and when I asked my guide he said it was for a definite reason.

"It would be too much . . . I would not dare," he continued to mutter. I especially noted his new habit of muttering, for it was not like him to talk to himself. We entered the laboratory in the attic, and I observed that detestable electrical machine, glowing with a sickly, sinister, violet luminosity. It was connected with a powerful chemical battery, but seemed to be receiving no current; for I recalled that in its experimental stage it had sputtered and purred when in action. In reply to my question Tillinghast mumbled that this permanent glow was not electrical in any sense that I could understand.

He now seated me near the machine, so that it was on my right, and turned a switch somewhere below the crowning cluster of glass bulbs. The usual sputtering began, turned to a whine, and terminated in a drone so soft as to suggest a return to silence. Meanwhile the luminosity increased, waned again, then assumed a pale, outré color or blend of colors which I could neither place nor describe. Tillinghast had been watching me, and noted my puzzled expression.

"Do you know what that is?" he whispered. "*That is ultra-violet.*" He chuckled oddly at my surprise. "You thought ultra-violet was invisible, and so it is—but you can see that and many other invisible things *now*.

"Listen to me! The waves from that thing are waking a thousand sleeping senses in us; senses which we inherit from eons of evolution from the state of detached electrons to the state of organic humanity. I have seen *truth,* and I intend to shew it to you. Do you wonder how it will seem? I will tell you." Here Tillinghast seated himself directly opposite me, blowing out his candle and staring hideously into my eyes. "Your existing sense-organs—ears first, I think—will pick up many of the impressions, for they are closely connected with the dormant organs. Then there will be others. You have heard of the pineal gland? I laugh at the shallow endocrinologist, fellow-dupe and fellow-parvenu of the Freudian. That gland is the great sense-organ of organs—*I have found out.* It is like sight in the end, and transmits visual pictures to the brain. If you are normal, that is the way you ought to get most of it . . . I mean get most of the evidence from *beyond.*"

I looked about the immense attic room with the sloping south wall, dimly lit by rays which the every-day eye cannot see. The far corners were all shadows, and the whole place took on a hazy unreality which obscured its nature and invited the imagination to symbolism and phantasm. During the interval that Tillinghast was silent I fancied myself in some vast and incredible temple of long-dead gods; some vague edifice of innumerable black stone columns reaching up from a floor of damp slabs to a cloudy height beyond the range of my vision. The picture was very vivid for a while, but gradually gave way to a more horrible conception; that of utter, absolute solitude in infinite, sightless, soundless space. There seemed to be a void, and nothing more, and I felt a childish fear which prompted me to draw from my hip pocket the revolver I always carried after dark since the night I was held up in East Providence. Then, from the farther-most regions of remoteness, the *sound* softly glided into existence. It was infinitely faint, subtly vibrant, and unmistakably musical, but held a quality of surpassing wildness which made its impact feel like a delicate torture of my whole body. I felt sensations like those one feels when accidentally scratching ground glass. Simultaneously there developed something like a cold draft, which apparently swept past me from the direction of the distant sound. As I waited breathlessly I perceived that both sound and wind were increasing; the effect being to give me an odd notion of myself as tied to a pair of rails in the path of a gigantic approaching locomotive. I began to speak to Tillinghast, and as I did so all the unusual impressions abruptly vanished. I saw only the man, the glowing machine, and the dim apartment. Tillinghast was grinning repulsively at the revolver which I had almost unconsciously drawn, but from his expression I was sure he had seen and heard as much as I, if not a great deal more. I whispered what I had experienced, and he bade me to remain as quiet and receptive as possible.

"Don't move," he cautioned, "for in these rays *we are able to be seen as well as to see.* I told you the servants left, but I didn't tell you *how.* It was that thick-witted housekeeper—she turned on the lights downstairs after I had warned her not to, and the wires picked up sympathetic vibrations. It must have been frightful—I could hear the screams up here in spite of all I was seeing and hearing from another direction, and later it was rather awful to find those empty heaps of clothes around the house. Mrs. Updike's clothes were close to the front hall switch—that's how I know she did it. It got them all. But so long as we don't move we're fairly safe. Remember we're dealing with a hideous world in which we are practically helpless. . . . *Keep still!*"

The combined shock of the revelation and of the abrupt command gave me a kind of paralysis, and in my terror my mind again opened to the impressions coming from what Tillinghast called "*beyond*." I was now in a vortex of sound and motion, with confused pictures before my eyes. I saw the blurred outlines of the room, but from some point in space there seemed to be pouring a seething column of unrecognizable shapes or clouds, penetrating the solid roof at a point ahead and to the right of me. Then I glimpsed the temple-like effect again, but this time the pillars reached up into an aerial ocean of light, which sent down one blinding beam along the path of the cloudy column I had seen before. After that the scene was almost wholly kaleidoscopic, and in the jumble of sights, sounds, and unidentified sense-impressions I felt that I was about to dissolve or in some way lose the solid form. One definite flash I shall always remember. I seemed for an instant to behold a patch of strange night sky filled with shining, revolving spheres, and as it receded I saw that the glowing suns formed a constellation or galaxy of settled shape; this shape being the distorted face of Crawford Tillinghast. At another time I felt the huge animate things brushing past me and occasionally *walking or drifting through my supposedly solid body,* and thought I saw Tillinghast look at them as though his better trained senses could catch them visually. I recalled what he had said of the pineal gland, and wondered what he saw with this preternatural eye.

Suddenly I myself became possessed of a kind of augmented sight. Over and above the luminous and shadowy chaos arose a picture which, though vague, held the elements of consistency and permanence. It was indeed somewhat familiar, for the unusual part was superimposed upon the usual terrestrial scene much as a cinema view may be thrown upon the painted curtain of a theater. I saw the attic laboratory, the electrical machine, and the unsightly form of Tillinghast opposite me; but of all the space unoccupied by familiar material objects not one particle was vacant. Indescribable shapes both alive and otherwise were mixed in disgusting disarray, and close to every known thing were whole worlds of alien, unknown entities. It likewise seemed that all the known things entered into the composition of other unknown things, and vice versa. Foremost among the living objects were great inky, jellyish monstrosities which flabbily quivered in harmony with the vibrations from the machine. They were present in loathsome profusion, and I saw to my horror that they *over-lapped;* that they were semi-fluid and capable of passing through one another and through what we know as solids. These things were never still, but seemed ever floating about with some malignant purpose. Sometimes they appeared to devour one another, the attacker launching itself at its victim and instantaneously obliterating the latter from sight. Shudderingly I felt that I knew what had obliterated the unfortunate servants, and could not exclude the things from my mind as I strove to observe other properties of the newly visible world that lies unseen around us. But Tillinghast had been watching me, and was speaking.

"You see them? You see them? You see the things that float and flop about you and through you every moment of your life? You see the creatures that form what men call the pure air and the blue sky? Have I not succeeded in breaking down the barrier; have I not shewn you worlds that no other living men have seen?" I heard him scream through the horrible chaos, and looked at the wild face thrust so offensively close to mine. His eyes were pits of flame, and they glared at me with what I now saw was overwhelming hatred. The machine droned detestably.

"You think those floundering things wiped out the servants? Fool, they are harmless! But the servants *are* gone, aren't they? You tried to stop me; you discouraged me when I needed every drop of encouragement I could get; you were afraid of the cosmic truth, you damned coward, but now I've got you! What swept up the servants? What made them scream so loud? . . . Don't know, eh? You'll know soon enough! Look at me—listen to what I say—do you suppose there are really any such things as time and magnitude? Do you fancy there are such things as form or matter? I tell you, I have struck depths that your little brain can't picture! I have seen beyond the bounds of infinity and drawn down daemons from the stars. . . . I have harnessed the shadows that stride from world to world to sow death and madness. . . . Space belongs to me, do you hear? Things are hunting me now— the things that devour and dissolve—but I know how to elude them. It is you they will get, as they got the servants. Stirring, dear sir? I told you it was dangerous to move. I have saved you so far by telling you to keep still—saved you to see more sights and to listen to me. If you had moved, they would have been at you long ago. Don't worry, they won't *hurt* you. They didn't hurt the servants—it was *seeing* that made the poor devils scream so. My pets are not pretty, for they come out of places where aesthetic standards are—*very different.* Disintegration is quite painless, I assure you—but *I want you to see them.* I almost saw them, but I knew how to stop. You are not curious? I always knew you were no scientist! Trembling, eh? Trembling with anxiety to see the ultimate things I have discovered? Why don't you move, then? Tired? Well, don't worry, my friend, *for they are coming.* . . . Look! Look, curse you, look! . . . It's just over your left shoulder. . . ."

What remains to be told is very brief, and may be familiar to you from the newspaper accounts. The police heard a shot in the old Tillinghast house and found us there—Tillinghast dead and me unconscious. They arrested me because the revolver was in my hand, but released me in three hours, after they found it was apoplexy which had finished Tillinghast and saw that my shot had been directed at the noxious machine which now lay hopelessly shattered on the laboratory floor. I did not tell very much of what I had seen, for I feared the coroner would be skeptical; but from the evasive outline I did give, the doctor told me that I had undoubtedly been hypnotized by the vindictive and homicidal madman.

I wish I could believe that doctor. It would help my shaky nerves if I could dismiss what I now have to think of the air and the sky about and above me. I never feel alone or comfortable, and a hideous sense of pursuit sometimes comes chillingly on me when I am weary. What prevents me from believing the doctor is this one simple fact—that the police never found the bodies of those servants whom they say Crawford Tillinghast murdered.

NYARLATHOTEP

Nyarlathotep . . . the crawling chaos . . . I am the last . . . I will tell the audient void. . . .

I do not recall distinctly when it began, but it was months ago. The general tension was horrible. To a season of political and social upheaval was added a strange and brooding apprehension of hideous physical danger; a danger widespread and all-embracing, such a danger as may be imagined only in the most terrible phantasms of the night. I recall that the people went about with pale and worried faces, and whispered warnings and prophecies which no one dared consciously repeat or acknowledge to himself that he had heard. A sense of monstrous guilt was upon the land, and out of the abysses between the stars swept chill currents that made men shiver in dark and lonely places. There was a daemoniac alteration in the sequence of the seasons—the autumn heat lingered fearsomely, and everyone felt that the world and perhaps the universe had passed from the control of known gods or forces to that of gods or forces which were unknown.

And it was then that Nyarlathotep came out of Egypt. Who he was, none could tell, but he was of the old native blood and looked like a Pharaoh. The fellahin knelt when they saw him, yet could not say why. He said he had risen up out of the blackness of twenty-seven centuries, and that he had heard messages from places not on this planet. Into the lands of civilization came Nyarlathotep, swarthy, slender, and sinister, always buying strange instruments of glass and metal and combining them into instruments yet stranger. He spoke much of the sciences—of electricity and psychology—and gave exhibitions of power which sent his spectators away speechless, yet which swelled his fame to exceeding magnitude. Men advised one another to see Nyarlathotep, and shuddered. And where Nyarlathotep went, rest vanished; for the small hours were rent with the screams of nightmare. Never before had the screams of nightmare been such a public problem; now the wise men almost wished they could forbid sleep in the small hours, that the shrieks of cities might less horribly disturb the pale, pitying moon as it glimmered on green waters gliding under bridges, and old steeples crumbling against a sickly sky.

I remember when Nyarlathotep came to my city—the great, the old, the terrible city of unnumbered crimes. My friend had told me of him, and of the impelling fascination and allurement of his revelations, and I burned with eagerness to explore his uttermost mysteries. My friend said they were horrible and impressive beyond my most fevered imaginings; that what was thrown on a screen in the darkened room prophesied things none but Nyarlathotep dared prophesy, and that in the sputter of his sparks there was taken from men that which had never been taken before yet which shewed only in the eyes. And I heard it hinted abroad that those who knew Nyarlathotep looked on sights which others saw not.

It was in the hot autumn that I went through the night with the restless crowds to see Nyarlathotep; through the stifling night and up the endless stairs into the choking room. And shadowed on a screen, I saw hooded forms amidst ruins, and yellow evil faces peering from behind fallen monuments. And I saw the world battling against blackness; against the waves of destruction from ultimate space; whirling, churning; struggling around the dimming, cooling sun. Then the sparks played amazingly around the heads of the spectators, and hair stood up on end whilst shadows more grotesque than I can tell came out and squatted on the heads. And when I, who was colder and more scientific than the rest, mumbled a trembling protest about "imposture" and "static electricity," Nyarlathotep drove us all out, down the dizzy stairs into the damp, hot, deserted midnight streets. I screamed aloud that I was *not* afraid; that I never could be afraid; and others screamed with me for solace. We swore to one another that the city *was* exactly the same, and still alive; and when the electric lights began to fade we cursed the company over and over again, and laughed at the queer faces we made.

I believe we felt something coming down from the greenish moon, for when we began to depend on its light we drifted into curious involuntary formations and seemed to know our destinations though we dared not think of them. Once we looked at the pavement and found the blocks loose and displaced by grass, with scarce a line of rusted metal to shew where the tramways had run. And again we saw a tram-car, lone, windowless, dilapidated, and almost on its side. When we gazed around the horizon, we could not find the third tower by the river, and noticed that the silhouette of the second tower was ragged at the top. Then we split up into narrow columns, each of which seemed drawn in a different direction. One disappeared in a narrow alley to the left, leaving only the echo of a shocking moan. Another filed down a weed-choked subway entrance, howling with a laughter that was mad. My own column was sucked toward the open country, and presently felt a chill which was not of the hot autumn; for as we stalked out on the dark moor, we beheld around us the hellish moon-glitter of evil snows. Trackless, inexplicable snows, swept asunder in one direction only, where lay a gulf all the blacker for its glittering walls. The column seemed very thin indeed as it plodded dreamily into the gulf. I lingered behind, for the black rift in the green-litten snow was frightful, and I thought I had heard the reverberations of a disquieting wail as my companions vanished; but my power to linger was slight. As if beckoned by those who had gone before, I half floated between the titanic snowdrifts, quivering and afraid, into the sightless vortex of the unimaginable.

Screamingly sentient, dumbly delirious, only the gods that were can tell. A sickened, sensitive shadow writhing in hands that are not hands, and whirled blindly past ghastly midnights of rotting creation, corpses of dead worlds with sores that were cities, charnel winds that brush the pallid stars and make them flicker low. Beyond the worlds vague ghosts of monstrous things; half-seen columns of unsanctified temples that rest on nameless rocks beneath space and reach up to dizzy vacua above the spheres of light and darkness. And through this revolting grave-yard of the universe the muffled, maddening beating of drums, and thin, monotonous whine of blasphemous flutes from inconceivable, unlighted chambers beyond Time; the detestable pounding and piping whereunto dance slowly, awkwardly, and absurdly the gigantic, tenebrous ultimate gods—the blind, voice-less, mindless gargoyles whose soul is Nyarlathotep.

EX OBLIVIONE

When the last days were upon me, and the ugly trifles of existence began to drive me to madness like the small drops of water that torturers let fall ceaselessly upon one spot of their victim's body, I loved the irradiate refuge of sleep. In my dreams I found a little of the beauty I had vainly sought in life, and wandered through old gardens and enchanted woods.

Once when the wind was soft and scented I heard the south calling, and sailed endlessly and languorously under strange stars.

Once when the gentle rain fell I glided in a barge down a sunless stream under the earth till I reached another world of purple twilight, iridescent arbors, and undying roses.

And once I walked through a golden valley that led to shadowy groves and ruins, and ended in a mighty wall green with antique vines, and pierced by a little gate of bronze.

Many times I walked through that valley, and longer and longer would I pause in the spectral half-light where the giant trees squirmed and twisted grotesquely, and the gray ground stretched damply from trunk to trunk, sometimes disclosing the mold-stained stones of buried temples. And always the goal of my fancies was the mighty vine-grown wall with the little gate of bronze therein.

After a while, as the days of waking became less and less bearable from their grayness and sameness, I would often drift in opiate peace through the valley and the shadowy groves, and wonder how I might seize them for my eternal dwelling-place, so that I need no more crawl back to a dull world stript of interest and new colors. And as I looked upon the little gate in the mighty wall, I felt that beyond it lay a dream-country from which, once it was entered, there would be no return.

So each night in sleep I strove to find the hidden latch of the gate in the ivyed antique wall, though it was exceedingly well hidden. And I would tell myself that the realm beyond the wall was not more lasting merely, but more lovely and radiant as well.

Then one night in the dream-city of Zakarion I found a yellowed papyrus filled with the thoughts of dream-sages who dwelt of old in that city, and who were too wise ever to be born in the waking world. Therein were written many things concerning the world of dream, and among them was lore of a golden valley and a sacred grove with temples, and a high wall pierced by a little bronze gate. When I saw this lore, I knew that it touched on the scenes I had haunted, and I therefore read long in the yellowed papyrus.

Some of the dream-sages wrote gorgeously of the wonders beyond the irrepassable gate, but others told of horror and disappointment. I knew not which to believe, yet longed more and more to cross forever into the unknown land; for doubt and secrecy are the lure of lures, and no new horror can be more terrible than the daily torture of the commonplace. So when I learned of the drug which would unlock the gate and drive me through, I resolved to take it when next I awaked.

Last night I swallowed the drug and floated dreamily into the golden valley and the shadowy groves; and when I came this time to the antique wall, I saw that the small gate of bronze was ajar. From beyond came a glow that weirdly lit the giant twisted trees and the tops of the buried temples, and I drifted on song-fully, expectant of the glories of the land from whence I should never return.

But as the gate swung wider and the sorcery of drug and dream pushed me through, I knew that all sights and glories were at an end; for in that new realm was neither land nor sea, but only the white void of unpeopled and illimitable space. So, happier than I had ever dared hoped to be, I dissolved again into that native infinity of crystal oblivion from which the daemon Life had called me for one brief and desolate hour.

THE QUEST OF IRANON

Into the granite city of Teloth wandered the youth, vine-crowned, his yellow hair glistening with myrrh and his purple robe torn with briers of the mountain Sidrak that lies across the antique bridge of stone. The men of Teloth are dark and stern, and dwell in square houses, and with frowns they asked the stranger whence he had come and what were his name and fortune. So the youth answered:

"I am Iranon, and come from Aira, a far city that I recall only dimly but seek to find again. I am a singer of songs that I learned in the far city, and my calling is to make beauty with the things remembered of childhood. My wealth is in little memories and dreams, and in hopes that I sing in gardens when the moon is tender and the west wind stirs the lotos-buds."

When the men of Teloth heard these things they whispered to one another; for though in the granite city there is no laughter or song, the stern men sometimes look to the Karthian hills in the spring and think of the lutes of distant Oonai whereof travelers have told. And thinking thus, they bade the stranger stay and sing in the square before the Tower of Mlin, though they liked not the color of his tattered robe, nor the myrrh in his hair, nor his chaplet of vine-leaves, nor the youth in his golden voice. At evening Iranon sang, and while he sang an old man prayed and a blind man said he saw a nimbus over the singer's head. But most of the men of Teloth yawned, and some laughed and some went away to sleep; for Iranon told nothing useful, singing only his memories, his dreams, and his hopes.

"I remember the twilight, the moon, and soft songs, and the window where I was rocked to sleep. And through the window was the street where the golden lights came, and where the shadows danced on houses of marble. I remember the square of moonlight on the floor, that was not like any other light, and the visions that danced in the moonbeams when my mother sang to me. And too, I remember the sun of morning bright above the many-colored hills in summer, and the sweetness of flowers borne on the south wind that made the trees sing.

"O Aira, city of marble and beryl, how many are thy beauties! How loved I the warm and fragrant groves across the hyaline Nithra, and the falls of the tiny Kra that flowed through the verdant valley! In those groves and in that vale the children wove wreaths for one another, and at dusk I dreamed strange dreams under the yath-trees on the mountain as I saw below me the lights of the city, and the curving Nithra reflecting a ribbon of stars.

"And in the city were palaces of veined and tinted marble, with golden domes and painted walls, and green gardens with cerulean pools and crystal fountains. Often I played in the gardens and waded in the pools, and lay and dreamed among the pale flowers under the trees. And sometimes at sunset I would climb the long hilly street to the citadel and the open place, and look down upon Aira, the magic city of marble and beryl, splendid in a robe of golden flame.

"Long have I missed thee, Aira, for I was but young when we went into exile; but my father was thy King and I shall come again to thee, for it is so decreed of Fate. All through seven lands have I sought thee, and some day shall I reign over thy groves and gardens, thy streets and palaces, and sing to men who shall know whereof I sing, and laugh not nor turn away. For I am Iranon, who was a Prince in Aira."

That night the men of Teloth lodged the stranger in a stable, and in the morning an archon came to him and told him to go to the shop of Athok the cobbler, and be apprenticed to him.

"But I am Iranon, a singer of songs," he said, "and have no heart for the cobbler's trade."

"All in Teloth must toil," replied the archon, "for that is the law." Then said Iranon,

"Wherefore do ye toil; is it not that ye may live and be happy? And if ye toil only that ye may toil more, when shall happiness

find you? Ye toil to live, but is not life made of beauty and song?
And if ye suffer no singers among you, where shall be the fruits
of your toil? Toil without song is like a weary journey without
an end. Were not death more pleasing?" But the archon was sullen
and did not understand, and rebuked the stranger.

"Thou art a strange youth, and I like not thy face nor thy
voice. The words thou speakest are blasphemy, for the gods of
Teloth have said that toil is good. Our gods have promised us a
haven of light beyond death, where there shall be rest without
end, and crystal coldness amidst which none shall vex his mind
with thought or his eyes with beauty. Go thou then to Athok
the cobbler or be gone out of the city by sunset. All here must
serve, and song is folly."

So Iranon went out of the stable and walked over the narrow
stone streets between the gloomy square houses of granite,
seeking something green in the air of spring. But in Teloth was
nothing green, for all was of stone. On the faces of men were
frowns, but by the stone embankment along the sluggish river
Zuro sat a young boy with sad eyes gazing into the waters to
spy green budding branches washed down from the hills by the
freshets. And the boy said to him:

"Art thou not indeed he of whom the archons tell, who seekest
a far city in a fair land? I am Romnod, and born of the blood of
Teloth, but am not old in the ways of the granite city, and yearn
daily for the warm groves and the distant lands of beauty and
song. Beyond the Karthian hills lieth Oonai, the city of lutes and
dancing, which men whisper of and say is both lovely and terrible.
Thither would I go were I old enough to find the way, and thither
shouldst thou go and thou wouldst sing and have men listen to
thee. Let us leave the city Teloth and fare together among the
hills of spring. Thou shalt shew me the ways of travel and I will
attend thy songs at evening when the stars one by one bring
dreams to the minds of dreamers. And peradventure it may be
that Oonai the city of lutes and dancing is even the fair Aira thou
seekest, for it is told that thou hast not known Aira since old

days, and a name often changeth. Let us go to Oonai, O Iranon of the golden head, where men shall know our longings and welcome us as brothers, nor ever laugh or frown at what we say." And Iranon answered:

"Be it so, small one; if any in this stone place yearn for beauty he must seek the mountains and beyond, and I would not leave thee to pine by the sluggish Zuro. But think not that delight and understanding dwell just across the Karthian hills, or in any spot thou canst find in a day's, or a year's, or a lustrum's journey. Behold, when I was small like thee I dwelt in the valley of Narthos by the frigid Xari, where none would listen to my dreams; and I told myself that when older I would go to Sinara on the southern slope, and sing to smiling dromedary-men in the market-place. But when I went to Sinara I found the dromedary-men all drunken and ribald, and saw that their songs were not as mine, so I traveled in a barge down the Xari to onyx-walled Jaren. And the soldiers at Jaren laughed at me and drove me out, so that I wandered to many other cities. I have seen Stethelos that is below the great cataract, and have gazed on the marsh where Sarnath once stood. I have been to Thraa, Ilarnek, and Kadatheron on the winding river Ai, and have dwelt long in Olathoë in the land of Lomar. But though I have had listeners sometimes, they have ever been few, and I know that welcome shall await me only in Aira, the city of marble and beryl where my father once ruled as King. So for Aira shall we seek, though it were well to visit distant and lute-blessed Oonai across the Karthian hills, which may indeed be Aira, though I think not. Aira's beauty is past imagining, and none can tell of it without rapture, whilst of Oonai the camel-drivers whisper leeringly."

At the sunset Iranon and small Romnod went forth from Teloth, and for long wandered amidst the green hills and cool forests. The way was rough and obscure, and never did they seem nearer to Oonai the city of lutes and dancing; but in the dusk as the stars came out Iranon would sing of Aira and its beauties and Romnod would listen, so that they were both happy after a fashion. They ate plentifully of fruit and red berries, and marked not the passing of time, but many years must have slipped away. Small Romnod was now not so small, and spoke deeply instead of shrilly, though Iranon was always the same, and decked his golden hair with vines and fragrant resins found in the woods. So it came to pass one day that Romnod seemed older than Iranon, though he had been very small when Iranon had found him watching for green budding branches in Teloth beside the sluggish stone-banked Zuro.

Then one night when the moon was full the travelers came to a mountain crest and looked down upon the myriad lights of Oonai. Peasants had told them they were near, and Iranon knew that this was not his native city of Aira. The lights of Oonai were not like those of Aira; for they were harsh and glaring, while the lights of Aira shine as softly and magically as shone the moonlight on the floor by the window where Iranon's mother once rocked him to sleep with song. But Oonai was a city of lutes and dancing, so Iranon and Romnod went down the steep slope that they might find men to whom songs and dreams would bring pleasure. And when they were come into the town they found rose-wreathed revelers bound from house to house and leaning from windows and balconies, who listened to the songs of Iranon and tossed him flowers and applauded when he was done. Then for a moment did Iranon believe he had found those who thought and felt even as he, though the town was not an hundredth as fair as Aira.

When dawn came Iranon looked about with dismay, for the domes of Oonai were not golden in the sun, but gray and dismal. And the men of Oonai were pale with reveling and dull with wine, and unlike the radiant men of Aira. But because the people had thrown him blossoms and acclaimed his songs Iranon stayed on, and with him Romnod, who liked the revelry of the town and wore in his dark hair roses and myrtle. Often at night Iranon sang to the revelers, but he was always as before, crowned only with the vine of the mountains and remembering the marble streets of Aira and the hyaline Nithra. In the frescoed halls of

the Monarch did he sing, upon a crystal dais raised over a floor
that was a mirror, and as he sang he brought pictures to his
hearers till the floor seemed to reflect old, beautiful, and half-
remembered things instead of the wine-reddened feasters who
pelted him with roses. And the King bade him put away his
tattered purple, and clothed him in satin and cloth-of-gold, with
rings of green jade and bracelets of tinted ivory, and lodged him
in a gilded and tapestried chamber on a bed of sweet carven
wood with canopies and coverlets of flower-embroidered silk.
Thus dwelt Iranon in Oonai, the city of lutes and dancing.

It is not known how long Iranon tarried in Oonai, but one
day the King brought to the palace some wild whirling dancers
from the Liranian desert, and dusky flute-players from Drinen in
the East, and after that the revelers threw their roses not so
much at Iranon as at the dancers and the flute-players. And day
by day that Romnod who had been a small boy in granite Teloth
grew coarser and redder with wine, till he dreamed less and less,
and listened with less delight to the songs of Iranon. But though
Iranon was sad he ceased not to sing, and at evening told again
his dreams of Aira, the city of marble and beryl. Then one night
the red and fattened Romnod snorted heavily amidst the poppied
silks of his banquet-couch and died writhing, whilst Iranon, pale
and slender, sang to himself in a far corner. And when Iranon
had wept over the grave of Romnod and strown it with green
budding branches, such as Romnod used to love, he put aside
his silks and gauds and went forgotten out of Oonai the city of
lutes and dancing clad only in the ragged purple in which he
had come, and garlanded with fresh vines from the mountains.

Into the sunset wandered Iranon, seeking still for his native
land and for men who would understand and cherish his songs
and dreams. In all the cities of Cydathria and in the lands beyond
the Bnazic desert gay-faced children laughed at his olden songs
and tattered robe of purple; but Iranon stayed ever young, and
wore wreaths upon his golden head whilst he sang of Aira, delight
of the past and hope of the future.

So came he one night to the squalid cot of an antique shepherd, bent and dirty, who kept lean flocks on a stony slope above a quicksand marsh. To this man Iranon spoke, as to so many others: "Canst thou tell me where I may find Aira, the city of marble and beryl, where flows the hyaline Nithra and where the falls of the tiny Kra sing to verdant valleys and hills forested with yath trees?" And the shepherd, hearing, looked long and strangely at Iranon, as if recalling something very far away in time, and noted each line of the stranger's face, and his golden hair, and his crown of vine-leaves. But he was old, and shook his head as he replied:

"O stranger, I have indeed heard the name of Aira, and the other names thou hast spoken, but they come to me from afar down the waste of long years. I heard them in my youth from the lips of a playmate, a beggar's boy given to strange dreams, who would weave long tales about the moon and the flowers and the west wind. We used to laugh at him, for we knew him from his birth though he thought himself a King's son. He was comely, even as thou, but full of folly and strangeness; and he ran away when small to find those who would listen gladly to his songs and dreams. How often hath he sung to me of lands that never were, and things that never can be! Of Aira did he speak much; of Aira and the river Nithra, and the falls of the tiny Kra. There would he ever say he once dwelt as a Prince, though here we knew him from his birth. Nor was there ever a marble city of Aira, nor those who could delight in strange songs, save in the dreams of mine old playmate Iranon who is gone."

And in the twilight, as the stars came out one by one and the moon cast on the marsh a radiance like that which a child sees quivering on the floor as he is rocked to sleep at evening, there walked into the lethal quicksands a very old man in tattered purple, crowned with withered vine-leaves and gazing ahead as if upon the golden domes of a fair city where dreams are understood. That night something of youth and beauty died in the elder world.

THE MOON-BOG

Somewhere, to what remote and fearsome region I know not, Denys Barry has gone. I was with him the last night he lived among men, and heard his screams when the thing came to him; but all the peasants and police in County Meath could never find him, or the others, though they searched long and far. And now I shudder when I hear the frogs piping in swamps, or see the moon in lonely places.

I had known Denys Barry well in America, where he had grown rich, and had congratulated him when he bought back the old castle by the bog at sleepy Kilderry. It was from Kilderry that his father had come, and it was there that he wished to enjoy his wealth among ancestral scenes. Men of his blood had once ruled over Kilderry and built and dwelt in the castle, but those days were very remote, so that for generations the castle had been empty and decaying. After he went to Ireland Barry wrote me often, and told me how under his care the gray castle was rising tower by tower to its ancient splendor; how the ivy was climbing slowly over the restored walls as it had climbed so many centuries ago, and how the peasants blessed him for bringing back the old days with his gold from over the sea. But in time there came troubles, and the peasants ceased to bless him, and fled away instead as from a doom. And then he sent a letter and asked me to visit him, for he was lonely in the castle with no one to speak to save the new servants and laborers he had brought from the north.

The bog was the cause of all these troubles, as Barry told me the night I came to the castle. I had reached Kilderry in the summer sunset, as the gold of the sky lighted the green of the hills and groves and the blue of the bog, where on a far islet a strange olden ruin glistened spectrally. That sunset was very beautiful, but the peasants at Ballylough had warned me against

it and said that Kilderry had become accursed, so that I almost
shuddered to see the high turrets of the castle gilded with fire.
Barry's motor had met me at the Ballylough station, for Kilderry
is off the railway. The villagers had shunned the car and the
driver from the north, but had whispered to me with pale faces
when they saw I was going to Kilderry. And that night, after our
reunion, Barry told me why.

The peasants had gone from Kilderry because Denys Barry
was to drain the great bog. For all his love of Ireland, America
had not left him untouched, and he hated the beautiful wasted
space where peat might be cut and land opened up. The legends
and superstitions of Kilderry did not move him, and he laughed
when the peasants first refused to help, and then cursed him and
went away to Ballylough with their few belongings as they saw
his determination. In their place he sent for laborers from the
north, and when the servants left he replaced them likewise. But
it was lonely among strangers, so Barry had asked me to come.

When I heard the fears which had driven the people from
Kilderry I laughed as loudly as my friend had laughed, for these
fears were of the vaguest, wildest, and most absurd character.
They had to do with some preposterous legend of the bog, and
of a grim guardian spirit that dwelt in the strange olden ruin on
the far islet I had seen in the sunset. There were tales of dancing
lights in the dark of the moon, and of chill winds when the night
was warm; of wraiths in white hovering over the waters, and of
an imagined city of stone deep down below the swampy surface.
But foremost among the weird fancies, and alone in its absolute
unanimity, was that of the curse awaiting him who should dare
to touch or drain the vast reddish morass. There were secrets,
said the peasants, which must not be uncovered; secrets that
had lain hidden since the plague came to the children of Partholan
in the fabulous years beyond history. In the *Book of Invaders*
it is told that these sons of the Greeks were all buried at Tallaght,
but old men in Kilderry said that one city was overlooked save
by its patron moon-goddess; so that only the wooded hills buried

it when the men of Nemed swept down from Scythia in their thirty ships.

Such were the idle tales which had made the villagers leave Kilderry, and when I heard them I did not wonder that Denys Barry had refused to listen. He had, however, a great interest in antiquities; and proposed to explore the bog thoroughly when it was drained. The white ruins on the islet he had often visited, but though their age was plainly great, and their contour very little like that of most ruins in Ireland, they were too dilapidated to tell the days of their glory. Now the work of drainage was ready to begin, and the laborers from the north were soon to strip the forbidden bog of its green moss and red heather, and kill the tiny shell-paved streamlets and quiet blue pools fringed with rushes.

After Barry had told me these things I was very drowsy, for the travels of the day had been wearying and my host had talked late into the night. A manservant shewed me to my room, which was in a remote tower overlooking the village, and the plain at the edge of the bog, and the bog itself; so that I could see from my windows in the moonlight the silent roofs from which the peasants had fled and which now sheltered the laborers from the north, and too, the parish church with its antique spire, and far out across the brooding bog the remote olden ruin on the islet gleaming white and spectral. Just as I dropped to sleep I fancied I heard faint sounds from the distance; sounds that were wild and half musical, and stirred me with a weird excitement which colored my dreams. But when I awaked next morning I felt it had all been a dream, for the visions I had seen were more wonderful than any sound of wild pipes in the night. Influenced by the legends that Barry had related, my mind had in slumber hovered around a stately city in a green valley, where marble streets and statues, villas and temples, carvings and inscriptions, all spoke in certain tones the glory that was Greece. When I told this dream to Barry we both laughed; but I laughed the louder, because he was perplexed about his laborers from the north.

For the sixth time they had all overslept, waking very slowly and dazedly, and acting as if they had not rested, although they were known to have gone early to bed the night before.

That morning and afternoon I wandered alone through the sun-gilded village and talked now and then with idle laborers, for Barry was busy with the final plans for beginning his work of drainage. The laborers were not as happy as they might have been, for most of them seemed uneasy over some dream which they had had, yet which they tried in vain to remember. I told them of my dream, but they were not interested till I spoke of the weird sounds I thought I had heard. Then they looked oddly at me, and said that they seemed to remember weird sounds, too.

In the evening Barry dined with me and announced that he would begin the drainage in two days. I was glad, for although I disliked to see the moss and the heather and the little streams and lakes depart, I had a growing wish to discern the ancient secrets the deep-matted peat might hide. And that night my dreams of piping flutes and marble peristyles came to a sudden and disquieting end; for upon the city in the valley I saw a pestilence descend, and then a frightful avalanche of wooded slopes that covered the dead bodies in the streets and left unburied only the temple of Artemis on the high peak, where the aged moon-priestess Cleis lay cold and silent with a crown of ivory on her silver head.

I have said that I awaked suddenly and in alarm. For some time I could not tell whether I was waking or sleeping, for the sound of flutes still rang shrilly in my ears; but when I saw on the floor the icy moonbeams and the outlines of a latticed Gothic window I decided I must be awake and in the castle at Kilderry. Then I heard a clock from some remote landing below strike the hour of two, and I knew I was awake. Yet still there came that monotonous piping from afar; wild, weird airs that made me think of some dance of fauns on distant Maenalus. It would not let me sleep, and in impatience I sprang up and paced the floor. Only by chance did I go to the north window and look out upon the silent village and the plain at the edge of the bog. I had no wish to gaze abroad, for I wanted to sleep; but the flutes tormented me, and I had to do or see something. How could I have suspected the thing I was to behold?

There in the moonlight that flooded the spacious plain was a spectacle which no mortal, having seen it, could ever forget. To the sound of reedy pipes that echoed over the bog there glided silently and eerily a mixed throng of swaying figures, reeling through such a revel as the Sicilians may have danced to Demeter in the old days under the harvest moon beside the Cyane. The wide plain, the golden moonlight, the shadowy moving forms, and above all the shrill monotonous piping, produced an effect which almost paralyzed me; yet I noted amidst my fear that half of these tireless, mechanical dancers were the laborers whom I had thought asleep, whilst the other half were strange airy beings in white, half indeterminate in nature, but suggesting pale wistful naiads from the haunted fountains of the bog. I do not know how long I gazed at this sight from the lonely turret window before I dropped suddenly in a dreamless swoon, out of which the high sun of morning aroused me.

My first impulse on awaking was to communicate all my fears and observations to Denys Barry, but as I saw the sunlight glowing through the latticed east window I became sure that there was no reality in what I thought I had seen. I am given to strange phantasms, yet am never weak enough to believe in them; so on this occasion contented myself with questioning the laborers, who slept very late and recalled nothing of the previous night save misty dreams of shrill sounds. This matter of the spectral piping harassed me greatly, and I wondered if the crickets of autumn had come before their time to vex the night and haunt the visions of men. Later in the day I watched Barry in the library poring over his plans for the great work which was to begin on the morrow, and for the first time felt a touch of the same kind of fear that had driven the peasants away. For some unknown reason I dreaded the thought of disturbing the ancient bog and its sunless secrets, and pictured terrible sights lying black under the unmeasured depth of age-old peat. That these secrets should be brought to light seemed injudicious, and I began to wish for an excuse to leave the castle and the village. I went so far as to talk casually to Barry on the subject, but did not dare continue after he gave his resounding laugh. So I was silent when the sun set fulgently over the far hills, and Kilderry blazed all red and gold in a flame that seemed a portent.

Whether the events of that night were of reality or illusion I shall never ascertain. Certainly they transcend anything we dream of in Nature and the universe; yet in no normal fashion can I explain those disappearances which were known to all men after it was over. I retired early and full of dread, and for a long time could not sleep in the uncanny silence of the tower. It was very dark, for although the sky was clear the moon was now well in the wane, and would not rise till the small hours. I thought as I lay there of Denys Barry, and of what would befall that bog when the day came, and found myself almost frantic with an impulse to rush out into the night, take Barry's car, and drive madly to Ballylough out of the menaced lands. But before my fears could crystallize into action I had fallen asleep, and gazed in dreams upon the city in the valley, cold and dead under a shroud of hideous shadow.

Probably it was the shrill piping that awaked me, yet that piping was not what I noticed first when I opened my eyes. I was lying with my back to the east window overlooking the bog, where the waning moon would rise, and therefore expected to see light cast on the opposite wall before me; but I had not looked for such a sight as now appeared. Light indeed glowed on the panels ahead, but it was not any light that the moon gives. Terrible and piercing was the shaft of ruddy refulgence that streamed through the Gothic window, and the whole chamber was brilliant with a splendor intense and unearthly. My immediate actions were peculiar for such a situation, but it is only in tales that a man does the dramatic and foreseen thing. Instead of looking out across the bog toward the source of the new light, I kept my eyes from the window in panic fear, and clumsily drew on my clothing with some dazed idea of escape. I remember seizing my revolver and hat, but before it was over I had lost them both without firing the one or donning the other. After a time the fascination of the red radiance overcame my fright, and I crept to the east window and looked out whilst the maddening, incessant piping whined and reverberated through the castle and over all the village.

Over the bog was a deluge of flaring light, scarlet and sinister, and pouring from the strange olden ruin on the far islet. The aspect of that ruin I cannot describe—I must have been mad, for it seemed to rise majestic and undecayed, splendid and column-cinctured, the flame-reflecting marble of its entablature piercing the sky like the apex of a temple on a mountain-top. Flutes shrieked and drums began to beat, and as I watched in awe and terror I thought I saw dark saltant forms silhouetted grotesquely against the vision of marble and effulgence. The effect was titanic—altogether unthinkable—and I might have stared indefinitely had not the sound of the piping seemed to grow stronger at my left. Trembling with a terror oddly mixed with ecstasy I crossed the circular room to the north window from which I could see the village and the plain at the edge of the bog. There my eyes dilated again with a wild wonder as great as if I had not just turned from a scene beyond the pale of Nature, for on the ghastly red-litten plain was moving a procession of beings in such a manner as none ever saw before save in nightmares.

Half gliding, half floating in the air, the white-clad bog-wraiths were slowly retreating toward the still waters and the island ruin in fantastic formations suggesting some ancient and solemn cere-monial dance. Their waving translucent arms, guided by the detestable piping of those unseen flutes, beckoned in uncanny rhythm to a throng of lurching laborers who followed dog-like with blind, brainless, floundering steps as if dragged by a clumsy but resistless daemon-will. As the naiads neared the bog, without altering their course, a new line of stumbling stragglers zigzagged drunkenly out of the castle from some door far below my window, groped sightlessly across the courtyard and through the intervening bit of village, and joined the floundering column of laborers on the plain. Despite their distance below me I at once knew they were the servants brought from the north, for I recognized the ugly and unwieldy form of the cook, whose very absurdness had now become unutterably tragic. The flutes piped horribly, and again I heard the beating of the drums from the direction of the island ruin. Then silently and gracefully the naiads reached the water and melted one by one into the ancient bog; while the line of followers, never checking their speed, splashed awkwardly after them and vanished amidst a tiny vortex of unwholesome bubbles which I could barely see in the scarlet light. And as the last pathetic straggler, the fat cook, sank heavily out of sight in that sullen pool, the flutes and the drums grew silent, and the blinding red rays from the ruins snapped instantaneously out, leaving the village of doom lone and desolate in the wan beams of a new-risen moon.

My condition was now one of indescribable chaos. Not knowing whether I was mad or sane, sleeping or waking, I was saved only by a merciful numbness. I believe I did ridiculous things such as offering prayers to Artemis, Latona, Demeter, Persephone, and Plouton. All that I recalled of a classic youth came to my lips as the horrors of the situation roused my deepest superstitions. I felt that I had witnessed the death of a whole village, and knew I was alone in the castle with Denys Barry, whose boldness had brought down a doom. As I thought of him new terrors convulsed me, and I fell to the floor; not fainting, but physically helpless. Then I felt the icy blast from the east window where the moon had risen, and began to hear the shrieks in the castle far below me. Soon those shrieks had attained a magnitude and quality which cannot be written of, and which make me faint as I think of them. All I can say is that they came from something I had known as a friend.

At some time during this shocking period the cold wind and the screaming must have roused me, for my next impression is of racing madly through inky rooms and corridors and out across the courtyard into the hideous night. They found me at dawn wandering mindless near Ballylough, but what unhinged me utterly was not any of the horrors I had seen or heard before. What I muttered about as I came slowly out of the shadows was a pair of fantastic incidents which occurred in my flight; incidents of no significance, yet which haunt me unceasingly when I am alone in certain marshy places or in the moonlight.

As I fled from that accursed castle along the bog's edge I heard a new sound; common, yet unlike any I had heard before at Kilderry. The stagnant waters, lately quite devoid of animal life, now teemed with a horde of slimy enormous frogs which piped shrilly and incessantly in tones strangely out of keeping with their size. They glistened bloated and green in the moon-beams, and seemed to gaze up at the fount of light. I followed the gaze of one very fat and ugly frog, and saw the second of the things which drove my senses away.

Stretching directly from the strange olden ruin on the far islet to the waning moon, my eyes seemed to trace a beam of faint quivering radiance having no reflection in the waters of the bog. And upward along that pallid path my fevered fancy pictured a thin shadow slowly writhing; a vague contorted shadow strug-gling as if drawn by unseen daemons. Crazed as I was, I saw in that awful shadow a monstrous resemblance—a nauseous, unbe-lievable caricature—a blasphemous effigy of him who had been Denys Barry.

THE OUTSIDER

That night the Baron dreamt of many a woe;
And all his warrior-guests, with shade and form
Of witch, and demon, and large coffin-worm,
Were long be-nightmared.
                              —Keats

Unhappy is he to whom the memories of childhood bring only fear and sadness. Wretched is he who looks back upon lone hours in vast and dismal chambers with brown hangings and maddening rows of antique books, or upon awed watches in twilight groves of grotesque, gigantic, and vine-encumbered trees that silently wave twisted branches far aloft. Such a lot the gods gave to me—to me, the dazed, the disappointed; the barren, the broken. And yet I am strangely content, and cling desperately to those sere memories, when my mind momentarily threatens to reach beyond to *the other.*

I know not where I was born, save that the castle was infinitely old and infinitely horrible; full of dark passages and having high ceilings where the eye could find only cobwebs and shadows. The stones in the crumbling corridors seemed always hideously damp, and there was an accursed smell everywhere, as of the piled-up corpses of dead generations. It was never light, so that I used sometimes to light candles and gaze steadily at them for relief; nor was there any sun outdoors, since the terrible trees grew high above the topmost accessible tower. There was one black tower which reached above the trees into the unknown outer sky, but that was partly ruined and could not be ascended save by a well-nigh impossible climb up the sheer wall, stone by stone.

I must have lived years in this place, but I cannot measure the time. Beings must have cared for my needs, yet I cannot recall any person except myself; or anything alive but the noiseless rats and bats and spiders. I think that whoever nursed me must have been shockingly aged, since my first conception of a living person was that of something mockingly like myself, yet distorted, shriveled, and decaying like the castle. To me there was nothing grotesque in the bones and skeletons that strowed some of the stone crypts deep down among the foundations. I fantastically associated these things with every-day events, and thought them more natural than the colored pictures of living beings which I found in many of the moldy books. From such books I learned all that I know. No teacher urged or guided me, and I do not recall hearing any human voice in all those years—not even my own; for although I had read of speech, I had never thought to try to speak aloud. My aspect was a matter equally unthought of, for there were no mirrors in the castle, and I merely regarded myself by instinct as akin to the youthful figures I saw drawn and painted in the books. I felt conscious of youth because I remembered so little.

Outside, across the putrid moat and under the dark mute trees, I would often lie and dream for hours about what I read in the books; and would longingly picture myself amidst gay crowds in the sunny world beyond the endless forest. Once I tried to escape from the forest, but as I went farther from the castle the shade grew denser and the air more filled with brooding fear; so that I ran frantically back lest I lose my way in a labyrinth of nighted silence.

So through endless twilights I dreamed and waited, though I knew not what I waited for. Then in the shadowy solitude my longing for light grew so frantic that I could rest no more, and I lifted entreating hands to the single black ruined tower that reached above the forest into the unknown outer sky. And at last I resolved to scale that tower, fall though I might; since it were better to glimpse the sky and perish, than to live without ever beholding day.

In the dank twilight I climbed the worn and aged stone stairs till I reached the level where they ceased, and thereafter clung perilously to small footholds leading upward. Ghastly and terrible was that dead, stairless cylinder of rock; black, ruined, and deserted, and sinister with startled bats whose wings made no noise. But more ghastly and terrible still was the slowness of my progress; for climb as I might, the darkness overhead grew no thinner, and a new chill as of haunted and venerable mold assailed me. I shivered as I wondered why I did not reach the light, and would have looked down had I dared. I fancied that night had come suddenly upon me, and vainly groped with one free hand for a window embrasure, that I might peer out and above, and try to judge the height I had attained.

All at once, after an infinity of awesome, sightless crawling up that concave and desperate precipice, I felt my head touch a solid thing, and I knew I must have gained the roof, or at least some kind of floor. In the darkness I raised my free hand and tested the barrier, finding it stone and immovable. Then came a deadly circuit of the tower, clinging to whatever holds the slimy wall could give; till finally my testing hand found the barrier yielding, and I turned upward again, pushing the slab or door with my head as I used both hands in my fearful ascent. There was no light revealed above, and as my hands went higher I knew that my climb was for the nonce ended; since the slab was the trap-door of an aperture leading to a level stone surface of greater circumference than the lower tower, no doubt the floor of some lofty and capacious observation chamber. I crawled through carefully, and tried to prevent the heavy slab from falling back into place; but failed in the latter attempt. As I lay exhausted on the stone floor I heard the eerie echoes of its fall, but hoped when necessary to pry it open again.

Believing I was now at a prodigious height, far above the accursed branches of the wood, I dragged myself up from the floor and fumbled about for windows, that I might look for the first time upon the sky, and the moon and stars of which I had read. But on every hand I was disappointed; since all that I found were vast shelves of marble, bearing odious oblong boxes of disturbing size. More and more I reflected, and wondered what hoary secrets might abide in this high apartment so many eons cut off from the castle below. Then unexpectedly my hands came upon a doorway, where hung a portal of stone, rough with strange chiseling. Trying it, I found it locked; but with a supreme burst of strength I overcame all obstacles and dragged it open inward. As I did so there came to me the purest ecstasy I have ever known; for shining tranquilly through an ornate grating of iron, and down a short stone passageway of steps that ascended from the newly found doorway, was the radiant full moon, which I had never before seen save in dreams and in vague visions I dared not call memories.

Fancying now that I had attained the very pinnacle of the castle, I commenced to rush up the few steps beyond the door; but the sudden veiling of the moon by a cloud caused me to stumble, and I felt my way more slowly in the dark. It was still very dark when I reached the grating—which I tried carefully and found unlocked, but which I did not open for fear of falling from the amazing height to which I had climbed. Then the moon came out.

Most daemoniacal of all shocks is that of the abysmally unexpected and grotesquely unbelievable. Nothing I had before undergone could compare in terror with what I now saw; with the bizarre marvels that sight implied. The sight itself was as simple as it was stupefying, for it was merely this: instead of a dizzying prospect of treetops seen from a lofty eminence, there stretched around me on a level through the grating nothing less than *the solid ground,* decked and diversified by marble slabs and columns, and overshadowed by an ancient stone church, whose ruined spire gleamed spectrally in the moonlight.

Half unconscious, I opened the grating and staggered out upon the white gravel path that stretched away in two directions. My mind, stunned and chaotic as it was, still held the frantic craving for light; and not even the fantastic wonder which had happened could stay my course. I neither knew nor cared whether my experience was insanity, dreaming, or magic; but was determined to gaze on brilliance and gaiety at any cost. I knew not who I was or what I was, or what my surroundings might be; though as I continued to stumble along I became conscious of a kind of fearsome latent memory that made my progress not wholly fortuitous. I passed under an arch out of that region of slabs and columns, and wandered through the open country; sometimes following the visible road, but sometimes leaving it curiously to tread across meadows where only occasional ruins bespoke the ancient presence of a forgotten road. Once I swam across a swift river where crumbling, mossy masonry told of a bridge long vanished.

Over two hours must have passed before I reached what seemed to be my goal, a venerable ivyed castle in a thickly wooded park; maddeningly familiar, yet full of perplexing strangeness to me. I saw that the moat was filled in, and that some of the well-known towers were demolished; whilst new wings existed to confuse the beholder. But what I observed with chief interest and delight were the open windows—gorgeously ablaze with light and sending forth sound of the gayest revelry. Advancing to one of these I looked in and saw an oddly dressed company, indeed; making merry, and speaking brightly to one another. I had never, seemingly, heard human speech before; and could guess only vaguely what was said. Some of the faces seemed to hold expressions that brought up incredibly remote recollections; others were utterly alien.

I now stepped through the low window into the brilliantly lighted room, stepping as I did so from my single bright moment of hope to my blackest convulsion of despair and realization. The nightmare was quick to come; for as I entered, there occurred immediately one of the most terrifying demonstrations I had ever conceived. Scarcely had I crossed the sill when there descended upon the whole company a sudden and unheralded fear of hideous intensity, distorting every face and evoking the most horrible screams from nearly every throat. Flight was universal, and in the clamor and panic several fell in a swoon and were dragged away by their madly fleeing companions. Many covered their eyes with their hands, and plunged blindly and awkwardly in their race to escape; overturning furniture and stumbling against the walls before they managed to reach one of the many doors.

The cries were shocking; and as I stood in the brilliant apartment alone and dazed, listening to their vanishing echoes, I trembled at the thought of what might be lurking near me unseen. At a casual inspection the room seemed deserted, but when I moved toward one of the alcoves I thought I detected a presence there—a hint of motion beyond the golden-arched doorway leading to another and somewhat similar room. As I approached the arch I began to perceive the presence more clearly; and then, with the first and last sound I ever uttered—a ghastly ululation that revolted me almost as poignantly as its noxious cause—I beheld in full, frightful vividness the inconceivable, indescribable, and unmentionable monstrosity which had by its simple appearance changed a merry company to a herd of delirious fugitives.

I cannot even hint what it was like, for it was a compound of all that is unclean, uncanny, unwelcome, abnormal, and detestable. It was the ghoulish shade of decay, antiquity, and desolation; the putrid, dripping eidolon of unwholesome revelation; the awful baring of that which the merciful earth should always hide. God knows it was not of this world—or no longer of this world—yet to my horror I saw in its eaten-away and bone-revealing outlines a leering, abhorrent travesty on the human shape; and in its moldy, disintegrating apparel an unspeakable quality that chilled me even more.

I was almost paralyzed, but not too much so to make a feeble effort toward flight; a backward stumble which failed to break the spell in which the nameless, voiceless monster held me. My eyes, bewitched by the glassy orbs which stared loathsomely into them, refused to close; though they were mercifully blurred, and shewed the terrible object but indistinctly after the first

shock. I tried to raise my hand to shut out the sight, yet so
stunned were my nerves that my arm could not fully obey my
will. The attempt, however, was enough to disturb my balance;
so that I had to stagger forward several steps to avoid falling. As
I did so I became suddenly and agonizingly aware of the *nearness*
of the carrion thing, whose hideous hollow breathing I half
fancied I could hear. Nearly mad, I found myself yet able to throw
out a hand to ward off the fetid apparition which pressed so
close; when in one cataclysmic second of cosmic nightmarishness
and hellish accident *my fingers touched the rotting outstretched
paw of the monster beneath the golden arch.*

I did not shriek, but all the fiendish ghouls that ride the
night-wind shrieked for me as in that same second there crashed
down upon my mind a single and fleeting avalanche of soul-
annihilating memory. I knew in that second all that had been; I
remembered beyond the frightful castle and the trees, and recognized the altered edifice in which I now stood; I recognized,
most terrible of all, the unholy abomination that stood leering
before me as I withdrew my sullied fingers from its own.

But in the cosmos there is balm as well as bitterness, and
that balm is nepenthe. In the supreme horror of that second I
forgot what had horrified me, and the burst of black memory
vanished in a chaos of echoing images. In a dream I fled from
that haunted and accursed pile, and ran swiftly and silently in
the moonlight. When I returned to the churchyard place of
marble and went down the steps I found the stone trap-door
immovable; but I was not sorry, for I had hated the antique
castle and the trees. Now I ride with the mocking and friendly
ghouls on the night-wind, and play by day amongst the catacombs of Nephren-Ka in the sealed and unknown valley of
Hadoth by the Nile. I know that light is not for me, save that
of the moon over the rock tombs of Neb, nor any gaiety save
the unnamed feasts of Nitokris beneath the Great Pyramid; yet
in my new wildness and freedom I almost welcome the bitterness of alienage.

For although nepenthe has calmed me, I know always that I am an outsider; a stranger in this century and among those who are still men. This I have known ever since I stretched out my fingers to the abomination within that great gilded frame; stretched out my fingers and touched *a cold and unyielding surface of polished glass.*

THE OTHER GODS

A top the tallest of earth's peaks dwell the gods of earth, and suffer no man to tell that he hath looked upon them. Lesser peaks they once inhabited; but ever the men from the plains would scale the slopes of rock and snow, driving the gods to higher and higher mountains till now only the last remains. When they left their older peaks they took with them all signs of themselves; save once, it is said, when they left a carven image on the face of the mountain which they called Ngranek.

But now they have betaken themselves to unknown Kadath in the cold waste where no man treads, and are grown stern, having no higher peak whereto to flee at the coming of men. They are grown stern, and where once they suffered men to displace them, they now forbid men to come, or coming, to depart. It is well for men that they know not of Kadath in the cold waste, else they would seek injudiciously to scale it.

Sometimes when earth's gods are homesick they visit in the still night the peaks where once they dwelt, and weep softly as they try to play in the olden way on remembered slopes. Men have felt the tears of the gods on white-capped Thurai, though they have thought it rain; and have heard the sighs of the gods in the plaintive dawn-winds of Lerion. In cloud-ships the gods are wont to travel, and wise cotters have legends that keep them from certain high peaks at night when it is cloudy, for the gods are not lenient as of old.

In Ulthar, which lies beyond the river Skai, once dwelt an old man avid to behold the gods of earth; a man deeply learned in the seven cryptical books of Hsan, and familiar with the Pnakotic Manuscripts of distant and frozen Lomar. His name was Barzai the Wise, and the villagers tell of how he went up a mountain on the night of the strange eclipse.

Barzai knew so much of the gods that he could tell of their

comings and goings, and guessed so many of their secrets that
he was deemed half a god himself. It was he who wisely advised
the burgesses of Ulthar when they passed their remarkable law
against the slaying of cats, and who first told the young priest
Atal where it is that black cats go at midnight on St. John's Eve.
Barzai was learned in the lore of earth's gods, and had gained a
desire to look upon their faces. He believed that his great secret
knowledge of gods could shield him from their wrath, so resolved
to go up to the summit of high and rocky Hatheg-Kla on a night
when he knew the gods would be there.

Hatheg-Kla is far in the stony desert beyond Hatheg, for
which it is named, and rises like a rock statue in a silent temple.
Around its peak the mists play always mournfully, for mists are
the memories of the gods, and the gods loved Hatheg-Kla when
they dwelt upon it in the old days. Often the gods of earth
visit Hatheg-Kla in their ships of cloud, casting pale vapors
over the slopes as they dance reminiscently on the summit
under a clear moon. The villagers of Hatheg say it is ill to climb
Hatheg-Kla at any time, and deadly to climb it by night when
pale vapors hide the summit and the moon; but Barzai heeded
them not when he came from neighboring Ulthar with the
young priest Atal, who was his disciple. Atal was only the son
of an innkeeper, and was sometimes afraid; but Barzai's father
had been a landgrave who dwelt in an ancient castle, so he
had no common superstition in his blood, and only laughed
at the fearful cotters.

Barzai and Atal went out of Hatheg into the stony desert
despite the prayers of peasants, and talked of earth's gods by
their campfires at night. Many days they traveled, and from afar
saw lofty Hatheg-Kla with his aureole of mournful mist. On the
thirteenth day they reached the mountain's lonely base, and Atal
spoke of his fears. But Barzai was old and learned and had no
fears, so led the way boldly up the slope that no man had scaled
since the time of Sansu, who is written of with fright in the
moldy Pnakotic Manuscripts.

The way was rocky, and made perilous by chasms, cliffs, and falling stones. Later it grew cold and snowy; and Barzai and Atal often slipped and fell as they hewed and plodded upward with staves and axes. Finally the air grew thin, and the sky changed color, and the climbers found it hard to breathe; but still they toiled up and up, marveling at the strangeness of the scene and thrilling at the thought of what would happen on the summit when the moon was out and the pale vapors spread around. For three days they climbed higher, higher, and higher toward the roof of the world; then they camped to wait for the clouding of the moon.

For four nights no clouds came, and the moon shone down cold through the thin mournful mists around the silent pinnacle. Then on the fifth night, which was the night of the full moon, Barzai saw some dense clouds far to the north, and stayed up with Atal to watch them draw near. Thick and majestic they sailed, slowly and deliberately onward; ranging themselves round the peak high above the watchers, and hiding the moon and the summit from view. For a long hour the watchers gazed, whilst the vapors swirled and the screen of clouds grew thicker and more restless. Barzai was wise in the lore of earth's gods, and listened hard for certain sounds, but Atal felt the chill of the vapors and the awe of the night, and feared much. And when Barzai began to climb higher and beckon eagerly, it was long before Atal would follow.

So thick were the vapors that the way was hard, and though Atal followed on at last, he could scarce see the gray shape of Barzai on the dim slope above in the clouded moonlight. Barzai forged very far ahead, and seemed despite his age to climb more easily than Atal; fearing not the steepness that began to grow too great for any save a strong and dauntless man, nor pausing at wide black chasms that Atal scarce could leap. And so they went up wildly over rocks and gulfs, slipping and stumbling, and sometimes awed at the vastness and horrible silence of bleak ice pinnacles and mute granite steeps.

Very suddenly Barzai went out of Atal's sight, scaling a hideous cliff that seemed to bulge outward and block the path for any climber not inspired of earth's gods. Atal was far below, and planning what he should do when he reached the place, when curiously he noticed that the light had grown strong, as if the cloudless peak and moonlit meeting-place of the gods were very near. And as he scrambled on toward the bulging cliff and litten sky he felt fears more shocking than any he had known before. Then through the high mists he heard the voice of unseen Barzai shouting wildly in delight:

"I have heard the gods! I have heard earth's gods singing in revelry on Hatheg-Kla! The voices of earth's gods are known to Barzai the Prophet! The mists are thin and the moon is bright, and I shall see the gods dancing wildly on Hatheg-Kla that they loved in youth! The wisdom of Barzai hath made him greater than earth's gods, and against his will their spells and barriers are as naught; Barzai will behold the gods, the proud gods, the secret gods, the gods of earth who spurn the sight of men!"

Atal could not hear the voices Barzai heard, but he was now close to the bulging cliff and scanning it for foot-holds. Then he heard Barzai's voice grow shriller and louder:

"The mists are very thin, and the moon casts shadows on the slope; the voices of earth's gods are high and wild, and they fear the coming of Barzai the Wise, who is greater than they. . . . The moon's light flickers, as earth's gods dance against it; I shall see the dancing forms of the gods that leap and howl in the moonlight. . . . The light is dimmer and the gods are afraid. . . ."

Whilst Barzai was shouting these things Atal felt a spectral change in the air, as if the laws of earth were bowing to greater laws; for though the way was steeper than ever, the upward path was now grown fearsomely easy, and the bulging cliff proved scarce an obstacle when he reached it and slid perilously up its convex face. The light of the moon had strangely failed, and as Atal plunged upward through the mists he heard Barzai the Wise shrieking in the shadows:

"The moon is dark, and the gods dance in the night; there is terror in the sky, for upon the moon hath sunk an eclipse foretold in no books of men or of earth's gods.... There is unknown magic on Hatheg-Kla, for the screams of the frightened gods have turned to laughter, and the slopes of ice shoot up endlessly into the black heavens whither I am plunging. . . . Hei! Hei! At last! *In the dim light I behold the gods of earth!*"

And now Atal, slipping dizzily up over inconceivable steeps, heard in the dark a loathsome laughing, mixed with such a cry as no man else ever heard save in the Phlegethon of unrelatable nightmares; a cry wherein reverberated the horror and anguish of a haunted lifetime packed into one atrocious moment:

"The *other* gods! The *other* gods! The gods of the outer hells that guard the feeble gods of earth! . . . Look away! . . . Go back! . . . Do not see! . . . Do not see! . . . The vengeance of the infinite abysses . . . That cursed, that damnable pit . . . Merciful gods of earth, *I am falling into the sky!*"

And as Atal shut his eyes and stopped his ears and tried to jump downward against the frightful pull from unknown heights, there resounded on Hatheg-Kla that terrible peal of thunder which awaked the good cotters of the plains and the honest burgesses of Hatheg and Nir and Ulthar, and caused them to behold through the clouds that strange eclipse of the moon that no book ever predicted. And when the moon came out at last Atal was safe on the lower snows of the mountain without sight of earth's gods, or of the *other* gods.

Now it is told in the moldy Pnakotic Manuscripts that Sansu found naught but wordless ice and rock when he climbed Hatheg-Kla in the youth of the world. Yet when the men of Ulthar and Nir and Hatheg crushed their fears and scaled that haunted steep by day in search of Barzai the Wise, they found graven in the naked stone of the summit a curious and Cyclopean symbol fifty cubits wide, as if the rock had been riven by some titanic chisel. And the symbol was like to one that learned men have discerned in those frightful parts of the

Pnakotic Manuscripts which are too ancient to be read. This they found.

Barzai the Wise they never found, nor could the holy priest Atal ever be persuaded to pray for his soul's repose. Moreover, to this day the people of Ulthar and Nir and Hatheg fear eclipses, and pray by night when pale vapors hide the mountain-top and the moon. And above the mists on Hatheg-Kla earth's gods sometimes dance reminiscently; for they know they are safe, and love to come from unknown Kadath in ships of cloud and play in the olden way, as they did when earth was new and men not given to the climbing of inaccessible places.

HYPNOS

To S. L.

Apropos of sleep, that sinister adventure of all our nights, we may say that men go to bed daily with an audacity that would be incomprehensible if we did not know that it is the result of ignorance of the danger.
—Baudelaire

May the merciful gods, if indeed there be such, guard those hours when no power of the will, or drug that the cunning of man devises, can keep me from the chasm of sleep. Death is merciful, for there is no return therefrom, but with him who has come back out of the nethermost chambers of night, haggard and knowing, peace rests nevermore. Fool that I was to plunge with such unsanctioned frenzy into mysteries no man was meant to penetrate; fool or god that *he* was—my only friend, who led me and went before me, and who in the end passed into terrors which may yet be mine.

We met, I recall, in a railway station, where he was the center of a crowd of the vulgarly curious. He was unconscious, having fallen in a kind of convulsion which imparted to his slight black-clad body a strange rigidity. I think he was then approaching forty years of age, for there were deep lines in the face, wan and hollow-cheeked, but oval and actually *beautiful;* and touches of gray in the thick, waving hair and small full beard which had once been of the deepest raven black. His brow was white as the marble of Pentelicus, and of a height and breadth almost godlike. I said to myself, with all the ardor of a sculptor, that this man was a faun's statue out of antique Hellas, dug from a temple's ruins and brought somehow to life in our stifling age only to feel the chill and pressure of devastating years. And when he opened his immense, sunken, and wildly luminous black eyes I knew he would be thenceforth my only friend—the only friend of one who had never possessed a friend before—for I saw that such eyes must have looked fully upon the grandeur and the terror of realms beyond normal consciousness and reality; realms which I had cherished in fancy, but vainly sought. So as I drove the crowd away I told him he must come home with me and be my teacher and leader in unfathomed mysteries, and he assented without speaking a word. Afterward I found that his voice was music—the music of deep viols and of crystalline spheres. We talked often in the night, and in the day, when I chiseled busts of him and carved miniature heads in ivory to immortalize his different expressions.

Of our studies it is impossible to speak, since they held so slight a connexion with anything of the world as living men conceive it. They were of that vaster and more appalling universe of dim entity and consciousness which lies deeper than matter, time, and space, and whose existence we suspect only in certain forms of sleep—those rare dreams beyond dreams which come never to common men, and but once or twice in the lifetime of imaginative men. The cosmos of our waking knowledge, born from such an universe as a bubble is born from the pipe of a jester, touches it only as such a bubble may touch its sardonic source when sucked back by the jester's whim. Men of learning suspect it little, and ignore it mostly. Wise men have interpreted dreams, and the gods have laughed. One man with Oriental eyes has said that all time and space are relative, and men have laughed. But even that man with Oriental eyes has done no more than suspect. I had wished and tried to do more than suspect, and my friend had tried and partly succeeded. Then we both tried together, and with exotic drugs courted terrible and forbidden dreams in the tower studio chamber of the old manor-house in hoary Kent.

Among the agonies of these after days is that chief of

torments—inarticulateness. What I learned and saw in those hours of impious exploration can never be told—for want of symbols or suggestions in any language. I say this because from first to last our discoveries partook only of the nature of *sensations;* sensations correlated with no impression which the nervous system of normal humanity is capable of receiving. They were sensations, yet within them lay unbelievable elements of time and space—things which at bottom possess no distinct and definite existence. Human utterance can best convey the general character of our experiences by calling them *plungings* or *soarings*; for in every period of revelation some part of our minds broke boldly away from all that is real and present, rushing aerially along shocking, unlighted, and fear-haunted abysses, and occasionally *tearing* through certain well-marked and typical obstacles describable only as viscous, uncouth clouds or vapors. In these black and bodiless flights we were sometimes alone and sometimes together. When we were together, my friend was always far ahead; I could comprehend his presence despite the absence of form by a species of pictorial memory whereby his face appeared to me, golden from a strange light and frightful with its weird beauty, its anomalously youthful cheeks, its burning eyes, its Olympian brow, and its shadowing hair and growth of beard.

Of the progress of time we kept no record, for time had become to us the merest illusion. I know only that there must have been something very singular involved, since we came at length to marvel why we did not grow old. Our discourse was unholy, and always hideously ambitious—no god or daemon could have aspired to discoveries and conquests like those which we planned in whispers. I shiver as I speak of them, and dare not be explicit; though I will say that my friend once wrote on paper a wish which he dared not utter with his tongue, and which made me burn the paper and look affrightedly out of the window at the spangled night sky. I will hint—only hint—that he had designs which involved the rulership of the visible universe and more; designs whereby the earth and the stars would move at his command, and the destinies of all living things be his. I affirm—I swear—that I had no share in these extreme aspirations. Anything my friend may have said or written to the contrary must be erroneous, for I am no man of strength to risk the unmentionable warfare in unmentionable spheres by which alone one might achieve success.

There was a night when winds from unknown spaces whirled us irresistibly into limitless vacua beyond all thought and entity. Perceptions of the most maddeningly untransmissible sort thronged upon us; perceptions of infinity which at the time convulsed us with joy, yet which are now partly lost to my memory and partly incapable of presentation to others. Viscous obstacles were clawed through in rapid succession, and at length I felt that we had been borne to realms of greater remoteness than any we had previously known. My friend was vastly in advance as we plunged into this awesome ocean of virgin ether, and I could see the sinister exultation on his floating, luminous, too youthful memory-face. Suddenly that face became dim and quickly disappeared, and in a brief space I found myself projected against an obstacle which I could not penetrate. It was like the others, yet incalculably denser; a sticky, clammy mass, if such terms can be applied to analogous qualities in a non-material sphere.

I had, I felt, been halted by a barrier which my friend and leader had successfully passed. Struggling anew, I came to the end of the drug-dream and opened my physical eyes to the tower studio in whose opposite corner reclined the pallid and still unconscious form of my fellow-dreamer, weirdly haggard and wildly beautiful as the moon shed gold-green light on his marble features. Then, after a short interval, the form in the corner stirred; and may pitying heaven keep from my sight and sound another thing like that which took place before me. I cannot tell you how he shrieked, or what vistas of unvisitable hells gleamed for a second in black eyes crazed with fright. I can only say that I fainted, and did not stir till he himself recovered and shook me in his frenzy for someone to keep away the horror and desolation.

That was the end of our voluntary searchings in the caverns of dream. Awed, shaken, and portentous, my friend who had been beyond the barrier warned me that we must never venture within those realms again. What he had seen, he dared not tell me; but he said from his wisdom that we must sleep as little as possible, even if drugs were necessary to keep us awake. That he was right, I soon learned from the unutterable fear which engulfed me whenever consciousness lapsed. After each short and inevitable sleep I seemed older, whilst my friend aged with a rapidity almost shocking. It is hideous to see wrinkles form and hair whiten almost before one's eyes. Our mode of life was now totally altered. Heretofore a recluse so far as I know—his true name and origin never having passed his lips—my friend now became frantic in his fear of solitude. At night he would not be alone, nor would the company of a few persons calm him. His sole relief was obtained in revelry of the most general and boisterous sort; so that few assemblies of the young and the gay were unknown to us. Our appearance and age seemed to excite in most cases a ridicule which I keenly resented, but which my friend considered a lesser evil than solitude. Especially was he afraid to be out of doors alone when the stars were shining, and if forced to this condition he would often glance furtively at the sky as if hunted by some monstrous thing therein. He did not always glance at the same place in the sky—it seemed to be a different place at different times. On spring evenings it would be low in the northeast. In the summer it would be nearly overhead. In the autumn it would be in the northwest. In winter it would be in the east, but mostly if in the small hours of morning. Midwinter evenings seemed least dreadful to him. Only after two years did I connect this fear with anything in particular; but then I began to see that he must be looking at a special spot on the celestial vault whose position at different times corresponded to the direction of his glance—a spot roughly marked by the constellation Corona Borealis.

We now had a studio in London, never separating, but never

discussing the days when we had sought to plumb the mysteries of the unreal world. We were aged and weak from our drugs, dissipations, and nervous overstrain, and the thinning hair and beard of my friend had become snow-white. Our freedom from long sleep was surprising, for seldom did we succumb more than an hour or two at a time to the shadow which had now grown so frightful a menace. Then came one January of fog and rain, when money ran low and drugs were hard to buy. My statues and ivory heads were all sold, and I had no means to purchase new materials, or energy to fashion them even had I possessed them. We suffered terribly, and on a certain night my friend sank into a deep-breathing sleep from which I could not awaken him. I can recall the scene now—the desolate, pitch-black garret studio under the eaves with the rain beating down; the ticking of the lone clock; the fancied ticking of our watches as they rested on the dressing-table; the creaking of some swaying shutter in a remote part of the house; certain distant city noises muffled by fog and space; and worst of all the deep, steady, sinister breathing of my friend on the couch—a rhythmical breathing which seemed to measure moments of supernal fear and agony for his spirit as it wandered in spheres forbidden, unimagined, and hideously remote.

The tension of my vigil became oppressive, and a wild train of trivial impressions and associations thronged through my almost unhinged mind. I heard a clock strike somewhere—not ours, for that was not a striking clock—and my morbid fancy found in this a new starting-point for idle wanderings. Clocks—time—space—infinity—and then my fancy reverted to the local as I reflected that even now, beyond the roof and the fog and the rain and the atmosphere, Corona Borealis was rising in the northeast. Corona Borealis, which my friend had appeared to dread, and whose scintillant semicircle of stars must even now be glowing unseen through the measureless abysses of ether. All at once my feverishly sensitive ears seemed to detect a new and wholly distinct component in the soft medley of drug-magnified sounds—a low and damnably insistent whine from very far away; droning, clamoring, mocking, calling, *from the northeast.*

But it was not that distant whine which robbed me of my faculties and set upon my soul such a seal of fright as may never in life be removed; not that which drew the shrieks and excited the convulsions which caused lodgers and police to break down the door. It was not what I *heard,* but what I *saw;* for in that dark, locked, shuttered, and curtained room there appeared from the black northeast corner a shaft of horrible red-gold light—a shaft which bore with it no glow to disperse the darkness, but which streamed only upon the recumbent head of the troubled sleeper, bringing out in hideous duplication the luminous and strangely youthful memory-face as I had known it in dreams of abysmal space and unshackled time, when my friend had pushed behind the barrier to those secret, innermost, and forbidden caverns of nightmare.

And as I looked, I beheld the head rise, the black, liquid, and deep-sunken eyes open in terror, and the thin, shadowed lips part as if for a scream too frightful to be uttered. There dwelt in that ghastly and flexible face, as it shone bodiless, luminous, and rejuvenated in the blackness, more of stark, teeming, brain-shattering fear than all the rest of heaven and earth has ever revealed to me. No word was spoken amidst the distant sound that grew nearer and nearer, but as I followed the memory-face's mad stare along that cursed shaft of light to its source, the source whence also the whining came, I too saw for an instant what it saw, and fell with ringing ears in that fit of shrieking and epilepsy which brought the lodgers and the police. Never could I tell, try as I might, what it actually was that I saw; nor could the still face tell, for although it must have seen more-than I did, it will never speak again. But always I shall guard against the mocking and insatiate Hypnos, lord of sleep, against the night sky, and against the mad ambitions of knowledge and philosophy.

Just what happened is unknown, for not only was my own mind unseated by the strange and hideous thing, but others were tainted with a forgetfulness which can mean nothing if not madness. They have said, I know not for what reason, that I never had a friend, but that art, philosophy, and insanity had filled all my tragic life. The lodgers and police on that night soothed me, and the doctor administered something to quiet me, nor did anyone see what a nightmare event had taken place. My stricken friend moved them to no pity, but what they found on the couch in the studio made them give me a praise which sickened me, and now a fame which I spurn in despair as I sit for hours, bald, gray-bearded, shriveled, palsied, drug-crazed, and broken, adoring and praying to the object they found.

For they deny that I sold the last of my statuary, and point with ecstasy at the thing which the shining shaft of light left cold, petrified, and unvocal. It is all that remains of my friend; the friend who led me on to madness and wreckage; a godlike head of such marble as only old Hellas could yield, young with the youth that is outside time, and with beauteous bearded face, curved, smiling lips, Olympian brow, and dense locks waving and poppy-crowned. They say that that haunting memory-face is modeled from my own, as it was at twenty-five, but upon the marble base is carven a single name in the letters of Attica—ΎΠΝΟΣ.

WHAT THE MOON BRINGS

I hate the moon—I am afraid of it—for when it shines on certain scenes familiar and loved it sometimes makes them unfamiliar and hideous.

It was in the spectral summer when the moon shone down on the old garden where I wandered; the spectral summer of narcotic flowers and humid seas of foliage that bring wild and many-colored dreams. And as I walked by the shallow crystal stream I saw unwonted ripples tipped with yellow light, as if those placid waters were drawn on in resistless currents to strange oceans that are not in the world. Silent and sparkling, bright and baleful, those moon-cursed waters hurried I knew not whither; whilst from the embowered banks white lotos-blossoms fluttered one by one in the opiate night-wind and dropped despairingly into the stream, swirling away horribly under the arched, carven bridge, and staring back with the sinister resignation of calm, dead faces.

And as I ran along the shore, crushing sleeping flowers with heedless feet and maddened ever by the fear of unknown things and the lure of the dead faces, I saw that the garden had no end under that moon; for where by day the walls were, there stretched now only new vistas of trees and paths, flowers and shrubs, stone idols and pagodas, and bendings of the yellow-litten stream past grassy banks and under grotesque bridges of marble. And the lips of the dead lotos-faces whispered sadly, and bade me follow, nor did I cease my steps till the stream became a river, and joined amidst marshes of swaying reeds and beaches of gleaming sand the shore of a vast and nameless sea.

Upon that sea the hateful moon shone, and over its unvocal waves weird perfumes brooded. And as I saw therein the lotos-faces vanish, I longed for nets that I might capture them and learn from them the secrets which the moon had brought upon the night. But when the moon went over to the west and the still tide ebbed from the sullen shore, I saw in that light old spires that the waves almost uncovered, and white columns gay with festoons of green seaweed. And knowing that to this sunken place all the dead had come, I trembled and did not wish again to speak with the lotos-faces.

Yet when I saw afar out in the sea a black condor descend from the sky to seek rest on a vast reef, I would fain have questioned him, and asked him of those whom I had known when they were alive. This I would have asked him had he not been so far away, but he was very far, and could not be seen at all when he drew nigh that gigantic reef.

So I watched the tide go out under that sinking moon, and saw gleaming the spires, the towers, and the roofs of that dead, dripping city. And as I watched, my nostrils tried to close against the perfume-conquering stench of the world's dead; for truly, in this unplaced and forgotten spot had all the flesh of the church-yards gathered for puffy sea-worms to gnaw and glut upon.

Over those horrors the evil moon now hung very low, but the puffy worms of the sea need no moon to feed by. And as I watched the ripples that told of the writhing of worms beneath, I felt a new chill from afar out whither the condor had flown, as if my flesh had caught a horror before my eyes had seen it.

Nor had my flesh trembled without cause, for when I raised my eyes I saw that the waters had ebbed very low, shewing much of the vast reef whose rim I had seen before. And when I saw that this reef was but the black basalt crown of a shocking eikon whose monstrous forehead now shone in the dim moonlight and whose vile hooves must paw the hellish ooze miles below, I shrieked and shrieked lest the hidden face rise above the waters, and lest the hidden eyes look at me after the slinking away of that leering and treacherous yellow moon.

And to escape this relentless thing I plunged gladly and unhesitatingly into the stinking shallows where amidst weedy walls and sunken streets fat sea-worms feast upon the world's dead.

AZATHOTH

When age fell upon the world, and wonder went out of the minds of men; when gray cities reared to smoky skies tall towers grim and ugly, in whose shadow none might dream of the sun or of spring's flowering meads; when learning stripped earth of her mantle of beauty, and poets sang no more save of twisted phantoms seen with bleared and inward-looking eyes; when these things had come to pass, and childish hopes had gone away forever, there was a man who traveled out of life on a quest into the spaces whither the world's dreams had fled.

Of the name and abode of this man but little is written, for they were of the waking world only; yet it is said that both were obscure. It is enough to know that he dwelt in a city of high walls where sterile twilight reigned, and that he toiled all day among shadow and turmoil, coming home at evening to a room whose one window opened not on the fields and groves but on a dim court where other windows stared in dull despair. From that casement one might see only walls and windows, except sometimes when one leaned far out and peered aloft at the small stars that passed. And because mere walls and windows must soon drive to madness a man who dreams and reads much, the dweller in that room used night after night to lean out and peer aloft to glimpse some fragment of things beyond the waking world and the grayness of tall cities. After years he began to call the slow-sailing stars by name, and to follow them in fancy when they glided regretfully out of sight; till at length his vision opened to many secret vistas whose existence no common eye suspects. And one night a mighty gulf was bridged, and the dream-haunted skies swelled down to the lonely watcher's window to merge with the close air of his room and make him a part of their fabulous wonder.

There came to that room wild streams of violet midnight glittering with dust of gold; vortices of dust and fire, swirling out of the ultimate spaces and heavy with perfumes from beyond the worlds. Opiate oceans poured there, litten by suns that the eye may never behold and having in their whirlpools strange dolphins and sea-nymphs of unrememberable deeps. Noiseless infinity eddied around the dreamer and wafted him away without even touching the body that leaned stiffly from the lonely window; and for days not counted in men's calendars the tides of far spheres bare him gently to join the dreams for which he longed; the dreams that men have lost. And in the course of many cycles they tenderly left him sleeping on a green sunrise shore; a green shore fragrant with lotos-blossoms and starred by red camalotes.

THE DESCENDANT

In London there is a man who screams when the church bells ring. He lives all alone with his streaked cat in Gray's Inn, and people call him harmlessly mad. His room is filled with books of the tamest and most puerile kind, and hour after hour he tries to lose himself in their feeble pages. All he seeks from life is not to think. For some reason thought is very horrible to him, and anything which stirs the imagination he flees as a plague. He is very thin and gray and wrinkled, but there are those who declare he is not nearly so old as he looks. Fear has its grisly claws upon him, and a sound will make him start with staring eyes and sweat-beaded forehead. Friends and companions he shuns, for he wishes to answer no questions. Those who once knew him as scholar and aesthete say it is very pitiful to see him now. He dropped them all years ago, and no one feels sure whether he left the country or merely sank from sight in some hidden byway. It is a decade now since he moved into Gray's Inn, and of where he had been he would say nothing till the night young Williams bought the *Necronomicon*.

Williams was a dreamer, and only twenty-three, and when he moved into the ancient house he felt a strangeness and a breath of cosmic wind about the gray wizened man in the next room. He forced his friendship where old friends dared not force theirs, and marveled at the fright that sat upon this gaunt, haggard watcher and listener. For that the man always watched and listened no one could doubt. He watched and listened with his mind more than with his eyes and ears, and strove every moment to drown something in his ceaseless poring over gay, insipid novels. And when the church bells rang he would stop his ears and scream, and the gray cat that dwelt with him would howl in unison till the last peal died reverberantly away.

But try as Williams would, he could not make his neighbor

speak of anything profound or hidden. The old man would not live up to his aspect and manner, but would feign a smile and a light tone and prattle feverishly and frantically of cheerful trifles; his voice every moment rising and thickening till at last it would split in a piping and incoherent falsetto. That his learning was deep and thorough, his most trivial remarks made abundantly clear; and Williams was not surprised to hear that he had been to Harrow and Oxford. Later it developed that he was none other than Lord Northam, of whose ancient hereditary castle on the Yorkshire coast so many odd things were told; but when Williams tried to talk of the castle, and of its reputed Roman origin, he refused to admit that there was anything unusual about it. He even tittered shrilly when the subject of the supposed under crypts, hewn out of the solid crag that frowns on the North Sea, was brought up.

So matters went till that night when Williams brought home the infamous *Necronomicon* of the mad Arab Abdul Alhazred. He had known of the dreaded volume since his sixteenth year, when his dawning love of the bizarre had led him to ask queer questions of a bent old bookseller in Chandos Street; and he had always wondered why men paled when they spoke of it. The old bookseller had told him that only five copies were known to have survived the shocked edicts of the priests and lawgivers against it and that all of these were locked up with frightened care by custodians who had ventured to begin a reading of the hateful black-letter. But now, at last, he had not only found an accessible copy but had made it his own at a ludicrously low figure. It was at a Jew's shop in the squalid precincts of Clare Market, where he had often bought strange things before, and he almost fancied the gnarled old Levite smiled amidst tangles of beard as the great discovery was made. The bulky leather cover with the brass clasp had been so prominently visible, and the price was so absurdly slight.

The one glimpse he had had of the title was enough to send him into transports, and some of the diagrams set in the vague Latin text excited the tensest and most disquieting recollections in his brain. He felt it was highly necessary to get the ponderous thing home and begin deciphering it, and bore it out of the shop with such precipitate haste that the old Jew chuckled disturbingly behind him. But when at last it was safe in his room he found the combination of black-letter and debased idiom too much for his powers as a linguist, and reluctantly called on his strange, frightened friend for help with the twisted, medieval Latin. Lord Northam was simpering inanities to his streaked cat, and started violently when the young man entered. Then he saw the volume and shuddered wildly, and fainted altogether when Williams uttered the title. It was when he regained his senses that he told his story; told his fantastic figment of madness in frantic whispers, lest his friend be not quick to burn the accursed book and give wide scattering to its ashes.

There must, Lord Northam whispered, have been something wrong at the start; but it would never have come to a head if he had not explored too far. He was the nineteenth Baron of a line whose beginnings went uncomfortably far back into the past—unbelievably far, if vague tradition could be heeded, for there were family tales of a descent from pre-Saxon times, when a certain Cnaeus Gabinius Capito, military tribune in the Third Augustan Legion then stationed at Lindum in Roman Britain, had been summarily expelled from his command for participation in certain rites unconnected with any known religion. Gabinius had, the rumor ran, come upon a cliffside cavern where strange folk met together and made the Elder Sign in the dark; strange folk whom the Britons knew not save in fear, and who were the last to survive from a great land in the west that had sunk, leaving only the islands with the raths and circles and shrines of which Stonehenge was the greatest. There was no certainty, of course, in the legend that Gabinius had built an impregnable fortress over the forbidden cave and founded a line which Pict and Saxon, Dane and Norman were powerless to obliterate; or in the tacit assumption that from this line sprang the bold companion and lieutenant of the Black Prince whom Edward Third created Baron of Northam. These things were not certain, yet they were often told; and in truth the stonework of Northam Keep did look alarmingly like the masonry of Hadrian's Wall. As a child Lord Northam had had peculiar dreams when sleeping in the older parts of the castle, and had acquired a constant habit of looking back through his memory for half-amorphous scenes and patterns and impressions which formed no part of his waking experience. He became a dreamer who found life tame and unsatisfying; a searcher for strange realms and relationships once familiar, yet lying nowhere in the visible regions of earth.

Filled with a feeling that our tangible world is only an atom in a fabric vast and ominous, and that unknown demesnes press on and permeate the sphere of the known at every point, Northam in youth and young manhood drained in turn the fonts of formal religion and occult mystery. Nowhere, however, could he find ease and content; and as he grew older the staleness and limitations of life became more and more maddening to him. During the 'nineties he dabbled in Satanism, and at all times he devoured avidly any doctrine or theory which seemed to promise escape from the close vistas of science and the dully unvarying laws of Nature. Books like Ignatius Donnelly's chimerical account of Atlantis he absorbed with zest, and a dozen obscure precursors of Charles Fort enthralled him with their vagaries. He would travel leagues to follow up a furtive village tale of abnormal wonder, and once went into the desert of Araby to seek a Nameless City of faint report, which no man has ever beheld. There rose within him the tantalizing faith that somewhere an easy gate existed, which if one found would admit him freely to those outer deeps whose echoes rattled so dimly at the back of his memory. It might be in the visible world, yet it might be only in his mind and soul. Perhaps he held within his own half-explored brain that cryptic link which would awaken him to elder and future lives in forgotten dimensions; which would bind him to the stars, and to the infinities and eternities beyond them.

COOL AIR

You ask me to explain why I am afraid of a draft of cool air; why I shiver more than others upon entering a cold room, and seem nauseated and repelled when the chill of evening creeps through the heat of a mild autumn day. There are those who say I respond to cold as others do to a bad odor, and I am the last to deny the impression. What I will do is to relate the most horrible circumstance I ever encountered, and leave it to you to judge whether or not this forms a suitable explanation of my peculiarity.

It is a mistake to fancy that horror is associated inextricably with darkness, silence, and solitude. I found it in the glare of mid-afternoon, in the clangor of a metropolis, and in the teeming midst of a shabby and commonplace rooming-house with a prosaic landlady and two stalwart men by my side. In the spring of 1923 I had secured some dreary and unprofitable magazine work in the city of New York; and being unable to pay any substantial rent, began drifting from one cheap boarding establishment to another in search of a room which might combine the qualities of decent cleanliness, endurable furnishings, and very reasonable price. It soon developed that I had only a choice between different evils, but after a time I came upon a house in West Fourteenth Street which disgusted me much less than the others I had sampled.

The place was a four-story mansion of brownstone, dating apparently from the late forties, and fitted with woodwork and marble whose stained and sullied splendor argued a descent from high levels of tasteful opulence. In the rooms, large and lofty, and decorated with impossible paper and ridiculously ornate stucco cornices, there lingered a depressing mustiness and hint of obscure cookery; but the floors were clean, the linen tolerably regular, and the hot water not too often cold or turned off, so that I came to regard it as at least a bearable place to hibernate till one might really live again. The landlady, a slatternly, almost bearded Spanish woman named Herrero, did not annoy me with gossip or with criticisms of the late-burning electric light in my third-floor front hall room; and my fellow-lodgers were as quiet and uncommunicative as one might desire, being mostly Spaniards a little above the coarsest and crudest grade. Only the din of street cars in the thoroughfare below proved a serious annoyance.

I had been there about three weeks when the first odd incident occurred. One evening at about eight I heard a spattering on the floor and became suddenly aware that I had been smelling the pungent odor of ammonia for some time. Looking about, I saw that the ceiling was wet and dripping; the soaking apparently proceeding from a corner on the side toward the street. Anxious to stop the matter at its source, I hastened to the basement to tell the landlady; and was assured by her that the trouble would quickly be set right.

"Doctair Muñoz," she cried as she rushed upstairs ahead of me, "he have speel hees chemicals. He ees too seeck for doctair heemself—seecker and seecker all the time—but he weel not have no othair for help. He ees vairy queer in hees seeckness—all day he take funnee-smelling baths, and he cannot get excite or warm. All hees own housework he do—hees leetle room are full of bottles and machines, and he do not work as doctair. But he was great once—my fathair in Barcelona have hear of heem—and only joost now he feex a arm of the plumber that get hurt of sudden. He nevair go out, only on roof, and my boy Esteban he breeng heem hees food and laundry and mediceens and chemicals. My Gawd, the sal-ammoniac that man use for keep heem cool!"

Mrs. Herrero disappeared up the staircase to the fourth floor, and I returned to my room. The ammonia ceased to drip, and as I cleaned up what had spilled and opened the window for air, I heard the landlady's heavy footsteps above me. Dr. Muñoz I had never heard, save for certain sounds as of some gasoline-driven mechanism; since his step was soft and gentle. I wondered for a moment what the strange affliction of this man might be, and whether his obstinate refusal of outside aid were not the result of a rather baseless eccentricity. There is, I reflected tritely, an infinite deal of pathos in the state of an eminent person who has come down in the world.

I might never have known Dr. Muñoz had it not been for the heart attack that suddenly seized me one forenoon as I sat writing in my room. Physicians had told me of the danger of those spells, and I knew there was no time to be lost; so remembering what the landlady had said about the invalid's help of the injured workman, I dragged myself upstairs and knocked feebly at the door above mine. My knock was answered in good English by a curious voice some distance to the right, asking my name and business; and these things being stated, there came an opening of the door next to the one I had sought.

A rush of cool air greeted me; and though the day was one of the hottest of late June, I shivered as I crossed the threshold into a large apartment whose rich and tasteful decoration surprised me in this nest of squalor and seediness. A folding couch now filled its diurnal role of sofa, and the mahogany furniture, sumptuous hangings, old paintings, and mellow book-shelves all bespoke a gentleman's study rather than a boarding-house bedroom. I now saw that the hall room above mine—the "leetle room" of bottles and machines which Mrs. Herrero had mentioned—was merely the laboratory of the doctor; and that his main living quarters lay in the spacious adjoining room whose convenient alcoves and large contiguous bathroom permitted him to hide all dressers and obtrusive utilitarian devices. Dr. Muñoz, most certainly, was a man of birth, cultivation, and discrimination.

The figure before me was short but exquisitely proportioned, and clad in somewhat formal dress of perfect cut and fit. A high-bred face of masterful though not arrogant expression was adorned by a short iron-gray full beard, and an old-fashioned pince-nez shielded the full, dark eyes and surmounted an aquiline nose which gave a Moorish touch to a physiognomy otherwise dominantly Celtiberian. Thick, well-trimmed hair that argued the punctual calls of a barber was parted gracefully above a high forehead; and the whole picture was one of striking intelligence and superior blood and breeding.

Nevertheless, as I saw Dr. Muñoz in that blast of cool air, I felt a repugnance which nothing in his aspect could justify. Only his lividly inclined complexion and coldness of touch could have afforded a physical basis for this feeling, and even these things should have been excusable considering the man's known invalidism. It might, too, have been the singular cold that alienated me; for such chilliness was abnormal on so hot a day, and the abnormal always excites aversion, distrust, and fear.

But repugnance was soon forgotten in admiration, for the strange physician's extreme skill at once became manifest despite the ice-coldness and shakiness of his bloodless-looking hands. He clearly understood my needs at a glance, and ministered to them with a master's deftness; the while reassuring me in a finely modulated though oddly hollow and timbreless voice that he was the bitterest of sworn enemies to death, and had sunk his fortune and lost all his friends in a lifetime of bizarre experiment devoted to its bafflement and extirpation. Something of the benevolent fanatic seemed to reside in him, and he rambled on almost garrulously as he sounded my chest and mixed a suitable draft of drugs fetched from the smaller laboratory room. Evidently he found the society of a well-born man a rare novelty in this dingy environment, and was moved to unaccustomed speech as memories of better days surged over him.

His voice, if queer, was at least soothing; and I could not even perceive that he breathed as the fluent sentences rolled urbanely out. He sought to distract my mind from my own seizure by speaking of his theories and experiments; and I remember his tactfully consoling me about my weak heart by insisting that will and consciousness are stronger than organic life itself, so that if a bodily frame be but originally healthy and carefully preserved, it may through a scientific enhancement of these qualities retain a kind of nervous animation despite the most serious impairments, defects, or even absences in the battery of specific organs. He might, he half jestingly said, some day teach me to live—or at least to possess some kind of conscious existence—without any heart at all! For his part, he was afflicted with a complication of maladies requiring a very exact regimen which included constant cold. Any marked rise in temperature might, if prolonged, affect him fatally; and the frigidity of his habitation—some 55 or 56 degrees Fahrenheit—was maintained by an absorption system of ammonia cooling, the gasoline engine of whose pumps I had often heard in my own room below.

Relieved of my seizure in a marvelously short while, I left the shivery place a disciple and devotee of the gifted recluse. After that I paid him frequent overcoated calls; listening while he told of secret researches and almost ghastly results, and trembling a bit when I examined the unconventional and astonishingly ancient volumes on his shelves. I was eventually, I may add, almost cured of my disease for all time by his skillful ministrations. It seems that he did not scorn the incantations of the medievalists, since he believed these cryptic formulae to contain rare psychological stimuli which might conceivably have singular effects on the substance of a nervous system from which organic pulsations had fled. I was touched by his account of the aged Dr. Torres of Valencia, who had shared his earlier experiments with him through the great illness of eighteen years before, whence his present disorders proceeded. No sooner had the venerable practitioner saved his colleague than he himself succumbed to the grim enemy he had fought. Perhaps the strain had been too great; for Dr. Muñoz made it whisperingly clear—though not in detail—that the methods of healing had been most extraordinary, involving scenes and processes not welcomed by elderly and conservative Galens.

As the weeks passed, I observed with regret that my new friend was indeed slowly but unmistakably losing ground physically, as Mrs. Herrero had suggested. The livid aspect of his countenance was intensified, his voice became more hollow and indistinct, his muscular motions were less perfectly co-ordinated, and his mind and will displayed less resilience and initiative. Of this sad change he seemed by no means unaware, and little by little his expression and conversation both took on a gruesome irony which restored in me something of the subtle repulsion I had originally felt.

He developed strange caprices, acquiring a fondness for exotic spices and Egyptian incense till his room smelled like the vault of a sepulchered Pharaoh in the Valley of Kings. At the same time his demands for cold air increased, and with my aid he amplified the ammonia piping of his room and modified the pumps and feed of his refrigerating machine till he could keep the temperature as low as 34° or 40° and finally even 28°; the bathroom and laboratory, of course, being less chilled, in order that water might not freeze, and that chemical processes might not be impeded. The tenant adjoining him complained of the icy air from around the connecting door, so I helped him fit heavy hangings to obviate the difficulty. A kind of growing horror, of outré and morbid cast, seemed to possess him. He talked of death incessantly, but laughed hollowly when such things as burial or funeral arrangements were gently suggested.

All in all, he became a disconcerting and even gruesome companion; yet in my gratitude for his healing I could not well abandon him to the strangers around him, and was careful to dust his room and attend to his needs each day, muffled in a heavy ulster which I bought especially for the purpose. I likewise did much of his shopping, and gasped in bafflement at some of the chemicals he ordered from druggists and laboratory supply houses.

An increasing and unexplained atmosphere of panic seemed to rise around his apartment. The whole house, as I have said, had a musty odor; but the smell in his room was worse—and in spite of all the spices and incense, and the pungent chemicals of the now incessant baths which he insisted on taking unaided. I perceived that it must be connected with his ailment, and shuddered when I reflected on what that ailment might be. Mrs. Herrero crossed herself when she looked at him, and gave him up unreservedly to me; not even letting her son Esteban continue to run errands for him. When I suggested other physicians, the sufferer would fly into as much of a rage as he seemed to dare to entertain. He evidently feared the physical effect of violent emotion, yet his will and driving force waxed rather than waned, and he refused to be confined to his bed. The lassitude of his earlier ill days gave place to a return of his fiery purpose, so that he seemed about to hurl defiance at the death-daemon even as that ancient enemy seized him. The pretence of eating, always curiously like a formality with him, he virtually abandoned; and mental power alone appeared to keep him from total collapse.

He acquired a habit of writing long documents of some sort, which he carefully sealed and filled with injunctions that I transmit them after his death to certain persons whom he named—for the most part lettered East Indians, but including a once celebrated French physician now generally thought dead, and about whom the most inconceivable things had been whispered. As it happened, I burned all these papers undelivered and unopened. His aspect and voice became utterly frightful, and his presence almost unbearable. One September day an unexpected glimpse of him induced an epileptic fit in a man who had come to repair his electric desk lamp; a fit for which he prescribed effectively whilst keeping himself well out of sight. That man, oddly enough, had been through the terrors of the Great War without having incurred any fright so thorough.

Then, in the middle of October, the horror of horrors came with stupefying suddenness. One night about eleven the pump of the refrigerating machine broke down, so that within three hours the process of ammonia cooling became impossible. Dr. Muñoz summoned me by thumping on the floor, and I worked desperately to repair the injury while my host cursed in a tone whose lifeless, rattling hollowness surpassed description. My amateur efforts, however, proved of no use; and when I had brought in a mechanic from a neighboring all-night garage we learned that nothing could be done till morning, when a new piston would have to be obtained. The moribund hermit's rage and fear, swelling to grotesque proportions, seemed likely to shatter what remained of his failing physique; and once a spasm caused him to clap his hands to his eyes and rush into the bathroom. He groped his way out with face tightly bandaged, and I never saw his eyes again.

The frigidity of the apartment was now sensibly diminishing, and at about 5 a.m. the doctor retired to the bathroom, commanding me to keep him supplied with all the ice I could obtain at all-night drug stores and cafeterias. As I would return from my sometimes discouraging trips and lay my spoils before the closed bathroom door, I could hear a restless splashing within, and a thick voice croaking out the order for "More— more!" At length a warm day broke, and the shops opened one by one. I asked Esteban either to help with the ice-fetching whilst I obtained the pump piston, or to order the piston while I continued with the ice; but instructed by his mother, he absolutely refused.

Finally I hired a seedy-looking loafer whom I encountered on the corner of Eighth Avenue to keep the patient supplied with ice from a little shop where I introduced him, and applied myself diligently to the task of finding a pump piston and engaging workmen competent to install it. The task seemed interminable, and I raged almost as violently as the hermit when I saw the hours slipping by in a breathless, foodless round of vain telephoning, and a hectic quest from place to place, hither and thither by subway and surface car. About noon I encountered a suitable supply house far downtown, and at approximately 1:30 p.m. arrived at my boarding-place with the necessary paraphernalia and two sturdy and intelligent mechanics. I had done all I could, and hoped I was in time.

Black terror, however, had preceded me. The house was in utter turmoil, and above the chatter of awed voices I heard a man praying in a deep basso. Fiendish things were in the air, and lodgers told over the beads of their rosaries as they caught the odor from beneath the doctor's closed door. The lounger I had hired, it seems, had fled screaming and mad-eyed not long after his second delivery of ice; perhaps as a result of excessive curiosity. He could not, of course, have locked the door behind him; yet it was now fastened, presumably from the inside. There was no sound within save a nameless sort of slow, thick dripping.

Briefly consulting with Mrs. Herrero and the workmen despite a fear that gnawed my inmost soul, I advised the breaking down of the door; but the landlady found a way to turn the key from the outside with some wire device. We had previously opened the doors of all the other rooms on that hall, and flung all the windows to the very top. Now, noses protected by handkerchiefs, we tremblingly invaded the accursed south room which blazed with the warm sun of early afternoon.

A kind of dark, slimy trail led from the open bathroom door to the hall door, and thence to the desk, where a terrible little pool had accumulated. Something was scrawled there in pencil in an awful, blind hand on a piece of paper hideously smeared as though by the very claws that traced the hurried last words. Then the trail led to the couch and ended unutterably.

What was, or had been, on the couch I cannot and dare not say here. But this is what I shiveringly puzzled out on the stickily smeared paper before I drew a match and burned it to a crisp; what I puzzled out in terror as the landlady and two mechanics rushed frantically from that hellish place to babble their incoherent stories at the nearest police station. The nauseous words seemed well-nigh incredible in that yellow sunlight, with the clatter of cars and motor trucks ascending clamorously from crowded Fourteenth Street, yet I confess that I believed them then. Whether I believe them now I honestly do not know. There are things about which it is better not to speculate, and all that

I can say is that I hate the smell of ammonia, and grow faint at a draft of unusually cool air.

"The end," ran that noisome scrawl, "is here. No more ice—the man looked and ran away. Warmer every minute, and the tissues can't last. I fancy you know—what I said about the will and the nerves and the preserved body after the organs ceased to work. It was good theory, but couldn't keep up indefinitely. There was a gradual deterioration I had not foreseen. Dr. Torres knew, but the shock killed him. He couldn't stand what he had to do—he had to get me in a strange, dark place when he minded my letter and nursed me back. And the organs never would work again. It had to be done my way—artificial preservation—*for you see I died that time eighteen years ago.*"

PICKMAN'S MODEL

You needn't think I'm crazy, Eliot—plenty of others have queerer prejudices than this. Why don't you laugh at Oliver's grandfather, who won't ride in a motor? If I don't like that damned subway, it's my own business; and we got here more quickly anyhow in the taxi. We'd have had to walk up the hill from Park Street if we'd taken the car.

I know I'm more nervous than I was when you saw me last year, but you don't need to hold a clinic over it. There's plenty of reason, God knows, and I fancy I'm lucky to be sane at all. Why the third degree? You didn't use to be so inquisitive.

Well, if you must hear it, I don't know why you shouldn't. Maybe you ought to, anyhow, for you kept writing me like a grieved parent when you heard I'd begun to cut the Art Club and keep away from Pickman. Now that he's disappeared I go around to the club once in a while, but my nerves aren't what they were.

No, I don't know what's become of Pickman, and I don't like to guess. You might have surmised I had some inside information when I dropped him—and that's why I don't want to think where he's gone. Let the police find what they can—it won't be much, judging from the fact that they don't know yet of the old North End place he hired under the name of Peters. I'm not sure that I could find it again myself—not that I'd ever try, even in broad daylight! Yes, I do know, or am afraid I know, why he maintained it. I'm coming to that. And I think you'll understand before I'm through why I don't tell the police. They would ask me to guide them, but I couldn't go back there even if I knew the way. There was something there—and now I can't use the subway or (and you may as well have your laugh at this, too) go down into cellars any more.

I should think you'd have known I didn't drop Pickman for

the same silly reasons that fussy old women like Dr. Reid or Joe Minot or Bosworth did. Morbid art doesn't shock me, and when a man has the genius Pickman had I feel it an honor to know him, no matter what direction his work takes. Boston never had a greater painter than Richard Upton Pickman. I said it at first and I say it still, and I never swerved an inch, either, when he shewed that "Ghoul Feeding." That, you remember, was when Minot cut him.

You know, it takes profound art and profound insight into Nature to turn out stuff like Pickman's. Any magazine-cover hack can splash paint around wildly and call it a nightmare or a Witches' Sabbath or a portrait of the devil, but only a great painter can make such a thing really scare or ring true. That's because only a real artist knows the actual anatomy of the terrible or the physiology of fear—the exact sort of lines and proportions that connect up with latent instincts or hereditary memories of fright, and the proper color contrasts and lighting effects to stir the dormant sense of strangeness. I don't have to tell you why a Fuseli really brings a shiver while a cheap ghost-story frontispiece merely makes us laugh. There's something those fellows catch—beyond life—that they're able to make us catch for a second. Doré had it. Sime has it. Angarola of Chicago has it. And Pickman had it as no man ever had it before or—I hope to heaven—ever will again.

Don't ask me what it is they see. You know, in ordinary art, there's all the difference in the world between the vital, breathing things drawn from Nature or models and the artificial truck that commercial small fry reel off in a bare studio by rule. Well, I should say that the really weird artist has a kind of vision which makes models, or summons up what amounts to actual scenes from the spectral world he lives in. Anyhow, he manages to turn out results that differ from the pretender's mince-pie dreams in just about the same way that the life painter's results differ from the concoctions of a correspondence-school cartoonist. If I had ever seen what Pickman saw—but no! Here, let's have a drink before we get any deeper. Gad, I wouldn't be alive if I'd ever seen what that man—if he was a man—saw!

You recall that Pickman's forte was faces. I don't believe anybody since Goya could put so much of sheer hell into a set of features or a twist of expression. And before Goya you have to go back to the medieval chaps who did the gargoyles and chimeras on Notre Dame and Mont Saint-Michel. They believed all sorts of things—and maybe they saw all sorts of things, too, for the Middle Ages had some curious phases. I remember your asking Pickman yourself once, the year before you went away, wherever in thunder he got such ideas and visions. Wasn't that a nasty laugh he gave you? It was partly because of that laugh that Reid dropped him. Reid, you know, had just taken up comparative pathology, and was full of pompous "inside stuff" about the biological or evolutionary significance of this or that mental or physical symptom. He said Pickman repelled him more and more every day, and almost frightened him toward the last—that the fellow's features and expression were slowly developing in a way he didn't like; in a way that wasn't human. He had a lot of talk about diet, and said Pickman must be abnormal and eccentric to the last degree. I suppose you told Reid, if you and he had any correspondence over it, that he'd let Pickman's paintings get on his nerves or harrow up his imagination. I know I told him that myself—then.

But keep in mind that I didn't drop Pickman for anything like this. On the contrary, my admiration for him kept growing; for that "Ghoul Feeding" was a tremendous achievement. As you know, the club wouldn't exhibit it, and the Museum of Fine Arts wouldn't accept it as a gift; and I can add that nobody would buy it, so Pickman had it right in his house till he went. Now his father has it in Salem—you know Pickman comes of old Salem stock, and had a witch ancestor hanged in 1692.

I got into the habit of calling on Pickman quite often, especially after I began making notes for a monograph on weird art. Probably it was his work which put the idea into my head, and anyhow, I found him a mine of data and suggestions when I came to develop it. He shewed me all the paintings and drawings he had about; including some pen-and-ink sketches that would, I verily believe, have got him kicked out of the club if many of the members had seen them. Before long I was pretty nearly a devotee, and would listen for hours like a schoolboy to art theories and philosophic speculations wild enough to qualify him for the Danvers asylum. My hero-worship, coupled with the fact that people generally were commencing to have less and less to do with him, made him get very confidential with me; and one evening he hinted that if I were fairly close-mouthed and none too squeamish, he might shew me something rather unusual—something a bit stronger than anything he had in the house.

"You know," he said, "there are things that won't do for Newbury Street—things that are out of place here, and that can't be conceived here, anyhow. It's my business to catch the overtones of the soul, and you won't find those in a parvenu set of artificial streets on made land. Back Bay isn't Boston—it isn't anything yet, because it's had no time to pick up memories and attract local spirits. If there are any ghosts here, they're the tame ghosts of a salt marsh and a shallow cove; and I want human ghosts—the ghosts of beings highly organized enough to have looked on hell and known the meaning of what they saw.

"The place for an artist to live is the North End. If any aesthete were sincere, he'd put up with the slums for the sake of the massed traditions. God, man! Don't you realize that places like that weren't merely *made*, but actually *grew?* Generation after generation lived and felt and died there, and in days when people weren't afraid to live and feel and die. Don't you know there was a mill on Copp's Hill in 1632, and that half the present streets were laid out by 1650? I can shew you houses that have stood two centuries and a half and more; houses that have witnessed what would make a modern house crumble into powder. What do moderns know of life and the forces behind it? You call the Salem witchcraft a delusion, but I'll wage my four-times-great-grandmother could have told you things. They hanged her on Gallows Hill, with Cotton Mather looking sanctimoniously on. Mather, damn him, was afraid somebody might succeed in kicking free of this accursed cage of monotony—I wish someone had laid a spell on him or sucked his blood in the night!

"I can shew you a house he lived in, and I can shew you another one he was afraid to enter in spite of all his fine bold talk. He knew things he didn't dare put into that stupid *Magnalia* or that puerile *Wonders of the Invisible World.* Look here, do you know the whole North End once had a set of tunnels that kept certain people in touch with each other's houses, and the burying-ground, and the sea? Let them prosecute and persecute above ground—things went on every day that they couldn't reach, and voices laughed at night that they couldn't place!

"Why, man, out of ten surviving houses built before 1700 and not moved since I'll wager that in eight I can shew you something queer in the cellar. There's hardly a month that you don't read of workmen finding bricked-up arches and wells leading nowhere in this or that old place as it comes down—you could see one near Henchman Street from the elevated last year. There were witches and what their spells summoned; pirates and what they brought in from the sea; smugglers; privateers—and I tell you, people knew how to live, and how to enlarge the bounds of life, in the old times! This wasn't the only world a bold and wise man could know—faugh! And to think of today in contrast, with such pale-pink brains that even a club of supposed artists gets shudders and convulsions if a picture goes beyond the feelings of a Beacon Street tea-table!

"The only saving grace of the present is that it's too damned stupid to question the past very closely. What do maps and records and guide-books really tell of the North End? Bah! At a guess I'll guarantee to lead you to thirty or forty alleys and networks of alleys north of Prince Street that aren't suspected by ten living beings outside of the foreigners that swarm them.

And what do those Dagoes know of their meaning? No, Thurber, these ancient places are dreaming gorgeously and overflowing with wonder and terror and escapes from the commonplace, and yet there's not a living soul to understand or profit by them. Or rather, there's only one living soul—for I haven't been digging around in the past for nothing!

"See here, you're interested in this sort of thing. What if I told you that I've got another studio up there, where I can catch the night-spirit of antique horror and paint things that I couldn't even think of in Newbury Street? Naturally I don't tell those cursed old maids at the club—with Reid, damn him, whispering even as it is that I'm a sort of monster bound down the toboggan of reverse evolution. Yes, Thurber, I decided long ago that one must paint terror as well as beauty from life, so I did some exploring in places where I had reason to know terror lives.

"I've got a place that I don't believe three living Nordic men besides myself have ever seen. It isn't so very far from the elevated as distance goes, but it's centuries away as the soul goes. I took it because of the queer old brick well in the cellar—one of the sort I told you about. The shack's almost tumbling down, so that nobody else would live there, and I'd hate to tell you how little I pay for it. The windows are boarded up, but I like that all the better, since I don't want daylight for what I do. I paint in the cellar, where the inspiration is thickest, but I've other rooms furnished on the ground floor. A Sicilian owns it, and I've hired it under the name of Peters.

"Now if you're game, I'll take you there tonight. I think you'd enjoy the pictures, for as I said, I've let myself go a bit there. It's no vast tour—I sometimes do it on foot, for I don't want to attract attention with a taxi in such a place. We can take the shuttle at the South Station for Battery Street, and after that the walk isn't much."

Well, Eliot, there wasn't much for me to do after that harangue but to keep myself from running instead of walking for the first vacant cab we could sight. We changed to the elevated at the

South Station, and at about twelve o'clock had climbed down the steps at Battery Street and struck along the old waterfront past Constitution Wharf. I didn't keep track of the cross streets, and can't tell you yet which it was we turned up, but I know it wasn't Greenough Lane.

When we did turn, it was to climb through the deserted length of the oldest and dirtiest alley I ever saw in my life, with crumbling-looking gables, broken small-paned windows, and archaic chimneys that stood out half-disintegrated against the moonlit sky. I don't believe there were three houses in sight that hadn't been standing in Cotton Mather's time—certainly I glimpsed at least two with an overhang, and once I thought I saw a peaked roof-line of the almost forgotten pre-gambrel type, though antiquarians tell us there are none left in Boston.

From that alley, which had a dim light, we turned to the left into an equally silent and still narrower alley with no light at all; and in a minute made what I think was an obtuse-angled bend toward the right in the dark. Not long after this Pickman produced a flashlight and revealed an antediluvian ten-paneled door that looked damnably worm-eaten. Unlocking it, he ushered me into a barren hallway with what was once splendid dark-oak paneling—simple, of course, but thrillingly suggestive of the times of Andros and Phipps and the Witchcraft. Then he took me through a door on the left, lighted an oil lamp, and told me to make myself at home.

Now, Eliot, I'm what the man in the street would call fairly "hard-boiled," but I'll confess that what I saw on the walls of that room gave me a bad turn. They were his pictures, you know—the ones he couldn't paint or even shew in Newbury Street—and he was right when he said he had "let himself go." Here—have another drink—I need one anyhow!

There's no use in my trying to tell you what they were like, because the awful, the blasphemous horror, and the unbelievable loathsomeness and moral fetor came from simple touches quite beyond the power of words to classify. There was none of the exotic technique you see in Sidney Sime, none of the trans-Saturnian landscapes and lunar fungi that Clark Ashton Smith uses to freeze the blood. The backgrounds were mostly old churchyards, deep woods, cliffs by the sea, brick tunnels, ancient paneled rooms, or simple vaults of masonry. Copp's Hill Burying Ground, which could not be many blocks away from this very house, was a favorite scene.

The madness and monstrosity lay in the figures in the foreground—for Pickman's morbid art was pre-eminently one of daemoniac portraiture. These figures were seldom completely human, but often approached humanity in varying degree. Most of the bodies, while roughly bipedal, had a forward slumping, and a vaguely canine cast. The texture of the majority was a kind of unpleasant rubberiness. Ugh! I can see them now! Their occupations—well, don't ask me to be too precise. They were usually feeding—I won't say on what. They were sometimes shewn in groups in cemeteries or underground passages, and often appeared to be in battle over their prey—or rather, their treasure-trove. And what damnable expressiveness Pickman sometimes gave the sightless faces of this charnel booty! Occasionally the things were shewn leaping through open windows at night, or squatting on the chests of sleepers, worrying at their throats. One canvas shewed a ring of them baying about a hanged witch on Gallows Hill, whose dead face held a close kinship to theirs.

But don't get the idea that it was all this hideous business of theme and setting which struck me faint. I'm not a three-year-old kid, and I'd seen much like this before. It was the *faces*, Eliot, those accursed *faces*, that leered and slavered out of the canvas with the very breath of life! By God, man, I verily believe they *were* alive! That nauseous wizard had waked the fires of hell in pigment, and his brush had been a nightmare-spawning wand. Give me that decanter, Eliot!

There was one thing called "The Lesson"—heaven pity me, that I ever saw it! Listen—can you fancy a squatting circle of nameless dog-like things in a churchyard teaching a small child

how to feed like themselves? The price of a changeling, I suppose—
you know the old myth about how the weird people leave their
spawn in cradles in exchange for the human babes they steal.
Pickman was shewing what happens to those stolen babes—how
they grow up—and then I began to see a hideous relationship in
the faces of the human and non-human figures. He was, in all his
gradations of morbidity between the frankly non-human and the
degradedly human, establishing a sardonic linkage and evolution.
The dog-things were developed from mortals!

And no sooner had I wondered what he made of their own
young as left with mankind in the form of changelings, than my
eye caught a picture embodying that very thought. It was that
of an ancient Puritan interior—a heavily beamed room with
lattice windows, a settle, and clumsy seventeenth-century furniture, with the family sitting about while the father read from the
Scriptures. Every face but one shewed nobility and reverence,
but that one reflected the mockery of the pit. It was that of a
young man in years, and no doubt belonged to a supposed son
of that pious father, but in essence it was the kin of the unclean
things. It was their changeling—and in a spirit of supreme irony
Pickman had given the features a very perceptible resemblance
to his own.

By this time Pickman had lighted a lamp in an adjoining room
and was politely holding open the door for me; asking me if I
would care to see his "modern studies." I hadn't been able to
give him much of my opinions—I was too speechless with fright
and loathing—but I think he fully understood and felt highly
complimented. And now I want to assure you again, Eliot, that
I'm no mollycoddle to scream at anything which shews a bit of
departure from the usual. I'm middle-aged and decently sophis-
ticated, and I guess you saw enough of me in France to know
I'm not easily knocked out. Remember, too, that I'd just about
recovered my wind and gotten used to those frightful pictures
which turned colonial New England into a kind of annex of hell.
Well, in spite of all this, that next room forced a real scream out

of me, and I had to clutch at the doorway to keep from keeling over. The other chamber had shewn a pack of ghouls and witches overrunning the world of our forefathers, but this one brought the horror right into our own daily life!

Gad, how that man could paint! There was a study called "Subway Accident," in which a flock of the vile things were clambering up from some unknown catacomb through a crack in the floor of the Boylston Street subway and attacking a crowd of people on the platform. Another shewed a dance on Copp's Hill among the tombs with the background of today. Then there were any number of cellar views, with monsters creeping in through holes and rifts in the masonry and grinning as they squatted behind barrels or furnaces and waited for their first victim to descend the stairs.

One disgusting canvas seemed to depict a vast cross-section of Beacon Hill, with ant-like armies of the mephitic monsters squeezing themselves through burrows that honeycombed the ground. Dances in the modern cemeteries were freely pictured, and another conception somehow shocked me more than all the rest—a scene in an unknown vault, where scores of the beasts crowded about one who held a well-known Boston guide-book and was evidently reading aloud. All were pointing to a certain passage, and every face seemed so distorted with epileptic and reverberant laughter that I almost thought I heard the fiendish echoes. The title of the picture was, "Holmes, Lowell, and Longfellow Lie Buried in Mount Auburn."

As I gradually steadied myself and got readjusted to this second room of deviltry and morbidity, I began to analyze some of the points in my sickening loathing. In the first place, I said to myself, these things repelled because of the utter inhumanity and callous cruelty they shewed in Pickman. The fellow must be a relentless enemy of all mankind to take such glee in the torture of brain and flesh and the degradation of the mortal tenement. In the second place, they terrified because of their very greatness. Their art was the art that convinced—when we saw the pictures we saw the daemons themselves and were afraid of them. And the queer part was, that Pickman got none of his power from the use of selectiveness or bizarrerie. Nothing was blurred, distorted, or conventionalized; outlines were sharp and life-like, and details were almost painfully defined. And the faces!

It was not any mere artist's interpretation that we saw; it was pandemonium itself, crystal clear in stark objectivity. That was it, by heaven! The man was not a fantaisiste or romanticist at all— he did not even try to give us the churning, prismatic ephemera of dreams, but coldly and sardonically reflected some stable, mechanistic, and well-established horror-world which he saw fully, brilliantly, squarely, and unfalteringly. God knows what that world can have been, or where he ever glimpsed the blasphemous shapes that loped and trotted and crawled through it; but whatever the baffling source of his images, one thing was plain. Pickman was in every sense—in conception and in execution—a thorough, painstaking, and almost scientific *realist*.

My host was now leading the way down cellar to his actual studio, and I braced myself for some hellish effects among the unfinished canvases. As we reached the bottom of the damp stairs he turned his flashlight to a corner of the large open space at hand, revealing the circular brick curb of what was evidently a great well in the earthen floor. We walked nearer, and I saw that it must be five feet across, with walls a good foot thick and some six inches above the ground level—solid work of the seventeenth century, or I was much mistaken. That, Pickman said, was the kind of thing he had been talking about—an aperture of the network of tunnels that used to undermine the hill. I noticed idly that it did not seem to be bricked up, and that a heavy disc of wood formed the apparent cover. Thinking of the things this well must have been connected with if Pickman's wild hints had not been mere rhetoric, I shivered slightly; then turned to follow him up a step and through a narrow door into a room of fair size, provided with a wooden floor and furnished as a studio. An acetylene gas outfit gave the light necessary for work.

The unfinished pictures on easels or propped against the walls were as ghastly as the finished ones upstairs, and shewed the painstaking methods of the artist. Scenes were blocked out with extreme care, and penciled guide lines told of the minute exactitude which Pickman used in getting the right perspective and proportions. The man was great—I say it even now, knowing as much as I do. A large camera on a table excited my notice, and Pickman told me that he used it in taking scenes for backgrounds, so that he might paint them from photographs in the studio instead of carting his outfit around the town for this or that view. He thought a photograph quite as good as an actual scene or model for sustained work, and declared he employed them regularly.

There was something very disturbing about the nauseous sketches and half-finished monstrosities that leered around from every side of the room, and when Pickman suddenly unveiled a huge canvas on the side away from the light I could not for my life keep back a loud scream—the second I had emitted that night. It echoed and echoed through the dim vaultings of that ancient and nitrous cellar, and I had to choke back a flood of reaction that threatened to burst out as hysterical laughter. Merciful Creator! Eliot, but I don't know how much was real and how much was feverish fancy. It doesn't seem to me that earth can hold a dream like that!

It was a colossal and nameless blasphemy with glaring red eyes, and it held in bony claws a thing that had been a man, gnawing at the head as a child nibbles at a stick of candy. Its position was a kind of crouch, and as one looked one felt that at any moment it might drop its present prey and seek a juicier morsel. But damn it all, it wasn't even the fiendish subject that made it such an immortal fountain-head of all panic—not that, nor the dog face with its pointed ears, bloodshot eyes, flat nose, and drooling lips. It wasn't the scaly claws nor the mold-caked body nor the half-hooved feet—none of these, though any one of them might well have driven an excitable man to madness.

It was the technique, Eliot—the cursed, the impious, the unnatural technique! As I am a living being, I never elsewhere saw the actual breath of life so fused into a canvas. The monster was there—it glared and gnawed and gnawed and glared—and I knew that only a suspension of Nature's laws could ever let a man paint a thing like that without a model—without some glimpse of the nether world which no mortal unsold to the Fiend has ever had.

Pinned with a thumb-tack to a vacant part of the canvas was a piece of paper now badly curled up—probably, I thought, a photograph from which Pickman meant to paint a background as hideous as the nightmare it was to enhance. I reached out to uncurl and look at it, when suddenly I saw Pickman start as if shot. He had been listening with peculiar intensity ever since my shocked scream had waked unaccustomed echoes in the dark cellar, and now he seemed struck with a fright which, though not comparable to my own, had in it more of the physical than of the spiritual. He drew a revolver and motioned me to silence, then stepped out into the main cellar and closed the door behind him.

I think I was paralyzed for an instant. Imitating Pickman's listening, I fancied I heard a faint scurrying sound somewhere, and a series of squeals or bleats in a direction I couldn't determine. I thought of huge rats and shuddered. Then there came a subdued sort of clatter which somehow set me all in gooseflesh—a furtive, groping kind of clatter, though I can't attempt to convey what I mean in words. It was like heavy wood falling on stone or brick—wood on brick—what did that make me think of?

It came again, and louder. There was a vibration as if the wood had fallen farther than it had fallen before. After that followed a sharp grating noise, a shouted gibberish from Pickman, and the deafening discharge of all six chambers of a revolver, fired spectacularly as a lion-tamer might fire in the air for effect. A muffled squeal or squawk, and a thud. Then more wood and brick grating, a pause, and the opening of the door—at which I'll confess I started violently. Pickman reappeared with his smoking weapon, cursing the bloated rats that infested the ancient well.

"The deuce knows what they eat, Thurber," he grinned, "for those archaic tunnels touched graveyard and witch-den and sea-coast. But whatever it is, they must have run short, for they were devilish anxious to get out. Your yelling stirred them up, I fancy. Better be cautious in these old places—our rodent friends are the one drawback, though I sometimes think they're a positive asset by way of atmosphere and color."

Well, Eliot, that was the end of the night's adventure. Pickman had promised to shew me the place, and heaven knows he had done it. He led me out of that tangle of alleys in another direction, it seems, for when we sighted a lamp post we were in a half-familiar street with monotonous rows of mingled tenement blocks and old houses. Charter Street, it turned out to be, but I was too flustered to notice just where we hit it. We were too late for the elevated, and walked back downtown through Hanover Street. I remember that walk. We switched from Tremont up Beacon, and Pickman left me at the corner of Joy, where I turned off. I never spoke to him again.

Why did I drop him? Don't be impatient. Wait till I ring for coffee. We've had enough of the other stuff, but I for one need something. No—it wasn't the paintings I saw in that place; though I'll swear they were enough to get him ostracized in nine-tenths of the homes and clubs of Boston, and I guess you won't wonder now why I have to steer clear of subways and cellars. It was—something I found in my coat the next morning. You know, the curled-up paper tacked to that frightful canvas in the cellar; the thing I thought was a photograph of some scene he meant to use as a background for that monster. That last scare had come while I was reaching to uncurl it, and it seems I had vacantly crumpled it into my pocket. But here's the coffee—take it black, Eliot, if you're wise.

Yes, that paper was the reason I dropped Pickman; Richard Upton Pickman, the greatest artist I have ever known—and the foulest being that ever leaped the bounds of life into the pits of myth and madness. Eliot—old Reid was right. He wasn't strictly human. Either he was born in strange shadow, or he'd found a way to unlock the forbidden gate. It's all the same now, for he's gone—back into the fabulous darkness he loved to haunt. Here, let's have the chandelier going.

Don't ask me to explain or even conjecture about what I burned. Don't ask me, either, what lay behind that mole-like scrambling Pickman was so keen to pass off as rats. There are secrets, you know, which might have come down from old Salem times, and Cotton Mather tells even stranger things. You know how damned life-like Pickman's paintings were—how we all wondered where he got those faces.

Well—that paper wasn't a photograph of any background, after all. What it shewed was simply the monstrous being he was painting on that awful canvas. It was the model he was using— and its background was merely the wall of the cellar studio in minute detail. But by God, Eliot, *it was a photograph from life*.

THE STRANGE HIGH
HOUSE IN THE MIST

In the morning mist comes up from the sea by the cliffs beyond
Kingsport. White and feathery it comes from the deep to its
brothers the clouds, full of dreams of dank pastures and caves of
leviathan. And later, in still summer rains on the steep roofs of
poets, the clouds scatter bits of those dreams, that men shall not
live without rumor of old, strange secrets, and wonders that planets
tell planets alone in the night. When tales fly thick in the grottoes
of tritons, and conches in seaweed cities blow wild tunes learned
from the Elder Ones, then great eager mists flock to heaven laden
with lore, and oceanward eyes on the rocks see only a mystic
whiteness, as if the cliff's rim were the rim of all earth, and the
solemn bells of buoys tolled free in the ether of faery.

Now north of archaic Kingsport the crags climb lofty and
curious, terrace on terrace, till the northernmost hangs in the
sky like a gray frozen wind-cloud. Alone it is, a bleak point jutting
in limitless space, for there the coast turns sharp where the great
Miskatonic pours out of the plains past Arkham, bringing woodland legends and little quaint memories of New England's hills.
The sea-folk in Kingsport look up at that cliff as other sea-folk
look up at the pole-star, and time the night's watches by the way
it hides or shews the Great Bear, Cassiopeia, and the Dragon.
Among them it is one with the firmament, and truly, it is hidden
from them when the mist hides the stars or the sun. Some of
the cliffs they love, as that whose grotesque profile they call
Father Neptune, or that whose pillared steps they term The
Causeway; but this one they fear because it is so near the sky.
The Portuguese sailors coming in from a voyage cross themselves
when they first see it, and the old Yankees believe it would be
much graver matter than death to climb it, if indeed that were

possible. Nevertheless there is an ancient house on that cliff, and at evening men see lights in the small-paned windows.

The ancient house has always been there, and people say One dwells therein who talks with the morning mists that come up from the deep, and perhaps sees singular things oceanward at those times when the cliff's rim becomes the rim of all earth, and solemn buoys toll free in the white ether of faery. This they tell from hearsay, for that forbidding crag is always unvisited, and natives dislike to train telescopes on it. Summer boarders have indeed scanned it with jaunty binoculars, but have never seen more than the gray primeval roof, peaked and shingled, whose eaves come nearly to the gray foundations, and the dim yellow light of the little windows peeping out from under those eaves in the dusk. These summer people do not believe that the same One has lived in the ancient house for hundreds of years, but cannot prove their heresy to any real Kingsporter. Even the Terrible Old Man who talks to leaden pendulums in bottles, buys groceries with centuried Spanish gold, and keeps stone idols in the yard of his antediluvian cottage in Water Street can only say these things were the same when his grandfather was a boy, and that must have been inconceivable ages ago, when Belcher or Shirley or Pownall or Bernard was Governor of His Majesty's Province of the Massachusetts-Bay.

Then one summer there came a philosopher into Kingsport. His name was Thomas Olney, and he taught ponderous things in a college by Narragansett Bay. With stout wife and romping children he came, and his eyes were weary with seeing the same things for many years, and thinking the same well-disciplined thoughts. He looked at the mists from the diadem of Father Neptune, and tried to walk into their white world of mystery along the titan steps of The Causeway. Morning after morning he would lie on the cliffs and look over the world's rim at the cryptical ether beyond, listening to spectral bells and the wild cries of what might have been gulls. Then, when the mist would lift and the sea stand out prosy with the smoke of steamers, he would sigh and descend to the town, where he loved to thread the narrow olden lanes up and down hill, and study the crazy tottering gables and odd pillared doorways which had sheltered so many generations of sturdy sea-folk. And he even talked with the Terrible Old Man, who was not fond of strangers, and was invited into his fearsomely archaic cottage where low ceilings and wormy paneling hear the echoes of disquieting soliloquies in the dark small hours.

Of course it was inevitable that Olney should mark the gray unvisited cottage in the sky, on that sinister northward crag which is one with the mists and the firmament. Always over Kingsport it hung, and always its mystery sounded in whispers through Kingsport's crooked alleys. The Terrible Old Man wheezed a tale that his father had told him, of lightning that shot one night *up from* that peaked cottage to the clouds of higher heaven; and Granny Orne, whose tiny gambrel-roofed abode in Ship Street is all covered with moss and ivy, croaked over something her grandmother had heard at second-hand, about shapes that flapped out of the eastern mists straight into the narrow single door of that unreachable place—for the door is set close to the edge of the crag toward the ocean, and glimpsed only from ships at sea.

At length, being avid for new strange things and held back by neither the Kingsporter's fear nor the summer boarder's usual indolence, Olney made a very terrible resolve. Despite a conservative training—or because of it, for humdrum lives breed wistful longings of the unknown—he swore a great oath to scale that avoided northern cliff and visit the abnormally antique gray cottage in the sky. Very plausibly his saner self argued that the place must be tenanted by people who reached it from inland along the easier ridge beside the Miskatonic's estuary. Probably they traded in Arkham, knowing how little Kingsport liked their habitation, or perhaps being unable to climb down the cliff on the Kingsport side. Olney walked out along the lesser cliffs to where the great crag leaped insolently up to consort with celestial things, and became very sure that no human feet could mount it or descend it on that beetling southern slope. East and north it rose thousands of feet vertically from the water, so only the western side, inland and toward Arkham, remained.

One early morning in August Olney set out to find a path to the inaccessible pinnacle. He worked northwest along pleasant back roads, past Hooper's Pond and the old brick powder-house to where the pastures slope up to the ridge above the Miskatonic and give a lovely vista of Arkham's white Georgian steeples across leagues of river and meadow. Here he found a shady road to Arkham, but no trail at all in the seaward direction he wished. Woods and fields crowded up to the high bank of the river's mouth, and bore not a sign of man's presence; not even a stone wall or a straying cow, but only the tall grass and giant trees and tangles of briers that the first Indian might have seen. As he climbed slowly east, higher and higher above the estuary on his left and nearer and nearer the sea, he found the way growing in difficulty; till he wondered how ever the dwellers in that disliked place managed to reach the world outside, and whether they came often to market in Arkham.

Then the trees thinned, and far below him on his right he saw the hills and antique roofs and spires of Kingsport. Even Central Hill was a dwarf from this height, and he could just make out the ancient graveyard by the Congregational Hospital, beneath which rumor said some terrible caves or burrows lurked. Ahead lay sparse grass and scrub blueberry bushes, and beyond them the naked rock of the crag and the thin peak of the dreaded gray cottage. Now the ridge narrowed, and Olney grew dizzy at his loneliness in the sky. South of him the frightful precipice above Kingsport, north of him the vertical drop of nearly a mile to the river's mouth. Suddenly a great chasm opened before him, ten feet deep, so that he had to let himself down by his hands and drop to a slanting floor, and then crawl perilously up a natural defile in the opposite wall. So this was the way the folk of the uncanny house journeyed betwixt earth and sky!

When he climbed out of the chasm a morning mist was gathering, but he clearly saw the lofty and unhallowed cottage ahead; walls as gray as the rock, and high peak standing bold against the milky white of the seaward vapors. And he perceived that there was no door on this landward end, but only a couple of small lattice windows with dingy bull's-eye panes leaded in seventeenth-century fashion. All around him was cloud and chaos, and he could see nothing below but the whiteness of illimitable space. He was alone in the sky with this queer and very disturbing house; and when he sidled around to the front and saw that the wall stood flush with the cliff's edge, so that the single narrow door was not to be reached save from the empty ether, he felt a distinct terror that altitude could not wholly explain. And it was very odd that shingles so worm-eaten could survive, or bricks so crumbled still form a standing chimney.

As the mist thickened, Olney crept around to the windows on the north and west and south sides, trying them but finding them all locked. He was vaguely glad they were locked, because the more he saw of that house the less he wished to get in. Then a sound halted him. He heard a lock rattle and bolt shoot, and a long creaking follow as if a heavy door were slowly and cautiously opened. This was on the oceanward side that he could not see, where the narrow portal opened on blank space thousands of feet in the misty sky above the waves.

Then there was heavy, deliberate tramping in the cottage, and Olney heard the windows opening, first on the north side opposite him, and then on the west just around the corner. Next would come the south windows, under the great low eaves on the side where he stood; and it must be said that he was more than uncomfortable as he thought of the detestable house on one side and the vacancy of upper air on the other. When a fumbling came in the nearer casements he crept around to the west again, flattening himself against the wall beside the now opened windows. It was plain that the owner had come home; but he had not come from the land, nor from any balloon or airship that could be imagined. Steps sounded again, and Olney edged round to the north; but before he could find a haven a voice called softly, and he knew he must confront his host.

Stuck out of a west window was a great black-bearded face whose eyes shone phosphorescently with the imprint of unheard-of sights. But the voice was gentle, and of a quaint olden kind, so that Olney did not shudder when a brown hand reached out to help him over the sill and into that low room of black oak wainscots and carved Tudor furnishings. The man was clad in very ancient garments, and had about him an unplaceable nimbus of sea-lore and dreams of tall galleons. Olney does not recall many of the wonders he told, or even who he was; but says that he was strange and kindly, and filled with the magic of unfathomed voids of time and space. The small room seemed green with a dim aqueous light, and Olney saw that the far windows to the east were not open, but shut against the misty ether with dull thick panes like the bottoms of old bottles.

That bearded host seemed young, yet looked out of eyes steeped in the elder mysteries; and from the tales of marvelous ancient things he related, it must be guessed that the village folk were right in saying he had communed with the mists of the sea and the clouds of the sky ever since there was any village to watch his taciturn dwelling from the plain below. And the day wore on, and still Olney listened to rumors of old times and far places, and heard how the Kings of Atlantis fought with the slippery blasphemies that wriggled out of rifts in ocean's floor, and how the pillared and weedy temple of Poseidonis is still glimpsed at midnight by lost ships, who know by its sight that they are lost. Years of the Titans were recalled, but the host grew timid when he spoke of the dim first age of chaos before the gods or even the Elder Ones were born, and when only *the other gods* came to dance on the peak of Hatheg-Kla in the stony desert near Ulthar, beyond the river Skai.

It was at this point that there came a knocking on the door; that ancient door of nail-studded oak beyond which lay only the abyss of white cloud. Olney started in fright, but the bearded man motioned him to be still, and tiptoed to the door to look out through a very small peep-hole. What he saw he did not like, so pressed his fingers to his lips and tiptoed around to shut and lock all the windows before returning to the ancient settle beside his guest. Then Olney saw lingering against the translucent squares of each of the little dim windows in succession a queer black outline as the caller moved inquisitively about before leaving; and he was glad his host had not answered the knocking. For there are strange objects in the great abyss, and the seeker of dreams must take care not to stir up or meet the wrong ones.

Then the shadows began to gather; first little furtive ones under the table, and then bolder ones in the dark paneled corners. And the bearded man made enigmatical gestures of prayer, and lit tall candles in curiously wrought brass candlesticks. Frequently he would glance at the door as if he expected someone, and at length his glance seemed answered by a singular rapping which must have followed some very ancient and secret code. This time he did not even glance through the peep-hole, but swung the great oak bar and shot the bolt, unlatching the heavy door and flinging it wide to the stars and the mist.

And then to the sound of obscure harmonies there floated into that room from the deep all the dreams and memories of earth's sunken Mighty Ones. And golden flames played about weedy locks, so that Olney was dazzled as he did them homage. Trident-bearing Neptune was there, and sportive tritons and fantastic nereids, and upon dolphins' backs was balanced a vast crenulate shell wherein rode the gray and awful form of primal Nodens, Lord of the Great Abyss. And the conches of the tritons gave weird blasts, and the nereids made strange sounds by striking on the grotesque resonant shells of unknown lurkers in black sea-caves. Then hoary Nodens reached forth a wizened hand and helped Olney and his host into the vast shell, whereat the conches and the gongs set up a wild and awesome clamor. And out into the limitless ether reeled that fabulous train, the noise of whose shouting was lost in the echoes of thunder.

All night in Kingsport they watched that lofty cliff when the storm and the mists gave them glimpses of it, and when toward the small hours the little dim windows went dark they whispered of dread and disaster.And Olney's children and stout wife prayed to the bland proper god of Baptists, and hoped that the traveler would borrow an umbrella and rubbers unless the rain stopped by morning. Then dawn swam dripping and mist-wreathed out of the sea, and the buoys tolled solemn in vortices of white ether. And at noon elfin horns rang over the ocean as Olney, dry and light-footed, climbed down from the cliffs to antique Kingsport with the look of far places in his eyes. He could not recall what he had dreamed in the sky-perched hut of that still nameless hermit, or say how he had crept down that crag untraversed by other feet. Nor could he talk of these matters at all save with the Terrible Old Man, who afterward mumbled queer things in his long white beard; vowing that the man who came down from that crag was not wholly the man who went up, and that somewhere under that gray peaked roof, or amidst inconceivable reaches of that sinister white mist, there lingered still the lost spirit of him who was Thomas Olney.

And ever since that hour, through dull dragging years of grayness and weariness, the philosopher has labored and eaten and slept and done uncomplaining the suitable deeds of a citizen. Not any more does he long for the magic of farther hills, or sigh for secrets that peer like green reefs from a bottomless sea. The sameness of his days no longer gives him sorrow, and well-disciplined thoughts have grown enough for his imagination. His good wife waxes stouter and his children older and prosier and more useful, and he never fails to smile correctly with pride when the occasion calls for it. In his glance there is not any restless light, and if he ever listens for solemn bells or far elfin horns it is only at night when old dreams are wandering. He has never seen Kingsport again, for his family disliked the funny old houses, and complained that the drains were impossibly bad. They have a trim bungalow now at Bristol Highlands, where no tall crags tower, and the neighbors are urban and modern.

But in Kingsport strange tales are abroad, and even the Terrible Old Man admits a thing untold by his grandfather. For now, when the wind sweeps boisterous out of the north past the high ancient house that is one with the firmament, there is broken at last that ominous brooding silence ever before the bane of Kingsport's maritime cotters. And old folk tell of pleasing voices heard singing there, and of laughter that swells with joys beyond earth's joys; and say that at evening the little low windows are brighter than formerly. They say, too, that the fierce aurora comes oftener to that spot, shining blue in the north with visions of frozen worlds while the crag and the cottage hang black and fantastic against wild coruscations. And the mists of the dawn are thicker, and sailors are not quite so sure that all the muffled seaward ringing is that of the solemn buoys.

Worst of all, though, is the shriveling of old fears in the hearts of Kingsport's young men, who grow prone to listen at night to the north wind's faint distant sounds. They swear no harm or pain can inhabit that high peaked cottage, for in the new voices gladness beats, and with them the tinkle of laughter and music. What tales the sea-mists may bring to that haunted and north-ernmost pinnacle they do not know, but they long to extract some hint of the wonders that knock at the cliff-yawning door when clouds are thickest. And patriarchs dread lest some day one by one they seek out that inaccessible peak in the sky, and learn what centuried secrets hide beneath the steep shingled roof which is part of the rocks and the stars and the ancient fears of Kingsport. That those venturesome youths will come back they do not doubt, but they think a light may be gone from their eyes, and a will from their hearts. And they do not wish quaint Kingsport with its climbing lanes and archaic gables to drag listless down the years while voice by voice the laughing chorus grows stronger and wilder in that unknown and terrible eyrie where mists and the dreams of mists stop to rest on their way from the sea to the skies.

They do not wish the souls of their young men to leave the pleasant hearths and gambrel-roofed taverns of old Kingsport, nor do they wish the laughter and song in that high rocky place to grow louder. For as the voice which has come has brought fresh mists from the sea and from the north fresh lights, so do they say that still other voices will bring more mists and more lights, till perhaps the olden gods (whose existence they hint only in whispers for fear the Congregational parson shall hear) may come out of the deep and from unknown Kadath in the cold waste and make their dwelling on that evilly appropriate crag so close to the gentle hills and valleys of quiet simple fisher-folk. This they do not wish, for to plain people things not of earth are unwelcome; and besides, the Terrible Old Man often recalls what Olney said about a knock that the lone dweller feared, and a shape seen black and inquisitive against the mist through those queer translucent windows of leaded bull's-eyes.

All these things, however, the Elder Ones only may decide; and meanwhile the morning mist still comes up by that lonely vertiginous peak with the steep ancient house, that gray low-eaved house where none is seen but where evening brings furtive lights while the north wind tells of strange revels. White and feathery it comes from the deep to its brothers the clouds, full of dreams of dank pastures and caves of leviathan. And when tales fly thick in the grottoes of tritons, and conches in seaweed cities blow wild tunes learned from the Elder Ones, then great eager vapors flock to heaven laden with lore; and Kingsport, nestling uneasy on its lesser cliffs below that awesome hanging sentinel of rock, sees oceanward only a mystic whiteness, as if the cliff's rim were the rim of all earth, and the solemn bells of the buoys tolled free in the ether of faery.

THE COLOR OUT OF SPACE

West of Arkham the hills rise wild, and there are valleys with deep woods that no axe has ever cut. There are dark narrow glens where the trees slope fantastically, and where thin brooklets trickle without ever having caught the glint of sunlight. On the gentler slopes there are farms, ancient and rocky, with squat, moss-coated cottages brooding eternally over old New England secrets in the lee of great ledges; but these are all vacant now, the wide chimneys crumbling and the shingled sides bulging perilously beneath low gambrel roofs.

The old folk have gone away, and foreigners do not like to live there. French-Canadians have tried it, Italians have tried it, and the Poles have come and departed. It is not because of anything that can be seen or heard or handled, but because of something that is imagined. The place is not good for the imagination, and does not bring restful dreams at night. It must be this which keeps the foreigners away, for old Ammi Pierce has never told them of anything he recalls from the strange days. Ammi, whose head has been a little queer for years, is the only one who still remains, or who ever talks of the strange days; and he dares to do this because his house is so near the open fields and the traveled roads around Arkham.

There was once a road over the hills and through the valleys, that ran straight where the blasted heath is now; but people ceased to use it and a new road was laid curving far toward the south. Traces of the old one can still be found amidst the weeds of a returning wilderness, and some of them will doubtless linger even when half the hollows are flooded for the new reservoir. Then the dark woods will be cut down and the blasted heath will slumber far below blue waters whose surface will mirror the sky and ripple in the sun. And the secrets of the strange days will be one with the deep's secrets; one with the hidden lore of old ocean, and all the mystery of primal earth.

When I went into the hills and vales to survey for the new reservoir they told me the place was evil. They told me this in Arkham, and because that is a very old town full of witch legends I thought the evil must be something which grandams had whispered to children through centuries. The name "blasted heath" seemed to me very odd and theatrical, and I wondered how it had come into the folklore of a Puritan people. Then I saw that dark westward tangle of glens and slopes for myself, and ceased to wonder at anything besides its own elder mystery. It was morning when I saw it, but shadow lurked always there. The trees grew too thickly, and their trunks were too big for any healthy New England wood. There was too much silence in the dim alleys between them, and the floor was too soft with the dank moss and mattings of infinite years of decay.

In the open spaces, mostly along the line of the old road, there were little hillside farms; sometimes with all the buildings standing, sometimes with only one or two, and sometimes with only a lone chimney or fast-filling cellar. Weeds and briers reigned, and furtive wild things rustled in the undergrowth. Upon everything was a haze of restlessness and oppression; a touch of the unreal and the grotesque, as if some vital element of perspective or chiaroscuro were awry. I did not wonder that the foreigners would not stay, for this was no region to sleep in. It was too much like a landscape of Salvator Rosa; too much like some forbidden woodcut in a tale of terror.

But even all this was not so bad as the blasted heath. I knew it the moment I came upon it at the bottom of a spacious valley; for no other name could fit such a thing, or any other thing fit such a name. It was as if the poet had coined the phrase from having seen this one particular region. It must, I thought as I viewed it, be the outcome of a fire; but why had nothing new ever grown over those five acres of gray desolation that sprawled open to the sky like a great spot eaten by acid in the woods and fields? It lay largely to the north of the ancient road line, but encroached a little on the other side. I felt an odd reluctance about approaching, and did so at last only because my business took me through and past it. There was no vegetation of any kind on that broad expanse, but only a fine gray dust or ash which no wind seemed ever to blow about. The trees near it were sickly and stunted, and many dead trunks stood or lay rotting at the rim. As I walked hurriedly by I saw the tumbled bricks and stones of an old chimney and cellar on my right, and the yawning black maw of an abandoned well whose stagnant vapors played strange tricks with the hues of the sunlight. Even the long, dark woodland climb beyond seemed welcome in contrast, and I marveled no more at the frightened whispers of Arkham people. There had been no house or ruin near; even in the old days the place must have been lonely and remote. And at twilight, dreading to repass that ominous spot, I walked circuitously back to the town by the curving road on the south. I vaguely wished some clouds would gather, for an odd timidity about the deep skyey voids above had crept into my soul.

In the evening I asked old people in Arkham about the blasted heath, and what was meant by that phrase "strange days" which so many evasively muttered. I could not, however, get any good answers, except that all the mystery was much more recent than I had dreamed. It was not a matter of old legendry at all, but something within the lifetime of those who spoke. It had happened in the 'eighties, and a family had disappeared or was killed. Speakers would not be exact; and because they all told me to pay no attention to old Ammi Pierce's crazy tales, I sought him out the next morning, having heard that he lived alone in the ancient tottering cottage where the trees first begin to get very thick. It was a fearsomely archaic place, and had begun to exude the faint miasmal odor which clings about houses that have stood too long. Only with persistent knocking could I rouse the aged man, and when he shuffled timidly to the door I could tell he was not glad to see me. He was not so feeble as I had expected;

but his eyes drooped in a curious way, and his unkempt clothing and white beard made him seem very worn and dismal. Not knowing just how he could best be launched on his tales, I feigned a matter of business; told him of my surveying, and asked vague questions about the district. He was far brighter and more educated than I had been led to think, and before I knew it had grasped quite as much of the subject as any man I had talked with in Arkham. He was not like other rustics I had known in the sections where reservoirs were to be. From him there were no protests at the miles of old wood and farmland to be blotted out, though perhaps there would have been had not his home lain outside the bounds of the future lake. Relief was all that he shewed; relief at the doom of the dark ancient valleys through which he had roamed all his life. They were better under water now—better under water since the strange days. And with this opening his husky voice sank low, while his body leaned forward and his right forefinger began to point shakily and impressively.

It was then that I heard the story, and as the rambling voice scraped and whispered on I shivered again and again despite the summer day. Often I had to recall the speaker from ramblings, piece out scientific points which he knew only by a fading parrot memory of professors' talk, or bridge over gaps where his sense of logic and continuity broke down. When he was done I did not wonder that his mind had snapped a trifle, or that the folk of Arkham would not speak much of the blasted heath. I hurried back before sunset to my hotel, unwilling to have the stars come out above me in the open; and the next day returned to Boston to give up my position. I could not go into that dim chaos of old forest and slope again, or face another time that gray blasted heath where the black well yawned deep beside the tumbled bricks and stones. The reservoir will soon be built now, and all those elder secrets will be safe forever under watery fathoms. But even then I do not believe I would like to visit that country by night—at least, not when the sinister stars are out; and nothing could bribe me to drink the new city water of Arkham.

It all began, old Ammi said, with the meteorite. Before that time there had been no wild legends at all since the witch trials, and even then these western woods were not feared half so much as the small island in the Miskatonic where the devil held court beside a curious stone altar older than the Indians. These were not haunted woods, and their fantastic dusk was never terrible till the strange days. Then there had come that white noontide cloud, that string of explosions in the air, and that pillar of smoke from the valley far in the wood. And by night all Arkham had heard of the great rock that fell out of the sky and bedded itself in the ground beside the well at the Nahum Gardner place. That was the house which had stood where the blasted heath was to come—the trim white Nahum Gardner house amidst its fertile gardens and orchards.

Nahum had come to town to tell people about the stone, and had dropped in at Ammi Pierce's on the way. Ammi was forty then, and all the queer things were fixed very strongly in his mind. He and his wife had gone with the three professors from Miskatonic University who hastened out the next morning to see the weird visitor from unknown stellar space, and had wondered why Nahum had called it so large the day before. It had shrunk, Nahum said as he pointed out the big brownish mound above the ripped earth and charred grass near the archaic well-sweep in his front yard; but the wise men answered that stones do not shrink. Its heat lingered persistently, and Nahum declared it had glowed faintly in the night. The professors tried it with a geologist's hammer and found it was oddly soft. It was, in truth, so soft as to be almost plastic; and they gouged rather than chipped a specimen to take back to the college for testing. They took it in an old pail borrowed from Nahum's kitchen, for even the small piece refused to grow cool. On the trip back they stopped at Ammi's to rest, and seemed thoughtful when Mrs. Pierce remarked that the fragment was growing smaller and burning the bottom of the pail. Truly, it was not large, but perhaps they had taken less than they thought.

The day after that—all this was in June of '82—the professors
had trooped out again in a great excitement. As they passed
Ammi's they told him what queer things the specimen had done,
and how it had faded wholly away when they put it in a glass
beaker. The beaker had gone, too, and the wise men talked of the
strange stone's affinity for silicon. It had acted quite unbelievably
in that well-ordered laboratory; doing nothing at all and shewing
no occluded gases when heated on charcoal, being wholly nega-
tive in the borax bead, and soon proving itself absolutely
non-volatile at any producible temperature, including that of the
oxy-hydrogen blowpipe. On an anvil it appeared highly malleable,
and in the dark its luminosity was very marked. Stubbornly refusing
to grow cool, it soon had the college in a state of real excitement;
and when upon heating before the spectroscope it displayed
shining bands unlike any known colors of the normal spectrum
there was much breathless talk of new elements, bizarre optical
properties, and other things which puzzled men of science are
wont to say when faced by the unknown.

Hot as it was, they tested it in a crucible with all the proper
reagents. Water did nothing. Hydrochloric acid was the same.
Nitric acid and even aqua regia merely hissed and spattered
against its torrid invulnerability. Ammi had difficulty in recalling
all these things, but recognized some solvents as I mentioned
them in the usual order of use. There were ammonia and caustic
soda, alcohol and ether, nauseous carbon disulfide and a dozen
others; but although the weight grew steadily less as time passed,
and the fragment seemed to be slightly cooling, there was no
change in the solvents to shew that they had attacked the
substance at all. It was a metal, though, beyond a doubt. It was
magnetic, for one thing; and after its immersion in the acid
solvents there seemed to be faint traces of the Widmannstätten
figures found on meteoric iron. When the cooling had grown
very considerable, the testing was carried on in glass; and it was
in a glass beaker that they left all the chips made of the original
fragment during the work. The next morning both chips and

beaker were gone without trace, and only a charred spot marked the place on the wooden shelf where they had been.

All this the professors told Ammi as they paused at his door, and once more he went with them to see the stony messenger from the stars, though this time his wife did not accompany him. It had now most certainly shrunk, and even the sober professors could not doubt the truth of what they saw. All around the dwindling brown lump near the well was a vacant space, except where the earth had caved in; and whereas it had been a good seven feet across the day before, it was now scarcely five. It was still hot, and the sages studied its surface curiously as they detached another and larger piece with hammer and chisel. They gouged deeply this time, and as they pried away the smaller mass they saw that the core of the thing was not quite homogeneous.

They had uncovered what seemed to be the side of a large colored globule imbedded in the substance. The color, which resembled some of the bands in the meteor's strange spectrum, was almost impossible to describe; and it was only by analogy that they called it color at all. Its texture was glossy, and upon tapping it appeared to promise both brittleness and hollowness. One of the professors gave it a smart blow with a hammer, and it burst with a nervous little pop. Nothing was emitted, and all trace of the thing vanished with the puncturing. It left behind a hollow spherical space about three inches across, and all thought it probable that others would be discovered as the enclosing substance wasted away.

Conjecture was vain; so after a futile attempt to find additional globules by drilling, the seekers left again with their new specimen—which proved, however, as baffling in the laboratory as its predecessor had been. Aside from being almost plastic, having heat, magnetism, and slight luminosity, cooling slightly in powerful acids, possessing an unknown spectrum, wasting away in air, and attacking silicon compounds with mutual destruction as a result, it presented no identifying features whatsoever; and at the end of the tests the college scientists were forced to own that they could not place it. It was nothing of this earth, but a piece of the great outside; and as such dowered with outside properties and obedient to outside laws.

That night there was a thunderstorm, and when the professors went out to Nahum's the next day they met with a bitter disappointment. The stone, magnetic as it had been, must have had some peculiar electrical property; for it had "drawn the lightning," as Nahum said, with a singular persistence. Six times within an hour the farmer saw the lightning strike the furrow in the front yard, and when the storm was over nothing remained but a ragged pit by the ancient well-sweep, half-choked with caved-in earth. Digging had borne no fruit, and the scientists verified the fact of the utter vanishment. The failure was total; so that nothing was left to do but go back to the laboratory and test again the disappearing fragment left carefully cased in lead. That fragment lasted a week, at the end of which nothing of value had been learned of it. When it had gone, no residue was left behind, and in time the professors felt scarcely sure they had indeed seen with waking eyes that cryptic vestige of the fathomless gulfs outside; that lone, weird message from other universes and other realms of matter, force, and entity.

As was natural, the Arkham papers made much of the incident with its collegiate sponsoring, and sent reporters to talk with Nahum Gardner and his family. At least one Boston daily also sent a scribe, and Nahum quickly became a kind of local celebrity. He was a lean, genial person of about fifty, living with his wife and three sons on the pleasant farmstead in the valley. He and Ammi exchanged visits frequently, as did their wives; and Ammi had nothing but praise for him after all these years. He seemed slightly proud of the notice his place had attracted, and talked often of the meteorite in the succeeding weeks. That July and August were hot, and Nahum worked hard at his haying in the ten-acre pasture across Chapman's Brook; his rattling wain wearing deep ruts in the shadowy lanes between. The labor tired him more than it had in other years, and he felt that age was beginning to tell on him.

Then fell the time of fruit and harvest. The pears and apples slowly ripened, and Nahum vowed that his orchards were prospering as never before. The fruit was growing to phenomenal size and unwonted gloss, and in such abundance that extra barrels were ordered to handle the future crop. But with the ripening came sore disappointment; for of all that gorgeous array of specious lusciousness not one single jot was fit to eat. Into the fine flavor of the pears and apples had crept a stealthy bitterness and sickishness, so that even the smallest of bites induced a lasting disgust. It was the same with the melons and tomatoes, and Nahum sadly saw that his entire crop was lost. Quick to connect events, he declared that the meteorite had poisoned the soil, and thanked heaven that most of the other crops were in the upland lot along the road.

Winter came early, and was very cold. Ammi saw Nahum less often than usual, and observed that he had begun to look worried. The rest of his family, too, seemed to have grown taciturn; and were far from steady in their churchgoing or their attendance at the various social events of the countryside. For this reserve or melancholy no cause could be found, though all the household confessed now and then to poorer health and a feeling of vague disquiet. Nahum himself gave the most definite statement of anyone when he said he was disturbed about certain footprints in the snow. They were the usual winter prints of red squirrels, white rabbits, and foxes, but the brooding farmer professed to see something not quite right about their nature and arrangement. He was never specific, but appeared to think that they were not as characteristic of the anatomy and habits of squirrels and rabbits and foxes as they ought to be. Ammi listened without interest to this talk until one night when he drove past Nahum's house in his sleigh on the way back from Clark's Corners. There had been a moon, and a rabbit had run across the road, and the leaps of that rabbit were longer than either Ammi or his horse liked. The latter, indeed, had almost run away when brought up by a firm rein. Thereafter Ammi gave

Nahum's tales more respect, and wondered why the Gardner dogs seemed so cowed and quivering every morning. They had, it developed, nearly lost the spirit to bark.

In February the McGregor boys from Meadow Hill were out shooting woodchucks, and not far from the Gardner place bagged a very peculiar specimen. The proportions of its body seemed slightly altered in a queer way impossible to describe, while its face had taken on an expression which no one ever saw in a woodchuck before. The boys were genuinely frightened, and threw the thing away at once, so that only their grotesque tales of it ever reached the people of the countryside. But the shying of the horses near Nahum's house had now become an acknowledged thing, and all the basis for a cycle of whispered legend was fast taking form.

People vowed that the snow melted faster around Nahum's than it did anywhere else, and early in March there was an awed discussion in Potter's general store at Clark's Corners. Stephen Rice had driven past Gardner's in the morning, and had noticed the skunk-cabbages coming up through the mud by the woods across the road. Never were things of such size seen before, and they held strange colors that could not be put into any words. Their shapes were monstrous, and the horse had snorted at an odor which struck Stephen as wholly unprecedented. That afternoon several persons drove past to see the abnormal growth, and all agreed that plants of that kind ought never to sprout in a healthy world. The bad fruit of the fall before was freely mentioned, and it went from mouth to mouth that there was poison in Nahum's ground. Of course it was the meteorite; and remembering how strange the men from the college had found that stone to be, several farmers spoke about the matter to them.

One day they paid Nahum a visit; but having no love of wild tales and folklore were very conservative in what they inferred. The plants were certainly odd, but all skunk-cabbages are more or less odd in shape and odor and hue. Perhaps some mineral element from the stone had entered the soil, but it would soon

be washed away. And as for the footprints and frightened horses—
of course this was mere country talk which such a phenomenon
as the aerolite would be certain to start. There was really nothing
for serious men to do in cases of wild gossip, for superstitious
rustics will say and believe anything. And so all through the
strange days the professors stayed away in contempt. Only one
of them, when given two phials of dust for analysis in a police
job over a year and a half later, recalled that the queer color of
that skunk-cabbage had been very like one of the anomalous
bands of light shewn by the meteor fragment in the college
spectroscope, and like the brittle globule found imbedded in the
stone from the abyss. The samples in this analysis case gave the
same odd bands at first, though later they lost the property.

The trees budded prematurely around Nahum's, and at night
they swayed ominously in the wind. Nahum's second son
Thaddeus, a lad of fifteen, swore that they swayed also when
there was no wind; but even the gossips would not credit this.
Certainly, however, restlessness was in the air. The entire Gardner
family developed the habit of stealthy listening, though not for
any sound which they could consciously name. The listening
was, indeed, rather a product of moments when consciousness
seemed half to slip away. Unfortunately such moments increased
week by week, till it became common speech that "something
was wrong with all Nahum's folks." When the early saxifrage
came out it had another strange color; not quite like that of the
skunk-cabbage, but plainly related and equally unknown to
anyone who saw it. Nahum took some blossoms to Arkham and
shewed them to the editor of the *Gazette,* but that dignitary did
no more than write a humorous article about them, in which
the dark fears of rustics were held up to polite ridicule. It was
a mistake of Nahum's to tell a stolid city man about the way the
great, overgrown mourning-cloak butterflies behaved in connexion
with these saxifrages.

April brought a kind of madness to the country folk, and
began that disuse of the road past Nahum's which led to its

ultimate abandonment. It was the vegetation. All the orchard trees blossomed forth in strange colors, and through the stony soil of the yard and adjacent pasturage there sprang up a bizarre growth which only a botanist could connect with the proper flora of the region. No sane wholesome colors were anywhere to be seen except in the green grass and leafage; but everywhere those hectic and prismatic variants of some diseased, underlying primary tone without a place among the known tints of earth. The Dutchman's breeches became a thing of sinister menace, and the bloodroots grew insolent in their chromatic perversion. Ammi and the Gardners thought that most of the colors had a sort of haunting familiarity, and decided that they reminded one of the brittle globule in the meteor. Nahum plowed and sowed the ten-acre pasture and the upland lot, but did nothing with the land around the house. He knew it would be of no use, and hoped that the summer's strange growths would draw all the poison from the soil. He was prepared for almost anything now, and had grown used to the sense of something near him waiting to be heard. The shunning of his house by neighbors told on him, of course; but it told on his wife more. The boys were better off, being at school each day; but they could not help being frightened by the gossip. Thaddeus, an especially sensitive youth, suffered the most.

In May the insects came, and Nahum's place became a nightmare of buzzing and crawling. Most of the creatures seemed not quite usual in their aspects and motions, and their nocturnal habits contradicted all former experience. The Gardners took to watching at night—watching in all directions at random for something . . . they could not tell what. It was then that they all owned that Thaddeus had been right about the trees. Mrs. Gardner was the next to see it from the window as she watched the swollen boughs of a maple against a moonlit sky. The boughs surely moved, and there was no wind. It must be the sap. Strangeness had come into everything growing now. Yet it was none of Nahum's family at all who made the next discovery.

Familiarity had dulled them, and what they could not see was glimpsed by a timid windmill salesman from Bolton who drove by one night in ignorance of the country legends. What he told in Arkham was given a short paragraph in the *Gazette*; and it was there that all the farmers, Nahum included, saw it first. The night had been dark and the buggy-lamps faint, but around a farm in the valley which everyone knew from the account must be Nahum's the darkness had been less thick. A dim though distinct luminosity seemed to inhere in all the vegetation, grass, leaves, and blossoms alike, while at one moment a detached piece of the phosphorescence appeared to stir furtively in the yard near the barn.

The grass had so far seemed untouched, and the cows were freely pastured in the lot near the house, but toward the end of May the milk began to be bad. Then Nahum had the cows driven to the uplands, after which the trouble ceased. Not long after this the change in grass and leaves became apparent to the eye. All the verdure was going gray, and was developing a highly singular quality of brittleness. Ammi was now the only person who ever visited the place, and his visits were becoming fewer and fewer. When school closed the Gardners were virtually cut off from the world, and sometimes let Ammi do their errands in town. They were failing curiously both physically and mentally, and no one was surprised when the news of Mrs. Gardner's madness stole around.

It happened in June, about the anniversary of the meteor's fall, and the poor woman screamed about things in the air which she could not describe. In her raving there was not a single specific noun, but only verbs and pronouns. Things moved and changed and fluttered, and ears tingled to impulses which were not wholly sounds. Something was taken away—she was being drained of something—something was fastening itself on her that ought not to be—someone must make it keep off—nothing was ever still in the night—the walls and windows shifted. Nahum did not send her to the county asylum, but let her wander about the house as long as she was harmless to herself and others. Even when her expression changed he did nothing. But when the boys grew afraid of her, and Thaddeus nearly fainted at the way she made faces at him, he decided to keep her locked in the attic. By July she had ceased to speak and crawled on all fours, and before that month was over Nahum got the mad notion that she was slightly luminous in the dark, as he now clearly saw was the case with the nearby vegetation.

It was a little before this that the horses had stampeded. Something had aroused them in the night, and their neighing and kicking in their stalls had been terrible. There seemed virtually nothing to do to calm them, and when Nahum opened the stable door they all bolted out like frightened woodland deer. It took a week to track all four, and when found they were seen to be quite useless and unmanageable. Something had snapped in their brains, and each one had to be shot for its own good. Nahum borrowed a horse from Ammi for his haying, but found it would not approach the barn. It shied, balked, and whinnied, and in the end he could do nothing but drive it into the yard while the men used their own strength to get the heavy wagon near enough the hayloft for convenient pitching. And all the while the vegetation was turning gray and brittle. Even the flowers whose hues had been so strange were graying now, and the fruit was coming out gray and dwarfed and tasteless. The asters and goldenrod bloomed gray and distorted, and the roses and zinneas and hollyhocks in the front yard were such blasphemous-looking things that Nahum's oldest boy Zenas cut them down. The strangely puffed insects died about that time, even the bees that had left their hives and taken to the woods.

By September all the vegetation was fast crumbling to a grayish powder, and Nahum feared that the trees would die before the poison was out of the soil. His wife now had spells of terrific screaming, and he and the boys were in a constant state of nervous tension. They shunned people now, and when school opened the boys did not go. But it was Ammi, on one of his rare visits, who first realized that the well water was no longer good. It had an evil taste that was not exactly fetid nor exactly salty, and Ammi advised his friend to dig another well on higher ground to use till the soil was good again. Nahum, however, ignored the warning, for he had by that time become calloused to strange and unpleasant things. He and the boys continued to use the tainted supply, drinking it as listlessly and mechanically as they ate their meager and ill-cooked meals and did their thankless and monotonous chores through the aimless days. There was something of stolid resignation about them all, as if they walked half in another world between lines of nameless guards to a certain and familiar doom.

Thaddeus went mad in September after a visit to the well. He had gone with a pail and had come back empty-handed, shrieking and waving his arms, and sometimes lapsing into an inane titter or a whisper about "the moving colors down there." Two in one family was pretty bad, but Nahum was very brave about it. He let the boy run about for a week until he began stumbling and hurting himself, and then he shut him in an attic room across the hall from his mother's. The way they screamed at each other from behind their locked doors was very terrible, especially to little Merwin, who fancied they talked in some terrible language that was not of earth. Merwin was getting frightfully imaginative, and his restlessness was worse after the shutting away of the brother who had been his greatest playmate.

Almost at the same time the mortality among the livestock commenced. Poultry turned grayish and died very quickly, their meat being found dry and noisome upon cutting. Hogs grew inordinately fat, then suddenly began to undergo loathsome changes which no one could explain. Their meat was of course useless, and Nahum was at his wit's end. No rural veterinary would approach his place, and the city veterinary from Arkham was openly baffled. The swine began growing gray and brittle and falling to pieces before they died, and their eyes and muzzles developed singular alterations. It was very inexplicable, for they had never been fed from the tainted vegetation. Then something struck the cows. Certain areas or sometimes the whole body would be uncannily shriveled or compressed, and atrocious collapses or disintegrations were common. In the last stages—and death was always the result—there would be a graying and turning brittle like that which beset the hogs. There could be no question of poison, for all the cases occurred in a locked and undisturbed barn. No bites of prowling things could have brought the virus, for what live beast of earth can pass through solid obstacles? It must be only natural disease—yet what disease could wreak such results was beyond any mind's guessing. When the harvest came there was not an animal surviving on the place, for the stock and poultry were dead and the dogs had run away. These dogs, three in number, had all vanished one night and were never heard of again. The five cats had left some time before, but their going was scarcely noticed since there now seemed to be no mice, and only Mrs. Gardner had made pets of the graceful felines.

On the nineteenth of October Nahum staggered into Ammi's house with hideous news. The death had come to poor Thaddeus in his attic room, and it had come in a way which could not be told. Nahum had dug a grave in the railed family plot behind the farm, and had put therein what he found. There could have been nothing from outside, for the small barred window and locked door were intact; but it was much as it had been in the barn. Ammi and his wife consoled the stricken man as best they could, but shuddered as they did so. Stark terror seemed to cling round the Gardners and all they touched, and the very presence of one in the house was a breath from regions unnamed and unnamable. Ammi accompanied Nahum home with the greatest reluctance, and did what he might to calm the hysterical sobbing of little Merwin. Zenas needed no calming. He had come of late to do nothing but stare into space and obey what his father told him; and Ammi thought that his fate was very merciful. Now and then Merwin's screams were answered faintly from the attic, and in response to an inquiring look Nahum said that his wife was getting very feeble. When night approached, Ammi managed to get away; for not even friendship could make him stay in that spot when the faint glow of the vegetation began and the trees may or may not have swayed without wind. It was really lucky for Ammi that he was not more imaginative. Even as things were, his mind was bent ever so slightly; but had he been able to connect and reflect upon all the portents around him he must inevitably have turned a total maniac. In the twilight he hastened home, the screams of the mad woman and the nervous child ringing horribly in his ears.

Three days later Nahum lurched into Ammi's kitchen in the early morning, and in the absence of his host stammered out a desperate tale once more, while Mrs. Pierce listened in a clutching fright. It was little Merwin this time. He was gone. He had gone out late at night with a lantern and pail for water, and had never come back. He'd been going to pieces for days, and hardly knew what he was about. Screamed at everything. There had been a frantic shriek from the yard then, but before the father could get to the door, the boy was gone. There was no glow from the lantern he had taken, and of the child himself no trace. At the time Nahum thought the lantern and pail were gone too; but when dawn came, and the man had plodded back from his all-night search of the woods and fields, he had found some very curious things near the well. There was a crushed and apparently somewhat melted mass of iron which had certainly been the lantern; while a bent bail and twisted iron hoops beside it, both half-fused, seemed to hint at the remnants of the pail. That was all. Nahum was past imagining, Mrs. Pierce was blank, and Ammi, when he had reached home and heard the tale, could give no guess. Merwin was gone, and there would be no use in telling the people around, who shunned all Gardners now. No use, either, in telling the city people at Arkham who laughed at everything. Thad was gone, and now Merwin was gone. Something was creeping and creeping and waiting to be seen and felt and heard. Nahum would go soon, and he wanted Ammi to look after his wife and Zenas if they survived him. It must all be a judgment of some sort; though he could not fancy what for, since he had always walked uprightly in the Lord's ways so far as he knew.

For over two weeks Ammi saw nothing of Nahum; and then, worried about what might have happened, he overcame his fears and paid the Gardner place a visit. There was no smoke from the great chimney, and for a moment the visitor was apprehensive of the worst. The aspect of the whole farm was shocking —grayish withered grass and leaves on the ground, vines falling in brittle wreckage from archaic walls and gables, and great bare trees clawing up at the gray November sky with a studied malevolence which Ammi could not but feel had come from some subtle change in the tilt of the branches. But Nahum was alive, after all. He was weak, and lying on a couch in the low-ceiled kitchen, but perfectly conscious and able to give simple orders to Zenas. The room was deadly cold; and as Ammi visibly shivered, the host shouted huskily to Zenas for more wood. Wood, indeed, was sorely needed; since the cavernous fireplace was unlit and empty, with a cloud of soot blowing about in the chill wind that came down the chimney. Presently Nahum asked him if the extra wood had made him any more comfortable, and then Ammi saw what had happened. The stoutest cord had broken at last, and the hapless farmer's mind was proof against more sorrow.

Questioning tactfully, Ammi could get no clear data at all about the missing Zenas. "In the well—he lives in the well—" was all that the clouded father would say. Then there flashed across the visitor's mind a sudden thought of the mad wife, and he changed his line of inquiry. "Nabby? Why, here she is!" was the surprised response of poor Nahum, and Ammi soon saw that he must search for himself. Leaving the harmless babbler on the couch, he took the keys from their nail beside the door and climbed the creaking stairs to the attic. It was very close and noisome up there, and no sound could be heard from any direction. Of the four doors in sight, only one was locked, and on this he tried various keys on the ring he had taken. The third key proved the right one, and after some fumbling Ammi threw open the low white door.

It was quite dark inside, for the window was small and half-obscured by the crude wooden bars; and Ammi could see nothing at all on the wide-planked floor. The stench was beyond enduring, and before proceeding further he had to retreat to another room and return with his lungs filled with breathable air. When he did enter he saw something dark in the corner, and upon seeing it more clearly he screamed outright. While he screamed he thought a momentary cloud eclipsed the window, and a second later he felt himself brushed as if by some hateful current of vapor. Strange colors danced before his eyes; and had not a present horror numbed him he would have thought of the globule in the meteor that the geologist's hammer had shattered, and of the morbid vegetation that had sprouted in the spring. As it was he thought only of the blasphemous monstrosity which confronted him, and which all too clearly had shared the nameless fate of young Thaddeus and the livestock. But the terrible thing about this horror was that it very slowly and perceptibly moved as it continued to crumble.

Ammi would give me no added particulars to this scene, but the shape in the corner does not reappear in his tale as a moving object. There are things which cannot be mentioned, and what is done in common humanity is sometimes cruelly judged by the law. I gathered that no moving thing was left in that attic room, and that to leave anything capable of motion there would have been a deed so monstrous as to damn any accountable being to eternal torment. Anyone but a stolid farmer would have fainted or gone mad, but Ammi walked conscious through that low doorway and locked the accursed secret behind him. There would be Nahum to deal with now; he must be fed and tended, and removed to some place where he could be cared for.

Commencing his descent of the dark stairs, Ammi heard a thud below him. He even thought a scream had been suddenly choked off, and recalled nervously the clammy vapor which had brushed by him in that frightful room above. What presence had his cry and entry started up? Halted by some vague fear, he heard still further sounds below. Indubitably there was a sort of heavy dragging, and a most detestably sticky noise as of some fiendish and unclean species of suction. With an associative sense goaded to feverish heights, he thought unaccountably of what he had seen upstairs. Good God! What eldritch dream-world was this into which he had blundered? He dared move neither backward nor forward, but stood there trembling at the black curve of the boxed-in staircase. Every trifle of the scene burned itself into his brain. The sounds, the sense of dread expectancy, the darkness, the steepness of the narrow steps—and merciful heaven! . . . the faint but unmistakable luminosity of all the woodwork in sight; steps, sides, exposed laths, and beams alike!

Then there burst forth a frantic whinny from Ammi's horse outside, followed at once by a clatter which told of a frenzied runaway. In another moment horse and buggy had gone beyond earshot, leaving the frightened man on the dark stairs to guess what had sent them. But that was not all. There had been another sound out there. A sort of liquid splash—water—it must have been the well. He had left Hero untied near it, and a buggy-wheel must have brushed the coping and knocked in a stone. And still the pale phosphorescence glowed in that detestably ancient woodwork. God! how old the house was! Most of it built before 1670, and the gambrel roof not later than 1730.

A feeble scratching on the floor downstairs now sounded distinctly, and Ammi's grip tightened on a heavy stick he had picked up in the attic for some purpose. Slowly nerving himself, he finished his descent and walked boldly toward the kitchen. But he did not complete the walk, because what he sought was no longer there. It had come to meet him, and it was still alive after a fashion. Whether it had crawled or whether it had been dragged by any external force, Ammi could not say; but the death had been at it. Everything had happened in the last half-hour, but collapse, graying, and disintegration were already far advanced.

There was a horrible brittleness, and dry fragments were scaling off. Ammi could not touch it, but looked horrifiedly into the distorted parody that had been a face. "What was it, Nahum—what was it?" he whispered, and the cleft, bulging lips were just able to crackle out a final answer.

"Nothin' . . . nothin' . . . the color . . . it burns . . . cold an' wet . . . but it burns . . . it lived in the well . . . I seen it . . . a kind o' smoke . . . jest like the flowers last spring . . . the well shone at night . . . Thad an' Mernie an' Zenas . . . everything alive . . . suckin' the life out of everything . . . in that stone . . . it must a' come in that stone . . . pizened the whole place . . . dun't know what it wants . . . that round thing them men from the college dug outen the stone . . . they smashed it . . . it was that same color . . . jest the same, like the flowers an' plants . . . must a' ben more of 'em . . . seeds . . . seeds . . . they growed . . . I seen it the fust time this week . . . must a' got strong on Zenas . . . he was a big boy, full o' life . . . it beats down your mind an' then gits ye . . . burns ye up . . . in the well water . . . you was right about that . . . evil water . . . Zenas never come back from the well . . . can't git away . . . draws ye . . . ye know summ'at's comin', but 'tain't no use . . . I seen it time an' agin senct Zenas was took . . . whar's Nabby, Ammi? . . . my head's no good . . . dun't know how long senct I fed her . . . it'll git her ef we ain't keerful . . . jest a color . . . her face is gettin' to hev that color sometimes towards night . . . an' it burns an' sucks . . . it come from some place whar things ain't as they is here . . . one o' them professors said so . . . he was right . . . look out, Ammi, it'll do suthin' more . . . sucks the life out . . ."

But that was all. That which spoke could speak no more because it had completely caved in. Ammi laid a red checked tablecloth over what was left and reeled out the back door into the fields. He climbed the slope to the ten-acre pasture and stumbled home by the north road and the woods. He could not pass that well from which his horse had run away. He had looked at it through the window, and had seen that no stone was missing from the rim. Then the lurching buggy had not dislodged anything after all—the splash had been something else—something which went into the well after it had done with poor Nahum. . . .

When Ammi reached his house the horse and buggy had arrived before him and thrown his wife into fits of anxiety. Reassuring her without explanations, he set out at once for Arkham and notified the authorities that the Gardner family was no more. He indulged in no details, but merely told of the deaths of Nahum and Nabby, that of Thaddeus being already known, and mentioned that the cause seemed to be the same strange ailment which had killed the livestock. He also stated that Merwin and Zenas had disappeared. There was considerable questioning at the police station, and in the end Ammi was compelled to take three officers to the Gardner farm, together with the coroner, the medical examiner, and the veterinary who had treated the diseased animals. He went much against his will, for the afternoon was advancing and he feared the fall of night over that accursed place, but it was some comfort to have so many people with him.

The six men drove out in a democrat-wagon, following Ammi's buggy, and arrived at the pest-ridden farmhouse about four o'clock. Used as the officers were to gruesome experiences, not one remained unmoved at what was found in the attic and under the red checked tablecloth on the floor below. The whole aspect of the farm with its gray desolation was terrible enough, but those two crumbling objects were beyond all bounds. No one could look long at them, and even the medical examiner admitted that there was very little to examine. Specimens could be analyzed, of course, so he busied himself in obtaining them—and here it develops that a very puzzling aftermath occurred at the college laboratory where the two phials of dust were finally taken. Under the spectroscope both samples gave off an unknown spectrum, in which many of the baffling bands were precisely like those which the strange meteor had yielded in the previous year. The property of emitting this spectrum vanished in a month, the dust thereafter consisting mainly of alkaline phosphates and carbonates.

Ammi would not have told the men about the well if he had

thought they meant to do anything then and there. It was getting toward sunset, and he was anxious to be away. But he could not help glancing nervously at the stony curb by the great sweep, and when a detective questioned him he admitted that Nahum had feared something down there—so much so that he had never even thought of searching it for Merwin or Zenas. After that nothing would do but that they empty and explore the well immediately, so Ammi had to wait trembling while pail after pail of rank water was hauled up and splashed on the soaking ground outside. The men sniffed in disgust at the fluid, and toward the last held their noses against the fetor they were uncovering. It was not so long a job as they had feared it would be, since the water was phenomenally low. There is no need to speak too exactly of what they found. Merwin and Zenas were both there, in part, though the vestiges were mainly skeletal. There were also a small deer and a large dog in about the same state, and a number of bones of smaller animals. The ooze and slime at the bottom seemed inexplicably porous and bubbling, and a man who descended on hand-holds with a long pole found that he could sink the wooden shaft to any depth in the mud of the floor without meeting any solid obstruction.

Twilight had now fallen, and lanterns were brought from the house. Then, when it was seen that nothing further could be gained from the well, everyone went indoors and conferred in the ancient sitting-room while the intermittent light of a spectral half-moon played wanly on the gray desolation outside. The men were frankly nonplussed by the entire case, and could find no convincing common element to link the strange vegetable conditions, the unknown disease of livestock and humans, and the unaccountable deaths of Merwin and Zenas in the tainted well. They had heard the common country talk, it is true; but could not believe that anything contrary to natural law had occurred. No doubt the meteor had poisoned the soil, but the illness of persons and animals who had eaten nothing grown in that soil was another matter. Was it the well water? Very possibly. It might be a good idea to analyze it. But what peculiar madness could have made both boys jump into the well? Their deeds were so similar—and the fragments shewed that they had both suffered from the gray brittle death. Why was everything so gray and brittle?

It was the coroner, seated near a window overlooking the yard, who first noticed the glow about the well. Night had fully set in, and all the abhorrent grounds seemed faintly luminous with more than the fitful moonbeams; but this new glow was something definite and distinct, and appeared to shoot up from the black pit like a softened ray from a searchlight, giving dull reflections in the little ground pools where the water had been emptied. It had a very queer color, and as all the men clustered round the window Ammi gave a violent start. For this strange beam of ghastly miasma was to him of no unfamiliar hue. He had seen that color before, and feared to think what it might mean. He had seen it in the nasty brittle globule in that aerolite two summers ago, had seen it in the crazy vegetation of the springtime, and had thought he had seen it for an instant that very morning against the small barred window of that terrible attic room where nameless things had happened. It had flashed there a second, and a clammy and hateful current of vapor had brushed past him—and then poor Nahum had been taken by something of that color. He had said so at the last—said it was the globule and the plants. After that had come the runaway in the yard and the splash in the well—and now that well was belching forth to the night a pale insidious beam of the same daemoniac tint.

It does credit to the alertness of Ammi's mind that he puzzled even at that tense moment over a point which was essentially scientific. He could not but wonder at his gleaning of the same impression from a vapor glimpsed in the daytime, against a window opening on the morning sky, and from a nocturnal exhalation seen as a phosphorescent mist against the black and blasted landscape. It wasn't right—it was against Nature—and he thought of those terrible last words of his stricken friend, "It come from some place whar things ain't as they is here . . . one o' them professors said so . . ."

All three horses outside, tied to a pair of shriveled saplings by the road, were now neighing and pawing frantically. The wagon driver started for the door to do something, but Ammi laid a shaky hand on his shoulder. "Dun't go out thar," he whispered. "They's more to this nor what we know. Nahum said somethin' lived in the well that sucks your life out. He said it must be some'at growed from a round ball like one we all seen in the meteor stone that fell a year ago June. Sucks an' burns, he said, an' is jest a cloud of color like that light out thar now, that ye can hardly see an' can't tell what it is. Nahum thought it feeds on everything livin' an' gits stronger all the time. He said he seen it this last week. It must be somethin' from away off in the sky like the men from the college last year says the meteor stone was. The way it's made an' the way it works ain't like no way o' God's world. It's some'at from beyond."

So the men paused indecisively as the light from the well grew stronger and the hitched horses pawed and whinnied in increasing frenzy. It was truly an awful moment; with terror in that ancient and accursed house itself, four monstrous sets of fragments—two from the house and two from the well—in the woodshed behind, and that shaft of unknown and unholy iridescence from the slimy depths in front. Ammi had restrained the driver on impulse, forgetting how uninjured he himself was after the clammy brushing of that colored vapor in the attic room, but perhaps it is just as well that he acted as he did. No one will ever know what was abroad that night; and though the blasphemy from beyond had not so far hurt any human of unweakened mind, there is no telling what it might not have done at that last moment, and with its seemingly increased strength and the special signs of purpose it was soon to display beneath the half-clouded moonlit sky.

All at once one of the detectives at the window gave a short, sharp gasp. The others looked at him, and then quickly followed his own gaze upward to the point at which its idle straying had been suddenly arrested. There was no need for words. What had been disputed in country gossip was disputable no longer, and it is because of the thing which every man of that party agreed in whispering later on that the strange days are never talked about in Arkham. It is necessary to premise that there was no wind at that hour of the evening. One did arise not long afterward, but there was absolutely none then. Even the dry tips of the lingering hedge-mustard, gray and blighted, and the fringe on the roof of the standing democrat-wagon were unstirred. And yet amid that tense, godless calm the high bare boughs of all the trees in the yard were moving. They were twitching morbidly and spasmodically, clawing in convulsive and epileptic madness at the moonlit clouds; scratching impotently in the noxious air as if jerked by some alien and bodiless line of linkage with subterrene horrors writhing and struggling below the black roots.

Not a man breathed for several seconds. Then a cloud of darker depth passed over the moon, and the silhouette of clutching branches faded out momentarily. At this there was a general cry; muffled with awe, but husky and almost identical from every throat. For the terror had not faded with the silhouette, and in a fearsome instant of deeper darkness the watchers saw wriggling at that treetop height a thousand tiny points of faint and unhallowed radiance, tipping each bough like the fire of St. Elmo or the flames that came down on the apostles' heads at Pentecost. It was a monstrous constellation of unnatural light, like a glutted swarm of corpse-fed fireflies dancing hellish sarabands over an accursed marsh; and its color was that same nameless intrusion which Ammi had come to recognize and dread. All the while the shaft of phosphorescence from the well was getting brighter and brighter, bringing to the minds of the huddled men a sense of doom and abnormality which far outraced any image their conscious minds could form. It was no longer *shining* out, it was *pouring* out; and as the shapeless stream of unplaceable color left the well it seemed to flow directly into the sky.

The veterinary shivered, and walked to the front door to drop the heavy extra bar across it. Ammi shook no less, and had to tug and point for lack of a controllable voice when he wished to draw notice to the growing luminosity of the trees. The neighing and stamping of the horses had become utterly frightful, but not a soul of that group in the old house would have ventured forth for any earthly reward. With the moments the shining of the trees increased, while their restless branches seemed to strain more and more toward verticality. The wood of the well-sweep was shining now, and presently a policeman dumbly pointed to some wooden sheds and bee-hives near the stone wall on the west. They were commencing to shine, too, though the tethered vehicles of the visitors seemed so far unaffected. Then there was a wild commotion and clopping in the road, and as Ammi quenched the lamp for better seeing they realized that the span of frantic grays had broke their sapling and run off with the democrat-wagon.

The shock served to loosen several tongues, and embarrassed whispers were exchanged. "It spreads on everything organic that's been around here," muttered the medical examiner. No one replied, but the man who had been in the well gave a hint that his long pole must have stirred up something intangible. "It was awful," he added. "There was no bottom at all. Just ooze and bubbles and the feeling of something lurking under there." Ammi's horse still pawed and screamed deafeningly in the road outside, and nearly drowned its owner's faint quaver as he mumbled his formless reflections. "It come from that stone . . . it growed down thar . . . it got everything livin' . . . it fed itself on 'em, mind and body . . . Thad an' Mernie, Zenas an' Nabby . . . Nahum was the last . . . they all drunk the water . . . it got strong on 'em . . . it come from beyond, whar things ain't like they be here . . . now it's goin' home. . . ."

At this point, as the column of unknown color flared suddenly stronger and began to weave itself into fantastic suggestions of shape which each spectator later described differently, there came from poor tethered Hero such a sound as no man before or since ever heard from a horse. Every person in that low-pitched sitting room stopped his ears, and Ammi turned away from the window in horror and nausea. Words could not convey it—when Ammi looked out again the hapless beast lay huddled inert on the moonlit ground between the splintered shafts of the buggy. That was the last of Hero till they buried him next day. But the present was no time to mourn, for almost at this instant a detective silently called attention to something terrible in the very room with them. In the absence of the lamplight it was clear that a faint phosphorescence had begun to pervade the entire apartment. It glowed on the broad-planked floor and the fragment of rag carpet, and shimmered over the sashes of the small-paned windows. It ran up and down the exposed corner-posts, coruscated about the shelf and mantel, and infected the very doors and furniture. Each minute saw it strengthen, and at last it was very plain that healthy living things must leave that house.

Ammi shewed them the back door and the path up through the fields to the ten-acre pasture. They walked and stumbled as in a dream, and did not dare look back till they were far away on the high ground. They were glad of the path, for they could not have gone the front way, by that well. It was bad enough passing the glowing barn and sheds, and those shining orchard trees with their gnarled, fiendish contours; but thank heaven the branches did their worst twisting high up. The moon went under some very black clouds as they crossed the rustic bridge over Chapman's Brook, and it was blind groping from there to the open meadows.

When they looked back toward the valley and the distant Gardner place at the bottom they saw a fearsome sight. All the farm was shining with the hideous unknown blend of color; trees, buildings, and even such grass and herbage as had not been wholly changed to lethal gray brittleness. The boughs were all straining skyward, tipped with tongues of foul flame, and lambent tricklings of the same monstrous fire were creeping about the ridgepoles of the house, barn, and sheds. It was a scene from a vision of Fuseli, and over all the rest reigned that riot of luminous amorphousness, that alien and undimensioned rainbow of cryptic poison from the well—seething, feeling, lapping, reaching, scintillating, straining, and malignly bubbling in its cosmic and unrecognizable chromaticism.

Then without warning the hideous thing shot vertically up toward the sky like a rocket or meteor, leaving behind no trail and disappearing through a round and curiously regular hole in the clouds before any man could gasp or cry out. No watcher can ever forget that sight, and Ammi stared blankly at the stars of Cygnus, Deneb twinkling above the others, where the unknown color had melted into the Milky Way. But his gaze was the next moment called swiftly to earth by the crackling in the valley. It was just that. Only a wooden ripping and crackling, and not an explosion, as so many others of the party vowed. Yet the outcome was the same, for in one feverish, kaleidoscopic instant there burst up from that doomed and accursed farm a gleamingly eruptive cataclysm of unnatural sparks and substance; blurring the glance of the few who saw it, and sending forth to the zenith a bombarding cloudburst of such colored and fantastic fragments as our universe must needs disown. Through quickly re-closing vapors they followed the great morbidity that had vanished, and in another second they had vanished too. Behind and below was only a darkness to which the men dared not return, and all about was a mounting wind which seemed to sweep down in black, frore gusts from interstellar space. It shrieked and howled, and lashed the fields and distorted woods in a mad cosmic frenzy, till soon the trembling party realized it would be no use waiting for the moon to shew what was left down there at Nahum's.

Too awed even to hint theories, the seven shaking men trudged back toward Arkham by the north road. Ammi was worse than his fellows, and begged them to see him inside his own kitchen, instead of keeping straight on to town. He did not wish to cross the nighted, wind-whipped woods alone to his home on the main road. For he had had an added shock that the others were spared, and was crushed forever with a brooding fear he dared not even mention for many years to come. As the rest of the watchers on that tempestuous hill had stolidly set their faces toward the road, Ammi had looked back an instant at the shadowed valley of desolation so lately sheltering his ill-starred friend. And from that stricken, far-away spot he had seen something feebly rise, only to sink down again upon the place from which the great shapeless horror had shot into the sky. It was just a color—but not any color of our earth or heavens. And because Ammi recognized that color, and knew that this last faint remnant must still lurk down there in the well, he has never been quite right since.

Ammi would never go near the place again. It is over half a century now since the horror happened, but he has never been there, and will be glad when the new reservoir blots it out. I shall be glad, too, for I do not like the way the sunlight changed color around the mouth of that abandoned well I passed. I hope the water will always be very deep—but even so, I shall never drink it. I do not think I shall visit the Arkham country hereafter. Three of the men who had been with Ammi returned the next morning to see the ruins by daylight, but there were not any real ruins. Only the bricks of the chimney, the stones of the cellar, some mineral and metallic litter here and there, and the rim of that nefandous well. Save for Ammi's dead horse, which they towed away and buried, and the buggy which they shortly returned to him, everything that had ever been living had gone. Five eldritch acres of dusty gray desert remained, nor has anything ever grown there since. To this day it sprawls open to the sky like a great spot eaten by acid in the woods and fields, and the few who have ever dared glimpse it in spite of the rural tales have named it "the blasted heath."

The rural tales are queer. They might be even queerer if city men and college chemists could be interested enough to analyze the water from that disused well, or the gray dust that no wind seems ever to disperse. Botanists, too, ought to study the stunted flora on the borders of that spot, for they might shed light on the country notion that the blight is spreading—little by little, perhaps an inch a year. People say the color of the neighboring herbage is not quite right in the spring, and that wild things leave queer prints in the light winter snow. Snow never seems quite so heavy on the blasted heath as it is elsewhere. Horses— the few that are left in this motor age—grow skittish in the silent valley; and hunters cannot depend on their dogs too near the splotch of grayish dust.

They say the mental influences are very bad, too. Numbers went queer in the years after Nahum's taking, and always they lacked the power to get away. Then the stronger-minded folk all left the region, and only the foreigners tried to live in the crumbling old homesteads. They could not stay, though; and one sometimes wonders what insight beyond ours their wild, weird stores of whispered magic have given them. Their dreams at night, they protest, are very horrible in that grotesque country; and surely the very look of the dark realm is enough to stir a morbid fancy. No traveler has ever escaped a sense of strangeness in those deep ravines, and artists shiver as they paint thick woods whose mystery is as much of the spirit as of the eye. I myself am curious about the sensation I derived from my one lone walk before Ammi told me his tale. When twilight came I had vaguely wished some clouds would gather, for an odd timidity about the deep skyey voids above had crept into my soul.

Do not ask me for my opinion. I do not know—that is all. There was no one but Ammi to question; for Arkham people will not talk about the strange days, and all three professors who saw the aerolite and its colored globule are dead. There were other globules—depend upon that. One must have fed itself and escaped, and probably there was another which was too late. No doubt it is still down the well—I know there was something wrong with the sunlight I saw above that miasmal brink. The rustics say the blight creeps an inch a year, so perhaps there is a kind of growth or nourishment even now. But whatever daemon hatchling is there, it must be tethered to something or else it would quickly spread. Is it fastened to the roots of those trees that claw the air? One of the current Arkham tales is about fat oaks that shine and move as they ought not to do at night.

What it is, only God knows. In terms of matter I suppose the thing Ammi described would be called a gas, but this gas obeyed laws that are not of our cosmos. This was no fruit of such worlds and suns as shine on the telescopes and photographic plates of our observatories. This was no breath from the skies whose motions and dimensions our astronomers measure or deem too vast to measure. It was just a color out of space—a frightful messenger from unformed realms of infinity beyond all Nature as we know it; from realms whose mere existence stuns the brain and numbs us with the black extra-cosmic gulfs it throws open before our frenzied eyes.

I doubt very much if Ammi consciously lied to me, and I do not think his tale was all a freak of madness as the townfolk had forewarned. Something terrible came to the hills and valleys on that meteor, and something terrible—though I know not in what proportion—still remains. I shall be glad to see the water come. Meanwhile I hope nothing will happen to Ammi. He saw so much of the thing—and its influence was so insidious. Why has he never been able to move away? How clearly he recalled those dying words of Nahum's—"can't git away ... draws ye ... ye know summ'at's comin', but 'tain't no use. . . ." Ammi is such a good old man—when the reservoir gang gets to work I must write the chief engineer to keep a sharp watch on him. I would hate to think of him as the gray, twisted, brittle monstrosity which persists more and more in troubling my sleep.

THE DREAMS IN
THE WITCH HOUSE

Whether the dreams brought on the fever or the fever brought on the dreams Walter Gilman did not know. Behind everything crouched the brooding, festering horror of the ancient town, and of the moldy, unhallowed garret gable where he wrote and studied and wrestled with figures and formulae when he was not tossing on the meager iron bed. His ears were growing sensitive to a preternatural and intolerable degree, and he had long ago stopped the cheap mantel clock whose ticking had come to seem like a thunder of artillery. At night the subtle stirring of the black city outside, the sinister scurrying of rats in the wormy partitions, and the creaking of hidden timbers in the centuried house, were enough to give him a sense of strident pandemonium. The darkness always teemed with unexplained sound—and yet he sometimes shook with fear lest the noises he heard should subside and allow him to hear certain other, fainter, noises which he suspected were lurking behind them.

He was in the changeless, legend-haunted city of Arkham, with its clustering gambrel roofs that sway and sag over attics where witches hid from the King's men in the dark, olden days of the Province. Nor was any spot in that city more steeped in macabre memory than the gable room which harbored him—for it was this house and this room which had likewise harbored old Keziah Mason, whose flight from Salem Gaol at the last no one was ever able to explain. That was in 1692—the jailer had gone mad and babbled of a small, white-fanged furry thing which scuttled out of Keziah's cell, and not even Cotton Mather could explain the curves and angles smeared on the gray stone walls with some red, sticky fluid.

Possibly Gilman ought not to have studied so hard.

Non-Euclidean calculus and quantum physics are enough to stretch any brain; and when one mixes them with folklore, and tries to trace a strange background of multi-dimensional reality behind the ghoulish hints of the Gothic tales and the wild whispers of the chimney-corner, one can hardly expect to be wholly free from mental tension. Gilman came from Haverhill, but it was only after he had entered college in Arkham that he began to connect his mathematics with the fantastic legends of elder magic. Something in the air of the hoary town worked obscurely on his imagination. The professors at Miskatonic had urged him to slacken up, and had voluntarily cut down his course at several points. Moreover, they had stopped him from consulting the dubious old books on forbidden secrets that were kept under lock and key in a vault at the university library. But all these precautions came late in the day, so that Gilman had some terrible hints from the dreaded *Necronomicon* of Abdul Alhazred, the fragmentary *Book of Eibon*, and the suppressed *Unaussprechlichen Kulten* of von Junzt to correlate with his abstract formulae on the properties of space and the linkage of dimensions known and unknown.

He knew his room was in the old Witch House—that, indeed, was why he had taken it. There was much in the Essex County records about Keziah Mason's trial, and what she had admitted under pressure to the Court of Oyer and Terminer had fascinated Gilman beyond all reason. She had told Judge Hathorne of lines and curves that could be made to point out directions leading through the walls of space to other spaces beyond, and had implied that such lines and curves were frequently used at certain midnight meetings in the dark valley of the white stone beyond Meadow Hill and on the unpeopled island in the river. She had spoken also of the Black Man, of her oath, and of her new secret name of Nahab. Then she had drawn those devices on the walls of her cell and vanished.

Gilman believed strange things about Keziah, and had felt a queer thrill on learning that her dwelling was still standing after more than 235 years. When he heard the hushed Arkham whispers about Keziah's persistent presence in the old house and the narrow streets, about the irregular human tooth-marks left on certain sleepers in that and other houses, about the childish cries heard near May-Eve, and Hallowmass, about the stench often noted in the old house's attic just after those dreaded seasons, and about the small, furry, sharp-toothed thing which haunted the moldering structure and the town and nuzzled people curiously in the black hours before dawn, he resolved to live in the place at any cost. A room was easy to secure; for the house was unpopular, hard to rent, and long given over to cheap lodgings. Gilman could not have told what he expected to find there, but he knew he wanted to be in the building where some circumstance had more or less suddenly given a mediocre old woman of the seventeenth century an insight into mathematical depths perhaps beyond the utmost modern delvings of Planck, Heisenberg, Einstein, and de Sitter.

He studied the timber and plaster walls for traces of cryptic designs at every accessible spot where the paper had peeled, and within a week managed to get the eastern attic room where Keziah was held to have practiced her spells. It had been vacant from the first—for no one had ever been willing to stay there long—but the Polish landlord had grown wary about renting it. Yet nothing whatever happened to Gilman till about the time of the fever. No ghostly Keziah flitted through the somber halls and chambers, no small furry thing crept into his dismal eyrie to nuzzle him, and no record of the witch's incantations rewarded his constant search. Sometimes he would take walks through shadowy tangles of unpaved musty-smelling lanes where eldritch brown houses of unknown age leaned and tottered and leered mockingly through narrow, small-paned windows. Here he knew strange things had happened once, and there was a faint suggestion behind the surface that everything of that monstrous past might not—at least in the darkest, narrowest, and most intricately crooked alleys—have utterly perished. He also rowed out twice to the ill-regarded island in the river, and made a sketch of the singular angles described by the moss-grown rows of gray standing stones whose origin was so obscure and immemorial.

Gilman's room was of good size but queerly irregular shape; the north wall slanting perceptibly inward from the outer to the inner end, while the low ceiling slanted gently downward in the same direction. Aside from an obvious rat-hole and the signs of other stopped-up ones, there was no access—nor any appearance of a former avenue of access—to the space which must have existed between the slanting wall and the straight outer wall on the house's north side, though a view from the exterior shewed where a window had been boarded up at a very remote date. The loft above the ceiling—which must have had a slanting floor—was likewise inaccessible. When Gilman climbed up a ladder to the cobwebbed level loft above the rest of the attic he found vestiges of a bygone aperture tightly and heavily covered with ancient planking and secured by the stout wooden pegs common in colonial carpentry. No amount of persuasion, however, could induce the stolid landlord to let him investigate either of these two closed spaces.

As time wore along, his absorption in the irregular wall and ceiling of his room increased; for he began to read into the odd angles a mathematical significance which seemed to offer vague clues regarding their purpose. Old Keziah, he reflected, might have had excellent reasons for living in a room with peculiar angles; for was it not through certain angles that she claimed to have gone outside the boundaries of the world of space we know? His interest gradually veered away from the unplumbed voids beyond the slanting surfaces, since it now appeared that the purpose of those surfaces concerned the side he was already on.

The touch of brain-fever and the dreams began early in February. For some time, apparently, the curious angles of Gilman's room had been having a strange, almost hypnotic effect on him; and as the bleak winter advanced he had found himself staring more and more intently at the corner where the down-slanting ceiling met the inward-slanting wall. About this period his inability to concentrate on his formal studies worried him considerably, his apprehensions about the mid-year examinations being very acute. But the exaggerated sense of hearing was scarcely less annoying. Life had become an insistent and almost unendurable cacophony, and there was that constant, terrifying impression of *other* sounds—perhaps from regions beyond life—trembling on the very brink of audibility. So far as concrete noises went, the rats in the ancient partitions were the worst. Sometimes their scratching seemed not only furtive but deliberate. When it came from beyond the slanting north wall it was mixed with a sort of dry rattling—and when it came from the century-closed loft above the slanting ceiling Gilman always braced himself as if expecting some horror which only bided its time before descending to engulf him utterly.

The dreams were wholly beyond the pale of sanity, and Gilman felt that they must be a result, jointly, of his studies in mathematics and in folklore. He had been thinking too much about the vague regions which his formulae told him must lie beyond the three dimensions we know, and about the possibility that old Keziah Mason—guided by some influence past all conjecture—had actually found the gate to those regions. The yellowed county records containing her testimony and that of her accusers were so damnably suggestive of things beyond human experience—and the descriptions of the darting little furry object which served as her familiar were so painfully realistic despite their incredible details.

That object—no larger than a good-sized rat and quaintly called by the townspeople "Brown Jenkin"—seemed to have been the fruit of a remarkable case of sympathetic herd-delusion, for in 1692 no less than eleven persons had testified to glimpsing it. There were recent rumors, too, with a baffling and disconcerting amount of agreement. Witnesses said it had long hair and the shape of a rat, but that its sharp-toothed, bearded face was evilly human while its paws were like tiny human hands. It took messages betwixt old Keziah and the devil, and was nursed on the witch's blood—which it sucked like a vampire. Its voice was a kind of loathsome titter, and it could speak all languages. Of all the bizarre monstrosities in Gilman's dreams, nothing filled him with greater panic and nausea than this blasphemous and diminutive hybrid, whose image flitted across his vision in a form a thousandfold more hateful than anything his waking mind had deduced from the ancient records and the modern whispers.

Gilman's dreams consisted largely in plunges through limitless abysses of inexplicably colored twilight and bafflingly disordered sound; abysses whose material and gravitational properties, and whose relation to his own entity, he could not even begin to explain. He did not walk or climb, fly or swim, crawl or wriggle; yet always experienced a mode of motion partly voluntary and partly involuntary. Of his own condition he could not well judge, for sight of his arms, legs, and torso seemed always cut off by some odd disarrangement of perspective; but he felt that his physical organization and faculties were somehow marvelously transmuted and obliquely projected—though not without a certain grotesque relationship to his normal proportions and properties.

The abysses were by no means vacant, being crowded with indescribably angled masses of alien-hued substance, some of which appeared to be organic while others seemed inorganic. A few of the organic objects tended to awake vague memories in the back of his mind, though he could form no conscious idea of what they mockingly resembled or suggested. In the later dreams he began to distinguish separate categories into which the organic objects appeared to be divided, and which seemed to involve in each case a radically different species of conduct-pattern and basic motivation. Of these categories one seemed to him to include objects slightly less illogical and irrelevant in their motions than the members of the other categories.

All the objects—organic and inorganic alike—were totally

beyond description or even comprehension. Gilman sometimes compared the inorganic masses to prisms, labyrinths, clusters of cubes and planes, and Cyclopean buildings; and the organic things struck him variously as groups of bubbles, octopi, centipedes, living Hindoo idols, and intricate Arabesques roused into a kind of ophidian animation. Everything he saw was unspeakably menacing and horrible; and whenever one of the organic entities appeared by its motions to be noticing him, he felt a stark, hideous fright which generally jolted him awake. Of how the organic entities moved, he could tell no more than of how he moved himself. In time he observed a further mystery—the tendency of certain entities to appear suddenly out of empty space, or to disappear totally with equal suddenness. The shrieking, roaring confusion of sound which permeated the abysses was past all analysis as to pitch, timbre, or rhythm; but seemed to be synchronous with vague visual changes in all the indefinite objects, organic and inorganic alike. Gilman had a constant sense of dread that it might rise to some unbearable degree of intensity during one or another of its obscure, relentlessly inevitable fluctuations.

But it was not in these vortices of complete alienage that he saw Brown Jenkin. That shocking little horror was reserved for certain lighter, sharper dreams which assailed him just before he dropped into the fullest depths of sleep. He would be lying in the dark fighting to keep awake when a faint lambent glow would seem to shimmer around the centuried room, shewing in a violet mist the convergence of angled planes which had seized his brain so insidiously. The horror would appear to pop out of the rat-hole in the corner and patter toward him over the sagging, wide-planked floor with evil expectancy in its tiny, bearded human face—but mercifully, this dream always melted away before the object got close enough to nuzzle him. It had hellishly long, sharp, canine teeth. Gilman tried to stop up the rat-hole every day, but each night the real tenants of the partitions would gnaw away the obstruction, whatever it might be. Once he had the landlord nail tin over it, but the next night the rats gnawed a fresh hole—in making which they pushed or dragged out into the room a curious little fragment of bone.

Gilman did not report his fever to the doctor, for he knew he could not pass the examinations if ordered to the college infirmary when every moment was needed for cramming. As it was, he failed in Calculus D and Advanced General Psychology, though not without hope of making up lost ground before the end of the term. It was in March when the fresh element entered his lighter preliminary dreaming, and the nightmare shape of Brown Jenkin began to be companioned by the nebulous blur which grew more and more to resemble a bent old woman. This addition disturbed him more than he could account for, but finally he decided that it was like an ancient crone whom he had twice actually encountered in the dark tangle of lanes near the abandoned wharves. On those occasions the evil, sardonic, and seemingly unmotivated stare of the beldame had set him almost shivering—especially the first time, when an overgrown rat darting across the shadowed mouth of a neighboring alley had made him think irrationally of Brown Jenkin. Now, he reflected, those nervous fears were being mirrored in his disordered dreams.

That the influence of the old house was unwholesome, he could not deny; but traces of his early morbid interest still held him there. He argued that the fever alone was responsible for his nightly phantasies, and that when the touch abated he would be free from the monstrous visions. Those visions, however, were of abhorrent vividness and convincingness, and whenever he awaked he retained a vague sense of having undergone much more than he remembered. He was hideously sure that in unrecalled dreams he had talked with both Brown Jenkin and the old woman, and that they had been urging him to go somewhere with them and to meet a third being of greater potency.

Toward the end of March he began to pick up in his mathematics, though other studies bothered him increasingly. He was getting an intuitive knack for solving Riemannian equations, and astonished Professor Upham by his comprehension of fourth-dimensional and other problems which had floored all the rest of the class. One afternoon there was a discussion of possible freakish curvatures in space, and of theoretical points of approach or even contact between our part of the cosmos and various other regions as distant as the farthest stars or the trans-galactic gulfs themselves—or even as fabulously remote as the tentatively conceivable cosmic units beyond the whole Einsteinian space-time continuum. Gilman's handling of this theme filled everyone with admiration, even though some of his hypothetical illustrations caused an increase in the always plentiful gossip about his nervous and solitary eccentricity. What made the students shake their heads was his sober theory that a man might—given mathematical knowledge admittedly beyond all likelihood of human acquirement—step deliberately from the earth to any other celestial body which might lie at one of an infinity of specific points in the cosmic pattern.

Such a step, he said, would require only two stages; first, a passage out of the three-dimensional sphere we know, and second, a passage back to the three-dimensional sphere at another point, perhaps one of infinite remoteness. That this could be accomplished without loss of life was in many cases conceivable. Any being from any part of three-dimensional space could probably survive in the fourth dimension; and its survival of the second stage would depend upon what alien part of three-dimensional space it might select for its re-entry. Denizens of some planets might be able to live on certain others—even planets belonging to other galaxies, or to similar-dimensional phases of other space-time continua—though of course there must be vast numbers of mutually uninhabitable even though mathematically juxtaposed bodies or zones of space.

It was also possible that the inhabitants of a given dimensional realm could survive entry to many unknown and incomprehensible realms of additional or indefinitely multiplied dimensions—be they within or outside the given space-time continuum—and that the converse would be likewise true. This was a matter for speculation, though one could be fairly certain that the type of mutation involved in a passage from any given dimensional plane to the next higher plane would not be destructive of biological integrity as we understand it. Gilman could not be very clear about his reasons for this last assumption, but his haziness here was more than overbalanced by his clearness on other complex points. Professor Upham especially liked his demonstration of the kinship of higher mathematics to certain phases of magical lore transmitted down the ages from an ineffable antiquity—human or pre-human—whose knowledge of the cosmos and its laws was greater than ours.

Around the first of April Gilman worried considerably because his slow fever did not abate. He was also troubled by what some of his fellow-lodgers said about his sleep-walking. It seemed that he was often absent from his bed, and that the creaking of his floor at certain hours of the night was remarked by the man in the room below. This fellow also spoke of hearing the tread of shod feet in the night; but Gilman was sure he must have been mistaken in this, since shoes as well as other apparel were always precisely in place in the morning. One could develop all sorts of aural delusions in this morbid old house—for did not Gilman himself, even in daylight, now feel certain that noises other than rat-scratchings came from the black voids beyond the slanting wall and above the slanting ceiling? His pathologically sensitive ears began to listen for faint footfalls in the immemorially sealed loft overhead, and sometimes the illusion of such things was agonizingly realistic.

However, he knew that he had actually become a somnambulist; for twice at night his room had been found vacant, though with all his clothing in place. Of this he had been assured by Frank Elwood, the one fellow-student whose poverty forced him to room in this squalid and unpopular house. Elwood had been studying in the small hours and had come up for help on a differential equation, only to find Gilman absent. It had been rather presumptuous of him to open the unlocked door after knocking had failed to rouse a response, but he had needed the help very badly and thought that his host would not mind a gentle prodding awake. On neither occasion, though, had Gilman been there—and when told of the matter he wondered where he could have been wandering, barefoot and with only his night-clothes on. He resolved to investigate the matter if reports of his sleep-walking continued, and thought of sprinkling flour on the floor of the corridor to see where his footsteps might lead. The door was the only conceivable egress, for there was no possible foothold outside the narrow window.

As April advanced Gilman's fever-sharpened ears were disturbed by the whining prayers of a superstitious loomfixer named Joe Mazurewicz, who had a room on the ground floor. Mazurewicz had told long, rambling stories about the ghost of old Keziah and the furry, sharp-fanged, nuzzling thing, and had said he was so badly haunted at times that only his silver crucifix—given him for the purpose by Father Iwanicki of St. Stanislaus' Church—could bring him relief. Now he was praying because the Witches' Sabbath was drawing near. May-Eve was Walpurgis-Night, when hell's blackest evil roamed the earth and all the slaves of Satan gathered for nameless rites and deeds. It was always a very bad time in Arkham, even though the fine folks up in Miskatonic Avenue and High and Saltonstall Streets pretended to know nothing about it.There would be bad doings—and a child or two would probably be missing. Joe knew about such things, for his grandmother in the old country had heard tales from her grandmother. It was wise to pray and count one's beads at this season. For three months Keziah and Brown Jenkin had not been near Joe's room, nor near Paul Choynski's room, nor anywhere else—and it meant no good when they held off like that. They must be up to something.

Gilman dropped in at a doctor's office on the 16th of the month, and was surprised to find his temperature was not as high as he had feared. The physician questioned him sharply, and advised him to see a nerve specialist. On reflection, he was glad he had not consulted the still more inquisitive college doctor. Old Waldron, who had curtailed his activities before, would have made him take a rest—an impossible thing now that he was so close to great results in his equations. He was certainly near the boundary between the known universe and the fourth dimension, and who could say how much farther he might go?

But even as these thoughts came to him he wondered at the source of his strange confidence. Did all of this perilous sense of imminence come from the formulae on the sheets he covered day by day? The soft, stealthy, imaginary footsteps in the sealed loft above were unnerving. And now, too, there was a growing feeling that somebody was constantly persuading him to do something terrible which he could not do. How about the somnambulism? Where did he go sometimes in the night? And what was that faint suggestion of sound which once in a while seemed to trickle through the maddening confusion of identifiable sounds even in broad daylight and full wakefulness? Its rhythm did not correspond to anything on earth, unless perhaps to the cadence of one or two unmentionable Sabbat-chants, and sometimes he feared it corresponded to certain attributes of the vague shrieking or roaring in those wholly alien abysses of dream.

The dreams were meanwhile getting to be atrocious. In the lighter preliminary phase the evil old woman was now of fiendish distinctness, and Gilman knew she was the one who had frightened him in the slums. Her bent back, long nose, and shriveled chin were unmistakable, and her shapeless brown garments were like those he remembered. The expression on her face was one of hideous malevolence and exultation, and when he awaked he could recall a croaking voice that persuaded and threatened. He must meet the Black Man, and go with them all to the throne of Azathoth at the center of ultimate Chaos. That was what she said. He must sign in his own blood the book of Azathoth and take a new secret name now that his independent delvings had gone so far. What kept him from going with her and Brown Jenkin and the other to the throne of Chaos where the thin flutes pipe mindlessly was the fact that he had seen the name "Azathoth" in the *Necronomicon,* and knew it stood for a primal evil too horrible for description.

The old woman always appeared out of thin air near the corner where the downward slant met the inward slant. She seemed to crystallize at a point closer to the ceiling than to the floor, and every night she was a little nearer and more distinct before the dream shifted. Brown Jenkin, too, was always a little nearer at the last, and its yellowish-white fangs glistened shockingly in that unearthly violet phosphorescence. Its shrill loathsome tittering stuck more and more in Gilman's head, and he could remember in the morning how it had pronounced the words "Azathoth" and "Nyarlathotep."

In the deeper dreams everything was likewise more distinct, and Gilman felt that the twilight abysses around him were those of the fourth dimension. Those organic entities whose motions seemed least flagrantly irrelevant and unmotivated were probably projections of life-forms from our own planet, including human beings. What the others were in their own dimensional sphere or spheres he dared not try to think. Two of the less irrelevantly moving things—a rather large congeries of iridescent, prolately spheroidal bubbles and a very much smaller polyhedron of unknown colors and rapidly shifting surface angles—seemed to take notice of him and follow him about or float ahead as he changed position among the titan prisms, labyrinths, cube-and-plane clusters, and quasi-buildings; and all the while the vague shrieking and roaring waxed louder and louder, as if approaching some monstrous climax of utterly unendurable intensity.

During the night of April 19–20 the new development occurred. Gilman was half-involuntarily moving about in the twilight abysses with the bubble-mass and the small polyhedron floating ahead, when he noticed the peculiarly regular angles formed by the edges of some gigantic neighboring prism-clusters.

In another second he was out of the abyss and standing tremulously on a rocky hillside bathed in intense, diffused green light. He was barefooted and in his night-clothes, and when he tried to walk discovered that he could scarcely lift his feet. A swirling vapor hid everything but the immediate sloping terrain from sight, and he shrank from the thought of the sounds that might surge out of that vapor.

Then he saw the two shapes laboriously crawling toward him—the old woman and the little furry thing. The crone strained up to her knees and managed to cross her arms in a singular fashion, while Brown Jenkin pointed in a certain direction with a horribly anthropoid fore paw which it raised with evident difficulty. Spurred by an impulse he did not originate, Gilman dragged himself forward along a course determined by the angle of the old woman's arms and the direction of the small monstrosity's paw, and before he had shuffled three steps he was back in the twilight abysses. Geometrical shapes seethed around him, and he fell dizzily and interminably. At last he woke in his bed in the crazily angled garret of the eldritch old house.

He was good for nothing that morning, and stayed away from all his classes. Some unknown attraction was pulling his eyes in a seemingly irrelevant direction, for he could not help staring at a certain vacant spot on the floor. As the day advanced the focus of his unseeing eyes changed position, and by noon he had conquered the impulse to stare at vacancy. About two o'clock he went out for lunch, and as he threaded the narrow lanes of the city he found himself turning always to the southeast. Only an effort halted him at a cafeteria in Church Street, and after the meal he felt the unknown pull still more strongly.

He would have to consult a nerve specialist after all—perhaps there was a connexion with his somnambulism—but meanwhile he might at least try to break the morbid spell himself. Undoubtedly he could still manage to walk away from the pull; so with great resolution he headed against it and dragged himself deliberately north along Garrison Street. By the time he had

reached the bridge over the Miskatonic he was in a cold perspiration, and he clutched at the iron railing as he gazed upstream
at the ill-regarded island whose regular lines of ancient standing
stones brooded sullenly in the afternoon sunlight.

Then he gave a start. For there was a clearly visible living
figure on that desolate island, and a second glance told him it
was certainly the strange old woman whose sinister aspect had
worked itself so disastrously into his dreams. The tall grass near
her was moving, too, as if some other living thing were crawling
close to the ground. When the old woman began to turn toward
him he fled precipitately off the bridge and into the shelter of
the town's labyrinthine waterfront alleys. Distant though the
island was, he felt that a monstrous and invincible evil could
flow from the sardonic stare of that bent, ancient figure in brown.

The southeastward pull still held, and only with tremendous
resolution could Gilman drag himself into the old house and up
the rickety stairs. For hours he sat silent and aimless, with his
eyes shifting gradually westward. About six o'clock his sharpened
ears caught the whining prayers of Joe Mazurewicz two floors
below, and in desperation he seized his hat and walked out into
the sunset-golden streets, letting the now directly southward pull
carry him where it might. An hour later darkness found him in
the open fields beyond Hangman's Brook, with the glimmering
spring stars shining ahead. The urge to walk was gradually
changing to an urge to leap mystically into space, and suddenly
he realized just where the source of the pull lay.

It was in the sky. A definite point among the stars had a claim
on him and was calling him. Apparently it was a point somewhere
between Hydra and Argo Navis, and he knew that he had been
urged toward it ever since he had awaked soon after dawn. In the
morning it had been underfoot; afternoon found it rising in
the southeast, and now it was roughly south but wheeling toward
the west. What was the meaning of this new thing? Was he going
mad? How long would it last? Again mustering his resolution,
Gilman turned and dragged himself back to the sinister old house.

Mazurewicz was waiting for him at the door, and seemed both anxious and reluctant to whisper some fresh bit of superstition. It was about the witch light. Joe had been out celebrating the night before—it was Patriots' Day in Massachusetts—and had come home after midnight. Looking up at the house from outside, he had thought at first that Gilman's window was dark; but then he had seen the faint violet glow within. He wanted to warn the gentleman about that glow, for everybody in Arkham knew it was Keziah's witch light which played near Brown Jenkin and the ghost of the old crone herself. He had not mentioned this before, but now he must tell about it because it meant that Keziah and her long-toothed familiar were haunting the young gentleman. Sometimes he and Paul Choynski and Landlord Dombrowski thought they saw that light seeping out of cracks in the sealed loft above the young gentleman's room, but they had all agreed not to talk about that. However, it would be better for the gentleman to take another room and get a crucifix from some good priest like Father Iwanicki.

As the man rambled on Gilman felt a nameless panic clutch at his throat. He knew that Joe must have been half drunk when he came home the night before, yet this mention of a violet light in the garret window was of frightful import. It was a lambent glow of this sort which always played about the old woman and the small furry thing in those lighter, sharper dreams which prefaced his plunge into unknown abysses, and the thought that a wakeful second person could see the dream-luminance was utterly beyond sane harborage. Yet where had the fellow got such an odd notion? Had he himself talked as well as walked around the house in his sleep? No, Joe said, he had not—but he must check up on this. Perhaps Frank Elwood could tell him something, though he hated to ask.

Fever—wild dreams—somnambulism—illusions of sounds—a pull toward a point in the sky—and now a suspicion of insane sleep-talking! He must stop studying, see a nerve specialist, and take himself in hand. When he climbed to the second story he paused at Elwood's door but saw that the other youth was out. Reluctantly he continued up to his garret room and sat down in the dark. His gaze was still pulled to the southwest, but he also found himself listening intently for some sound in the closed loft above, and half imagining that an evil violet light seeped down through an infinitesimal crack in the low, slanting ceiling.

That night as Gilman slept the violet light broke upon him with heightened intensity, and the old witch and small furry thing—getting closer than ever before—mocked him with inhuman squeals and devilish gestures. He was glad to sink into the vaguely roaring twilight abysses, though the pursuit of that iridescent bubble-congeries and that kaleidoscopic little polyhedron was menacing and irritating. Then came the shift as vast converging planes of a slippery-looking substance loomed above and below him—a shift which ended in a flash of delirium and a blaze of unknown, alien light in which yellow, carmine, and indigo were madly and inextricably blended.

He was half lying on a high, fantastically balustraded terrace above a boundless jungle of outlandish, incredible peaks, balanced planes, domes, minarets, horizontal discs poised on pinnacles, and numberless forms of still greater wildness—some of stone and some of metal—which glittered gorgeously in the mixed, almost blistering glare from a polychromatic sky. Looking upward he saw three stupendous discs of flame, each of a different hue, and at a different height above an infinitely distant curving horizon of low mountains. Behind him tiers of higher terraces towered aloft as far as he could see. The city below stretched away to the limits of vision, and he hoped that no sound would well up from it.

The pavement from which he easily raised himself was of a veined, polished stone beyond his power to identify, and the tiles were cut in bizarre-angled shapes which struck him as less asymmetrical than based on some unearthly symmetry whose laws he could not comprehend. The balustrade was chest-high, delicate, and fantastically wrought, while along the rail were ranged at short intervals little figures of grotesque design and exquisite workmanship. They, like the whole balustrade, seemed to be made of some sort of shining metal whose color could not be guessed in this chaos of mixed effulgences; and their nature utterly defied conjecture. They represented some ridged, barrel-shaped object with thin horizontal arms radiating spoke-like from a central ring, and with vertical knobs or bulbs projecting from the head and base of the barrel. Each of these knobs was the hub of a system of five long, flat, triangularly tapering arms arranged around it like the arms of a starfish—nearly horizontal, but curving slightly away from the central barrel. The base of the bottom knob was fused to the long railing with so delicate a point of contact that several figures had been broken off and were missing. The figures were about four and a half inches in height, while the spiky arms gave them a maximum diameter of about two and a half inches.

When Gilman stood up the tiles felt hot to his bare feet. He was wholly alone, and his first act was to walk to the balustrade and look dizzily down at the endless, Cyclopean city almost two thousand feet below. As he listened he thought a rhythmic confusion of faint musical pipings covering a wide tonal range welled up from the narrow streets beneath, and he wished he might discern the denizens of the place. The sight turned him giddy after a while, so that he would have fallen to the pavement had he not clutched instinctively at the lustrous balustrade. His right hand fell on one of the projecting figures, the touch seeming to steady him slightly. It was too much, however, for the exotic delicacy of the metal-work, and the spiky figure snapped off under his grasp. Still half-dazed, he continued to clutch it as his other hand seized a vacant space on the smooth railing.

But now his oversensitive ears caught something behind him, and he looked back across the level terrace. Approaching him softly though without apparent furtiveness were five figures, two of which were the sinister old woman and the fanged, furry little animal. The other three were what sent him unconscious—for they were living entities about eight feet high, shaped precisely like the spiky images on the balustrade, and propelling themselves by a spider-like wriggling of their lower set of starfish-arms.

Gilman awakened in his bed, drenched by a cold perspiration and with a smarting sensation in his face, hands, and feet. Springing to the floor, he washed and dressed in frantic haste, as if it were necessary for him to get out of the house as quickly as possible. He did not know where he wished to go, but felt that once more he would have to sacrifice his classes. The odd pull toward that spot in the sky between Hydra and Argo had abated, but another of even greater strength had taken its place. Now he felt that he must go north—infinitely north. He dreaded to cross the bridge that gave a view of the desolate island in the Miskatonic, so went over the Peabody Avenue bridge. Very often he stumbled, for his eyes and ears were chained to an extremely lofty point in the blank blue sky.

After about an hour he got himself under better control, and saw that he was far from the city. All around him stretched the bleak emptiness of salt marshes, while the narrow road ahead led to Innsmouth—that ancient, half-deserted town which Arkham people were so curiously unwilling to visit. Though the northward pull had not diminished, he resisted it as he had resisted the other pull, and finally found that he could almost balance the one against the other. Plodding back to town and getting some coffee at a soda fountain, he dragged himself into the public library and browsed aimlessly among the lighter magazines. Once he met some friends who remarked how oddly sunburned he looked, but he did not tell them of his walk. At three o'clock he took some lunch at a restaurant, noting meanwhile that the pull had either lessened or divided itself. After that he killed the time at a cheap cinema show, seeing the inane performance over and over again without paying any attention to it.

About nine at night he drifted homeward and stumbled into the ancient house. Joe Mazurewicz was whining unintelligible prayers, and Gilman hastened up to his own garret chamber without pausing to see if Elwood was in. It was when he turned on the feeble electric light that the shock came. At once he saw there was something on the table which did not belong there, and a second look left no room for doubt. Lying on its side—for it could not stand up alone—was the exotic spiky figure which in his monstrous dream he had broken off the fantastic balustrade. No detail was missing. The ridged, barrel-shaped center, the thin, radiating arms, the knobs at each end, and the flat, slightly outward-curving starfish-arms spreading from those knobs—all were there. In the electric light the color seemed to be a kind of iridescent gray veined with green, and Gilman could see amidst his horror and bewilderment that one of the knobs ended in a jagged break corresponding to its former point of attachment to the dream-railing.

Only his tendency toward a dazed stupor prevented him from screaming aloud. This fusion of dream and reality was too much to bear. Still dazed, he clutched at the spiky thing and staggered downstairs to Landlord Dombrowski's quarters. The whining prayers of the superstitious loomfixer were still sounding through the moldy halls, but Gilman did not mind them now. The landlord was in, and greeted him pleasantly. No, he had not seen that thing before and did not know anything about it. But his wife had said she found a funny tin thing in one of the beds when she fixed the rooms at noon, and maybe that was it. Dombrowski called her, and she waddled in. Yes, that was the thing. She had found it in the young gentleman's bed—on the side next the wall. It had looked very queer to her, but of course the young gentleman had lots of queer things in his room—books and curios and pictures and markings on paper. She certainly knew nothing about it.

So Gilman climbed upstairs again in a mental turmoil, convinced that he was either still dreaming or that his somnambulism had run to incredible extremes and led him to depredations in unknown places. Where had he got this outré thing? He did not recall seeing it in any museum in Arkham. It must have been somewhere, though; and the sight of it as he snatched it in his sleep must have caused the odd dream-picture of the balustraded terrace. Next day he would make some very guarded inquiries—and perhaps see the nerve specialist.

Meanwhile he would try to keep track of his somnambulism. As he went upstairs and across the garret hall he sprinkled about some flour which he had borrowed—with a frank admission as to its purpose—from the landlord. He had stopped at Elwood's door on the way, but had found all dark within. Entering his room, he placed the spiky thing on the table, and lay down in complete mental and physical exhaustion without pausing to undress. From the closed loft above the slanting ceiling he thought he heard a faint scratching and padding, but he was too disorganized even to mind it. That cryptical pull from the north was getting very strong again, though it seemed now to come from a lower place in the sky.

In the dazzling violet light of dream the old woman and the fanged, furry thing came again and with a greater distinctness than on any former occasion. This time they actually reached him, and he felt the crone's withered claws clutching at him. He was pulled out of bed and into empty space, and for a moment he heard a rhythmic roaring and saw the twilight amorphousness of the vague abysses seething around him. But that moment was very brief, for presently he was in a crude, windowless little space with rough beams and planks rising to a peak just above his head, and with a curious slanting floor underfoot. Propped level on that floor were low cases full of books of every degree of antiquity and disintegration, and in the center were a table and bench, both apparently fastened in place. Small objects of unknown shape and nature were ranged on the tops of the cases, and in the flaming violet light Gilman thought he saw a counterpart of the spiky image which had puzzled him so horribly. On the left the floor fell abruptly away, leaving a black triangular gulf out of which, after a second's dry rattling, there presently climbed the hateful little furry thing with the yellow fangs and bearded human face.

The evilly grinning beldame still clutched him, and beyond the table stood a figure he had never seen before—a tall, lean man of dead black coloration but without the slightest sign of negroid features; wholly devoid of either hair or beard, and wearing as his only garment a shapeless robe of some heavy black fabric. His feet were indistinguishable because of the table and bench, but he must have been shod, since there was a clicking whenever he changed position. The man did not speak, and bore no trace of expression on his small, regular features. He merely pointed to a book of prodigious size which lay open on the table, while the beldame thrust a huge gray quill into Gilman's right hand. Over everything was a pall of intensely maddening fear, and the climax was reached when the furry thing ran up the dreamer's clothing to his shoulders and then down his left arm, finally biting him sharply in the wrist just below his cuff. As the blood spurted from this wound Gilman lapsed into a faint.

He awaked on the morning of the 22nd with a pain in his left wrist, and saw that his cuff was brown with dried blood. His recollections were very confused, but the scene with the black man in the unknown space stood out vividly. The rats must have bitten him as he slept, giving rise to the climax of that frightful dream. Opening the door, he saw that the flour on the corridor floor was undisturbed except for the huge prints of the loutish fellow who roomed at the other end of the garret. So he had not been sleep-walking this time. But something would have to be done about those rats. He would speak to the landlord about them. Again he tried to stop up the hole at the base of the slanting wall, wedging in a candlestick which seemed of about the right size. His ears were ringing horribly, as if with the residual echoes of some horrible noise heard in dreams.

As he bathed and changed clothes he tried to recall what he had dreamed after the scene in the violet-litten space, but nothing definite would crystallize in his mind. That scene itself must have corresponded to the sealed loft overhead, which had begun to attack his imagination so violently, but later impressions were faint and hazy. There were suggestions of the vague, twilight abysses, and of still vaster, blacker abysses beyond them—abysses in which all fixed suggestions of form were absent. He had been taken there by the bubble-congeries and the little polyhedron which always dogged him; but they, like himself, had changed to wisps of milky, barely luminous mist in this farther void of ultimate blackness. Something else had gone on ahead—a larger wisp which now and then condensed into nameless approximations of form—and he thought that their progress had not been in a straight line, but rather along the alien curves and spirals of some ethereal vortex which obeyed laws unknown to the physics and mathematics of any conceivable cosmos. Eventually there had been a hint of vast, leaping shadows, of a monstrous, half-acoustic pulsing, and of the thin, monotonous piping of an unseen flute—but that was all. Gilman decided he had picked up that last conception from what he had read in the *Necronomicon* about the mindless entity Azathoth, which rules all time and space from a curiously environed black throne at the center of Chaos.

When the blood was washed away the wrist wound proved very slight, and Gilman puzzled over the location of the two tiny punctures. It occurred to him that there was no blood on the bedspread where he had lain—which was very curious in view of the amount on his skin and cuff. Had he been sleep-walking within his room, and had the rat bitten him as he sat in some chair or paused in some less rational position? He looked in every corner for brownish drops or stains, but did not find any. He had better, he thought, sprinkle flour within the room as well as outside the door—though after all no further proof of his sleep-walking was needed. He knew he did walk—and the thing to do now was to stop it. He must ask Frank Elwood for help. This morning the strange pulls from space seemed lessened, though they were replaced by another sensation even more inexplicable. It was a vague, insistent impulse to fly away from his present situation, but held not a hint of the specific direction in which he wished to fly. As he picked up the strange spiky image on the table he thought the older northward pull grew a trifle stronger; but even so, it was wholly overruled by the newer and more bewildering urge.

He took the spiky image down to Elwood's room, steeling himself against the whines of the loomfixer which welled up from the ground floor. Elwood was in, thank heaven, and appeared to be stirring about. There was time for a little conversation before leaving for breakfast and college, so Gilman hurriedly poured forth an account of his recent dreams and fears. His host was very sympathetic, and agreed that something ought to be done. He was shocked by his guest's drawn, haggard aspect, and noticed the queer, abnormal-looking sunburn which others had remarked during the past week. There was not much, though, that he could say. He had not seen Gilman on any sleep-walking expedition, and had no idea what the curious image could be. He had, though, heard the French-Canadian who lodged just under Gilman talking to Mazurewicz one evening. They were telling each other how badly they dreaded the coming of Walpurgis-Night, now only a few days off; and were exchanging pitying comments about the poor, doomed young gentleman. Desrochers, the fellow under Gilman's room, had spoken of nocturnal footsteps both shod and unshod, and of the violet light he saw one night when he had stolen fearfully up to peer through Gilman's keyhole. He had not dared to peer, he told Mazurewicz, after he had glimpsed that light through the cracks around the door. There had been soft talking, too—and as he began to describe it his voice had sunk to an inaudible whisper.

Elwood could not imagine what had set these superstitious creatures gossiping, but supposed their imaginations had been roused by Gilman's late hours and somnolent walking and talking on the one hand, and by the nearness of traditionally feared May-Eve on the other hand. That Gilman talked in his sleep was plain, and it was obviously from Desrochers' keyhole-listenings that the delusive notion of the violet dream-light had got abroad. These simple people were quick to imagine they had seen any odd thing they had heard about. As for a plan of action—Gilman had better move down to Elwood's room and avoid sleeping alone. Elwood would, if awake, rouse him whenever he began to talk or rise in his sleep. Very soon, too, he must see the specialist. Meanwhile they would take the spiky image around to the various museums and to certain professors; seeking identification and stating that it had been found in a public rubbish-can. Also, Dombrowski must attend to the poisoning of those rats in the walls.

Braced up by Elwood's companionship, Gilman attended classes that day. Strange urges still tugged at him, but he could sidetrack them with considerable success. During a free period he shewed the queer image to several professors, all of whom were intensely interested, though none of them could shed any light upon its nature or origin. That night he slept on a couch which Elwood had had the landlord bring to the second-story room, and for the first time in weeks was wholly free from disquieting dreams. But the feverishness still hung on, and the whines of the loomfixer were an unnerving influence.

During the next few days Gilman enjoyed an almost perfect immunity from morbid manifestations. He had, Elwood said, shewed no tendency to talk or rise in his sleep; and meanwhile the landlord was putting rat-poison everywhere. The only disturbing element was the talk among the superstitious foreigners, whose imaginations had become highly excited. Mazurewicz was always trying to make him get a crucifix, and finally forced one upon him which he said had been blessed by the good Father Iwanicki. Desrochers, too, had something to say—in fact, he insisted that cautious steps had sounded in the now vacant room above him on the first and second nights of Gilman's absence from it. Paul Choynski thought he heard sounds in the halls and on the stairs at night, and claimed that his door had been softly tried, while Mrs. Dombrowski vowed she had seen Brown Jenkin for the first time since All-Hallows. But such naive reports could mean very little, and Gilman let the cheap metal crucifix hang idly from a knob on his host's dresser.

For three days Gilman and Elwood canvassed the local museums in an effort to identify the strange spiky image, but always without success. In every quarter, however, interest was intense; for the utter alienage of the thing was a tremendous challenge to scientific curiosity. One of the small radiating arms was broken off and subjected to chemical analysis, and the result is still talked about in college circles. Professor Ellery found platinum, iron, and tellurium in the strange alloy; but mixed with these were at least three other apparent elements of high atomic weight which chemistry was absolutely powerless to classify. Not only did they fail to correspond with any known element, but they did not even fit the vacant places reserved for probable elements in the periodic system. The mystery remains unsolved to this day, though the image is on exhibition at the museum of Miskatonic University.

On the morning of April 27 a fresh rat-hole appeared in the room where Gilman was a guest, but Dombrowski tinned it up during the day. The poison was not having much effect, for scratchings and scurryings in the walls were virtually undiminished. Elwood was out late that night, and Gilman waited up for him. He did not wish to go to sleep in a room alone—especially since he thought he had glimpsed in the evening twilight the repellent old woman whose image had become so horribly transferred to his dreams. He wondered who she was, and what had been near her rattling the tin can in a rubbish-heap at the mouth of a squalid courtyard. The crone had seemed to notice him and leer evilly at him—though perhaps this was merely his imagination.

The next day both youths felt very tired, and knew they would sleep like logs when night came. In the evening they drowsily discussed the mathematical studies which had so completely and perhaps harmfully engrossed Gilman, and speculated about the linkage with ancient magic and folklore which seemed so darkly probable. They spoke of old Keziah Mason, and Elwood agreed that Gilman had good scientific grounds for thinking she might have stumbled on strange and significant information. The hidden cults to which these witches belonged often guarded and handed down surprising secrets from elder, forgotten eons; and it was by no means impossible that Keziah had actually mastered the art of passing through dimensional gates. Tradition emphasizes the uselessness of material barriers in halting a witch's motions; and who can say what underlies the old tales of broomstick rides through the night?

Whether a modern student could ever gain similar powers from mathematical research alone, was still to be seen. Success, Gilman added, might lead to dangerous and unthinkable situations; for who could foretell the conditions pervading an adjacent but normally inaccessible dimension? On the other hand, the picturesque possibilities were enormous. Time could not exist in certain belts of space, and by entering and remaining in such a belt one might preserve one's life and age indefinitely; never suffering organic metabolism or deterioration except for slight amounts incurred during visits to one's own or similar planes. One might, for example, pass into a timeless dimension and emerge at some remote period of the earth's history as young as before.

Whether anybody had ever managed to do this, one could hardly conjecture with any degree of authority. Old legends are hazy and ambiguous, and in historic times all attempts at crossing forbidden gaps seem complicated by strange and terrible alliances with beings and messengers from outside. There was the immemorial figure of the deputy or messenger of hidden and terrible powers—the "Black Man" of the witch-cult, and the "Nyarlathotep" of the *Necronomicon*. There was, too, the baffling problem of the lesser messengers or intermediaries—the quasi-animals and queer hybrids which legend depicts as witches' familiars. As

Gilman and Elwood retired, too sleepy to argue further, they heard Joe Mazurewicz reel into the house half-drunk, and shuddered at the desperate wildness of his whining prayers.

That night Gilman saw the violet light again. In his dream he had heard a scratching and gnawing in the partitions, and thought that someone fumbled clumsily at the latch. Then he saw the old woman and the small furry thing advancing toward him over the carpeted floor. The beldame's face was alight with inhuman exultation, and the little yellow-toothed morbidity tittered mockingly as it pointed at the heavily sleeping form of Elwood on the other couch across the room. A paralysis of fear stifled all attempts to cry out. As once before, the hideous crone seized Gilman by the shoulders, yanking him out of bed and into empty space. Again the infinitude of the shrieking twilight abysses flashed past him, but in another second he thought he was in a dark, muddy, unknown alley of fetid odors, with the rotting walls of ancient houses towering up on every hand.

Ahead was the robed black man he had seen in the peaked space in the other dream, while from a lesser distance the old woman was beckoning and grimacing imperiously. Brown Jenkin was rubbing itself with a kind of affectionate playfulness around the ankles of the black man, which the deep mud largely concealed. There was a dark open doorway on the right, to which the black man silently pointed. Into this the grimacing crone started, dragging Gilman after her by his pajama sleeve. There were evil-smelling staircases which creaked ominously, and on which the old woman seemed to radiate a faint violet light; and finally a door leading off a landing. The crone fumbled with the latch and pushed the door open, motioning to Gilman to wait and disappearing inside the black aperture.

The youth's oversensitive ears caught a hideous strangled cry, and presently the beldame came out of the room bearing a small, senseless form which she thrust at the dreamer as if ordering him to carry it. The sight of this form, and the expression on its face, broke the spell. Still too dazed to cry out, he plunged recklessly down the noisome staircase and into the mud outside; halting only when seized and choked by the waiting black man. As consciousness departed he heard the faint, shrill tittering of the fanged, rat-like abnormality.

On the morning of the 29th Gilman awaked into a maelstrom of horror. The instant he opened his eyes he knew something was terribly wrong, for he was back in his old garret room with the slanting wall and ceiling, sprawled on the now unmade bed. His throat was aching inexplicably, and as he struggled to a sitting posture he saw with growing fright that his feet and pajama-bottoms were brown with caked mud. For the moment his recollections were hopelessly hazy, but he knew at least that he must have been sleep-walking. Elwood had been lost too deeply in slumber to hear and stop him. On the floor were confused muddy prints, but oddly enough they did not extend all the way to the door. The more Gilman looked at them, the more peculiar they seemed; for in addition to those he could recognize as his there were some smaller, almost round markings—such as the legs of a large chair or table might make, except that most of them tended to be divided into halves. There were also some curious muddy rat-tracks leading out of a fresh hole and back into it again. Utter bewilderment and the fear of madness racked Gilman as he staggered to the door and saw that there were no muddy prints outside. The more he remembered of his hideous dream the more terrified he felt, and it added to his desperation to hear Joe Mazurewicz chanting mournfully two floors below.

Descending to Elwood's room he roused his still-sleeping host and began telling of how he had found himself, but Elwood could form no idea of what might really have happened. Where Gilman could have been, how he got back to his room without making tracks in the hall, and how the muddy, furniture-like prints came to be mixed with his in the garret chamber, were wholly beyond conjecture. Then there were those dark, livid marks on his throat, as if he had tried to strangle himself. He put his hands up to them, but found that they did not even approximately fit. While they were talking Desrochers dropped in to say that he had heard a terrific clattering overhead in the dark small hours. No, there had been no one on the stairs after midnight—though just before midnight he had heard faint footfalls in the garret, and cautiously descending steps he did not like. It was, he added, a very bad time of year for Arkham. The young gentleman had better be sure to wear the crucifix Joe Mazurewicz had given him. Even the daytime was not safe, for after dawn there had been strange sounds in the house—especially a thin, childish wail hastily choked off.

Gilman mechanically attended classes that morning, but was wholly unable to fix his mind on his studies. A mood of hideous apprehension and expectancy had seized him, and he seemed to be awaiting the fall of some annihilating blow. At noon he lunched at the University Spa, picking up a paper from the next seat as he waited for dessert. But he never ate that dessert; for an item on the paper's first page left him limp, wild-eyed, and able only to pay his check and stagger back to Elwood's room.

There had been a strange kidnapping the night before in Orne's Gangway, and the two-year-old child of a clod-like laundry worker named Anastasia Wolejko had completely vanished from sight. The mother, it appeared, had feared the event for some time; but the reasons she assigned for her fear were so grotesque that no one took them seriously. She had, she said, seen Brown Jenkin about the place now and then ever since early in March, and knew from its grimaces and titterings that little Ladislas must be marked for sacrifice at the awful Sabbat on Walpurgis-Night. She had asked her neighbor Mary Czanek to sleep in the room and try to protect the child, but Mary had not dared. She could not tell the police, for they never believed such things. Children had been taken that way every year ever since she could remember. And her friend Pete Stowacki would not help because he wanted the child out of the way anyhow.

But what threw Gilman into a cold perspiration was the report of a pair of revelers who had been walking past the mouth of the gangway just after midnight. They admitted they had been drunk, but both vowed they had seen a crazily dressed trio furtively entering the dark passageway. There had, they said, been a huge robed negro, a little old woman in rags, and a young white man in his night-clothes. The old woman had been dragging the youth, while around the feet of the negro a tame rat was rubbing and weaving in the brown mud.

Gilman sat in a daze all the afternoon, and Elwood—who had meanwhile seen the papers and formed terrible conjectures from them—found him thus when he came home. This time neither could doubt but that something hideously serious was closing in around them. Between the phantasms of nightmare and the realities of the objective world a monstrous and unthinkable relationship was crystallizing, and only stupendous vigilance could avert still more direful developments. Gilman must see a specialist sooner or later, but not just now, when all the papers were full of this kidnapping business.

Just what had really happened was maddeningly obscure, and for a moment both Gilman and Elwood exchanged whispered theories of the wildest kind. Had Gilman unconsciously succeeded better than he knew in his studies of space and its dimensions? Had he actually slipped outside our sphere to points unguessed and unimaginable? Where—if anywhere—had he been on those nights of daemoniac alienage? The roaring twilight abysses—the green hillside—the blistering terrace—the pulls from the stars—the ultimate black vortex—the black man—the muddy alley and the stairs—the old witch and the fanged, furry horror—the bubble-congeries and the little polyhedron—the strange sunburn—the wrist wound—the unexplained image—the muddy feet—the throat-marks—the tales and fears of the superstitious foreigners—what did all this mean? To what extent could the laws of sanity apply to such a case?

There was no sleep for either of them that night, but next day they both cut classes and drowsed. This was April 30th, and with the dusk would come the hellish Sabbat-time which all the foreigners and the superstitious old folk feared. Mazurewicz came home at six o'clock and said people at the mill were whispering that the Walpurgis-revels would be held in the dark ravine beyond Meadow Hill where the old white stone stands in a place queerly void of all plant-life. Some of them had even told the police and advised them to look there for the missing Wolejko child, but they did not believe anything would be done. Joe insisted that the poor young gentleman wear his nickel-chained crucifix, and Gilman put it on and dropped it inside his shirt to humor the fellow.

Late at night the two youths sat drowsing in their chairs, lulled by the rhythmical praying of the loomfixer on the floor below. Gilman listened as he nodded, his preternaturally sharpened hearing seeming to strain for some subtle, dreaded murmur beyond the noises in the ancient house. Unwholesome recollections of things in the *Necronomicon* and the Black Book welled up, and he found himself swaying to infandous rhythms said to pertain to the blackest ceremonies of the Sabbat and to have an origin outside the time and space we comprehend.

Presently he realized what he was listening for—the hellish chant of the celebrants in the distant black valley. How did he know so much about what they expected? How did he know the time when Nahab and her acolyte were due to bear the brimming bowl which would follow the black cock and the black goat? He saw that Elwood had dropped asleep, and tried to call out and waken him. Something, however, closed his throat. He was not his own master. Had he signed the black man's book after all?

Then his fevered, abnormal hearing caught the distant, windborne notes. Over miles of hill and field and alley they came, but he recognized them none the less. The fires must be lit, and the dancers must be starting in. How could he keep himself from going? What was it that had enmeshed him? Mathematics—folklore—the house—old Keziah—Brown Jenkin . . . and now he saw that there was a fresh rat-hole in the wall near his couch.

Above the distant chanting and the nearer praying of Joe Mazurewicz came another sound—a stealthy, determined scratching in the partitions. He hoped the electric lights would not go out. Then he saw the fanged, bearded little face in the rat-hole—the accursed little face which he at last realized bore such a shocking, mocking resemblance to old Keziah's—and heard the faint fumbling at the door.

The screaming twilight abysses flashed before him, and he felt himself helpless in the formless grasp of the iridescent bubble-congeries. Ahead raced the small, kaleidoscopic polyhedron, and all through the churning void there was a heightening and acceleration of the vague tonal pattern which seemed to foreshadow some unutterable and unendurable climax. He seemed to know what was coming—the monstrous burst of Walpurgis-rhythm in whose cosmic timbre would be concentrated all the primal, ultimate space-time seethings which lie behind the massed spheres of matter and sometimes break forth in measured reverberations that penetrate faintly to every layer of entity and give hideous significance throughout the worlds to certain dreaded periods.

But all this vanished in a second. He was again in the cramped, violet-litten peaked space with the slanting floor, the low cases of ancient books, the bench and table, the queer objects, and the triangular gulf at one side. On the table lay a small white figure—an infant boy, unclothed and unconscious—while on the other side stood the monstrous, leering old woman with a gleaming, grotesque-hafted knife in her right hand, and a queerly proportioned pale metal bowl covered with curiously chased designs and having delicate lateral handles in her left. She was intoning some croaking ritual in a language which Gilman could not understand, but which seemed like something guardedly quoted in the *Necronomicon.*

As the scene grew clear he saw the ancient crone bend forward and extend the empty bowl across the table—and unable to control his own motions, he reached far forward and took it in both hands, noticing as he did so its comparative lightness. At the same moment the disgusting form of Brown Jenkin scrambled up over the brink of the triangular black gulf on his left. The crone now motioned him to hold the bowl in a certain position while she raised the huge, grotesque knife above the small white victim as high as her right hand could reach. The fanged, furry thing began tittering a continuation of the unknown ritual, while the witch croaked loathsome responses. Gilman felt a gnawing, poignant abhorrence shoot through his mental and emotional paralysis, and the light metal bowl shook in his grasp. A second later the downward motion of the knife broke the spell completely, and he dropped the bowl with a resounding bell-like clangor while his hands darted out frantically to stop the monstrous deed.

In an instant he had edged up the slanting floor around the end of the table and wrenched the knife from the old woman's claws; sending it clattering over the brink of the narrow triangular gulf. In another instant, however, matters were reversed; for those murderous claws had locked themselves tightly around his own throat, while the wrinkled face was twisted with insane fury. He felt the chain of the cheap crucifix grinding into his neck, and in his peril wondered how the sight of the object itself would affect the evil creature. Her strength was altogether superhuman, but as she continued her choking he reached feebly in his shirt and drew out the metal symbol, snapping the chain and pulling it free.

At sight of the device the witch seemed struck with panic, and her grip relaxed long enough to give Gilman a chance to break it entirely. He pulled the steel-like claws from his neck, and would have dragged the beldame over the edge of the gulf had not the claws received a fresh access of strength and closed in again. This time he resolved to reply in kind, and his own hands reached out for the creature's throat. Before she saw what he was doing he had the chain of the crucifix twisted about her neck, and a moment later he had tightened it enough to cut off her breath. During her last struggle he felt something bite at his ankle, and saw that Brown Jenkin had come to her aid. With one savage kick he sent the morbidity over the edge of the gulf and heard it whimper on some level far below.

Whether he had killed the ancient crone he did not know, but he let her rest on the floor where she had fallen. Then, as he turned away, he saw on the table a sight which nearly snapped the last thread of his reason. Brown Jenkin, tough of sinew and with four tiny hands of daemoniac dexterity, had been busy while the witch was throttling him, and his efforts had been in vain. What he had prevented the knife from doing to the victim's chest, the yellow fangs of the furry blasphemy had done to a wrist—and the bowl so lately on the floor stood full beside the small lifeless body.

In his dream-delirium Gilman heard the hellish, alien-rhythmed chant of the Sabbat coming from an infinite distance, and knew the black man must be there. Confused memories mixed themselves with his mathematics, and he believed his subconscious mind held the *angles* which he needed to guide him back to the normal world—alone and unaided for the first time. He felt sure he was in the immemorially sealed loft above his own room, but whether he could ever escape through the slanting floor or the long-stopped egress he doubted greatly. Besides, would not an escape from a dream-loft bring him merely into a dream-house—an abnormal projection of the actual place he sought? He was wholly bewildered as to the relation betwixt dream and reality in all his experiences.

The passage through the vague abysses would be frightful, for the Walpurgis-rhythm would be vibrating, and at last he would have to hear that hitherto veiled cosmic pulsing which he so mortally dreaded. Even now he could detect a low, monstrous shaking whose tempo he suspected all too well. At Sabbat-time it always mounted and reached through to the worlds to summon the initiate to nameless rites. Half the chants of the Sabbat were patterned on this faintly overheard pulsing which no earthly ear could endure in its unveiled spatial fulness. Gilman wondered, too, whether he could trust his instinct to take him back to the right part of space. How could he be sure he would not land on that green-litten hillside of a far planet, on the tesselated terrace above the city of tentacled monsters somewhere beyond the galaxy, or in the spiral black vortices of that ultimate void of Chaos wherein reigns the mindless daemon-sultan Azathoth?

Just before he made the plunge the violet light went out and left him in utter blackness. The witch—old Keziah—Nahab—that must have meant her death. And mixed with the distant chant of the Sabbat and the whimpers of Brown Jenkin in the gulf below he thought he heard another and wilder whine from unknown depths. Joe Mazurewicz—the prayers against the Crawling Chaos now turning to an inexplicably triumphant shriek—worlds of sardonic actuality impinging on vortices of febrile dream—Iä! Shub-Niggurath! The Goat with a Thousand Young . . .

They found Gilman on the floor of his queerly angled old garret room long before dawn, for the terrible cry had brought Desrochers and Choynski and Dombrowski and Mazurewicz at once, and had even wakened the soundly sleeping Elwood in his chair. He was alive, and with open, staring eyes, but seemed largely unconscious. On his throat were the marks of murderous hands, and on his left ankle was a distressing rat-bite. His clothing was badly rumpled, and Joe's crucifix was missing. Elwood trembled, afraid even to speculate on what new form his friend's sleep-walking had taken. Mazurewicz seemed half-dazed because of a "sign" he said he had had in response to his prayers, and he crossed himself frantically when the squealing and whimpering of a rat sounded from beyond the slanting partition.

When the dreamer was settled on his couch in Elwood's room they sent for Dr. Malkowski—a local practitioner who would repeat no tales where they might prove embarrassing—and he gave Gilman two hypodermic injections which caused him to relax in something like natural drowsiness. During the day the patient regained consciousness at times and whispered his newest dream disjointedly to Elwood. It was a painful process, and at its very start brought out a fresh and disconcerting fact.

Gilman—whose ears had so lately possessed an abnormal sensitiveness—was now stone deaf. Dr. Malkowski, summoned again in haste, told Elwood that both ear-drums were ruptured, as if by the impact of some stupendous sound intense beyond all human conception or endurance. How such a sound could have been heard in the last few hours without arousing all the Miskatonic Valley was more than the honest physician could say.

Elwood wrote his part of the colloquy on paper, so that a fairly easy communication was maintained. Neither knew what to make of the whole chaotic business, and decided it would be better if they thought as little as possible about it. Both, though, agreed that they must leave this ancient and accursed house as soon as it could be arranged. Evening papers spoke of a police raid on some curious revelers in a ravine beyond Meadow Hill just before dawn, and mentioned that the white stone there was an object of age-long superstitious regard. Nobody had been caught, but among the scattering fugitives had been glimpsed a huge negro. In another column it was stated that no trace of the missing child Ladislas Wolejko had been found.

The crowning horror came that very night. Elwood will never forget it, and was forced to stay out of college the rest of the term because of the resulting nervous breakdown. He had thought he heard rats in the partitions all the evening, but paid little attention to them. Then, long after both he and Gilman had retired, the atrocious shrieking began. Elwood jumped up, turned on the lights, and rushed over to his guest's couch. The occupant was emitting sounds of veritably inhuman nature, as if racked by some torment beyond description. He was writhing under the bedclothes, and a great red stain was beginning to appear on the blankets.

Elwood scarcely dared to touch him, but gradually the screaming and writhing subsided. By this time Dombrowski, Choynski, Desrochers, Mazurewicz, and the top-floor lodger were all crowding into the doorway, and the landlord had sent his wife back to telephone for Dr. Malkowski. Everybody shrieked when a large rat-like form suddenly jumped out from beneath the ensanguined bedclothes and scuttled across the floor to a fresh, open hole close by. When the doctor arrived and began to pull down those frightful covers Walter Gilman was dead.

It would be barbarous to do more than suggest what had killed Gilman. There had been virtually a tunnel through his body—something had eaten his heart out. Dombrowski, frantic at the failure of his constant rat-poisoning efforts, cast aside all thought of his lease and within a week had moved with all his older lodgers to a dingy but less ancient house in Walnut Street. The worst thing for a while was keeping Joe Mazurewicz quiet; for the brooding loomfixer would never stay sober, and was constantly whining and muttering about spectral and terrible things.

It seems that on that last hideous night Joe had stooped to look at the crimson rat-tracks which led from Gilman's couch to the nearby hole. On the carpet they were very indistinct, but a piece of open flooring intervened between the carpet's edge and the base-board. There Mazurewicz had found something monstrous—or thought he had, for no one else could quite agree with him despite the undeniable queerness of the prints. The tracks on the flooring were certainly vastly unlike the average prints of a rat, but even Choynski and Desrochers would not admit that they were like the prints of four tiny human hands.

The house was never rented again. As soon as Dombrowski left it the pall of its final desolation began to descend, for people shunned it both on account of its old reputation and because of the new fetid odor. Perhaps the ex-landlord's rat-poison had worked after all, for not long after his departure the place became a neighborhood nuisance. Health officials traced the smell to the closed spaces above and beside the eastern garret room, and agreed that the number of dead rats must be enormous. They decided, however, that it was not worth their while to hew open and disinfect the long-sealed spaces; for the fetor would soon be over, and the locality was not one which encouraged fastidious standards. Indeed, there were always vague local tales of unexplained stenches upstairs in the Witch House just after May-Eve and Hallowmass. The neighbors grumblingly acquiesced in the inertia—but the fetor none the less formed an additional count against the place. Toward the last the house was condemned as an habitation by the building inspector.

Gilman's dreams and their attendant circumstances have never been explained. Elwood, whose thoughts on the entire episode are sometimes almost maddening, came back to college the next autumn and graduated in the following June. He found the spectral gossip of the town much diminished, and it is indeed a fact that—notwithstanding certain reports of a ghostly tittering in the deserted house which lasted almost as long as that edifice itself—no fresh appearances either of old Keziah or of Brown Jenkin have been muttered of since Gilman's death. It is rather fortunate that Elwood was not in Arkham in that later year when certain events abruptly renewed the local whispers about elder horrors. Of course he heard about the matter afterward and suffered untold torments of black and bewildered speculation; but even that was not as bad as actual nearness and several possible sights would have been.

In March, 1931, a gale wrecked the roof and great chimney of the vacant Witch House, so that a chaos of crumbling bricks, blackened, moss-grown shingles, and rotting planks and timbers crashed down into the loft and broke through the floor beneath. The whole attic story was choked with debris from above, but no one took the trouble to touch the mess before the inevitable razing of the decrepit structure. That ultimate step came in the following December, and it was when Gilman's old room was cleared out by reluctant, apprehensive workmen that the gossip began.

Among the rubbish which had crashed through the ancient slanting ceiling were several things which made the workmen pause and call in the police. Later the police in turn called in the coroner and several professors from the university. There were bones—badly crushed and splintered, but clearly recognizable as human—whose manifestly modern date conflicted puzzlingly with the remote period at which their only possible lurking-place, the low, slant-floored loft overhead, had supposedly been sealed from all human access. The coroner's physician decided that some belonged to a small child, while certain others—found mixed with shreds of rotten brownish cloth—belonged to a rather undersized, bent female of advanced years. Careful sifting of debris also disclosed many tiny bones of rats caught in the collapse, as well as older rat-bones gnawed by small fangs in a fashion now and then highly productive of controversy and reflection.

Other objects found included the mingled fragments of many books and papers, together with a yellowish dust left from the total disintegration of still older books and papers. All, without exception, appeared to deal with black magic in its most advanced and horrible forms; and the evidently recent date of certain items is still a mystery as unsolved as that of the modern human bones. An even greater mystery is the absolute homogeneity of the crabbed, archaic writing found on a wide range of papers whose conditions and watermarks suggest age differences of at least 150 to 200 years. To some, though, the greatest mystery of all is the variety of utterly inexplicable objects—objects whose shapes, materials, types of workmanship, and purposes baffle all conjecture—found scattered amidst the wreckage in evidently diverse states of injury. One of these things—which excited several Miskatonic professors profoundly—is a badly damaged monstrosity plainly resembling the strange image which Gilman gave to the college museum, save that it is larger, wrought of some peculiar bluish stone instead of metal, and possessed of a singularly angled pedestal with undecipherable hieroglyphics.

Archeologists and anthropologists are still trying to explain the bizarre designs chased on a crushed bowl of light metal whose inner side bore ominous brownish stains when found. Foreigners and credulous grandmothers are equally garrulous about the modern nickel crucifix with broken chain mixed in the rubbish and shiveringly identified by Joe Mazurewicz as that which he had given poor Gilman many years before. Some believe this crucifix was dragged up to the sealed loft by rats, while others think it must have been on the floor in some corner of Gilman's old room all the time. Still others, including Joe himself, have theories too wild and fantastic for sober credence.

When the slanting wall of Gilman's room was torn out, the once sealed triangular space between that partition and the house's north wall was found to contain much less structural debris, even in proportion to its size, than the room itself; though it had a ghastly layer of older materials which paralyzed the wreckers with horror. In brief, the floor was a veritable ossuary of the bones of small children—some fairly modern, but others extending back in infinite gradations to a period so remote that crumbling was almost complete. On this deep bony layer rested a knife of great size, obvious antiquity, and grotesque, ornate, and exotic design—above which the debris was piled.

In the midst of this debris, wedged between a fallen plank and a cluster of cemented bricks from the ruined chimney, was an object destined to cause more bafflement, veiled fright, and openly superstitious talk in Arkham than anything else discovered in the haunted and accursed building. This object was the partly crushed skeleton of a huge, diseased rat, whose abnormalities of form are still a topic of debate and source of singular reticence among the members of Miskatonic's department of comparative anatomy. Very little concerning this skeleton has leaked out, but the workmen who found it whisper in shocked tones about the long, brownish hairs with which it was associated.

The bones of the tiny paws, it is rumored, imply prehensile characteristics more typical of a diminutive monkey than of a rat; while the small skull with its savage yellow fangs is of the utmost anomalousness, appearing from certain angles like a miniature, monstrously degraded parody of a human skull. The workmen crossed themselves in fright when they came upon this blasphemy, but later burned candles of gratitude in St. Stanislaus' Church because of the shrill, ghostly tittering they felt they would never hear again.

THE CASE OF
CHARLES DEXTER WARD

*The essential Saltes of Animals may be so
prepared and preserved, that an ingenious Man
may have the whole Ark of Noah in his own
Studie, and raise the fine Shape of an Animal out
of its Ashes at his Pleasure; and by the lyke
Method from the essential Saltes of humane Dust,
a Philosopher may, without any criminal
Necromancy, call up the Shape of any dead
Ancestour from the Dust whereinto his Bodie
has been incinerated.*
—Borellus

I. A Result and a Prologue

1

From a private hospital for the insane near Providence, Rhode Island, there recently disappeared an exceedingly singular person. He bore the name of Charles Dexter Ward, and was placed under restraint most reluctantly by the grieving father who had watched his aberration grow from a mere eccentricity to a dark mania involving both a possibility of murderous tendencies and a profound and peculiar change in the apparent contents of his mind. Doctors confess themselves quite baffled by his case, since it presented oddities of a general physiological as well as psychological character.

In the first place, the patient seemed oddly older than his twenty-six years would warrant. Mental disturbance, it is true, will age one rapidly; but the face of this young man had taken on a subtle cast which only the very aged normally acquire. In the second place, his organic processes shewed a certain queerness of proportion which nothing in medical experience can parallel. Respiration and heart action had a baffling lack of symmetry; the voice was lost, so that no sounds above a whisper were possible; digestion was incredibly prolonged and minimized, and neural reactions to standard stimuli bore no relation at all to anything heretofore recorded, either normal or pathological. The skin had a morbid chill and dryness, and the cellular structure of the tissue seemed exaggeratedly coarse and loosely knit. Even a large olive birthmark on the right hip had disappeared, whilst there had formed on the chest a very peculiar mole or blackish spot of which no trace existed before. In general, all physicians agree that in Ward the processes of metabolism had become retarded to a degree beyond precedent.

Psychologically, too, Charles Ward was unique. His madness held no affinity to any sort recorded in even the latest and most exhaustive of treatises, and was conjoined to a mental force which would have made him a genius or a leader had it not been twisted into strange and grotesque forms. Dr. Willett, who was Ward's family physician, affirms that the patient's gross mental capacity, as gauged by his response to matters outside the sphere of his insanity, had actually increased since the seizure. Ward, it is true, was always a scholar and an antiquarian; but even his most brilliant early work did not shew the prodigious grasp and insight displayed during his last examinations by the alienists. It was, indeed, a difficult matter to obtain a legal commitment to the hospital, so powerful and lucid did the youth's mind seem; and only on the evidence of others, and on the strength of many abnormal gaps in his stock of information as distinguished from his intelligence, was he finally placed in confinement. To the very moment of his vanishment he was an omnivorous reader and as great a conversationalist as his poor voice permitted; and shrewd observers, failing to foresee his escape, freely predicted that he would not be long in gaining his discharge from custody.

Only Dr. Willett, who brought Charles Ward into the world and had watched his growth of body and mind ever since, seemed frightened at the thought of his future freedom. He had had a terrible experience and had made a terrible discovery which he dared not reveal to his skeptical colleagues. Willett, indeed, presents a minor mystery all his own in his connexion with the case. He was the last to see the patient before his flight, and emerged from that final conversation in a state of mixed horror and relief which several recalled when Ward's escape became known three hours later. That escape itself is one of the unsolved wonders of Dr. Waite's hospital. A window open above a sheer drop of sixty feet could hardly explain it, yet after that talk with Willett the youth was undeniably gone. Willett himself has no public explanations to offer, though he seems strangely easier in mind than before the escape. Many, indeed, feel that he would like to say more if he thought any considerable number would believe him. He had found Ward in his room, but shortly after his departure the attendants knocked in vain. When they opened the door the patient was not there, and all they found was the open window with a chill April breeze blowing in a cloud of fine bluish-gray dust that almost choked them. True, the dogs howled some time before; but that was while Willett was still present, and they had caught nothing and shewn no disturbance later on. Ward's father was told at once over the telephone, but he seemed more saddened than surprised. By the time Dr. Waite called in person, Dr. Willett had been talking with him, and both disavowed any knowledge or complicity in the escape. Only from certain closely confidential friends of Willett and the senior Ward have any clues been gained, and even these are too wildly fantastic for general credence. The one fact which remains is that up to the present time no trace of the missing madman has been unearthed.

Charles Ward was an antiquarian from infancy, no doubt gaining his taste from the venerable town around him, and from the relics of the past which filled every corner of his parents' old mansion in Prospect Street on the crest of the hill. With the years his devotion to ancient things increased; so that history, genealogy, and the study of colonial architecture, furniture, and craftsmanship at length crowded everything else from his sphere of interests. These tastes are important to remember in considering his madness; for although they do not form its absolute nucleus, they play a prominent part in its superficial form. The gaps of information which the alienists noticed were all related to modern matters, and were invariably offset by a correspondingly excessive though outwardly concealed knowledge of bygone matters as brought out by adroit questioning; so that one would have fancied the patient literally transferred to a former age through some obscure sort of auto-hypnosis. The odd thing was that Ward seemed no longer interested in the antiquities he knew so well. He had, it appears, lost his regard for them through sheer familiarity; and all his final efforts were obviously bent toward mastering those common facts of the modern world which had been so totally and unmistakably expunged from his brain. That this wholesale deletion had occurred, he did his best to hide; but it was clear to all who watched him that his whole program of reading and conversation was determined by a frantic wish to imbibe such knowledge of his own life and of the ordinary practical and cultural background of the twentieth century as ought to have been his by virtue of his birth in 1902 and his education in the schools of our own time. Alienists are now wondering how, in view of his vitally impaired range of data, the escaped patient manages to cope with the complicated world of today; the dominant opinion being that he is "lying low" in some humble and unexacting position till his stock of modern information can be brought up to the normal.

The beginning of Ward's madness is a matter of dispute among alienists. Dr. Lyman, the eminent Boston authority, places it in 1919 or 1920, during the boy's last year at the Moses Brown School, when he suddenly turned from the study of the past to the study of the occult, and refused to qualify for college on the ground that he had individual researches of much greater importance to make. This is certainly borne out by Ward's altered habits at the time, especially by his continual search through town records and among old burying-grounds for a certain grave dug in 1771; the grave of an ancestor named Joseph Curwen, some of whose papers he professed to have found behind the paneling of a very old house in Olney Court, on Stampers' Hill, which Curwen was known to have built and occupied. It is, broadly speaking, undeniable that the winter of 1919–20 saw a great change in Ward; whereby he abruptly stopped his general antiquarian pursuits and embarked on a desperate delving into occult subjects both at home and abroad, varied only by this strangely persistent search for his forefather's grave.

From this opinion, however, Dr. Willett substantially dissents; basing his verdict on his close and continuous knowledge of the patient, and on certain frightful investigations and discoveries which he made toward the last. Those investigations and discoveries have left their mark upon him; so that his voice trembles when he tells them, and his hand trembles when he tries to write of them. Willett admits that the change of 1919–20 would ordinarily appear to mark the beginning of a progressive decadence which culminated in the horrible and uncanny alienation of 1928; but believes from personal observation that a finer distinction must be made. Granting freely that the boy was always ill-balanced temperamentally, and prone to be unduly susceptible and enthusiastic in his responses to phenomena around him, he refuses to concede that the early alteration marked the actual passage from sanity to madness; crediting instead Ward's own statement that he had discovered or rediscovered something whose effect on human thought was likely to be marvelous and profound. The true madness, he is certain, came with a later change; after the Curwen portrait and the ancient papers had been unearthed; after a trip to strange foreign places had been made, and some terrible invocations chanted under strange and secret circumstances; after certain *answers* to these invocations had been plainly indicated, and a frantic letter penned under agonizing and inexplicable conditions; after the wave of vampirism and the ominous Pawtuxet gossip; and after the patient's memory commenced to exclude contemporary images whilst his voice failed and his physical aspect underwent the subtle modification so many subsequently noticed.

It was only about this time, Willett points out with much acuteness, that the nightmare qualities became indubitably linked with Ward; and the doctor feels shudderingly sure that enough solid evidence exists to sustain the youth's claim regarding his crucial discovery. In the first place, two workmen of high intelligence saw Joseph Curwen's ancient papers found. Secondly, the boy once shewed Dr. Willett those papers and a page of the Curwen diary, and each of the documents had every appearance of genuineness. The hole where Ward claimed to have found them was long a visible reality, and Willett had a very convincing final glimpse of them in surroundings which can scarcely be believed and can never perhaps be proved. Then there were the mysteries and coincidences of the Orne and Hutchinson letters, and the problem of the Curwen penmanship and of what the detectives brought to light about Dr. Allen; these things, and the terrible message in medieval minuscules found in Willett's pocket when he gained consciousness after his shocking experience.

And most conclusive of all, there are the two hideous *results* which the doctor obtained from a certain pair of formulae during his final investigations; results which virtually proved the authenticity of the papers and of their monstrous implications at the same time that those papers were borne forever from human knowledge.

2

One must look back at Charles Ward's earlier life as at something belonging as much to the past as the antiquities he loved so keenly. In the autumn of 1918, and with a considerable show of zest in the military training of the period, he had begun his junior year at the Moses Brown School, which lies very near his home. The old main building, erected in 1819, had always charmed his youthful antiquarian sense; and the spacious park in which the academy is set appealed to his sharp eye for land-scape. His social activities were few; and his hours were spent mainly at home, in rambling walks, in his classes and drills, and in pursuit of antiquarian and genealogical data at the City Hall, the State House, the Public Library, the Athenaeum, the Historical Society, the John Carter Brown and John Hay Libraries of Brown University, and the newly opened Shepley Library in Benefit Street. One may picture him yet as he was in those days; tall, slim, and blond, with studious eyes and a slight stoop, dressed somewhat carelessly, and giving a dominant impression of harm-less awkwardness rather than attractiveness.

His walks were always adventures in antiquity, during which he managed to recapture from the myriad relics of a glamorous old city a vivid and connected picture of the centuries before. His home was a great Georgian mansion atop the well-nigh precipitous hill that rises just east of the river; and from the rear windows of its rambling wings he could look dizzily out over all the clustered spires, domes, roofs, and skyscraper summits of the lower town to the purple hills of the countryside beyond. Here he was born, and from the lovely classic porch of the double-bayed brick facade his nurse had first wheeled him in his carriage; past the little white farmhouse of two hundred years before that the town had long ago overtaken, and on toward the stately colleges along the shady, sumptuous street, whose old square brick mansions and smaller wooden houses with narrow, heavy-columned Doric porches dreamed solid and exclusive amidst their generous yards and gardens.

He had been wheeled, too, along sleepy Congdon Street, one tier lower down on the steep hill, and with all its eastern homes on high terraces. The small wooden houses averaged a greater age here, for it was up this hill that the growing town had climbed; and in these rides he had imbibed something of the color of a quaint colonial village. The nurse used to stop and sit on the benches of Prospect Terrace to chat with policemen; and one of the child's first memories was of the great westward sea of hazy roofs and domes and steeples and far hills which he saw one winter afternoon from that great railed embankment, all violet and mystic against a fevered, apocalyptic sunset of reds and golds and purples and curious greens. The vast marble dome of the State House stood out in massive silhouette, its crowning statue haloed fantastically by a break in one of the tinted stratus clouds that barred the flaming sky.

When he was larger his famous walks began; first with his impatiently dragged nurse, and then alone in dreamy meditation. Farther and farther down that almost perpendicular hill he would venture, each time reaching older and quainter levels of the ancient city. He would hesitate gingerly down vertical Jenckes Street with its bank walls and colonial gables to the shady Benefit Street corner, where before him was a wooden antique with an Ionic-pilastered pair of doorways, and beside him a prehistoric gambrel-roofer with a bit of primal farmyard remaining, and the great Judge Durfee house with its fallen vestiges of Georgian grandeur. It was getting to be a slum here; but the titan elms cast a restoring shadow over the place, and the boy used to stroll south past the long lines of the pre-Revolutionary homes with their great central chimneys and classic portals. On the eastern side they were set high over basements with railed double flights of stone steps, and the young Charles could picture them as they were when the street was new, and red heels and periwigs set off the painted pediments whose signs of wear were now becoming so visible.

Westward the hill dropped almost as steeply as above, down to the old "Town Street" that the founders had laid out at the river's edge in 1636. Here ran innumerable little lanes with leaning, huddled houses of immense antiquity; and fascinated though he was, it was long before he dared to thread their archaic verticality for fear they would turn out a dream or a gateway to unknown terrors. He found it much less formidable to continue along Benefit Street past the iron fence of St. John's hidden churchyard and the rear of the 1761 Colony House and the moldering bulk of the Golden Ball Inn where Washington stopped. At Meeting Street—the successive Gaol Lane and King Street of other periods—he would look upward to the east and see the arched flight of steps to which the highway had to resort in climbing the slope, and downward to the west, glimpsing the old brick colonial schoolhouse that smiles across the road at the ancient Sign of Shakespear's Head where the *Providence Gazette and Country-Journal* was printed before the Revolution. Then came the exquisite First Baptist Church of 1775, luxurious with its matchless Gibbs steeple, and the Georgian roofs and cupolas hovering by. Here and to the southward the neighborhood became better, flowering at last into a marvelous group of early mansions; but still the little ancient lanes led off down the precipice to the west, spectral in their many-gabled archaism and dipping to a riot of iridescent decay where the wicked old waterfront recalls its proud East India days amidst polyglot vice and squalor, rotting wharves, and blear-eyed ship-chandleries, with such surviving alley names as Packet, Bullion, Gold, Silver, Coin, Doubloon, Sovereign, Guilder, Dollar, Dime, and Cent.

Sometimes, as he grew taller and more adventurous, young Ward would venture down into this maelstrom of tottering houses, broken transoms, tumbling steps, twisted balustrades, swarthy faces, and nameless odors; winding from South Main to South Water, searching out the docks where the bay and sound steamers still touched, and returning northward at this lower level past the steep-roofed 1816 warehouses and the broad square at the Great Bridge, where the 1773 Market House still stands firm on its ancient arches. In that square he would pause to drink in the bewildering beauty of the old town as it rises on its eastward bluff, decked with its two Georgian spires and crowned by the vast new Christian Science dome as London is crowned by St. Paul's. He liked mostly to reach this point in the late afternoon, when the slanting sunlight touches the Market House and the ancient hill roofs and belfries with gold, and throws magic around the dreaming wharves where Providence Indiamen used to ride at anchor. After a long look he would grow almost dizzy with a poet's love for the sight, and then he would scale the slope homeward in the dusk past the old white church and up the narrow precipitous ways where yellow gleams would begin to peep out in small-paned windows and through fanlights set high over double flights of steps with curious wrought-iron railings.

At other times, and in later years, he would seek for vivid contrasts; spending half a walk in the crumbling colonial regions northwest of his home, where the hill drops to the lower eminence of Stampers' Hill with its ghetto and negro quarter clustering round the place where the Boston stage coach used to start before the Revolution, and the other half in the gracious southerly realm about George, Benevolent, Power, and Williams Streets, where the old slope holds unchanged the fine estates and bits of walled garden and steep green lane in which so many fragrant memories linger. These rambles, together with the diligent studies which accompanied them, certainly account for a large amount of the antiquarian lore which at last crowded the modern world from Charles Ward's mind; and illustrate the mental soil upon which fell, in that fateful winter of 1919–20, the seeds that came to such strange and terrible fruition.

Dr. Willett is certain that, up to this ill-omened winter of first change, Charles Ward's antiquarianism was free from every trace of the morbid. Graveyards held for him no particular attraction beyond their quaintness and historic value, and of anything like violence or savage instinct he was utterly devoid. Then, by insidious degrees, there appeared to develop a curious sequel to one of his genealogical triumphs of the year before; when he had discovered among his maternal ancestors a certain very long-lived man named Joseph Curwen, who had come from Salem in March of 1692, and about whom a whispered series of highly peculiar and disquieting stories clustered.

Ward's great-great-grandfather Welcome Potter had in 1785 married a certain "Ann Tillinghast, daughter of Mrs. Eliza, daughter to Capt. James Tillinghast," of whose paternity the family had preserved no trace. Late in 1918, whilst examining a volume of original town records in manuscript, the young genealogist encountered an entry describing a legal change of name, by which in 1772 a Mrs. Eliza Curwen, widow of Joseph Curwen, resumed, along with her seven-year-old daughter Ann, her maiden name of Tillinghast; on the ground "that her Husband's name was become a publick Reproach by Reason of what was knowne after his Decease; the which confirming an antient common Rumour, tho' not to be credited by a loyall Wife till so proven as to be wholely past Doubting." This entry came to light upon the accidental separation of two leaves which had been carefully pasted together and treated as one by a labored revision of the page numbers.

It was at once clear to Charles Ward that he had indeed discovered a hitherto unknown great-great-great-grandfather. The discovery doubly excited him because he had already heard vague reports and seen scattered allusions relating to this person; about whom there remained so few publicly available records, aside from those becoming public only in modern times, that it almost seemed as if a conspiracy had existed to blot him from memory. What did appear, moreover, was of such a singular and provocative nature that one could not fail to imagine curiously what it was that the colonial recorders were so anxious to conceal and forget; or to suspect that the deletion had reasons all too valid.

Before this, Ward had been content to let his romancing about old Joseph Curwen remain in the idle stage; but having discovered his own relationship to this apparently "hushed-up" character, he proceeded to hunt out as systematically as possible whatever he might find concerning him. In this excited quest he eventually succeeded beyond his highest expectations; for old letters, diaries, and sheaves of unpublished memoirs in cobwebbed Providence garrets and elsewhere yielded many illuminating passages which their writers had not thought it worth their while to destroy. One important sidelight came from a point as remote as New York, where some Rhode Island colonial correspondence was stored in the Museum at Fraunces'Tavern.The really crucial thing, though, and what in Dr. Willett's opinion formed the definite source of Ward's undoing, was the matter found in August 1919 behind the paneling of the crumbling house in Olney Court. It was that, beyond a doubt, which opened up those black vistas whose end was deeper than the pit.

II. An Antecedent and a Horror

1

Joseph Curwen, as revealed by the rambling legends embodied in what Ward heard and unearthed, was a very astonishing, enigmatic, and obscurely horrible individual. He had fled from Salem to Providence—that universal haven of the odd, the free, and the dissenting—at the beginning of the great witchcraft panic; being in fear of accusation because of his solitary ways and queer chemical or alchemical experiments. He was a color-less-looking man of about thirty, and was soon found qualified to become a freeman of Providence; thereafter buying a home lot just north of Gregory Dexter's at about the foot of Olney Street. His house was built on Stampers' Hill west of the Town Street, in what later became Olney Court; and in 1761 he replaced this with a larger one, on the same site, which is still standing.

Now the first odd thing about Joseph Curwen was that he did not seem to grow much older than he had been on his arrival. He engaged in shipping enterprises, purchased wharfage near Mile-End Cove, helped rebuild the Great Bridge in 1713, and in 1723 was one of the founders of the Congregational

Church on the hill; but always did he retain the nondescript aspect of a man not greatly over thirty or thirty-five. As decades mounted up, this singular quality began to excite wide notice; but Curwen always explained it by saying that he came of hardy forefathers, and practiced a simplicity of living which did not wear him out. How such simplicity could be reconciled with the inexplicable comings and goings of the secretive merchant, and with the queer gleaming of his windows at all hours of night, was not very clear to the townsfolk; and they were prone to assign other reasons for his continued youth and longevity. It was held, for the most part, that Curwen's incessant mixings and boilings of chemicals had much to do with his condition. Gossip spoke of the strange substances he brought from London and the Indies on his ships or purchased in Newport, Boston, and New York; and when old Dr. Jabez Bowen came from Rehoboth and opened his apothecary shop across the Great Bridge at the Sign of the Unicorn and Mortar, there was ceaseless talk of the drugs, acids, and metals that the taciturn recluse incessantly bought or ordered from him. Acting on the assumption that Curwen possessed a wondrous and secret medical skill, many sufferers of various sorts applied to him for aid; but though he appeared to encourage their belief in a non-committal way, and always gave them odd-colored potions in response to their requests, it was observed that his ministrations to others seldom proved of benefit. At length, when over fifty years had passed since the stranger's advent, and without producing more than five years' apparent change in his face and physique, the people began to whisper more darkly; and to meet more than half way that desire for isolation which he had always shewn.

Private letters and diaries of the period reveal, too, a multitude of other reasons why Joseph Curwen was marveled at, feared, and finally shunned like a plague. His passion for graveyards, in which he was glimpsed at all hours and under all conditions, was notorious; though no one had witnessed any deed on his part which could actually be termed ghoulish. On the Pawtuxet Road he had a farm, at which he generally lived during the summer, and to which he would frequently be seen riding at various odd times of the day or night. Here his only visible servants, farmers, and caretakers were a sullen pair of aged Narragansett Indians; the husband dumb and curiously scarred, and the wife of a very repulsive cast of countenance, probably due to a mixture of negro blood. In the lean-to of this house was the laboratory where most of the chemical experiments were conducted. Curious porters and teamers who delivered bottles, bags, or boxes at the small rear door would exchange accounts of the fantastic flasks, crucibles, alembics, and furnaces they saw in the low shelved room; and prophesied in whispers that the close-mouthed "chymist"—by which they meant *alchemist*—would not be long in finding the Philosopher's Stone. The nearest neighbors to this farm—the Fenners, a quarter of a mile away—had still queerer things to tell of certain sounds which they insisted came from the Curwen place in the night. There were cries, they said, and sustained howlings; and they did not like the large number of livestock which thronged the pastures, for no such amount was needed to keep a lone old man and a very few servants in meat, milk, and wool. The identity of the stock seemed to change from week to week as new droves were purchased from the Kingstown farmers. Then, too, there was something very obnoxious about a certain great stone outbuilding with only high narrow slits for windows.

Great Bridge idlers likewise had much to say of Curwen's town house in Olney Court; not so much the fine new one built in 1761, when the man must have been nearly a century old, but the first low gambrel-roofed one with the windowless attic and shingled sides, whose timbers he took the peculiar precaution of burning after its demolition. Here there was less mystery, it is true; but the hours at which lights were seen, the secretiveness of the two swarthy foreigners who comprised the only menservants, the hideous indistinct mumbling of the incredibly aged French housekeeper, the large amounts of food seen to enter a door within which only four persons lived, and the *quality* of certain voices often heard in muffled conversation at highly unseasonable times, all combined with what was known of the Pawtuxet farm to give the place a bad name.

In choicer circles, too, the Curwen home was by no means undiscussed; for as the newcomer had gradually worked into the church and trading life of the town, he had naturally made acquaintances of the better sort, whose company and conversation he was well fitted by education to enjoy. His birth was known to be good, since the Curwens or Corwins of Salem needed no introduction in New England. It developed that Joseph Curwen had traveled much in very early life, living for a time in England and making at least two voyages to the Orient; and his speech, when he deigned to use it, was that of a learned and cultivated Englishman. But for some reason or other Curwen did not care for society. Whilst never actually rebuffing a visitor, he always reared such a wall of reserve that few could think of anything to say to him which would not sound inane.

There seemed to lurk in his bearing some cryptic, sardonic arrogance, as if he had come to find all human beings dull through having moved among stranger and more potent entities. When Dr. Checkley the famous wit came from Boston in 1738 to be rector of King's Church, he did not neglect calling on one of whom he soon heard so much; but left in a very short while because of some sinister undercurrent he detected in his host's discourse. Charles Ward told his father, when they discussed Curwen one winter evening, that he would give much to learn what the mysterious old man had said to the sprightly cleric, but that all diarists agree concerning Dr. Checkley's reluctance to repeat anything he had heard. The good man had been hideously shocked, and could never recall Joseph Curwen without a visible loss of the gay urbanity for which he was famed.

More definite, however, was the reason why another man of taste and breeding avoided the haughty hermit. In 1746 Mr. John Merritt, an elderly English gentleman of literary and scientific leanings, came from Newport to the town which was so rapidly overtaking it in standing, and built a fine country seat on the Neck in what is now the heart of the best residence section. He lived in considerable style and comfort, keeping the first coach and liveried servants in town, and taking great pride in his telescope, his microscope, and his well-chosen library of English and Latin books. Hearing of Curwen as the owner of the best library in Providence, Mr. Merritt early paid him a call, and was more cordially received than most other callers at the house had been. His admiration for his host's ample shelves, which besides the Greek, Latin, and English classics were equipped with a remarkable battery of philosophical, mathematical, and scientific works including Paracelsus, Agricola, van Helmont, Sylvius, Glauber, Boyle, Boerhaave, Becher, and Stahl, led Curwen to suggest a visit to the farmhouse and laboratory whither he had never invited anyone before; and the two drove out at once in Mr. Merritt's coach.

Mr. Merritt always confessed to seeing nothing really horrible at the farmhouse, but maintained that the titles of the books in the special library of thaumaturgical, alchemical, and theological subjects which Curwen kept in a front room were alone sufficient to inspire him with a lasting loathing. Perhaps, however, the facial expression of the owner in exhibiting them contributed much of the prejudice. The bizarre collection, besides a host of standard works which Mr. Merritt was not too alarmed to envy, embraced nearly all the cabbalists, daemonologists, and magicians known to man; and was a treasure-house of lore in the doubtful realms of alchemy and astrology. Hermes Trismegistus in Mesnard's edition, the *Turba Philosophorum*, Geber's *Liber Investigationis*, and Artephius' *Key of Wisdom* all were there; with the cabbalistic *Zohar*, Peter Jammy's set of Albertus Magnus, Raymond Lully's *Ars Magna et Ultima* in Zetzner's edition, Roger Bacon's

Thesaurus Chemicus, Fludd's *Clavis Alchimiae,* and Trithemius'
De Lapide Philosophico crowding them close. Medieval Jews
and Arabs were represented in profusion, and Mr. Merritt turned
pale when, upon taking down a fine volume conspicuously
labeled as the *Qanoon-e-Islam,* he found it was in truth the
forbidden *Necronomicon* of the mad Arab Abdul Alhazred, of
which he had heard such monstrous things whispered some
years previously after the exposure of nameless rites at the
strange little fishing village of Kingsport, in the Province of the
Massachusetts-Bay.

But oddly enough, the worthy gentleman owned himself most
impalpably disquieted by a mere minor detail. On the huge
mahogany table there lay face downward a badly worn copy of
Borellus, bearing many cryptical marginalia and interlineations
in Curwen's hand. The book was open at about its middle, and
one paragraph displayed such thick and tremulous pen-strokes
beneath the lines of mystic black-letter that the visitor could not
resist scanning it through. Whether it was the nature of the
passage underscored, or the feverish heaviness of the strokes
which formed the underscoring, he could not tell; but something
in that combination affected him very badly and very peculiarly.
He recalled it to the end of his days, writing it down from
memory in his diary and once trying to recite it to his close
friend Dr. Checkley till he saw how greatly it disturbed the urbane
rector. It read:

> The essential Saltes of Animals may be so prepared
> and preserved, that an ingenious Man may have the
> whole Ark of Noah in his own Studie, and raise the
> fine Shape of an Animal out of its Ashes at his
> Pleasure; and by the lyke Method from the essential
> Saltes of humane Dust, a Philosopher may, without
> any criminal Necromancy, call up the Shape of any
> dead Ancestour from the Dust whereinto his Bodie
> has been incinerated.

It was near the docks along the southerly part of the Town Street, however, that the worst things were muttered about Joseph Curwen. Sailors are superstitious folk; and the seasoned salts who manned the infinite rum, slave, and molasses sloops, the rakish privateers, and the great brigs of the Browns, Crawfords, and Tillinghasts, all made strange furtive signs of protection when they saw the slim, deceptively young-looking figure with its yellow hair and slight stoop entering the Curwen warehouse in Doubloon Street or talking with captains and supercargoes on the long quay where the Curwen ships rode restlessly. Curwen's own clerks and captains hated and feared him, and all his sailors were mongrel riff-raff from Martinique, St. Eustatius, Havana, or Port Royal. It was, in a way, the frequency with which these sailors were replaced which inspired the acutest and most tangible part of the fear in which the old man was held. A crew would be turned loose in the town on shore leave, some of its members perhaps charged with this errand or that; and when reassembled it would be almost sure to lack one or more men. That many of the errands had concerned the farm on the Pawtuxet Road, and that few of the sailors had ever been seen to return from that place, was not forgotten; so that in time it became exceedingly difficult for Curwen to keep his oddly assorted hands. Almost invariably several would desert soon after hearing the gossip of the Providence wharves, and their replacement in the West Indies became an increasingly great problem to the merchant.

In 1760 Joseph Curwen was virtually an outcast, suspected of vague horrors and daemoniac alliances which seemed all the more menacing because they could not be named, understood, or even proved to exist. The last straw may have come from the affair of the missing soldiers in 1758, for in March and April of that year two Royal regiments on their way to New France were quartered in Providence, and depleted by an inexplicable process far beyond the average rate of desertion. Rumor dwelt on the frequency with which Curwen was wont to be seen talking with the red-coated strangers; and as several of them began to be missed, people thought of the odd conditions among his own seamen. What would have happened if the regiments had not been ordered on, no one can tell.

Meanwhile the merchant's worldly affairs were prospering. He had a virtual monopoly of the town's trade in saltpeter, black pepper, and cinnamon, and easily led any other one shipping establishment save the Browns in his importation of brassware, indigo, cotton, woolens, salt, rigging, iron, paper, and English goods of every kind. Such shopkeepers as James Green, at the Sign of the Elephant in Cheapside, the Russells, at the Sign of the Golden Eagle across the Bridge, or Clark and Nightingale at the Frying-Pan and Fish near the New Coffee-House, depended almost wholly upon him for their stock; and his arrangements with the local distillers, the Narragansett dairymen and horse-breeders, and the Newport candle-makers, made him one of the prime exporters of the Colony.

Ostracized though he was, he did not lack for civic spirit of a sort. When the Colony House burned down, he subscribed handsomely to the lotteries by which the new brick one—still standing at the head of its parade in the old main street—was built in 1761. In that same year, too, he helped rebuild the Great Bridge after the October gale. He replaced many of the books of the public library consumed in the Colony House fire, and bought heavily in the lottery that gave the muddy Market Parade and deep-rutted Town Street their pavement of great round stones with a brick footwalk or "causey" in the middle. About this time, also, he built the plain but excellent new house whose doorway is still such a triumph of carving. When the Whitefield adherents broke off from Dr. Cotton's hill church in 1743 and founded Deacon Snow's church across the Bridge, Curwen had gone with them; though his zeal and attendance soon abated. Now, however, he cultivated piety once more; as if to dispel the shadow which had thrown him into isolation and would soon begin to wreck his business fortunes if not sharply checked.

2

The sight of this strange, pallid man, hardly middle-aged in aspect yet certainly not less than a full century old, seeking at last to emerge from a cloud of fright and detestation too vague to pin down or analyze, was at once a pathetic, a dramatic, and a contemptible thing. Such is the power of wealth and of surface gestures, however, that there came indeed a slight abatement in the visible aversion displayed toward him; especially after the rapid disappearances of his sailors abruptly ceased. He must likewise have begun to practice an extreme care and secrecy in his graveyard expeditions, for he was never again caught at such wanderings; whilst the rumors of uncanny sounds and maneuvers at his Pawtuxet farm diminished in proportion. His rate of food consumption and cattle replacement remained abnormally high; but not until modern times, when Charles Ward examined a set of his accounts and invoices in the Shepley Library, did it occur to any person—save one embittered youth, perhaps—to make dark comparisons between the large number of Guinea blacks he imported until 1766, and the disturbingly small number for whom he could produce bona fide bills of sale either to slave-dealers at the Great Bridge or to the planters of the Narragansett Country. Certainly, the cunning and ingenuity of this abhorred character were uncannily profound, once the necessity for their exercise had become impressed upon him.

But of course the effect of all this belated mending was necessarily slight. Curwen continued to be avoided and distrusted, as indeed the one fact of his continued air of youth at a great age would have been enough to warrant; and he could see that in the end his fortunes would be likely to suffer. His elaborate studies and experiments, whatever they may have been, apparently required a heavy income for their maintenance; and since a change of environment would deprive him of the trading advantages he had gained, it would not have profited him to begin anew in a different region just then. Judgment demanded that he patch up his relations with the townsfolk of Providence, so that his presence might no longer be a signal for hushed conversation, transparent excuses of errands elsewhere, and a general atmosphere of constraint and uneasiness. His clerks, being now reduced to the shiftless and impecunious residue whom no one else would employ, were giving him much worry; and he held to his sea-captains and mates only by shrewdness in gaining some kind of ascendancy over them—a mortgage, a promissory note, or a bit of information very pertinent to their welfare. In many cases, diarists have recorded with some awe, Curwen shewed almost the power of a wizard in unearthing family secrets for questionable use. During the final five years of his life it seemed as though only direct talks with the long-dead could possibly have furnished some of the data which he had so glibly at his tongue's end.

About this time the crafty scholar hit upon a last desperate expedient to regain his footing in the community. Hitherto a complete hermit, he now determined to contract an advantageous marriage; securing as a bride some lady whose unquestioned position would make all ostracism of his home impossible. It may be that he also had deeper reasons for wishing an alliance; reasons so far outside the known cosmic sphere that only papers found a century and a half after his death caused anyone to suspect them; but of this nothing certain can ever be learned. Naturally he was aware of the horror and indignation with which any ordinary courtship of his would be received, hence he looked about for some likely candidate upon whose parents he might exert a suitable pressure. Such candidates, he found, were not at all easy to discover; since he had very particular requirements in the way of beauty, accomplishments, and social security. At length his survey narrowed down to the household of one of his best and oldest ship-captains, a widower of high birth and unblemished standing named Dutee Tillinghast, whose only daughter Eliza seemed dowered with every conceivable advantage save prospects as an heiress. Capt. Tillinghast was completely under the domination of Curwen; and consented, after a terrible interview in his cupolaed house on Power's Lane hill, to sanction the blasphemous alliance.

Eliza Tillinghast was at that time eighteen years of age, and had been reared as gently as the reduced circumstances of her father permitted. She had attended Stephen Jackson's school opposite the Court-House Parade; and had been diligently instructed by her mother, before the latter's death of smallpox in 1757, in all the arts and refinements of domestic life. A sampler of hers, worked in 1753 at the age of nine, may still be found in the rooms of the Rhode Island Historical Society. After her mother's death she had kept the house, aided only by one old black woman. Her arguments with her father concerning the proposed Curwen marriage must have been painful indeed; but of these we have no record. Certain it is that her engagement to young Ezra Weeden, second mate of the Crawford packet *Enterprise,* was dutifully broken off, and that her union with Joseph Curwen took place on the seventh of March, 1763, in the Baptist church, in the presence of one of the most distinguished assemblages which the town could boast; the ceremony being performed by the younger Samuel Winsor. The *Gazette* mentioned the event very briefly, and in most surviving copies the item in question seems to be cut or torn out. Ward found a single intact copy after much search in the archives of a private collector of note, observing with amusement the meaningless urbanity of the language:

> Monday evening last, Mr. Joseph Curwen, of this Town, Merchant, was married to Miss Eliza Tillinghast, Daughter of Capt. Dutee Tillinghast, a young Lady who has real Merit, added to a beautiful Person, to grace the connubial State and perpetuate its Felicity.

The collection of Durfee-Arnold letters, discovered by Charles Ward shortly before his first reputed madness in the private collection of Melville F. Peters, Esq., of George St., and covering this and a somewhat antecedent period, throws vivid light on the outrage done to public sentiment by this ill-assorted match. The social influence of the Tillinghasts, however, was not to be denied; and once more Joseph Curwen found his house frequented by persons whom he could never otherwise have induced to cross his threshold. His acceptance was by no means complete, and his bride was socially the sufferer through her forced venture; but at all events the wall of utter ostracism was somewhat worn down. In his treatment of his wife the strange bridegroom astonished both her and the community by displaying an extreme graciousness and consideration. The new house in Olney Court was now wholly free from disturbing manifestations, and although Curwen was much absent at the Pawtuxet farm which his wife never visited, he seemed more like a normal citizen than at any other time in his long years of residence. Only one person remained in open enmity with him, this being the youthful ship's officer whose engagement to Eliza Tillinghast had been so abruptly broken. Ezra Weeden had frankly vowed vengeance; and though of a quiet and ordinarily mild disposition, was now gaining a hate-bred, dogged purpose which boded no good to the usurping husband.

On the seventh of May, 1765, Curwen's only child Ann was born; and was christened by the Rev. John Graves of King's Church, of which both husband and wife had become communicants shortly after their marriage, in order to compromise between their respective Congregational and Baptist affiliations. The record of this birth, as well as that of the marriage two years before, was stricken from most copies of the church and town annals where it ought to appear; and Charles Ward located both with the greatest difficulty after his discovery of the widow's change of name had apprised him of his own relationship, and engendered the feverish interest which culminated in his madness. The birth entry, indeed, was found very curiously through correspondence with the heirs of the loyalist Dr. Graves, who had taken with him a duplicate set of records when he left his pastorate at the outbreak of the Revolution. Ward had tried this source because he knew that his great-great-grandmother Ann Tillinghast Potter had been an Episcopalian.

Shortly after the birth of his daughter, an event he seemed to welcome with a fervor greatly out of keeping with his usual coldness, Curwen resolved to sit for a portrait. This he had painted by a very gifted Scotsman named Cosmo Alexander, then a resident of Newport, and since famous as the early teacher of Gilbert Stuart. The likeness was said to have been executed on a wall-panel of the library of the house in Olney Court, but neither of the two old diaries mentioning it gave any hint of its ultimate disposition. At this period the erratic scholar shewed signs of unusual abstraction, and spent as much time as he possibly could at his farm on the Pawtuxet Road. He seemed, it was stated, in a condition of suppressed excitement or suspense; as if expecting some phenomenal thing or on the brink of some strange discovery. Chemistry or alchemy would appear to have played a great part, for he took from his house to the farm the greater number of his volumes on that subject.

His affectation of civic interest did not diminish, and he lost no opportunities for helping such leaders as Stephen Hopkins, Joseph Brown, and Benjamin West in their efforts to raise the cultural tone of the town, which was then much below the level of Newport in its patronage of the liberal arts. He had helped Daniel Jenckes found his bookshop in 1763, and was thereafter his best customer; extending aid likewise to the struggling *Gazette* that appeared each Wednesday at the Sign of Shakespear's Head. In politics he ardently supported Governor Hopkins against the Ward party whose prime strength was in Newport, and his really eloquent speech at Hacker's Hall in 1765 against the setting off of North Providence as a separate town with a pro-Ward vote in the General Assembly did more than any other one thing to wear down the prejudice against him. But Ezra Weeden, who watched him closely, sneered cynically at all this outward activity; and freely swore it was no more than a mask for some nameless traffick with the blackest gulfs of Tartarus. The revengeful youth

began a systematic study of the man and his doings whenever
he was in port; spending hours at night by the wharves with a
dory in readiness when he saw lights in the Curwen warehouses,
and following the small boat which would sometimes steal quietly
off and down the bay. He also kept as close a watch as possible
on the Pawtuxet farm, and was once severely bitten by the dogs
the old Indian couple loosed upon him.

3

In 1766 came the final change in Joseph Curwen. It was very
sudden, and gained wide notice amongst the curious townsfolk;
for the air of suspense and expectancy dropped like an old cloak,
giving instant place to an ill-concealed exaltation of perfect
triumph. Curwen seemed to have difficulty in restraining himself
from public harangues on what he had found or learned or made;
but apparently the need of secrecy was greater than the longing
to share his rejoicing, for no explanation was ever offered by
him. It was after this transition, which appears to have come
early in July, that the sinister scholar began to astonish people
by his possession of information which only their long-dead
ancestors would seem to be able to impart.

But Curwen's feverish secret activities by no means ceased
with this change. On the contrary, they tended rather to increase;
so that more and more of his shipping business was handled by
the captains whom he now bound to him by ties of fear as
potent as those of bankruptcy had been. He altogether abandoned
the slave trade, alleging that its profits were constantly decreasing.
Every possible moment was spent at the Pawtuxet farm; though
there were rumors now and then of his presence in places which,
though not actually near graveyards, were yet so situated in
relation to graveyards that thoughtful people wondered just how
thorough the old merchant's change of habits really was. Ezra
Weeden, though his periods of espionage were necessarily brief

and intermittent on account of his sea voyaging, had a vindictive persistence which the bulk of the practical townsfolk and farmers lacked; and subjected Curwen's affairs to a scrutiny such as they had never had before.

Many of the odd maneuvers of the strange merchant's vessels had been taken for granted on account of the unrest of the times, when every colonist seemed determined to resist the provisions of the Sugar Act which hampered a prominent traffick. Smuggling and evasion were the rule in Narragansett Bay, and nocturnal landings of illicit cargoes were continuous commonplaces. But Weeden, night after night following the lighters or small sloops which he saw steal off from the Curwen warehouses at the Town Street docks, soon felt assured that it was not merely His Majesty's armed ships which the sinister skulker was anxious to avoid. Prior to the change in 1766 these boats had for the most part contained chained negroes, who were carried down and across the bay and landed at an obscure point on the shore just north of Pawtuxet; being afterward driven up the bluff and across country to the Curwen farm, where they were locked in that enormous stone outbuilding which had only high narrow slits for windows. After that change, however, the whole program was altered. Importation of slaves ceased at once, and for a time Curwen abandoned his midnight sailings. Then, about the spring of 1767, a new policy appeared. Once more the lighters grew wont to put out from the black, silent docks, and this time they would go down the bay some distance, perhaps as far as Namquit Point, where they would meet and receive cargo from strange ships of considerable size and widely varied appearance. Curwen's sailors would then deposit this cargo at the usual point on the shore, and transport it overland to the farm; locking it in the same cryptical stone building which had formerly received the negroes. The cargo consisted almost wholly of boxes and cases, of which a large proportion were oblong and heavy and disturbingly suggestive of coffins.

Weeden always watched the farm with unremitting assiduity; visiting it each night for long periods, and seldom letting a week go by without a sight except when the ground bore a footprint-revealing snow. Even then he would often walk as close as possible in the traveled road or on the ice of the neighboring river to see what tracks others might have left. Finding his own vigils interrupted by nautical duties, he hired a tavern companion named Eleazar Smith to continue the survey during his absences; and between them the two could have set in motion some extraordinary rumors. That they did not do so was only because they knew the effect of publicity would be to warn their quarry and make further progress impossible. Instead, they wished to learn something definite before taking any action. What they did learn must have been startling indeed, and Charles Ward spoke many times to his parents of his regret at Weeden's later burning of his notebooks. All that can be told of their discoveries is what Eleazar Smith jotted down in a none too coherent diary, and what other diarists and letter-writers have timidly repeated from the statements which they finally made—and according to which the farm was only the outer shell of some vast and revolting menace, of a scope and depth too profound and intangible for more than shadowy comprehension.

It is gathered that Weeden and Smith became early convinced that a great series of tunnels and catacombs, inhabited by a very sizeable staff of persons besides the old Indian and his wife, underlay the farm. The house was an old peaked relic of the middle seventeenth century with enormous stack chimney and diamond-paned lattice windows, the laboratory being in a lean-to toward the north, where the roof came nearly to the ground. This building stood clear of any other; yet judging by the different voices heard at odd times within, it must have been accessible through secret passages beneath. These voices, before 1766, were mere mumblings and negro whisperings and frenzied screams, coupled with curious chants or invocations. After that date, however, they assumed a very singular and terrible cast as they ran the gamut betwixt dronings of dull acquiescence and explosions of frantic pain or fury, rumblings of conversation and whines of entreaty, pantings of eagerness and shouts of protest. They appeared to be in different languages, all known to Curwen, whose rasping accents were frequently distinguishable in reply, reproof, or threatening. Sometimes it seemed that several persons must be in the house; Curwen, certain captives, and the guards of those captives. There were voices of a sort that neither Weeden nor Smith had ever heard before despite their wide knowledge of foreign parts, and many that they did seem to place as belonging to this or that nationality. The nature of the conversations seemed always a kind of catechism, as if Curwen were extorting some sort of information from terrified or rebellious prisoners.

Weeden had many verbatim reports of overheard scraps in his notebook, for English, French, and Spanish, which he knew, were frequently used; but of these nothing has survived. He did, however, say that besides a few ghoulish dialogues in which the past affairs of Providence families were concerned, most of the questions and answers he could understand were historical or scientific; occasionally pertaining to very remote places and ages. Once, for example, an alternately raging and sullen figure was questioned in French about the Black Prince's massacre at Limoges in 1370, as if there were some hidden reason which he ought to know. Curwen asked the prisoner—if prisoner it were—whether the order to slay was given because of the Sign of the Goat found on the altar in the ancient Roman crypt beneath the Cathedral, or whether the Dark Man of the Haute Vienne Coven had spoken the Three Words. Failing to obtain replies, the inquisitor had seemingly resorted to extreme means; for there was a terrific shriek followed by silence and muttering and a bumping sound.

None of these colloquies were ever ocularly witnessed, since the windows were always heavily draped. Once, though, during a discourse in an unknown tongue, a shadow was seen on the curtain which startled Weeden exceedingly; reminding him of one of the puppets in a show he had seen in the autumn of 1764 in Hacker's Hall, when a man from Germantown,

Pennsylvania, had given a clever mechanical spectacle advertised as a "View of the Famous City of Jerusalem, in which are represented Jerusalem, the Temple of Solomon, his Royal Throne, the noted Towers, and Hills, likewise the Sufferings of Our Saviour from the Garden of Gethsemane to the Cross on the Hill of Golgotha; an artful piece of Statuary, Worthy to be seen by the Curious." It was on this occasion that the listener, who had crept close to the window of the front room whence the speaking proceeded, gave a start which roused the old Indian pair and caused them to loose the dogs on him. After that no more conversations were ever heard in the house, and Weeden and Smith concluded that Curwen had transferred his field of action to regions below.

That such regions in truth existed, seemed amply clear from many things. Faint cries and groans unmistakably came up now and then from what appeared to be the solid earth in places far from any structure; whilst hidden in the bushes along the river-bank in the rear, where the high ground sloped steeply down to the valley of the Pawtuxet, there was found an arched oaken door in a frame of heavy masonry, which was obviously an entrance to caverns within the hill. When or how these catacombs could have been constructed, Weeden was unable to say; but he frequently pointed out how easily the place might have been reached by bands of unseen workmen from the river. Joseph Curwen put his mongrel seamen to diverse uses indeed! During the heavy spring rains of 1769 the two watchers kept a sharp eye on the steep river-bank to see if any subterrene secrets might be washed to light, and were rewarded by the sight of a profusion of both human and animal bones in places where deep gullies had been worn in the banks. Naturally there might be many explanations of such things in the rear of a stock farm, and in a locality where old Indian burying-grounds were common, but Weeden and Smith drew their own inferences.

It was in January 1770, whilst Weeden and Smith were still debating vainly on what, if anything, to think or do about the whole bewildering business, that the incident of the *Fortaleza* occurred. Exasperated by the burning of the revenue sloop *Liberty* at Newport during the previous summer, the customs fleet under Admiral Wallace had adopted an increased vigilance concerning strange vessels; and on this occasion His Majesty's armed schooner *Cygnet,* under Capt. Charles Leslie, captured after a short pursuit one early morning the scow *Fortaleza* of Barcelona, Spain, under Capt. Manuel Arruda, bound according to its log from Grand Cairo, Egypt, to Providence. When searched for contraband material, this ship revealed the astonishing fact that its cargo consisted exclusively of Egyptian mummies, consigned to "Sailor A. B. C.," who would come to remove his goods in a lighter just off Namquit Point and whose identity Capt. Arruda felt himself in honor bound not to reveal. The Vice-Admiralty Court at Newport, at a loss what to do in view of the non-contraband nature of the cargo on the one hand and of the unlawful secrecy of the entry on the other hand, compromised on Collector Robinson's recommendation by freeing the ship but forbidding it a port in Rhode Island waters. There were later rumors of its having been seen in Boston Harbor, though it never openly entered the Port of Boston.

This extraordinary incident did not fail of wide remark in Providence, and there were not many who doubted the existence of some connexion between the cargo of mummies and the sinister Joseph Curwen. His exotic studies and his curious chemical importations being common knowledge, and his fondness for graveyards being common suspicion; it did not take much imagination to link him with a freakish importation which could not conceivably have been destined for anyone else in the town. As if conscious of this natural belief, Curwen took care to speak casually on several occasions of the chemical value of the balsams found in mummies; thinking perhaps that he might make the affair seem less unnatural, yet stopping just short of admitting his participation. Weeden and Smith, of course, felt no doubt whatsoever of the significance of the thing; and indulged in the wildest theories concerning Curwen and his monstrous labors.

The following spring, like that of the year before, had heavy rains; and the watchers kept careful track of the river-bank behind the Curwen farm. Large sections were washed away, and a certain number of bones discovered; but no glimpse was afforded of any actual subterranean chambers or burrows. Something was rumored, however, at the village of Pawtuxet about a mile below, where the river flows in falls over a rocky terrace to join the placid landlocked cove. There, where quaint old cottages climbed the hill from the rustic bridge, and fishing-smacks lay anchored at their sleepy docks, a vague report went round of things that were floating down the river and flashing into sight for a minute as they went over the falls. Of course the Pawtuxet is a long river which winds through many settled regions abounding in graveyards, and of course the spring rains had been very heavy; but the fisherfolk about the bridge did not like the wild way that one of the things stared as it shot down to the still water below, or the way that another half cried out although its condition had greatly departed from that of objects which normally cry out. That rumor sent Smith—for Weeden was just then at sea—in haste to the river-bank behind the farm; where surely enough there remained the evidences of an extensive cave-in. There was, however, no trace of a passage into the steep bank; for the miniature avalanche had left behind a solid wall of mixed earth and shrubbery from aloft. Smith went to the extent of some experimental digging, but was deterred by lack of success— or perhaps by fear of possible success. It is interesting to speculate on what the persistent and revengeful Weeden would have done had he been ashore at the time.

4

By the autumn of 1770 Weeden decided that the time was ripe to tell others of his discoveries; for he had a large number of facts to link together, and a second eye-witness to refute the possible charge that jealousy and vindictiveness had spurred his fancy. As his first confidant he selected Capt. James Mathewson of the *Enterprise*, who on the one hand knew him well enough not to doubt his veracity, and on the other hand was sufficiently influential in the town to be heard in turn with respect. The colloquy took place in an upper room of Sabin's Tavern near the docks, with Smith present to corroborate virtually every statement; and it could be seen that Capt. Mathewson was tremendously impressed. Like nearly everyone else in the town, he had had black suspicions of his own anent Joseph Curwen; hence it needed only this confirmation and enlargement of data to convince him absolutely. At the end of the conference he was very grave, and enjoined strict silence upon the two younger men. He would, he said, transmit the information separately to some ten or so of the most learned and prominent citizens of Providence; ascertaining their views and following whatever advice they might have to offer. Secrecy would probably be essential in any case, for this was no matter that the town constables or militia could cope with; and above all else the excitable crowd must be kept in ignorance, lest there be enacted in these already troublous times a repetition of that frightful Salem panic of less than a century before which had first brought Curwen hither.

The right persons to tell, he believed, would be Dr. Benjamin West, whose pamphlet on the late transit of Venus proved him a scholar and keen thinker; Rev. James Manning, President of the College which had just moved up from Warren and was temporarily housed in the new King Street schoolhouse awaiting the completion of its building on the hill above Presbyterian-Lane; ex-Governor Stephen Hopkins, who had been a member of the Philosophical Society at Newport, and was a man of very broad perceptions; John Carter, publisher of the *Gazette*; all four of the Brown brothers, John, Joseph, Nicholas, and Moses, who formed the recognized local magnates, and of whom Joseph was an amateur scientist of parts; old Dr. Jabez Bowen, whose erudition was considerable, and who had much first-hand knowledge of Curwen's odd purchases; and Capt. Abraham Whipple, a privateersman of phenomenal boldness and energy who could be counted on to lead in any active measures needed. These men, if favorable, might eventually be brought together for collective deliberation; and with them would rest the responsibility of deciding whether or not to inform the Governor of the Colony, Joseph Wanton of Newport, before taking action.

The mission of Capt. Mathewson prospered beyond his highest expectations; for whilst he found one or two of the chosen confidants somewhat skeptical of the possible ghastly side of Weeden's tale, there was not one who did not think it necessary to take some sort of secret and co-ordinated action. Curwen, it was clear, formed a vague potential menace to the welfare of the town and Colony; and must be eliminated at any cost. Late in December 1770 a group of eminent townsmen met at the home of Stephen Hopkins and debated tentative measures. Weeden's notes, which he had given to Capt. Mathewson, were carefully read; and he and Smith were summoned to give testimony anent details. Something very like fear seized the whole assemblage before the meeting was over, though there ran through that fear a grim determination which Capt. Whipple's bluff and resonant profanity best expressed. They would not notify the Governor, because a more than legal course seemed necessary. With hidden powers of uncertain extent apparently at his disposal, Curwen was not a man who could safely be warned to leave town. Nameless reprisals might ensue, and even if the sinister creature complied, the removal would be no more than the shifting of an unclean burden to another place. The times were lawless, and men who had flouted the King's revenue forces for years were not the ones to balk at sterner things when duty impelled. Curwen must be surprised at his Pawtuxet farm by a large raiding-party of seasoned privateersmen and given one decisive chance to explain himself. If he proved a madman, amusing himself with shrieks and imaginary conversations in different voices, he would be properly confined. If something graver appeared, and if the underground horrors indeed turned out to be real, he and all with him must die. It could be done quietly, and even the widow and her father need not be told how it came about.

While these serious steps were under discussion there occurred in the town an incident so terrible and inexplicable that for a time little else was mentioned for miles around. In the middle of a moonlight January night with heavy snow underfoot there resounded over the river and up the hill a shocking series of cries which brought sleepy heads to every window; and people around Weybosset Point saw a great white thing plunging frantically along the badly cleared space in front of the Turk's Head. There was a baying of dogs in the distance, but this subsided as soon as the clamor of the awakened town became audible. Parties of men with lanterns and muskets hurried out to see what was happening, but nothing rewarded their search. The next morning, however, a giant, muscular body, stark naked, was found on the jams of ice around the southern piers of the Great Bridge, where the Long Dock stretched out beside Abbott's distill-house, and the identity of this object became a theme for endless speculation and whispering. It was not so much the younger as the older folk who whispered, for only in the patriarchs did that rigid face with horror-bulging eyes strike any chord of memory. They, shaking as they did so, exchanged furtive murmurs of wonder and fear; for in those stiff, hideous features lay a resemblance so marvelous as to be almost an identity—and that identity was with a man who had died full fifty years before.

Ezra Weeden was present at the finding; and remembering the baying of the night before, set out along Weybosset Street and across Muddy Dock Bridge whence the sound had come. He had a curious expectancy, and was not surprised when, reaching the edge of the settled district where the street merged into the Pawtuxet Road, he came upon some very curious tracks in the snow. The naked giant had been pursued by dogs and many booted men, and the returning tracks of the hounds and their masters could be easily traced. They had given up the chase upon coming too near the town. Weeden smiled grimly, and as a perfunctory detail traced the footprints back to their source. It was the Pawtuxet farm of Joseph Curwen, as he well knew it would be; and he would have given much had the yard been less confusingly trampled. As it was, he dared not seem too interested in full daylight. Dr. Bowen, to whom Weeden went at once with his report, performed an autopsy on the strange corpse, and discovered peculiarities which baffled him utterly. The digestive tracts of the huge man seemed never to have been in use, whilst the whole skin had a coarse, loosely knit texture impossible to account for. Impressed by what the old men whispered of this body's likeness to the long-dead blacksmith Daniel Green, whose great-grandson Aaron Hoppin was a supercargo in Curwen's employ, Weeden asked casual questions till he found where Green was buried. That night a party of ten visited the old North Burying Ground opposite Herrenden's Lane and opened a grave. They found it vacant, precisely as they had expected.

Meanwhile arrangements had been made with the post riders to intercept Joseph Curwen's mail, and shortly before the incident of the naked body there was found a letter from one Jedediah Orne of Salem which made the co-operating citizens think deeply. Parts of it, copied and preserved in the private archives of the Smith family where Charles Ward found it, ran as follows:

> I delight that you continue in ye Gett'g at Olde Matters in your Way, and doe not think better was done at Mr. Hutchinson's in Salem-Village. Certainely, there was Noth'g butt ye liveliest Awfulness in that which H. rais'd upp from What he cou'd gather onlie a part of. What you sente, did not Worke, whether because of Any Thing miss'g, or because ye Wordes were not Righte from my Speak'g or yr

Copy'g. I alone am at a Loss. I have not ye Chymicall
art to followe Borellus, and owne my Self confounded
by ye VII. Booke of ye Necronomicon that you
recommende. But I wou'd have you Observe what
was tolde to us aboute tak'g Care whom to calle
up, for you are Sensible what Mr. Mather writ in ye
Magnalia of ——, and can judge how truely that
Horrendous thing is reported. I say to you againe,
doe not call up Any that you can not put downe;
by the Which I meane, Any that can in Turne call
up somewhat against you, whereby your Powerfullest
Devices may not be of use. Ask of the Lesser, lest
the Greater shall not wish to Answer, and shall
commande more than you. I was frighted when I
read of your know'g what Ben Zariatnatmik hadde
in his ebony Boxe, for I was conscious who must
have tolde you. And againe I ask that you shalle
write me as Jedediah and not Simon. In this
Community a Man may not live too long, and you
knowe my Plan by which I came back as my Son.
I am desirous you will Acquaint me with what ye
Blacke Man learnt from Sylvanus Cocidius in ye
Vault, under ye Roman Wall, and will be oblig'd for
ye Lend'g of ye MS. you speak of.

Another and unsigned letter from Philadelphia provoked equal
thought, especially for the following passage:

I will observe what you say respecting the sending
of Accounts only by yr Vessels, but can not always
be certain when to expect them. In the Matter spoke
of, I require onlie one more thing; but wish to be
sure I apprehend you exactly. You inform me, that
no Part must be missing if the finest Effects are to
be had, but you can not but know how hard it is

to be sure. It seems a great Hazard and Burthen to
take away the whole Box, and in Town (i.e. St. Peter's,
St. Paul's, St. Mary's, or Christ Church) it can scarce
be done at all. But I know what Imperfections were
in the one I rais'd up October last, and how many
live Specimens you were forc'd to imploy before
you hit upon the right Mode in the year 1766; so
will be guided by you in all Matters. I am impatient
for yr Brig, and inquire daily at Mr. Biddle's Wharf.

A third suspicious letter was in an unknown tongue and even
an unknown alphabet. In the Smith diary found by Charles Ward
a single oft-repeated combination of characters is clumsily copied;
and authorities at Brown University have pronounced the
alphabet Amharic or Abyssinian, although they do not recognize
the word. None of these epistles was ever delivered to Curwen,
though the disappearance of Jedediah Orne from Salem as
recorded shortly afterward shewed that the Providence men took
certain quiet steps. The Pennsylvania Historical Society also has
some curious letters received by Dr. Shippen regarding the presence of an unwholesome character in Philadelphia. But more
decisive steps were in the air, and it is in the secret assemblages
of sworn and tested sailors and faithful old privateersmen in the
Brown warehouses by night that we must look for the main
fruits of Weeden's disclosures. Slowly and surely a plan of
campaign was under development which would leave no trace
of Joseph Curwen's noxious mysteries.

Curwen, despite all precautions, apparently felt that something
was in the wind; for he was now remarked to wear an unusually
worried look. His coach was seen at all hours in the town and
on the Pawtuxet Road, and he dropped little by little the air of
forced geniality with which he had latterly sought to combat
the town's prejudice. The nearest neighbors to his farm, the
Fenners, one night remarked a great shaft of light shooting into
the sky from some aperture in the roof of that cryptical stone

building with the high, excessively narrow windows; an event which they quickly communicated to John Brown in Providence. Mr. Brown had become the executive leader of the select group bent on Curwen's extirpation, and had informed the Fenners that some action was about to be taken. This he deemed needful because of the impossibility of their not witnessing the final raid; and he explained his course by saying that Curwen was known to be a spy of the customs officers at Newport, against whom the hand of every Providence shipper, merchant, and farmer was openly or clandestinely raised. Whether the ruse was wholly believed by neighbors who had seen so many queer things is not certain; but at any rate the Fenners were willing to connect any evil with a man of such queer ways. To them Mr. Brown had entrusted the duty of watching the Curwen farmhouse, and of regularly reporting every incident which took place there.

5

The probability that Curwen was on guard and attempting unusual things, as suggested by the odd shaft of light, precipitated at last the action so carefully devised by the band of serious citizens. According to the Smith diary a company of about 100 men met at 10 p.m. on Friday, April 12th, 1771, in the great room of Thurston's Tavern at the Sign of the Golden Lion on Weybosset Point across the Bridge. Of the guiding group of prominent men in addition to the leader John Brown there were present Dr. Bowen, with his case of surgical instruments, President Manning without the great periwig (the largest in the Colonies) for which he was noted, Governor Hopkins, wrapped in his dark cloak and accompanied by his seafaring brother Esek, whom he had initiated at the last moment with the permission of the rest, John Carter, Capt. Mathewson, and Capt. Whipple, who was to lead the actual raiding party. These chiefs conferred apart in a rear chamber, after which Capt. Whipple emerged to the great room and gave the gathered seamen their last oaths and instructions. Eleazar Smith was with the leaders as they sat in the rear apartment awaiting the arrival of Ezra Weeden, whose duty was to keep track of Curwen and report the departure of his coach for the farm.

About 10:30 a heavy rumble was heard on the Great Bridge, followed by the sound of a coach in the street outside; and at that hour there was no need of waiting for Weeden in order to know that the doomed man had set out for his last night of unhallowed wizardry. A moment later, as the receding coach clattered faintly over the Muddy Dock Bridge, Weeden appeared; and the raiders fell silently into military order in the street, shouldering the firelocks, fowling-pieces, or whaling harpoons which they had with them. Weeden and Smith were with the party, and of the deliberating citizens there were present for active service Capt. Whipple, the leader, Capt. Esek Hopkins, John Carter, President Manning, Capt. Mathewson, and Dr. Bowen; together with Moses Brown, who had come up at the eleventh hour though absent from the preliminary session in the tavern. All these freemen and their hundred sailors began the long march without delay, grim and a trifle apprehensive as they left the Muddy Dock behind and mounted the gentle rise of Broad Street toward the Pawtuxet Road. Just beyond Elder Snow's church some of the men turned back to take a parting look at Providence lying outspread under the early spring stars. Steeples and gables rose dark and shapely, and salt breezes swept up gently from the cove north of the Bridge. Vega was climbing above the great hill across the water, whose crest of trees was broken by the roof-line of the unfinished College edifice. At the foot of that hill, and along the narrow mounting lanes of its side, the old town dreamed; Old Providence, for whose safety and sanity so monstrous and colossal a blasphemy was about to be wiped out.

An hour and a quarter later the raiders arrived, as previously agreed, at the Fenner farmhouse; where they heard a final report on their intended victim. He had reached his farm over half an hour before, and the strange light had soon afterward shot once into the sky, but there were no lights in any visible windows. This was always the case of late. Even as this news was given another great glare arose toward the south, and the party realized that they had indeed come close to the scene of awesome and unnatural wonders. Capt. Whipple now ordered his force to separate into three divisions; one of twenty men under Eleazar Smith to strike across to the shore and guard the landing-place against possible reinforcements for Curwen until summoned by a messenger for desperate service, a second of twenty men under Capt. Esek Hopkins to steal down into the river valley behind the Curwen farm and demolish with axes or gunpowder the oaken door in the high, steep bank, and the third to close in on the house and adjacent buildings themselves. Of this division one third was to be led by Capt. Mathewson to the cryptical stone edifice with high narrow windows, another third to follow Capt. Whipple himself to the main farmhouse, and the remaining third to preserve a circle around the whole group of buildings until summoned by a final emergency signal.

The river party would break down the hillside door at the sound of a single whistle-blast, then waiting and capturing anything which might issue from the regions within. At the sound of two whistle-blasts it would advance through the aperture to oppose the enemy or join the rest of the raiding contingent. The party at the stone building would accept these respective signals in an analogous manner; forcing an entrance at the first, and at the second descending whatever passage into the ground might be discovered, and joining the general or focal warfare expected to take place within the caverns. A third or emergency signal of three blasts would summon the immediate reserve from its general guard duty; its twenty men dividing equally and entering the unknown depths through both farmhouse and stone building. Capt. Whipple's belief in the existence of catacombs was absolute, and he took no alternative into consideration when making his plans. He had with him a whistle of great power and shrillness, and did not fear any upsetting or misunderstanding of signals. The final reserve at the landing, of course, was nearly out of the whistle's range; hence would require a special messenger if needed for help. Moses Brown and John Carter went with Capt. Hopkins to the river-bank, while President Manning was detailed with Capt. Mathewson to the stone building. Dr. Bowen, with Ezra Weeden, remained in Capt. Whipple's party which was to storm the farmhouse itself. The attack was to begin as soon as a messenger from Capt. Hopkins had joined Capt. Whipple to notify him of the river party's readiness. The leader would then deliver the loud single blast, and the various advance parties would commence their simultaneous attack on three points. Shortly before 1 a.m. the three divisions left the Fenner farmhouse; one to guard the landing, another to seek the river valley and the hillside door, and the third to subdivide and attend to the actual buildings of the Curwen farm.

Eleazar Smith, who accompanied the shore-guarding party, records in his diary an uneventful march and a long wait on the bluff by the bay; broken once by what seemed to be the distant sound of the signal whistle and again by a peculiar muffled blend of roaring and crying and a powder blast which seemed to come from the same direction. Later on one man thought he caught some distant gunshots, and still later Smith himself felt the throb of titanic and thunderous words resounding in upper air. It was just before dawn that a single haggard messenger with wild eyes and a hideous unknown odor about his clothing appeared and told the detachment to disperse quietly to their homes and never again think or speak of the night's doings or of him who had been Joseph Curwen. Something about the bearing of the messenger carried a conviction which his mere words could never have conveyed; for though he was a seaman well known to many of them, there was something obscurely lost or gained in his soul which set him for evermore apart. It was the same later on when they met other old companions who had gone into that zone of horror. Most of them had lost or gained something imponderable and indescribable. They had seen or heard or felt something which was not for human creatures, and could not forget it. From them there was never any gossip, for to even the commonest of mortal instincts there are terrible boundaries. And from that single messenger the party at the shore caught a nameless awe which almost sealed their own lips. Very few are the rumors which ever came from any of them, and Eleazar Smith's diary is the only written record which has survived from that whole expedition which set forth from the Sign of the Golden Lion under the stars.

Charles Ward, however, discovered another vague sidelight in some Fenner correspondence which he found in New London, where he knew another branch of the family had lived. It seems that the Fenners, from whose house the doomed farm was distantly visible, had watched the departing columns of raiders; and had heard very clearly the angry barking of the Curwen dogs, followed by the first shrill blast which precipitated the attack. This blast had been followed by a repetition of the great shaft of light from the stone building, and in another moment, after a quick sounding of the second signal ordering a general invasion, there had come a subdued prattle of musketry followed by a horrible roaring cry which the correspondent Luke Fenner had represented in his epistle by the characters *"Waaaahrrrrr— R'waaahrrr."* This cry, however, had possessed a quality which no mere writing could convey, and the correspondent mentions that his mother fainted completely at the sound. It was later repeated less loudly, and further but more muffled evidences of gunfire ensued; together with a loud explosion of powder from the direction of the river. About an hour afterward all the dogs began to bark frightfully, and there were vague ground rumblings so marked that the candlesticks tottered on the mantelpiece. A strong smell of sulfur was noted; and Luke Fenner's father declared that he heard the third or emergency whistle signal, though the others failed to detect it. Muffled musketry sounded again, followed by a deep scream less piercing but even more horrible than those which had preceded it; a kind of throaty, nastily plastic cough or gurgle whose quality as a scream must have come more from its continuity and psychological import than from its actual acoustic value.

Then the flaming thing burst into sight at a point where the Curwen farm ought to lie, and the human cries of desperate and frightened men were heard. Muskets flashed and cracked, and the flaming thing fell to the ground. A second flaming thing appeared, and a shriek of human origin was plainly distinguished. Fenner wrote that he could even gather a few words belched in frenzy: "Almighty, protect thy lamb!" Then there were more shots, and the second flaming thing fell. After that came silence for about three-quarters of an hour; at the end of which time little Arthur Fenner, Luke's brother, exclaimed that he saw "a red fog" going up to the stars from the accursed farm in the distance. No one but the child can testify to this, but Luke admits the significant coincidence implied by the panic of almost convulsive fright which at the same moment arched the backs and stiffened the fur of the three cats then within the room.

Five minutes later a chill wind blew up, and the air became suffused with such an intolerable stench that only the strong freshness of the sea could have prevented its being noticed by the shore party or by any wakeful souls in Pawtuxet village. This stench was nothing which any of the Fenners had ever encountered before, and produced a kind of clutching, amorphous fear beyond that of the tomb or the charnel-house. Close upon it came the awful voice which no hapless hearer will ever be able to forget. It thundered out of the sky like a doom, and windows rattled as its echoes died away. It was deep and musical; powerful as a bass organ, but evil as the forbidden books of the Arabs. What it said no man can tell, for it spoke in an unknown tongue, but this is the writing Luke Fenner set down to portray the daemoniac intonations: "DEESMEES-JESHET-BONE DOSEFE DUVEMA-ENITEMOSS." Not till the year 1919 did any soul link this crude transcript with anything else in mortal knowledge, but Charles Ward paled as he recognized what Mirandola had denounced in shudders as the ultimate horror among black magic's incantations.

An unmistakably human shout or deep chorused scream seemed to answer this malign wonder from the Curwen farm, after which the unknown stench grew complex with an added odor equally intolerable. A wailing distinctly different from the scream now burst out, and was protracted ululantly in rising and falling paroxysms. At times it became almost articulate, though no auditor could trace any definite words; and at one point it seemed to verge toward the confines of diabolic and hysterical laughter. Then a yell of utter, ultimate fright and stark madness wrenched from scores of human throats—a yell which came strong and clear despite the depth from which it must have burst; after which darkness and silence ruled all things. Spirals of acrid smoke ascended to blot out the stars, though no flames appeared and no buildings were observed to be gone or injured on the following day.

Toward dawn two frightened messengers with monstrous and unplaceable odors saturating their clothing knocked at the Fenner door and requested a keg of rum, for which they paid very well indeed. One of them told the family that the affair of Joseph Curwen was over, and that the events of the night were not to be mentioned again. Arrogant as the order seemed, the aspect of him who gave it took away all resentment and lent it a fearsome authority; so that only these furtive letters of Luke Fenner, which he urged his Connecticut relative to destroy, remain to tell what was seen and heard. The non-compliance of that relative, whereby the letters were saved after all, has alone kept the matter from a merciful oblivion. Charles Ward had one detail to add as a result of a long canvass of Pawtuxet residents for ancestral traditions. Old Charles Slocum of that village said that there was known to his grandfather a queer rumor concerning a charred, distorted body found in the fields a week after the death of Joseph Curwen was announced. What kept the talk alive was the notion that this body, so far as could be seen in its burned and twisted condition, was neither thoroughly human nor wholly allied to any animal which Pawtuxet folk had ever seen or read about.

6

Not one man who participated in that terrible raid could ever be induced to say a word concerning it, and every fragment of the vague data which survives comes from those outside the final fighting party. There is something frightful in the care with which these actual raiders destroyed each scrap which bore the least allusion to the matter. Eight sailors had been killed, but although their bodies were not produced their families were satisfied with the statement that a clash with customs officers had occurred. The same statement also covered the numerous cases of wounds, all of which were extensively bandaged and treated only by Dr. Jabez Bowen, who had accompanied the party. Hardest to explain was the nameless odor clinging to all the raiders, a thing which was discussed for weeks. Of the citizen leaders, Capt. Whipple and Moses Brown were most severely hurt, and letters of their wives testify the bewilderment which their reticence and close guarding of their bandages produced. Psychologically every participant was aged, sobered, and shaken. It is fortunate that they were all strong men of action and simple, orthodox religionists, for with more subtle introspectiveness and mental complexity they would have fared ill indeed. President Manning was the most disturbed; but even he outgrew the darkest shadow, and smothered memories in prayers. Every man of those leaders had a stirring part to play in later years, and it is perhaps fortunate that this is so. Little more than a twelvemonth afterward Capt. Whipple led the mob who burned the revenue ship *Gaspee*, and in this bold act we may trace one step in the blotting out of unwholesome images.

There was delivered to the widow of Joseph Curwen a sealed leaden coffin of curious design, obviously found ready on the spot when needed, in which she was told her husband's body lay. He had, it was explained, been killed in a customs battle about which it was not politic to give details. More than this no tongue ever uttered of Joseph Curwen's end, and Charles Ward had only a single hint wherewith to construct a theory. This hint was the merest thread—a shaky underscoring of a passage in Jedediah Orne's confiscated letter to Curwen, as partly copied in Ezra Weeden's handwriting. The copy was found in the possession of Smith's descendants; and we are left to decide whether Weeden gave it to his companion after the end, as a mute clue to the abnormality which had occurred, or whether, as is more probable, Smith had it before, and added the underscoring himself from what he had managed to extract from his friend by shrewd guessing and adroit cross-questioning. The underlined passage is merely this:

> *I say to you againe, doe not call up Any that you can not put downe; by the Which I meane, Any that can in Turne call up somewhat against you, whereby your Powerfullest Devices may not be of use. Ask of the Lesser, lest the Greater shall not wish to Answer, and shall commande more than you.*

In the light of this passage, and reflecting on what last unmentionable allies a beaten man might try to summon in his direst extremity, Charles Ward may well have wondered whether any citizen of Providence killed Joseph Curwen.

The deliberate effacement of every memory of the dead man from Providence life and annals was vastly aided by the influence of the raiding leaders. They had not at first meant to be so thorough, and had allowed the widow and her father and child to remain in ignorance of the true conditions; but Capt. Tillinghast was an astute man, and soon uncovered enough rumors to whet his horror and cause him to demand that his daughter and granddaughter change their name, burn the library and all remaining papers, and chisel the inscription from the slate slab above Joseph Curwen's grave. He knew Capt. Whipple well, and probably extracted more hints from that bluff mariner than anyone else ever gained respecting the end of the accused sorcerer.

From that time on the obliteration of Curwen's memory became increasingly rigid, extending at last by common consent even to the town records and files of the *Gazette*. It can be compared in spirit only to the hush that lay on Oscar Wilde's name for a decade after his disgrace, and in extent only to the fate of that sinful King of Runazar in Lord Dunsany's tale, whom the Gods decided must not only cease to be, but must cease ever to have been.

Mrs. Tillinghast, as the widow became known after 1772, sold the house in Olney Court and resided with her father in Power's Lane till her death in 1817. The farm at Pawtuxet, shunned by every living soul, remained to molder through the years; and seemed to decay with unaccountable rapidity. By 1780 only the stone and brickwork were standing, and by 1800 even these had fallen to shapeless heaps. None ventured to pierce the tangled shrubbery on the river-bank behind which the hillside door may have lain, nor did any try to frame a definite image of the scenes amidst which Joseph Curwen departed from the horrors he had wrought.

Only robust old Capt. Whipple was heard by alert listeners to mutter once in a while to himself, "Pox on that ———, but he had no business to laugh while he screamed. 'Twas as though the damn'd ——— had some'at up his sleeve. For half a crown I'd burn his ——— house."

III. A Search and an Evocation

1

Charles Ward, as we have seen, first learned in 1918 of his descent from Joseph Curwen. That he at once took an intense interest in everything pertaining to the bygone mystery is not to be wondered at; for every vague rumor that he had heard of Curwen now became something vital to himself, in whom flowed Curwen's blood. No spirited and imaginative genealogist could have done otherwise than begin forthwith an avid and systematic collection of Curwen data.

In his first delvings there was not the slightest attempt at secrecy; so that even Dr. Lyman hesitates to date the youth's madness from any period before the close of 1919. He talked freely with his family—though his mother was not particularly pleased to own an ancestor like Curwen—and with the officials of the various museums and libraries he visited. In applying to private families for records thought to be in their possession he made no concealment of his object, and shared the somewhat amused skepticism with which the accounts of the old diarists and letter-writers were regarded. He often expressed a keen wonder as to what really had taken place a century and a half before at that Pawtuxet farmhouse whose site he vainly tried to find, and what Joseph Curwen really had been.

When he came across the Smith diary and archives and encountered the letter from Jedediah Orne he decided to visit Salem and look up Curwen's early activities and connexions there, which he did during the Easter vacation of 1919. At the Essex Institute, which was well known to him from former sojourns in the glamorous old town of crumbling Puritan gables and clustered gambrel roofs, he was very kindly received, and unearthed there a considerable amount of Curwen data. He found that his ancestor was born in Salem-Village, now Danvers, seven miles from town, on the eighteenth of February (O.S.) 1662-3; and that he had run away to sea at the age of fifteen, not appearing again for nine years, when he returned with the speech, dress, and manners of a native Englishman and settled in Salem proper. At that time he had little to do with his family, but spent most of his hours with the curious books he had brought from Europe, and the strange chemicals which came for him on ships from England, France, and Holland. Certain trips of his into the country were the objects of much local inquisitiveness, and were whisperingly associated with vague rumors of fires on the hills at night.

Curwen's only close friends had been one Edward Hutchinson of Salem-Village and one Simon Orne of Salem. With these men he was often seen in conference about the Common, and visits among them were by no means infrequent. Hutchinson had a house well out toward the woods, and it was not altogether liked by sensitive people because of the sounds heard there at night. He was said to entertain strange visitors, and the lights seen from his windows were not always of the same color. The knowledge he displayed concerning long-dead persons and long-forgotten events was considered distinctly unwholesome, and he disappeared about the time the witchcraft panic began, never to be heard from again. At that time Joseph Curwen also departed, but his settlement in Providence was soon learned of. Simon Orne lived in Salem until 1720, when his failure to grow visibly old began to excite attention. He thereafter disappeared, though thirty years later his precise counterpart and self-styled son turned up to claim his property. The claim was allowed on the strength of documents in Simon Orne's known hand, and Jedediah Orne continued to dwell in Salem till 1771, when certain letters from Providence citizens to the Rev. Thomas Barnard and others brought about his quiet removal to parts unknown.

Certain documents by and about all of these strange characters were available at the Essex Institute, the Court House, and the Registry of Deeds, and included both harmless commonplaces such as land titles and bills of sale, and furtive fragments of a more provocative nature. There were four or five unmistakable allusions to them on the witchcraft trial records; as when one Hepzibah Lawson swore on July 10, 1692, at the Court of Oyer and Terminer under Judge Hathorne, that "fortie Witches and the Blacke Man were wont to meete in the Woodes behind Mr. Hutchinson's house," and one Amity How declared at a session of August 8th before Judge Gedney that "Mr. G. B. (Rev. George Burroughs) on that

Nighte putt ye Divell his Marke upon Bridget S., Jonathan A., *Simon O.*, Deliverance W., *Joseph C.*, Susan P., Mehitable C., and Deborah B." Then there was a catalog of Hutchinson's uncanny library as found after his disappearance, and an unfinished manuscript in his handwriting, couched in a cipher none could read. Ward had a photostatic copy of this manuscript made, and began to work casually on the cipher as soon as it was delivered to him. After the following August his labors on the cipher became intense and feverish, and there is reason to believe from his speech and conduct that he hit upon the key before October or November. He never stated, though, whether or not he had succeeded.

But of the greatest immediate interest was the Orne material. It took Ward only a short time to prove from identity of penmanship a thing he had already considered established from the text of the letter to Curwen; namely, that Simon Orne and his supposed son were one and the same person. As Orne had said to his correspondent, it was hardly safe to live too long in Salem, hence he resorted to a thirty-year sojourn abroad, and did not return to claim his lands except as a representative of a new generation. Orne had apparently been careful to destroy most of his correspondence, but the citizens who took action in 1771 found and preserved a few letters and papers which excited their wonder. There were cryptic formulae and diagrams in his and other hands which Ward now either copied with care or had photographed, and one extremely mysterious letter in a chirography that the searcher recognized from items in the Registry of Deeds as positively Joseph Curwen's.

This Curwen letter, though undated as to the year, was evidently not the one in answer to which Orne had written the confiscated missive; and from internal evidence Ward placed it not much later than 1750. It may not be amiss to give the text in full, as a sample of the style of one whose history was so dark and terrible. The recipient is addressed as "Simon," but a line (whether drawn by Curwen or Orne Ward could not tell) is run through the word.

Prouidence, I. May (Ut. vulgo)

Brother:—

My honor'd Antient ffriende, due Respects and earnest
Wishes to Him whom we serue for yr eternall Power.
I am just come upon That which you ought to knowe,
concern'g the Matter of the Laste Extremitie and what
to doe regard'g yt. I am not dispos'd to followe you
in go'g Away on acct. of my Yeares, for Prouidence
hath not ye Sharpeness of ye Bay in hunt'g oute
uncommon Things and bringinge to Tryall. I am ty'd
up in Shippes and Goodes, and cou'd not doe as you
did, besides the Whiche my ffarme at Patuxet hath
under it What you Knowe, that wou'd not waite for
my com'g Backe as an Other.

But I am not unreadie for harde ffortunes, as I haue
tolde you, and haue longe work'd upon ye Way of get'g
Backe after ye Laste. I laste Night strucke on ye Wordes
that bringe up YOGGE-SOTHOTHE, and sawe for ye
firste Time that fface spoke of by Ibn Schacabao in ye
——. And IT said, that ye III Psalme in ye Liber-
Damnatus holdes ye Clauicle. With Sunne in V House,
Saturne in Trine, drawe ye Pentagram of Fire, and saye
ye ninth Uerse thrice. This Uerse repeate eache
Roodemas and Hallow's Eue; and ye Thing will breede
in ye Outside Spheres.

*And of ye Seede of Olde shal One be borne who
shal looke Backe, tho' know'g not what he seekes.*

Yett will this availe Nothing if there be no Heir, and
if the Saltes, or the Way to make the Saltes, bee not
Readie for his Hande; and here I will owne, I have not
taken needed Stepps nor founde Much. Ye Process is
plaguy harde to come neare; and it uses up such a
Store of Specimens, I am harde putte to it to get Enough,
notwithstand'g the Sailors I have from ye Indies. Ye
People aboute are become curious, but I can stande

them off. Ye Gentry are worse than the Populace, be'g more Circumstantiall in their Accts. and more believ'd in what they tell. That Parson and Mr. Merritt have talk'd some, I am fearfull, but no Thing soe far is Dangerous. Ye Chymical substances are easie of get'g, there be'g II. goode Chymists in Towne, Dr. Bowen and Sam: Carew. I am foll'g oute what Borellus saith, and haue Helpe in Abdool Al-Hazred his VII. Booke. Whatever I gette, you shal haue. And in ye meane while, do not neglect to make use of ye Wordes I haue here giuen. I haue them Righte, but if you Desire to see HIM, imploy the Writings on ye Piece of —— that I am putt'g in this Packet. Saye ye Uerses every Roodmas and Hallow's Eue; and if yr Line runn out not, *one shall bee in yeares to come that shal looke backe and use what Saltes or Stuff for Saltes you shal leaue him.* Job XIV. XIV.

I rejoice you are again at Salem, and hope I may see you not longe hence. I have a goode Stallion, and am think'g of get'g a Coach, there be'g one (Mr. Merritt's) in Prouidence already, tho' ye Roades are bad. If you are dispos'd to Travel, doe not pass me bye. From Boston take ye Post Rd. thro' Dedham, Wrentham, and Attleborough, goode Tavernes be'g at all these Townes. Stop at Mr. Bolcom's in Wrentham, where ye Beddes are finer than Mr. Hatch's, but eate at ye other House for their Cooke is better. Turne into Prou. by Patucket ffalls, and ye Rd. past Mr. Sayles's Tavern. My House opp. Mr. Epenetus Olney's Tavern off ye Towne Street, Ist on ye N. side of Olney's Court. Distance from Boston Stone abt. XLIV Miles.

Sir, I am yr olde and true ffriend and Servt. in *Almousin-Metraton.*

Josephus C.

To Mr. Simon Orne,
William's-Lane, in Salem.

This letter, oddly enough, was what first gave Ward the exact location of Curwen's Providence home; for none of the records encountered up to that time had been at all specific. The discovery was doubly striking because it indicated as the newer Curwen house built in 1761 on the site of the old, a dilapidated building still standing in Olney Court and well known to Ward in his antiquarian rambles over Stampers' Hill. The place was indeed only a few squares from his own home on the great hill's higher ground, and was now the abode of a negro family much esteemed for occasional washing, housecleaning, and furnace-tending services. To find, in distant Salem, such sudden proof of the significance of this familiar rookery in his own family history, was a highly impressive thing to Ward; and he resolved to explore the place immediately upon his return. The more mystical phases of the letter, which he took to be some extravagant kind of symbolism, frankly baffled him; though he noted with a thrill of curiosity that the Biblical passage referred to—Job 14, 14—was the familiar verse, "If a man die, shall he live again? All the days of my appointed time will I wait, till my change come."

2

Young Ward came home in a state of pleasant excitement, and spent the following Saturday in a long and exhaustive study of the house in Olney Court. The place, now crumbling with age, had never been a mansion; but was a modest two-and-a-half story wooden town house of the familiar Providence colonial type, with plain peaked roof, large central chimney, and artistically carved doorway with rayed fanlight, triangular pediment, and trim Doric pilasters. It had suffered but little alteration externally, and Ward felt he was gazing on something very close to the sinister matters of his quest.

The present negro inhabitants were known to him, and he was very courteously shewn about the interior by old Asa and his stout wife Hannah. Here there was more change than the outside indicated, and Ward saw with regret that fully half of the fine scroll-and-urn overmantels and shell-carved cupboard linings were gone, whilst much of the fine wainscotting and bolection molding was marked, hacked, and gouged, or covered up altogether with cheap wall-paper. In general, the survey did not yield as much as Ward had somehow expected; but it was at least exciting to stand within the ancestral walls which had housed such a man of horror as Joseph Curwen. He saw with a thrill that a monogram had been very carefully effaced from the ancient brass knocker.

From then until after the close of school Ward spent his time on the photostatic copy of the Hutchinson cipher and the accumulation of local Curwen data. The former still proved unyielding; but of the latter he obtained so much, and so many clues to similar data elsewhere, that he was ready by July to make a trip to New London and New York to consult old letters whose presence in those places was indicated. This trip was very fruitful, for it brought him the Fenner letters with their terrible description of the Pawtuxet farmhouse raid, and the Nightingale-Talbot letters in which he learned of the portrait painted on a panel of the Curwen library. This matter of the portrait interested him particularly, since he would have given much to know just what Joseph Curwen looked like; and he decided to make a second search of the house in Olney Court to see if there might not be some trace of the ancient features beneath peeling coats of later paint or layers of moldy wall-paper.

Early in August that search took place, and Ward went carefully over the walls of every room sizeable enough to have been by any possibility the library of the evil builder. He paid especial attention to the large panels of such overmantels as still remained; and was keenly excited after about an hour, when on a broad area above the fireplace in a spacious ground-floor room he became certain that the surface brought out by the peeling of several coats of paint was sensibly darker than any ordinary interior paint or the wood beneath it was likely to have been. A few more careful tests with a thin knife, and he knew that he had come upon an oil portrait of great extent. With truly scholarly restraint the youth did not risk the damage which an immediate attempt to uncover the hidden picture with the knife might have done, but just retired from the scene of his discovery to enlist expert help. In three days he returned with an artist of long experience, Mr. Walter C. Dwight, whose studio is near the foot of College Hill; and that accomplished restorer of paintings set to work at once with proper methods and chemical substances. Old Asa and his wife were duly excited over their strange visitors, and were properly reimbursed for this invasion of their domestic hearth.

As day by day the work of restoration progressed, Charles Ward looked on with growing interest at the lines and shades gradually unveiled after their long oblivion. Dwight had begun at the bottom; hence since the picture was a three-quarter-length one, the face did not come out for some time. It was meanwhile seen that the subject was a spare, well-shaped man with dark-blue coat, embroidered waistcoat, black satin small-clothes, and white silk stockings, seated in a carved chair against the background of a window with wharves and ships beyond. When the head came out it was observed to bear a neat Albemarle wig, and to possess a thin, calm, undistinguished face which seemed somehow familiar to both Ward and the artist. Only at the very last, though, did the restorer and his client begin to gasp with astonishment at the details of that lean, pallid visage, and to recognize with a touch of awe the dramatic trick which heredity had played. For it took the final bath of oil and the final stroke of the delicate scraper to bring out fully the expression which centuries had hidden; and to confront the bewildered Charles Dexter Ward, dweller in the past, with his own living features in the countenance of his horrible great-great-great-grandfather.

Ward brought his parents to see the marvel he had uncovered, and his father at once determined to purchase the picture despite its execution on stationary paneling. The resemblance to the boy, despite an appearance of rather greater age, was marvelous; and it could be seen that through some trick of atavism the physical contours of Joseph Curwen had found precise duplication after a century and a half. Mrs. Ward's resemblance to her ancestor was not at all marked, though she could recall relatives who had some of the facial characteristics shared by her son and by the bygone Curwen. She did not relish the discovery, and told her husband that he had better burn the picture instead of bringing it home. There was, she averred, something unwholesome about it; not only intrinsically, but in its very resemblance to Charles. Mr. Ward, however, was a practical man of power and affairs—a cotton manufacturer with extensive mills at Riverpoint in the Pawtuxet Valley—and not one to listen to feminine scruples. The picture impressed him mightily with its likeness to his son, and he believed the boy deserved it as a present. In this opinion, it is needless to say, Charles most heartily concurred; and a few days later Mr. Ward located the owner of the house—a small rodent-featured person with a guttural accent—and obtained the whole mantel and overmantel bearing the picture at a curtly fixed priced which cut short the impending torrent of unctuous haggling.

It now remained to take off the paneling and remove it to the Ward home, where provisions were made for its thorough restoration and installation with an electric mock-fireplace in Charles's third-floor study or library. To Charles was left the task of superintending this removal, and on the twenty-eighth of August he accompanied two expert workmen from the Crooker decorating firm to the house in Olney Court, where the mantel and portrait-bearing overmantel were detached with great care and precision for transportation in the company's motor truck. There was left a space of exposed brickwork marking the chimney's course, and in this young Ward observed a cubical recess about a foot square, which must have lain directly behind the head of the portrait. Curious as to what such a space might mean or contain, the youth approached and looked within; finding beneath the deep coatings of dust and soot some loose yellowed papers, a crude, thick copybook, and a few moldering textile shreds which may have formed the ribbon binding the rest together. Blowing away the bulk of the dirt and cinders, he took up the book and looked at the bold inscription on its cover. It was in a hand which he had learned to recognize at the Essex Institute, and proclaimed the volume as the *"Journall and Notes of Jos: Curwen, Gent., of Providence-Plantations, Late of Salem."*

Excited beyond measure by his discovery, Ward shewed the book to the two curious workmen beside him. Their testimony is absolute as to the nature and genuineness of the finding, and Dr. Willett relies on them to help establish his theory that the youth was not mad when he began his major eccentricities. All the other papers were likewise in Curwen's handwriting, and one of them seemed especially portentous because of its inscription: *"To Him Who Shal Come After, & How He May Gett Beyonde Time & ye Spheres."* Another was in a cipher; the same, Ward hoped, as the Hutchinson cipher which had hitherto baffled him. A third, and here the searcher rejoiced, seemed to be a key to the cipher; whilst the fourth and fifth were addressed respectively to "Edw: Hutchinson, Armiger" and "Jedediah Orne, Esq.," "or Their Heir or Heirs, or Those Represent'g Them." The sixth and last was inscribed: *"Joseph Curwen his Life and Travells Bet'n ye yeares 1678 and 1687: Of Whither He Voyag'd, Where He Stay'd, Whom He Sawe, and What He Learnt."*

3

We have now reached the point from which the more academic school of alienists date Charles Ward's madness. Upon his discovery the youth had looked immediately at a few of the inner pages of the book and manuscripts, and had evidently seen something which impressed him tremendously.

Indeed, in shewing the titles to the workmen he appeared to guard the text itself with peculiar care, and to labor under a perturbation for which even the antiquarian and genealogical significance of the find could hardly account. Upon returning home he broke the news with an almost embarrassed air, as if he wished to convey an idea of its supreme importance without having to exhibit the evidence itself. He did not even shew the titles to his parents, but simply told them that he had found some documents in Joseph Curwen's handwriting, "mostly in cipher," which would have to be studied very carefully before yielding up their true meaning. It is unlikely that he would have shewn what he did to the workmen, had it not been for their unconcealed curiosity. As it was he doubtless wished to avoid any display of peculiar reticence which would increase their discussion of the matter.

That night Charles Ward sat up in his room reading the new-found book and papers, and when day came he did not desist. His meals, on his urgent request when his mother called to see what was amiss, were sent up to him; and in the afternoon he appeared only briefly when the men came to install the Curwen picture and mantelpiece in his study. The next night he slept in snatches in his clothes, meanwhile wrestling feverishly with the unraveling of the cipher manuscript. In the morning his mother saw that he was at work on the photostatic copy of the Hutchinson cipher, which he had frequently shewn her before; but in response to her query he said that the Curwen key could not be applied to it. That afternoon he abandoned his work and watched the men fascinatedly as they finished their installation of the picture with its woodwork above a cleverly realistic electric log, setting the mock-fireplace and overmantel a little out from the north wall as if a chimney existed, and boxing in the sides with paneling to match the room's. The front panel holding the picture was sawn and hinged to allow cupboard space behind it. After the workmen went he moved his work into the study and sat down before it with his eyes half on the cipher and half on the portrait which stared back at him like a year-adding and century-recalling mirror.

His parents, subsequently recalling his conduct at this period, give interesting details anent the policy of concealment which he practiced. Before servants he seldom hid any paper which he might be studying, since he rightly assumed that Curwen's intricate and archaic chirography would be too much for them. With his parents, however, he was more circumspect; and unless the manuscript in question were a cipher, or a mere mass of cryptic symbols and unknown ideographs (as that entitled *"To Him Who Shal Come After* etc." seemed to be), he would cover it with some convenient paper until his caller had departed. At night he kept the papers under lock and key in an antique cabinet of his, where he also placed them whenever he left the room. He soon resumed fairly regular hours and habits, except that his long walks and other outside interests seemed to cease. The opening of school, where he now began his senior year, seemed a great bore to him; and he frequently asserted his determination never to bother with college. He had, he said, important special investigations to make, which would provide him with more avenues toward knowledge and the humanities than any university which the world could boast.

Naturally, only one who had always been more or less studious, eccentric, and solitary could have pursued this course for many days without attracting notice. Ward, however, was constitutionally a scholar and a hermit; hence his parents were less surprised than regretful at the close confinement and secrecy he adopted. At the same time, both his father and mother thought it odd that he would shew them no scrap of his treasure-trove, nor give any connected account of such data as he had deciphered. This reticence he explained away as due to a wish to wait until he might announce some connected revelation, but as the weeks passed without further disclosures there began to grow up between the youth and his family a kind of constraint; intensified in his mother's case by her manifest disapproval of all Curwen delvings.

During October Ward began visiting the libraries again, but no longer for the antiquarian matter of his former days. Witchcraft and magic, occultism and daemonology, were what he sought now; and when Providence sources proved unfruitful he would take the train for Boston and tap the wealth of the great library in Copley Square, the Widener Library at Harvard, or the Zion Research Library in Brookline, where certain rare works on Biblical subjects are available. He bought extensively, and fitted up a whole additional set of shelves in his study for newly acquired works on uncanny subjects; while during the Christmas holidays he made a round of out-of-town trips including one to Salem to consult certain records at the Essex Institute.

About the middle of January, 1920, there entered Ward's bearing an element of triumph which he did not explain, and he was no more found at work upon the Hutchinson cipher. Instead, he inaugurated a dual policy of chemical research and record-scanning; fitting up for the one a laboratory in the unused attic of the house, and for the latter haunting all the sources of vital statistics in Providence. Local dealers in drugs and scientific supplies, later questioned, gave astonishingly queer and meaningless catalogs of the substances and instruments he purchased; but clerks at the State House, the City Hall, and the various libraries agree as to the definite object of his second interest. He was searching intensely and feverishly for the grave of Joseph Curwen, from whose slate slab an older generation had so wisely blotted the name.

Little by little there grew upon the Ward family the conviction that something was wrong. Charles had had freaks and changes of minor interests before, but this growing secrecy and absorption in strange pursuits was unlike even him. His school work was the merest pretence; and although he failed in no test, it could be seen that the old application had all vanished. He had other concernments now; and when not in his new laboratory with a score of obsolete alchemical books, could be found either poring over old burial records down town or glued to his volumes of occult lore in his study, where the startlingly—one almost fancied increasingly—similar features of Joseph Curwen stared blandly at him from the great overmantel on the north wall.

Late in March Ward added to his archive-searching a ghoulish series of rambles about the various ancient cemeteries of the city. The cause appeared later, when it was learned from City Hall clerks that he had probably found an important clue. His quest had suddenly shifted from the grave of Joseph Curwen to that of one Naphthali Field; and this shift was explained when, upon going over the files that he had been over, the investigators actually found a fragmentary record of Curwen's burial which had escaped the general obliteration, and which stated that the curious leaden coffin had been interred "10 ft. S. and 5 ft. W. of Naphthali Field's grave in ye—." The lack of a specified burying-ground in the surviving entry greatly complicated the search, and Naphthali Field's grave seemed as elusive as that of Curwen; but here no systematic effacement had existed, and one might reasonably be expected to stumble on the stone itself even if its record had perished. Hence the rambles—from which St. John's (the former King's) Churchyard and the ancient Congregational burying-ground in the midst of Swan Point Cemetery were excluded, since other statistics had shewn that the only Naphthali Field (*obiit* 1729), whose grave could have been meant, had been a Baptist.

4

It was toward May when Dr. Willett, at the request of the senior Ward, and fortified with all the Curwen data which the family had gleaned from Charles in his non-secretive days, talked with the young man. The interview was of little value or conclusiveness, for Willett felt at every moment that Charles was thoroughly master of himself and in touch with matters of real importance; but it at least forced the secretive youth to offer some rational explanation of his recent demeanor. Of a pallid, impassive type not easily shewing embarrassment, Ward seemed quite ready to discuss his pursuits, though not to reveal their object. He stated that the papers of his ancestor had contained some remarkable secrets of early scientific knowledge, for the most part in cipher, of an apparent scope comparable only to the discoveries of Friar Bacon and perhaps surpassing even those. They were, however, meaningless except when correlated with a body of learning now wholly obsolete; so that their immediate presentation to a world equipped only with modern science would rob them of all impressiveness and dramatic significance. To take their vivid place in the history of human thought they must first be correlated by one familiar with the background out of which they evolved, and to this task of correlation Ward was now devoting himself. He was seeking to acquire as fast as possible those neglected arts of old which a true interpreter of the Curwen data must possess, and hoped in time to make a full announcement and presentation of the utmost interest to mankind and to the world of thought. Not even Einstein, he declared, could more profoundly revolutionize the current conception of things.

As to his graveyard search, whose object he freely admitted, but the details of whose progress he did not relate, he said he had reason to think that Joseph Curwen's mutilated headstone bore certain mystic symbols—carved from directions in his will and ignorantly spared by those who had effaced the name—which were absolutely essential to the final solution of his cryptic system. Curwen, he believed, had wished to guard his secret with care; and had consequently distributed the data in an exceedingly curious fashion. When Dr. Willett asked to see the mystic documents, Ward displayed much reluctance and tried to put him off with such things as photostatic copies of the Hutchinson cipher and Orne formulae and diagrams; but finally shewed him the exteriors of some of the real Curwen finds—the *"Journall and Notes,"* the cipher (title in cipher also), and the formula-filled message *"To Him Who Shal Come After"*—and let him glance inside such as were in obscure characters.

He also opened the diary at a page carefully selected for its innocuousness and gave Willett a glimpse of Curwen's connected handwriting in English. The doctor noted very closely the crabbed and complicated letters, and the general aura of the seventeenth century which clung round both penmanship and style despite the writer's survival into the eighteenth century, and became quickly certain that the document was genuine. The text itself was relatively trivial, and Willett recalled only a fragment:

> Wedn. 16 Octr. 1754. My Sloope the *Wakeful* this Day putt in from London with XX newe Men pick'd up in ye Indies, Spaniards from Martineco and 2 Dutch Men from Surinam. Ye Dutch Men are like to Desert from have'g hearde Somewhat ill of these Ventures, but I will see to ye Inducing of them to Staye. ffor Mr. Knight Dexter of ye Boy and Book 120 Pieces Camblets, 100 Pieces Assrtd. Cambleteens, 20 Pieces blue Duffles, 100 Pieces Shalloons, 50 Pieces Calamancoes, 300 Pieces each, Shendsoy and Humhums. ffor Mr. Green at ye Elephant 50 Gallon Cyttles, 20 Warm'g Pannes, 15 Bake Cyttles, 10 pr. Smoke'g Tonges. ffor Mr. Perrigo 1 Sett of Awles, ffor Mr. Nightingale 50 Reames prime Foolscap. Say'd ye SABAOTH thrice last Nighte but None appear'd. I must heare more from Mr. H. in Transylvania, tho' it is Harde reach'g him and exceeding strange he can not give me the Use of what he hath so well us'd these hundred yeares. Simon hath not Writ these V. Weekes, but I expecte soon hear'g from him.

When upon reaching this point Dr. Willett turned the leaf he was quickly checked by Ward, who almost snatched the book from his grasp. All that the doctor had a chance to see on the newly opened page was a brief pair of sentences; but these, strangely enough, lingered tenaciously in his memory. They ran: "Ye Verse from Liber-Damnatus be'g spoke V Roodmasses and IV Hallows-Eves, I am Hopeful ye Thing is breed'g Outside ye Spheres. It will drawe One who is to Come, if I can make sure he shal bee, and he shall think on Past thinges and look back thro' all ye yeares, against ye which I must have ready ye Saltes or That to make 'em with."

Willett saw no more, but somehow this small glimpse gave a new and vague terror to the painted features of Joseph Curwen which stared blandly down from the overmantel. Ever after that he entertained the odd fancy—which his medical skill of course assured him was only a fancy—that the eyes of the portrait had a sort of wish, if not an actual tendency, to follow young Charles Ward as he moved about the room. He stopped before leaving to study the picture closely, marveling at its resemblance to Charles and memorizing every minute detail of the cryptical, colorless face, even down to a slight scar or pit in the smooth brow above the right eye. Cosmo Alexander, he decided, was a painter worthy of the Scotland that produced Raeburn, and a teacher worthy of his illustrious pupil Gilbert Stuart.

Assured by the doctor that Charles's mental health was in no danger, but that on the other hand he was engaged in researches which might prove of real importance, the Wards were more lenient than they might otherwise have been when during the following June the youth made positive his refusal to attend college. He had, he declared, studies of much more vital importance to pursue; and intimated a wish to go abroad the following year in order to avail himself of certain sources of data not existing in America. The senior Ward, while denying this latter wish as absurd for a boy of only eighteen, acquiesced regarding the university; so that after a none too brilliant graduation from the Moses Brown School there ensued for Charles a three-year period of intensive occult study and graveyard searching. He became recognized as an eccentric, and dropped even more completely from the sight of his family's friends than he had been before; keeping close to his work and only occasionally making trips to other cities to consult obscure records. Once he went south to talk with a strange old mulatto who dwelt in a swamp and about whom a newspaper had printed a curious article. Again he sought a small village in the Adirondacks whence reports of certain odd ceremonial practices had come. But still his parents forbade him the trip to the Old World which he desired.

Coming of age in April, 1923, and having previously inherited a small competence from his maternal grandfather, Ward determined at last to take the European trip hitherto denied him. Of his proposed itinerary he would say nothing save that the needs of his studies would carry him to many places, but he promised to write his parents fully and faithfully. When they saw he could not be dissuaded, they ceased all opposition and helped as best they could; so that in June the young man sailed for Liverpool with the farewell blessings of his father and mother, who accompanied him to Boston and waved him out of sight from the White Star pier in Charlestown. Letters soon told of his safe arrival, and of his securing good quarters in Great Russell Street, London; where he proposed to stay, shunning all family friends, till he had exhausted the resources of the British Museum in a certain direction. Of his daily life he wrote but little, for there was little to write. Study and experiment consumed all his time, and he mentioned a laboratory which he had established in one of his rooms. That he said nothing of antiquarian rambles in the glamorous old city with its luring skyline of ancient domes and steeples and its tangles of roads and alleys whose mystic convolutions and sudden vistas alternately beckon and surprise, was taken by his parents as a good index of the degree to which his new interests had engrossed his mind.

In June, 1924, a brief note told of his departure for Paris, to which he had before made one or two flying trips for material in the Bibliothèque Nationale. For three months thereafter he sent only postal cards, giving an address in the Rue St. Jacques and referring to a special search among rare manuscripts in the library of an unnamed private collector. He avoided acquaintances, and no tourists brought back reports of having seen him. Then came a silence, and in October the Wards received a picture card from Prague, Czecho-Slovakia, stating that Charles was in that ancient town for the purpose of conferring with a certain very aged man supposed to be the last living possessor of some very curious medieval information. He gave an address in the Neustadt, and announced no move till the following January; when he dropped several cards from Vienna telling of his passage through that city on the way toward a more easterly region whither one of his correspondents and fellow-delvers into the occult had invited him.

The next card was from Klausenburg in Transylvania, and told of Ward's progress toward his destination. He was going to visit a Baron Ferenczy, whose estate lay in the mountains east of Rakus; and was to be addressed at Rakus in the care of that nobleman. Another card from Rakus a week later, saying that his host's carriage had met him and that he was leaving the village for the mountains, was his last message for a considerable time; indeed, he did not reply to his parents' frequent letters until May, when he wrote to discourage the plan of his mother for a meeting in London, Paris, or Rome during the summer, when the elder Wards were planning to travel in Europe. His researches, he said, were such that he could not leave his present quarters; while the situation of Baron Ferenczy's castle did not favor visits. It was on a crag in the dark wooded mountains, and the region was so shunned by the country folk that normal people could not help feeling ill at ease. Moreover, the Baron was not a person likely to appeal to correct and conservative New England gentlefolk. His aspect and manners had idiosyncrasies, and his age was so great as to be disquieting. It would be better, Charles said, if his parents would wait for his return to Providence; which could scarcely be far distant.

That return did not, however, take place until May, 1926, when after a few heralding cards the young wanderer quietly slipped into New York on the *Homeric* and traversed the long miles to Providence by motor-coach, eagerly drinking in the green rolling hills, the fragrant, blossoming orchards, and the white steepled towns of vernal Connecticut; his first taste of ancient New England in nearly four years. When the coach crossed the Pawcatuck and entered Rhode Island amidst the faery goldenness of a late spring afternoon his heart beat with quickened force, and the entry to Providence along Reservoir and Elmwood avenues was a breathless and wonderful thing despite the depths of forbidden lore to which he had delved. At the high square where Broad, Weybosset, and Empire Streets join, he saw before and below him in the fire of sunset the pleasant, remembered houses and domes and steeples of the old town; and his head swam curiously as the vehicle rolled down the terminal behind the Biltmore, bringing into view the great dome and soft, roof-pierced greenery of the ancient hill across the river, and the tall colonial spire of the First Baptist Church limned pink in the magic evening light against the fresh springtime verdure of its precipitous background.

Old Providence! It was this place and the mysterious forces of its long, continuous history which had brought him into being, and which had drawn him back toward marvels and secrets whose boundaries no prophet might fix. Here lay the arcana, wondrous or dreadful as the case might be, for which all his years of travel and application had been preparing him. A taxicab whirled him through Post Office Square with its glimpse of the river, the old Market House, and the head of the bay, and up the steep curved slope of Waterman Street to Prospect, where the vast gleaming dome and sunset-flushed Ionic columns of the Christian Science Church beckoned north-ward. Then eight squares past the fine old estates his childish eyes had known, and the quaint brick sidewalks so often trodden by his youthful feet. And at last the little white overtaken farmhouse

on the right, on the left the classic Adam porch and stately bayed
facade of the great brick house where he was born. It was
twilight, and Charles Dexter Ward had come home.

5

A school of alienists slightly less academic than Dr. Lyman's
assign to Ward's European trip the beginning of his true
madness. Admitting that he was sane when he started, they
believe that his conduct upon returning implies a disastrous
change. But even to this claim Dr. Willett refuses to accede.
There was, he insists, something later; and the queernesses of
the youth at this stage he attributes to the practice of rituals
learned abroad—odd enough things, to be sure, but by no means
implying mental aberration on the part of their celebrant. Ward
himself, though visibly aged and hardened, was still normal in
his general reactions; and in several talks with Willett displayed
a balance which no madman—even an incipient one—could
feign continuously for long. What elicited the notion of insanity
at this period were the *sounds* heard at all hours from Ward's
attic laboratory, in which he kept himself most of the time.
There were chantings and repetitions, and thunderous decla-
mations in uncanny rhythms; and although these sounds were
always in Ward's own voice, there was something in the quality
of that voice, and in the accents of the formulae it pronounced,
which could not but chill the blood of every hearer. It was
noticed that Nig, the venerable and beloved black cat of the
household, bristled and arched his back perceptibly when
certain of the tones were heard.

The odors occasionally wafted from the laboratory were
likewise exceedingly strange. Sometimes they were very noxious,
but more often they were aromatic, with a haunting, elusive
quality which seemed to have the power of inducing fantastic
images. People who smelled them had a tendency to glimpse

momentary mirages of enormous vistas, with strange hills or endless avenues of sphinxes and hippogriffs stretching off into infinite distance. Ward did not resume his old-time rambles, but applied himself diligently to the strange books he had brought home, and to equally strange delvings within his quarters; explaining that European sources had greatly enlarged the possibilities of his work, and promising great revelations in the years to come. His older aspect increased to a startling degree his resemblance to the Curwen portrait in his library; and Dr. Willett would often pause by the latter after a call, marveling at the virtual identity, and reflecting that only the small pit above the picture's right eye now remained to differentiate the long-dead wizard from the living youth. These calls of Willett's, undertaken at the request of the senior Wards, were curious affairs. Ward at no time repulsed the doctor, but the latter saw that he could never reach the young man's inner psychology. Frequently he noted peculiar things about; little wax images of grotesque design on the shelves or tables, and the half-erased remnants of circles, triangles, and pentagrams in chalk or charcoal on the cleared central space of the large room. And always in the night those rhythms and incantations thundered, till it became very difficult to keep servants or suppress furtive talk of Charles's madness.

In January, 1927, a peculiar incident occurred. One night about midnight, as Charles was chanting a ritual whose weird cadence echoed unpleasantly through the house below, there came a sudden gust of chill wind from the bay, and a faint, obscure trembling of the earth which everyone in the neighborhood noted. At the same time the cat exhibited phenomenal traces of fright, while dogs bayed for as much as a mile around. This was the prelude to a sharp thunderstorm, anomalous for the season, which brought with it such a crash that Mr. and Mrs. Ward believed the house had been struck. They rushed upstairs to see what damage had been done, but Charles met them at the door to the attic; pale, resolute, and portentous, with an almost fearsome combination of triumph and seriousness on his face. He assured them that the house had not really been struck, and that the storm would soon be over. They paused, and looking through a window saw that he was indeed right; for the lightning flashed farther and farther off, whilst the trees ceased to bend in the strange frigid gust from the water. The thunder sank to a sort of dull mumbling chuckle and finally died away. Stars came out, and the stamp of triumph on Charles Ward's face crystallized into a very singular expression.

For two months or more after this incident Ward was less confined than usual to his laboratory. He exhibited a curious interest in the weather, and made odd inquiries about the date of the spring thawing of the ground. One night late in March he left the house after midnight, and did not return till almost morning; when his mother, being wakeful, heard a rumbling motor draw up to the carriage entrance. Muffled oaths could be distinguished, and Mrs. Ward, rising and going to the window, saw four dark figures removing a long, heavy box from a truck at Charles's direction and carrying it within by the side door. She heard labored breathing and ponderous footfalls on the stairs, and finally a dull thumping in the attic; after which the footfalls descended again, and the four men reappeared outside and drove off in their truck.

The next day Charles resumed his strict attic seclusion, drawing down the dark shades of his laboratory windows and appearing to be working on some metal substance. He would open the door to no one, and steadfastly refused all proffered food. About noon a wrenching sound followed by a terrible cry and a fall were heard, but when Mrs. Ward rapped at the door her son at length answered faintly, and told her that nothing had gone amiss. The hideous and indescribable stench now welling out was absolutely harmless and unfortunately necessary. Solitude was the one prime essential, and he would appear later for dinner. That afternoon, after the conclusion of some odd hissing sounds which came from behind the locked portal, he did finally appear; wearing an extremely haggard aspect and forbidding anyone to enter the laboratory upon any pretext. This, indeed, proved the beginning of a new policy of secrecy; for never afterward was any other person permitted to visit either the mysterious garret workroom or the adjacent storeroom which he cleaned out, furnished roughly, and added to his inviolably private domain as a sleeping apartment. Here he lived, with books brought up from his library beneath, till the time he purchased the Pawtuxet bungalow and moved to it all his scientific effects.

In the evening Charles secured the paper before the rest of the family and damaged part of it through an apparent accident. Later on Dr. Willett, having fixed the date from statements by various members of the household, looked up an intact copy at the *Journal* office and found that in the destroyed section the following small item had occurred:

NOCTURNAL DIGGERS SURPRISED IN NORTH BURIAL GROUND

Robert Hart, night watchman at the North Burial Ground, this morning discovered a party of several men with a motor truck in the oldest part of the cemetery, but apparently frightened them off before they had accomplished whatever their object may have been.

The discovery took place at about four o'clock, when Hart's attention was attracted by the sound of a motor outside his shelter. Investigating, he saw a large truck on the main drive several rods away; but could not reach it before the sound of his feet on the gravel had revealed his approach. The men hastily placed a large box in the truck and drove away toward the street before they could be overtaken; and since no known grave was disturbed,

Hart believes that this box was an object which they wished to bury.

The diggers must have been at work for a long while before detection, for Hart found an enormous hole dug at a considerable distance back from the roadway in the lot of Amasa Field, where most of the old stones have long ago disappeared. The hole, a place as large and deep as a grave, was empty; and did not coincide with any interment mentioned in the cemetery records.

Sergt. Riley of the Second Station viewed the spot and gave the opinion that the hole was dug by bootleggers rather gruesomely and ingeniously seeking a safe cache for liquor in a place not likely to be disturbed. In reply to questions Hart said he thought the escaping truck had headed up Rochambeau Avenue, though he could not be sure.

During the next few days Ward was seldom seen by his family. Having added sleeping quarters to his attic realm, he kept closely to himself there, ordering food brought to the door and not taking it in until after the servant had gone away. The droning of monotonous formulae and the chanting of bizarre rhythms recurred at intervals, while at other times occasional listeners could detect the sound of tinkling glass, hissing chemicals, running water, or roaring gas flames. Odors of the most unplaceable quality, wholly unlike any before noted, hung at times around the door; and the air of tension observable in the young recluse whenever he did venture briefly forth was such as to excite the keenest speculation. Once he made a hasty trip to the Athenaeum for a book he required, and again he hired a messenger to fetch him a highly obscure volume from Boston. Suspense was written portentously over the whole situation, and both the family and Dr. Willett confessed themselves wholly at a loss what to do or think about it.

6

Then on the fifteenth of April a strange development occurred. While nothing appeared to grow different in kind, there was certainly a very terrible difference in degree; and Dr. Willett somehow attaches great significance to the change. The day was Good Friday, a circumstance of which the servants made much, but which others quite naturally dismiss as an irrelevant coincidence. Late in the afternoon young Ward began repeating a certain formula in a singularly loud voice, at the same time burning some substance so pungent that its fumes escaped over the entire house. The formula was so plainly audible in the hall outside the locked door that Mrs. Ward could not help memorizing it as she waited and listened anxiously, and later on she was able to write it down at Dr. Willett's request. It ran as follows, and experts have told Dr. Willett that its very close analogue can be found in the mystic writings of "Eliphas Levi," that cryptic soul who crept through a crack in the forbidden door and glimpsed the frightful vistas of the void beyond:

Per Adonai Eloim, Adonai Jehova,
Adonai Sabaoth, Metraton On Agla Mathon,
verbum pythonicum, mysterium salamandrae,
conventus sylvorum, antra gnomorum,
daemonia Coeli Gad, Almousin, Gibor, Jehosua,
Evam, Zariatnatmik, veni, veni, veni.

This had been going on for two hours without change or intermission when over all the neighborhood a pandaemoniac howling of dogs set in. The extent of this howling can be judged from the space it received in the papers the next day, but to those in the Ward household it was overshadowed by the odor which instantly followed it; a hideous, all-pervasive odor which none of them had ever smelled before or have ever smelled since. In the midst of this mephitic flood there came a very perceptible flash like that of lightning, which would have been blinding and impressive but for the daylight around; and then was heard *the voice* that no listener can ever forget because of its thunderous remoteness, its incredible depth, and its eldritch dissimilarity to Charles Ward's voice. It shook the house, and was clearly heard by at least two neighbors above the howling of the dogs. Mrs. Ward, who had been listening in despair outside her son's locked laboratory, shivered as she recognized its hellish import; for Charles had told her of its evil fame in dark books, and of the manner in which it had thundered, according to the Fenner letters, above the doomed Pawtuxet farmhouse on the night of Joseph Curwen's annihilation. There was no mistaking that nightmare phrase, for Charles had described it too vividly in the old days when he had talked frankly of his Curwen investigations. And yet it was only this fragment of an archaic and forgotten language: "*DIES MIES JESCHET BOENE DOESEF DOUVEMA ENITEMAUS.*"

Close upon this thundering there came a momentary darkening of the daylight, though sunset was still an hour distant, and then a puff of added odor different from the first but equally unknown and intolerable. Charles was chanting again now and his mother could hear syllables that sounded like "Yi-nash-Yog-Sothoth-he-lgeb-fi-throdog"—ending in a "Yah!" whose maniacal force mounted in an ear-splitting crescendo. A second later all previous memories were effaced by the wailing scream which burst out with frantic explosiveness and gradually changed form to a paroxysm of diabolic and hysterical laughter. Mrs. Ward, with the mingled fear and blind courage of maternity, advanced and knocked affrightedly at the concealing panels, but obtained no sign of recognition. She knocked again, but paused nervelessly as a second shriek arose, this one unmistakably in the familiar voice of her son, *and sounding concurrently with the still bursting cachinnations of that other voice.* Presently she fainted, although she is still unable to recall the precise and immediate cause. Memory sometimes makes merciful deletions.

Mr. Ward returned from the business section at about quarter past six; and not finding his wife downstairs, was told by the frightened servants that she was probably watching at Charles's door, from which the sounds had been far stranger than ever before. Mounting the stairs at once, he saw Mrs. Ward stretched at full length on the floor of the corridor outside the laboratory; and realizing that she had fainted, hastened to fetch a glass of water from a set bowl in a neighboring alcove. Dashing the cold fluid in her face, he was heartened to observe an immediate response on her part, and was watching the bewildered opening of her eyes when a chill shot through him and threatened to reduce him to the very state from which she was emerging. For the seemingly silent laboratory was not as silent as it had appeared to be, but held the murmurs of a tense, muffled conversation in tones too low for comprehension, yet of a quality profoundly disturbing to the soul.

It was not, of course, new for Charles to mutter formulae; but this muttering was definitely different. It was so palpably a dialogue, or imitation of a dialogue, with the regular alteration of inflections suggesting question and answer, statement and response. One voice was undisguisedly that of Charles, but the other had a depth and hollowness which the youth's best powers of ceremonial mimicry had scarcely approached before. There was something hideous, blasphemous, and abnormal about it, and but for a cry from his recovering wife which cleared his mind by arousing his protective instincts it is not likely that Theodore Howland Ward could have maintained for nearly a year more his old boast that he had never fainted. As it was, he seized his wife in his arms and bore her quickly downstairs before she could notice the voices which had so horribly disturbed him. Even so, however, he was not quick enough to escape catching something himself which caused him to stagger dangerously with his burden. For Mrs. Ward's cry had evidently been heard by others than he, and there had come from behind the locked door the first distinguishable words which that masked and terrible colloquy had yielded. They were merely an excited caution in Charles's own voice, but somehow their implications held a nameless fright for the father who overheard them. The phrase was just this: *"Sshh!—Write!"*

Mr. and Mrs. Ward conferred at some length after dinner, and the former resolved to have a firm and serious talk with Charles that very night. No matter how important the object, such conduct could no longer be permitted; for these latest developments transcended every limit of sanity and formed a menace to the order and nervous well-being of the entire household. The youth must indeed have taken complete leave of his senses, since only downright madness could have prompted the wild screams and imaginary conversations in assumed voices which the present day had brought forth. All this must be stopped, or Mrs. Ward would be made ill and the keeping of servants become an impossibility.

Mr. Ward rose at the close of the meal and started upstairs for Charles's laboratory. On the third floor, however, he paused at the sounds which he heard proceeding from the now disused library of his son. Books were apparently being flung about and papers wildly rustled, and upon stepping to the door Mr. Ward beheld the youth within, excitedly assembling a vast armful of literary matter of every size and shape. Charles's aspect was very drawn and haggard, and he dropped his entire load with a start at the sound of his father's voice. At the elder man's command he sat down, and for some time listened to the admonitions he had so long deserved. There was no scene. At the end of the lecture he agreed that his father was right, and that his noises, mutterings, incantations, and chemical odors were indeed inexcusable nuisances. He agreed to a policy of greater quiet, though insisting on a prolongation of his extreme privacy. Much of his future work, he said, was in any case purely book research; and he could obtain quarters elsewhere for any such vocal rituals as might be necessary at a later stage. For the fright and fainting of his mother he expressed the keenest contrition, and explained that the conversation later heard was part of an elaborate symbolism designed to create a certain mental atmosphere. His use of abstruse technical terms somewhat bewildered Mr. Ward, but the parting impression was one of undeniable sanity and poise despite a mysterious tension of the utmost gravity. The interview was really quite inconclusive, and as Charles picked up his armful and left the room Mr. Ward hardly knew what to make of the entire business. It was as mysterious as the death of poor old Nig, whose stiffening form had been found an hour before in the basement, with staring eyes and fear-distorted mouth.

Driven by some vague detective instinct, the bewildered parent now glanced curiously at the vacant shelves to see what his son had taken up to the attic. The youth's library was plainly and rigidly classified, so that one might tell at a glance the books or at least the kind of books which had been withdrawn. On this occasion Mr. Ward was astonished to find that nothing of the occult or the antiquarian, beyond what had been previously removed, was missing. These new withdrawals were all modern items; histories, scientific treatises, geographies, manuals of literature, philosophic works, and certain contemporary newspapers and magazines. It was a very curious shift from Charles Ward's recent run of reading, and the father paused in a growing vortex of perplexity and an engulfing sense of strangeness. The strangeness was a very poignant sensation, and almost clawed at his chest as he strove to see just what was wrong around him. Something was indeed wrong, and tangibly as well as spiritually so. Ever since he had been in this room he had known that something was amiss, and at last it dawned upon him what it was.

On the north wall rose still the ancient carved overmantel from the house in Olney Court, but to the cracked and precariously restored oils of the large Curwen portrait disaster had come. Time and unequal heating had done their work at last, and at some time since the room's last cleaning the worst had happened. Peeling clear of the wood, curling tighter and tighter, and finally crumbling into small bits with what must have been malignly silent suddenness, the portrait of Joseph Curwen had resigned forever its staring surveillance of the youth it so strangely resembled, and now lay scattered on the floor as a thin coating of fine bluish-gray dust.

IV. A Mutation and a Madness

1

In the week following that memorable Good Friday Charles Ward was seen more often than usual, and was continually carrying books between his library and the attic laboratory. His actions were quiet and rational, but he had a furtive, hunted look which his mother did not like, and developed an incredibly ravenous appetite as gauged by his demands upon the cook. Dr. Willett had been told of those Friday noises and happenings, and on the following Tuesday had a long conversation with the youth in the library where the picture stared no more. The interview was, as always, inconclusive; but Willett is still ready to swear that the youth was sane and himself at the time. He held out promises of an early revelation, and spoke of the need of securing a laboratory elsewhere. At the loss of the portrait he grieved singularly little considering his first enthusiasm over it, but seemed to find something of positive humor in its sudden crumbling.

About the second week Charles began to be absent from the house for long periods, and one day when good old black Hannah came to help with the spring cleaning she mentioned his frequent visits to the old house in Olney Court, where he would come with a large valise and perform curious delvings in the cellar. He was always very liberal to her and to old Asa, but seemed more worried than he used to be; which grieved her very much, since she had watched him grow up from birth. Another report of his doings came from Pawtuxet, where some friends of the family saw him at a distance a surprising number of times. He seemed to haunt the resort and canoe-house of Rhodes-on-the-Pawtuxet, and subsequent inquiries by Dr. Willett at that place brought out the fact that his purpose was always to secure access to the rather hedged-in river-bank, along which he would walk toward the north, usually not reappearing for a very long while.

Late in May came a momentary revival of ritualistic sounds in the attic laboratory which brought a stern reproof from Mr. Ward and a somewhat distracted promise of amendment from Charles. It occurred one morning, and seemed to form a resumption of the imaginary conversation noted on that turbulent Good Friday. The youth was arguing or remonstrating hotly with himself, for there suddenly burst forth a perfectly distinguishable series of clashing shouts in differentiated tones like alternate demands and denials which caused Mrs. Ward to run upstairs and listen at the door. She could hear no more than a fragment whose only plain words were "must have it red for three months," and upon her knocking all sounds ceased at once. When Charles was later questioned by his father he said that there were certain conflicts of spheres of consciousness which only great skill could avoid, but which he would try to transfer to other realms.

About the middle of June a queer nocturnal incident occurred. In the early evening there had been some noise and thumping in the laboratory upstairs, and Mr. Ward was on the point of investigating when it suddenly quieted down. That midnight, after the family had retired, the butler was nightlocking the front door when according to his statement Charles appeared somewhat blunderingly and uncertainly at the foot of the stairs with a large suitcase and made signs that he wished egress. The youth spoke no word, but the worthy Yorkshireman caught one sight of his fevered eyes and trembled causelessly. He opened the door and young Ward went out, but in the morning he presented his resignation to Mrs. Ward. There was, he said, something unholy in the glance Charles had fixed on him. It was no way for a young gentleman to look at an honest person, and he could not possibly stay another night. Mrs. Ward allowed the man to depart, but she did not value his statement highly. To fancy Charles in a savage state that night was quite ridiculous, for as long as she had remained awake she had heard faint sounds from the laboratory above; sounds as if of sobbing and pacing, and of a sighing which told only of despair's profoundest depths. Mrs. Ward had grown used to listening for sounds in the night, for the mystery of her son was fast driving all else from her mind.

The next evening, much as on another evening nearly three months before, Charles Ward seized the newspaper very early and accidentally lost the main section. The matter was not recalled till later, when Dr. Willett began checking up loose ends and searching out missing links here and there. In the *Journal* office he found the section which Charles had lost, and marked two items as of possible significance. They were as follows:

MORE CEMETERY DELVING

It was this morning discovered by Robert Hart, night watchman at the North Burial Ground, that ghouls were again at work in the ancient portion of the cemetery. The grave of Ezra Weeden, who was born in 1740 and died in 1824, according to his uprooted and savagely splintered slate headstone, was found excavated and rifled, the work being evidently done with a spade stolen from an adjacent tool-shed.

Whatever the contents may have been after more than a century of burial, all was gone except a few slivers of decayed wood. There were no wheel tracks, but the police have measured a single set of footprints which they found in the vicinity, and which indicate the boots of a man of refinement.

Hart is inclined to link this incident with the digging discovered last March, when a party in a motor truck were frightened away after making a deep excavation; but Sergt. Riley of the Second

Station discounts this theory and points to vital differences in the two cases. In March the digging had been in a spot where no grave was known; but this time a well-marked and cared-for grave had been rifled with every evidence of deliberate purpose, and with a conscious malignity expressed in the splintering of the slab which had been intact up to the day before.

Members of the Weeden family, notified of the happening, expressed their astonishment and regret; and were wholly unable to think of any enemy who would care to violate the grave of their ancestor. Hazard Weeden of 598 Angell Street recalls a family legend according to which Ezra Weeden was involved in some very peculiar circumstances, not dishonorable to himself, shortly before the Revolution; but of any modern feud or mystery he is frankly ignorant. Inspector Cunningham has been assigned to the case, and hopes to uncover some valuable clues in the near future.

DOGS NOISY IN PAWTUXET

Residents of Pawtuxet were aroused about 3 a.m. today by a phenomenal baying of dogs which seemed to center near the river just north of Rhodes-on-the-Pawtuxet. The volume and quality of the howling were unusually odd, according to most who heard it; and Fred Lemdin, night watchman at Rhodes, declares it was mixed with something very like the shrieks of a man in mortal terror and agony. A sharp and very brief thunderstorm, which seemed to strike somewhere near the bank of the river, put an end to the disturbance. Strange and unpleasant odors, probably from the oil tanks along the bay, are popularly linked with this incident; and may have had their share in exciting the dogs.

The aspect of Charles now became very haggard and hunted, and all agreed in retrospect that he may have wished at this period to make some statement or confession from which sheer terror withheld him. The morbid listening of his mother in the night brought out the fact that he made frequent sallies abroad under cover of darkness, and most of the more academic alienists unite at present in charging him with the revolting cases of vampirism which the press so sensationally reported about this time, but which have not yet been definitely traced to any known perpetrator. These cases, too recent and celebrated to need detailed mention, involved victims of every age and type and seemed to cluster around two distinct localities; the residential hill and the North End, near the Ward home, and the suburban districts across the Cranston line near Pawtuxet. Both late wayfarers and sleepers with open windows were attacked, and those who lived to tell the tale spoke unanimously of a lean, lithe, leaping monster with burning eyes which fastened its teeth in the throat or upper arm and feasted ravenously.

Dr. Willett, who refuses to date the madness of Charles Ward as far back as even this, is cautious in attempting to explain these horrors. He has, he declares, certain theories of his own; and limits his positive statements to a peculiar kind of negation. "I will not," he says, "state who or what I believe perpetrated these attacks and murders, but I will declare that Charles Ward was innocent of them. I have reason to be sure he was ignorant of the taste of blood, as indeed his continued anemic decline and increasing pallor prove better than any verbal argument. Ward meddled with terrible things, but he has paid for it, and he was never a monster or a villain. As for now—I don't like to think. A change came, and I'm content to believe that the old Charles

Ward died with it. His soul did, anyhow, for that mad flesh that vanished from Waite's hospital had another."

Willett speaks with authority, for he was often at the Ward home attending Mrs. Ward, whose nerves had begun to snap under the strain. Her nocturnal listening had bred some morbid hallucinations which she confided to the doctor with hesitancy, and which he ridiculed in talking to her, although they made him ponder deeply when alone. These delusions always concerned the faint sounds which she fancied she heard in the attic laboratory and bedroom, and emphasized the occurrence of muffled sighs and sobbings at the most impossible times. Early in July Willett ordered Mrs. Ward to Atlantic City for an indefinite recuperative sojourn, and cautioned both Mr. Ward and the haggard and elusive Charles to write her only cheering letters. It is probably to this enforced and reluctant escape that she owes her life and continued sanity.

2

Not long after his mother's departure Charles Ward began negotiating for the Pawtuxet bungalow. It was a squalid little wooden edifice with a concrete garage, perched high on the sparsely settled bank of the river slightly above Rhodes, but for some odd reason the youth would have nothing else. He gave the real-estate agencies no peace till one of them secured it for him at an exorbitant price from a somewhat reluctant owner, and as soon as it was vacant he took possession under cover of darkness, transporting in a great closed van the entire contents of his attic laboratory, including the books both weird and modern which he had borrowed from his study. He had this van loaded in the black small hours, and his father recalls only a drowsy realization of stifled oaths and stamping feet on the night the goods were taken away. After that Charles moved back to his own old quarters on the third floor, and never haunted the attic again.

To the Pawtuxet bungalow Charles transferred all the secrecy with which he had surrounded his attic realm, save that he now appeared to have two sharers of his mysteries; a villainous-looking Portuguese half-caste from the South Main St. waterfront who acted as a servant, and a thin, scholarly stranger with dark glasses and a stubbly full beard of dyed aspect whose status was evidently that of a colleague. Neighbors vainly tried to engage these odd persons in conversation. The mulatto Gomes spoke very little English, and the bearded man, who gave his name as Dr. Allen, voluntarily followed his example. Ward himself tried to be more affable, but succeeded only in provoking curiosity with his rambling accounts of chemical research. Before long queer tales began to circulate regarding the all-night burning of lights; and somewhat later, after this burning had suddenly ceased, there rose still queerer tales of disproportionate orders of meat from the butcher's and of the muffled shouting, declamation, rhythmic chanting, and screaming supposed to come from some very deep cellar below the place. Most distinctly the new and strange household was bitterly disliked by the honest bourgeoisie of the vicinity, and it is not remarkable that dark hints were advanced connecting the hated establishment with the current epidemic of vampiristic attacks and murders; especially since the radius of that plague seemed now confined wholly to Pawtuxet and the adjacent streets of Edgewood.

Ward spent most of his time at the bungalow, but slept occasionally at home and was still reckoned a dweller beneath his father's roof. Twice he was absent from the city on week-long trips, whose destinations have not yet been discovered. He grew steadily paler and more emaciated even than before, and lacked some of his former assurance when repeating to Dr. Willett his old, old story of vital research and future revelations. Willett often waylaid him at his father's house, for the elder Ward was deeply worried and perplexed, and wished his son to get as much sound oversight as could be managed in the case of so secretive and independent an adult. The doctor still insists that the youth was sane even as late as this, and adduces many a conversation to prove his point.

About September the vampirism declined, but in the following January Ward almost became involved in serious trouble. For some time the nocturnal arrival and departure of motor trucks at the Pawtuxet bungalow had been commented upon, and at this juncture an unforeseen hitch exposed the nature of at least one item of their contents. In a lonely spot near Hope Valley had occurred one of the frequent sordid waylayings of trucks by "hi-jackers" in quest of liquor shipments, but this time the robbers had been destined to receive the greater shock. For the long cases they seized proved upon opening to contain some exceedingly gruesome things; so gruesome, in fact, that the matter could not be kept quiet amongst the denizens of the underworld. The thieves had hastily buried what they discovered, but when the State Police got wind of the matter a careful search was made. A recently arrested vagrant, under promise of immunity from prosecution on any additional charge, at last consented to guide a party of troopers to the spot; and there was found in that hasty cache a very hideous and shameful thing. It would not be well for the national—or even the international—sense of decorum if the public were ever to know what was uncovered by that awestruck party. There was no mistaking it, even by these far from studious officers; and telegrams to Washington ensued with feverish rapidity.

The cases were addressed to Charles Ward at his Pawtuxet bungalow, and State and Federal officials at once paid him a very forceful and serious call. They found him pallid and worried with his two odd companions, and received from him what seemed to be a valid explanation and evidence of innocence. He had needed certain anatomical specimens as part of a program of research whose depth and genuineness anyone who had known him in the last decade could prove, and had ordered the required kind and number from agencies which he had thought as reasonably legitimate as such things can be. Of the *identity* of the specimens he had known absolutely nothing, and was properly shocked when the inspectors hinted at the monstrous effect on public sentiment and national dignity which a knowledge of the matter would produce. In this statement he was firmly sustained by his bearded colleague Dr. Allen, whose oddly hollow voice carried even more conviction than his own nervous tones; so that in the end the officials took no action, but carefully set down the New York name and address which Ward gave them as a basis for a search which came to nothing. It is only fair to add that the specimens were quickly and quietly restored to their proper places, and that the general public will never know of their blasphemous disturbance.

On February 9, 1928, Dr. Willett received a letter from Charles Ward which he considers of extraordinary importance, and about which he has frequently quarreled with Dr. Lyman. Lyman believes that this note contains positive proof of a well-developed case of *dementia praecox,* but Willett on the other hand regards it as the last perfectly sane utterance of the hapless youth. He calls especial attention to the normal character of the penmanship; which though shewing traces of shattered nerves, is nevertheless distinctly Ward's own. The text in full is as follows:

> 100 Prospect St.
> Providence, R.I.,
> February 8, 1928.

Dear Dr. Willett:—

I feel that at last the time has come for me to make the disclosures which I have so long promised you, and for which you have pressed me so often. The patience you have shewn in waiting, and the confidence you have shewn in my mind and integrity, are things I shall never cease to appreciate.

And now that I am ready to speak, I must own with humiliation that no triumph such as I dreamed of can ever be mine. Instead of triumph I have found terror, and my talk with you will not be a boast of victory but a plea for help and advice in saving both myself and the world from a horror beyond all human conception or calculation. You recall what those Fenner letters said of the old raiding party at Pawtuxet. That must all be done again, and quickly. Upon us depends more than can be put into words—all civilization, all natural law, perhaps even the fate of the solar system and the universe. I have brought to light a monstrous abnormality, but I did it for the sake of knowledge. Now for the sake of all life and Nature you must help me thrust it back into the dark again.

I have left that Pawtuxet place forever, and we must extirpate everything existing there, alive or dead. I shall not go there again, and you must not believe it if you ever hear that I am there. I will tell you why I say this when I see you. I have come home for good, and wish you would call on me at the very first moment that you can spare five or six hours continuously to hear what I have to say. It will take that long—and believe me when I tell you that you never had a more genuine professional duty than this. My life and reason are the very least things which hang in the balance.

I dare not tell my father, for he could not grasp the whole thing. But I have told him of my danger, and he has four men from a detective agency watching the house. I don't know how much good they can do, for they have against them forces which even you could scarcely envisage or acknowledge. So come quickly if you wish to see me alive and hear how you may help to save the cosmos from stark hell.

Any time will do—I shall not be out of the house. Don't telephone ahead, for there is no telling who or what may try to intercept you. And let us pray to whatever gods there be that nothing may prevent this meeting.

In utmost gravity and desperation,
Charles Dexter Ward.

P.S. Shoot Dr. Allen on sight *and dissolve
his body in acid.* Don't burn it.

Dr. Willett received this note about 10:30 a.m., and immediately arranged to spare the whole late afternoon and evening for the momentous talk, letting it extend on into the night as long as might be necessary. He planned to arrive about four o'clock, and through all the intervening hours was so engulfed in every sort of wild speculation that most of his tasks were very mechanically performed. Maniacal as the letter would have sounded to a stranger, Willett had seen too much of Charles Ward's oddities to dismiss it as sheer raving. That something very subtle, ancient, and horrible was hovering about he felt quite sure, and the reference to Dr. Allen could almost be comprehended in view of what Pawtuxet gossip said of Ward's enigmatical colleague. Willett had never seen the man, but had heard much of his aspect and bearing, and could not but wonder what sort of eyes those much-discussed dark glasses might conceal.

Promptly at four Dr. Willett presented himself at the Ward residence, but found to his annoyance that Charles had not adhered to his determination to remain indoors. The guards were there, but said that the young man seemed to have lost part of his timidity. He had that morning done much apparently frightened arguing and protesting over the telephone, one of the detectives said, replying to some unknown voice with phrases such as "I am very tired and must rest a while," "I can't receive anyone for some time, you'll have to excuse me," "Please postpone decisive action till we can arrange some sort of compromise," or "I am very sorry, but I must take a complete vacation from everything; I'll talk with you later." Then, apparently gaining boldness through meditation, he had slipped out so quietly that no one had seen him depart or knew that he had gone until he returned about one o'clock and entered the house without a word. He had gone upstairs, where a bit of his fear must have surged back; for he was heard to cry out in a highly terrified fashion upon entering his library, afterward trailing off into a kind of choking gasp. When, however, the butler had gone to inquire what the trouble was, he had appeared at the door with a great show of boldness, and had silently gestured the man away in a manner that terrified him unaccountably. Then he had evidently done some rearranging of his shelves, for a great clattering and thumping and creaking ensued; after which he had reappeared and left at once. Willett inquired whether or not any message had been left, but was told that there was none. The butler seemed queerly disturbed about something in Charles's appearance and manner, and asked solicitously if there was much hope for a cure of his disordered nerves.

For almost two hours Dr. Willett waited vainly in Charles Ward's library, watching the dusty shelves with their wide gaps where books had been removed, and smiling grimly at the paneled overmantel on the north wall, whence a year before the suave features of old Joseph Curwen had looked mildly down. After a time the shadows began to gather, and the sunset cheer gave place to a vague growing terror which flew shadowlike before the night. Mr. Ward finally arrived, and shewed much surprise and anger at his son's absence after all the pains which had been taken to guard him. He had not known of Charles's appointment, and promised to notify Willett when the youth returned. In bidding the doctor goodnight he expressed his utter perplexity at his son's condition, and urged his caller to do all he could to restore the boy to normal poise. Willett was glad to escape from that library, for something frightful and unholy seemed to haunt it; as if the vanished picture had left behind a legacy of evil. He had never liked that picture; and even now, strong-nerved though he was, there lurked a quality in its vacant panel which made him feel an urgent need to get out into the pure air as soon as possible.

3

The next morning Willett received a message from the senior Ward, saying that Charles was still absent. Mr. Ward mentioned that Dr. Allen had telephoned him to say that Charles would remain at Pawtuxet for some time, and that he must not be disturbed. This was necessary because Allen himself was suddenly called away for an indefinite period, leaving the researches in need of Charles's constant oversight. Charles sent his best wishes, and regretted any bother his abrupt change of plans might have caused. In listening to this message Mr. Ward heard Dr. Allen's voice for the first time, and it seemed to excite some vague and elusive memory which could not be actually placed, but which was disturbing to the point of fearfulness.

Faced by these baffling and contradictory reports, Dr. Willett was frankly at a loss what to do. The frantic earnestness of Charles's note was not to be denied, yet what could one think of its writer's immediate violation of his own expressed policy? Young Ward had written that his delvings had become blasphemous and menacing, that they and his bearded colleague must be extirpated at any cost, and that he himself would never return to their final scene; yet according to latest advices he had forgotten all this and was back in the thick of the mystery. Common sense bade one leave the youth alone with his freakishness, yet some deeper instinct would not permit the impression of that frenzied letter to subside. Willett read it over again, and could not make its essence sound as empty and insane as both its bombastic verbiage and its lack of fulfillment would seem to imply. Its terror was too profound and real, and in conjunction with what the doctor already knew evoked too vivid hints of monstrosities from beyond time and space to permit of any cynical explanation. There were nameless horrors abroad; and no matter how little one might be able to get at them, one ought to stand prepared for any sort of action at any time.

For over a week Dr. Willett pondered on the dilemma which

seemed thrust upon him, and became more and more inclined to pay Charles a call at the Pawtuxet bungalow. No friend of the youth had ever ventured to storm this forbidden retreat, and even his father knew of its interior only from such descriptions as he chose to give; but Willett felt that some direct conversation with his patient was necessary. Mr. Ward had been receiving brief and non-committal typed notes from his son, and said that Mrs. Ward in her Atlantic City retirement had had no better word. So at length the doctor resolved to act; and despite a curious sensation inspired by old legends of Joseph Curwen, and by more recent revelations and warnings from Charles Ward, set boldly out for the bungalow on the bluff above the river.

Willett had visited the spot before through sheer curiosity, though of course never entering the house or proclaiming his presence; hence knew exactly the route to take. Driving out Broad Street one early afternoon toward the end of February in his small motor, he thought oddly of the grim party which had taken that selfsame road a hundred and fifty-seven years before on a terrible errand which none might ever comprehend.

The ride through the city's decaying fringe was short, and trim Edgewood and sleepy Pawtuxet presently spread out ahead. Willett turned to the right down Lockwood Street and drove his car as far along that rural road as he could, then alighted and walked north to where the bluff towered above the lovely bends of the river and the sweep of misty downlands beyond. Houses were still few here, and there was no mistaking the isolated bungalow with its concrete garage on a high point of land at his left. Stepping briskly up the neglected gravel walk he rapped at the door with a firm hand, and spoke without a tremor to the evil Portuguese mulatto who opened it to the width of a crack.

He must, he said, see Charles Ward at once on vitally important business. No excuse would be accepted, and a repulse would mean only a full report of the matter to the elder Ward. The mulatto still hesitated, and pushed against the door when Willett attempted to open it; but the doctor merely raised his voice and renewed his demands. Then there came from the dark interior a husky whisper which somehow chilled the hearer through and through though he did not know why he feared it. "Let him in, Tony," it said, "we may as well talk now as ever." But disturbing as was the whisper, the greater fear was that which immediately followed. The floor creaked and the speaker hove in sight—and the owner of those strange and resonant tones was seen to be no other than Charles Dexter Ward.

The minuteness with which Dr. Willett recalled and recorded his conversation of that afternoon is due to the importance he assigns to this particular period. For at last he concedes a vital change in Charles Dexter Ward's mentality, and believes that the youth now spoke from a brain hopelessly alien to the brain whose growth he had watched for six and twenty years. Controversy with Dr. Lyman has compelled him to be very specific, and he definitely dates the madness of Charles Ward from the time the typewritten notes began to reach his parents. Those notes are not in Ward's normal style; not even in the style of that last frantic letter to Willett. Instead, they are strange and archaic, as if the snapping of the writer's mind had released a flood of tendencies and impressions picked up unconsciously through boyhood antiquarianism. There is an obvious effort to be modern, but the spirit and occasionally the language are those of the past.

The past, too, was evident in Ward's every tone and gesture as he received the doctor in that shadowy bungalow. He bowed, motioned Willett to a seat, and began to speak abruptly in that strange whisper which he sought to explain at the very outset.

"I am grown phthisical," he began, "from this cursed river air. You must excuse my speech. I suppose you are come from my father to see what ails me, and I hope you will say nothing to alarm him."

Willett was studying these scraping tones with extreme care, but studying even more closely the face of the speaker. Something, he felt, was wrong; and he thought of what the family had told him about the fright of that Yorkshire butler one night. He wished it were not so dark, but did not request that any blind be opened. Instead, he merely asked Ward why he had so belied the frantic note of little more than a week before.

"I was coming to that," the host replied. "You must know, I am in a very bad state of nerves, and do and say queer things I cannot account for. As I have told you often, I am on the edge of great matters; and the bigness of them has a way of making me light-headed. Any man might well be frighted of what I have found, but I am not to be put off for long. I was a dunce to have that guard and stick at home; for having gone this far, my place is here. I am not well spoke of by my prying neighbors, and perhaps I was led by weakness to believe myself what they say of me. There is no evil to any in what I do, so long as I do it rightly. Have the goodness to wait six months, and I'll shew you what will pay your patience well.

"You may as well know I have a way of learning old matters from things surer than books, and I'll leave you to judge the importance of what I can give to history, philosophy, and the arts by reason of the doors I have access to. My ancestor had all this when those witless peeping Toms came and murdered him. I now have it again, or am coming very imperfectly to have a part of it. This time nothing must happen, and least of all through any idiot fears of my own. Pray forget all I writ you, Sir, and have no fear of this place or any in it. Dr. Allen is a man of fine parts, and I owe him an apology for anything ill I have said of him. I wish I had no need to spare him, but there were things he had to do elsewhere. His zeal is equal to mine in all those matters, and I suppose that when I feared the work I feared him too as my greatest helper in it."

Ward paused, and the doctor hardly knew what to say or think. He felt almost foolish in the face of this calm repudiation of the letter; and yet there clung to him the fact that while the present discourse was strange and alien and indubitably mad, the note itself had been tragic in its naturalness and likeness to the Charles Ward he knew. Willett now tried to turn the talk on early matters, and recall to the youth some past events which would restore a familiar mood; but in this process he obtained only the most grotesque results. It was the same with all the alienists later on. Important sections of Charles Ward's store of mental images, mainly those touching modern times and his own personal life, had been unaccountably expunged; whilst all the massed antiquarianism of his youth had welled up from some profound subconsciousness to engulf the contemporary and the individual. The youth's intimate knowledge of elder things was abnormal and unholy, and he tried his best to hide it. When Willett would mention some favorite object of his boyhood archaistic studies he often shed by pure accident such a light as no normal mortal could conceivably be expected to possess, and the doctor shuddered as the glib allusion glided by.

It was not wholesome to know so much about the way the fat sheriff's wig fell off as he leaned over at the play in Mr. Douglass' Histrionick Academy in King Street on the eleventh of February, 1762, which fell on a Thursday; or about how the actors cut the text of Steele's *Conscious Lovers* so badly that one was almost glad the Baptist-ridden legislature closed the theater a fortnight later. That Thomas Sabin's Boston coach was "damn'd uncomfortable" old letters may well have told; but what healthy antiquarian could recall how the creaking of Epenetus Olney's new signboard (the gaudy crown he set up after he took to calling his tavern the Crown Coffee House) was exactly like the first few notes of the new jazz piece all the radios in Pawtuxet were playing?

Ward, however, would not be quizzed long in this vein. Modern and personal topics he waved aside quite summarily, whilst regarding antique affairs he soon shewed the plainest boredom. What he wished clearly enough was only to satisfy his visitor enough to make him depart without the intention of returning. To this end he offered to shew Willett the entire house, and at once proceeded to lead the doctor through every room from cellar to attic. Willett looked sharply, but noted that the visible books were far too few and trivial ever to have filled the wide gaps on Ward's shelves at home, and that the meager so-called "laboratory" was the flimsiest sort of a blind. Clearly there were a library and a laboratory elsewhere; but just where, it was impossible to say. Essentially defeated in his quest for something he could not name, Willett returned to town before evening and told the senior Ward everything which had occurred. They agreed that the youth must be definitely out of his mind, but decided that nothing drastic need be done just then. Above all, Mrs. Ward must be kept in as complete an ignorance as her son's own strange typed notes would permit.

Mr. Ward now determined to call in person upon his son, making it wholly a surprise visit. Dr. Willett took him in his car one evening, guiding him to within sight of the bungalow and waiting patiently for his return. The session was a long one, and the father emerged in a very saddened and perplexed state. His reception had developed much like Willett's, save that Charles had been an excessively long time in appearing after the visitor had forced his way into the hall and sent the Portuguese away with an imperative demand; and in the bearing of the altered son there was no trace of filial affection. The lights had been dim, yet even so the youth had complained that they dazzled him outrageously. He had not spoken out loud at all, averring that his throat was in very poor condition; but in his hoarse whisper there was a quality so vaguely disturbing that Mr. Ward could not banish it from his mind.

Now definitely leagued together to do all they could toward the youth's mental salvation, Mr. Ward and Dr. Willett set about collecting every scrap of data which the case might afford. Pawtuxet gossip was the first item they studied, and this was relatively easy to glean since both had friends in that region. Dr. Willett obtained the most rumors because people talked more frankly to him than to a parent of the central figure, and from all he heard he could tell that young Ward's life had become indeed a strange one. Common tongues would not dissociate his household from the vampirism of the previous summer, while the nocturnal comings and goings of the motor trucks provided their share of dark speculation. Local tradesmen spoke of the queerness of the orders brought them by the evil-looking mulatto, and in particular of the inordinate amounts of meat and fresh blood secured from the two butcher shops in the immediate neighborhood. For a household of only three, these quantities were quite absurd.

Then there was the matter of the sounds beneath the earth. Reports of these things were harder to pin down, but all the vague hints tallied in certain basic essentials. Noises of a ritual nature positively existed, and at times when the bungalow was dark. They might, of course, have come from the known cellar; but rumor insisted that there were deeper and more spreading crypts. Recalling the ancient tales of Joseph Curwen's catacombs, and assuming for granted that the present bungalow had been selected because of its situation on the old Curwen site as revealed in one or another of the documents found behind the picture, Willett and Mr. Ward gave this phase of the gossip much attention; and searched many times without success for the door in the river-bank which old manuscripts mentioned. As to popular opinions of the bungalow's various inhabitants, it was soon plain that the Brava Portuguese was loathed, the bearded and spectacled Dr. Allen feared, and the pallid young scholar disliked to a profound extent. During the last week or two Ward had obviously changed much, abandoning his attempts at affability and speaking only in hoarse but oddly repellent whispers on the few occasions that he ventured forth.

Such were the shreds and fragments gathered here and there; and over these Mr. Ward and Dr. Willett held many long and serious conferences. They strove to exercise deduction, induction, and constructive imagination to their utmost extent; and to correlate every known fact of Charles's later life, including the frantic letter which the doctor now shewed the father, with the meager documentary evidence available concerning old Joseph Curwen. They would have given much for a glimpse of the papers Charles had found, for very clearly the key to the youth's madness lay in what he had learned of the ancient wizard and his doings.

4

And yet, after all, it was from no step of Mr. Ward's or Dr. Willett's that the next move in this singular case proceeded. The father and the physician, rebuffed and confused by a shadow too shapeless and intangible to combat, had rested uneasily on their oars while the typed notes of young Ward to his parents grew fewer and fewer. Then came the first of the month with its customary financial adjustments, and the clerks at certain banks began a peculiar shaking of heads and telephoning from one to the other. Officials who knew Charles Ward by sight went down to the bungalow to ask why every check of his appearing at this juncture was a clumsy forgery, and were reassurred less than they ought to have been when the youth hoarsely explained that his hand had lately been so much affected by a nervous shock as to make normal writing impossible. He could, he said, form no written characters at all except with great difficulty; and could prove it by the fact that he had been forced to type all his recent letters, even those to his father and mother, who would bear out the assertion.

What made the investigators pause in confusion was not this circumstance alone, for that was nothing unprecedented or fundamentally suspicious; nor even the Pawtuxet gossip, of which one or two of them had caught echoes. It was the muddled discourse of the young man which nonplussed them, implying as it did a virtually total loss of memory concerning important monetary matters which he had had at his fingertips only a month or two before. Something was wrong; for despite the apparent coherence and rationality of his speech, there could be no normal reason for this ill-concealed blankness on vital points. Moreover, although none of these men knew Ward well, they could not help observing the change in his language and manner. They had heard he was an antiquarian, but even the most hopeless antiquarians do not make daily use of obsolete phraseology and gestures. Altogether, this combination of hoarseness, palsied hands, bad memory, and altered speech and bearing must represent some disturbance or malady of genuine gravity, which no doubt formed the basis of the prevailing odd rumors; and after their departure the party of officials decided that a talk with the senior Ward was imperative.

So on the sixth of March, 1928, there was a long and serious conference in Mr. Ward's office, after which the utterly bewildered father summoned Dr. Willett in a kind of helpless resignation. Willett looked over the strained and awkward signatures of the checks, and compared them in his mind with the penmanship of that last frantic note. Certainly, the change was radical and profound, and yet there was something damnably familiar about the new writing. It had crabbed and archaic tendencies of a very curious sort, and seemed to result from a type of stroke utterly different from that which the youth had always used. It was strange—but where had he seen it before? On the whole, it was obvious that Charles was insane. Of that there could be no doubt. And since it appeared unlikely that he could handle his property or continue to deal with the outside world much longer, something must quickly be done toward his oversight and possible cure. It was then that the alienists were called in, Drs. Peck and Waite of Providence and Dr. Lyman of Boston, to whom Mr. Ward and Dr. Willett gave the most exhaustive possible history of the case, and who conferred at length in the now unused library of their young patient, examining what books and papers of his were left in order to gain some further notion of his habitual mental cast. After scanning this material and examining the ominous note to Willett they all agreed that Charles Ward's studies had been enough to unseat or at least to warp any ordinary intellect, and wished most heartily that they could see his more intimate volumes and documents; but this latter they knew they could do, if at all, only after a scene at the bungalow itself. Willett now reviewed the whole case with febrile energy; it being at this time that he obtained the statements of the workmen who had seen Charles find the Curwen documents, and that he collated the incidents of the destroyed newspaper items, looking up the latter at the *Journal* office.

On Thursday, the eighth of March, Drs. Willett, Peck, Lyman, and Waite, accompanied by Mr. Ward, paid the youth their momentous call; making no concealment of their object and questioning the now acknowledged patient with extreme minuteness. Charles, though he was inordinately long in answering the summons and was still redolent of strange and noxious laboratory odors when he did finally make his agitated appearance, proved a far from recalcitrant subject; and admitted freely that his memory and balance had suffered somewhat from close application to abstruse studies. He offered no resistance when his removal to other quarters was insisted upon; and seemed, indeed, to display a high degree of intelligence as apart from mere memory. His conduct would have sent his interviewers away in bafflement had not the persistently archaic trend of his speech and unmistakable replacement of modern by ancient ideas in his consciousness marked him out as one definitely removed from the normal. Of his work he would say no more to the group of doctors than he had formerly said to his family and to Dr. Willett, and his frantic note of the previous month he dismissed as mere nerves and hysteria. He insisted that this shadowy bungalow possessed no library or laboratory beyond the visible ones, and waxed abstruse in explaining the absence from the house of such odors as now saturated all his clothing. Neighborhood gossip he attributed to nothing more than the cheap inventiveness of baffled curiosity. Of the whereabouts of Dr. Allen he said he did not feel at liberty to speak definitely, but assured his inquisitors that the bearded and spectacled man would return when needed. In paying off the stolid Brava who resisted all questioning by the visitors, and in closing the bungalow which still seemed to hold such nighted secrets, Ward shewed no sign of nervousness save a barely noticed tendency to pause as though listening for something very faint. He was apparently animated by a calmly philosophic resignation, as if his removal were the merest transient incident which would cause the least trouble if facilitated and disposed of once and for all. It was clear that he trusted to his obviously unimpaired keenness of absolute mentality to overcome all the embarrassments into which his twisted memory, his lost voice and handwriting, and his secretive and eccentric behavior had led him. His mother, it was agreed, was not to be told of the change; his father supplying typed notes in his name. Ward was taken to the restfully and picturesquely situated private hospital maintained by Dr. Waite on Conanicut Island in the bay, and subjected to the closest scrutiny and questioning by all the physicians connected with the case. It was then that the physical oddities were noticed; the slackened metabolism, the altered skin, and the disproportionate neural reactions. Dr. Willett was the most perturbed of the various examiners, for he had attended Ward all his life and could appreciate with terrible keenness the extent of his physical disorganization. Even the familiar olive mark on his hip was gone, while on his chest was a great black mole or cicatrix which had never been there before, and which made Willett wonder whether the youth had ever submitted to any of the "witch markings" reputed to be inflicted at certain unwholesome nocturnal meetings in wild and lonely places. The doctor could not keep his mind off a certain transcribed witch-trial record from Salem which Charles had shewn him in the old non-secretive days, and which read: "Mr. G. B. on that Nighte putt ye Divell his Marke upon Bridget S., Jonathan A., Simon O., Deliverance W., Joseph C., Susan P., Mehitable C., and Deborah B." Ward's face, too, troubled him horribly, till at length he suddenly discovered why he was horrified. For above the young man's right eye was something which he had never previously noticed—a small scar or pit precisely like that in the crumbled painting of old Joseph Curwen, and perhaps attesting some hideous ritualistic inoculation to which both had submitted at a certain stage of their occult careers.

While Ward himself was puzzling all the doctors at the hospital a very strict watch was kept on all mail addressed either to him or to Dr. Allen, which Mr. Ward had ordered delivered at the family home. Willett had predicted that very little would be found, since any communications of a vital nature would probably have been exchanged by messenger; but in the latter part of March there did come a letter from Prague for Dr. Allen which gave both the doctor and the father deep thought. It was in a very crabbed and archaic hand; and though clearly not the effort of a foreigner, shewed almost as singular a departure from modern English as the speech of young Ward himself. It read:

> Kleinstrasse 11,
> Altstadt, Prague,
> 11th Feby. 1928.

Brother in Almousin-Metraton:—

I this day receiv'd yr mention of what came up from the Salts I sent you. It was wrong, and meanes clearly that ye Headstones had been chang'd when Barnabas gott me the Specimen. It is often so, as you must be sensible of from the Thing you gott from ye Kings Chapell ground in 1769 and what H. gott from Olde Bury'g Point in 1690, that was like to ende him. I gott such a Thing in Aegypt 75 yeares gone, from the which came that Scar ye Boy saw on me here in 1924. As I told you longe ago, do not calle up That which you can not put downe; either from dead Saltes or out of ye Spheres beyond. Have ye Wordes for laying at all times readie, and stopp not to be sure when there is any Doubte of *Whom* you have. Stones are all chang'd now in Nine groundes out of 10. You are never sure till you question. I this day heard from H., who has had Trouble with the Soldiers. He is like to be sorry Transylvania is pass'd from Hungary to Roumania, and wou'd change his Seat if the Castel weren't so fulle of What we Knowe. But of this he hath doubtless writ you. In my next Send'g there will be Somewhat from a Hill tomb from ye East that will delight you greatly. Meanwhile forget not I am desirous of B. F. if you can possibly get him for me. You know G. in Philada. better than I. Have him up firste if you will, but doe not use him soe hard he will be Difficult, for I must speake to him in ye End.

Yogg-Sothoth Neblod Zin
Simon O.

To Mr. J. C. in
Providence.

Mr. Ward and Dr. Willett paused in utter chaos before this apparent bit of unrelieved insanity. Only by degrees did they absorb what it seemed to imply. So the absent Dr. Allen, and not Charles Ward, had come to be the leading spirit at Pawtuxet? That must explain the wild reference and denunciation in the youth's last frantic letter. And what of this addressing of the bearded and spectacled stranger as "Mr. J. C."? There was no escaping the inference, but there are limits to possible monstrosity. Who was "Simon O."; the old man Ward had visited in Prague four years previously? Perhaps, but in the centuries behind there had been another Simon O.— Simon Orne, alias Jedediah, of Salem, who vanished in 1771, *and whose peculiar handwriting Dr. Willett now unmistakably recognized from the photostatic copies of the Orne formulae which Charles had once shewn him.* What horrors and mysteries, what contradictions and contraventions of Nature, had come back after a century and a half to harass Old Providence with her clustered spires and domes?

The father and the old physician, virtually at a loss what to do or think, went to see Charles at the hospital and questioned him as delicately as they could about Dr. Allen, about the Prague visit, and about what he had learned of Simon or Jedediah Orne of Salem. To all these inquiries the youth was politely non-committal, merely barking in his hoarse whisper that he had found Dr. Allen to have a remarkable spiritual rapport with certain souls from the past, and that any correspondent the bearded man might have in Prague would probably be similarly gifted. When they left, Mr. Ward and Dr. Willett realized to their chagrin that they had really been the ones under catechism; and that without imparting anything vital himself, the confined youth had adroitly pumped them of everything the Prague letter had contained.

Drs. Peck, Waite, and Lyman were not inclined to attach much importance to the strange correspondence of young Ward's companion; for they knew the tendency of kindred eccentrics and monomaniacs to band together, and believed that Charles or Allen had merely unearthed an expatriated counterpart—perhaps one who had seen Orne's handwriting and copied it in an attempt to pose as the bygone character's reincarnation. Allen himself was perhaps a similar case, and may have persuaded the youth into accepting him as an avatar of the long-dead Curwen. Such things had been known before, and on the same basis the hard-headed doctors disposed of Willett's growing disquiet about Charles Ward's present handwriting, as studied from unpremeditated specimens obtained by various ruses. Willett thought he had placed its odd familiarity at last, and that what it vaguely resembled was the bygone penmanship of old Joseph Curwen himself; but this the other physicians regarded as a phase of imitativeness only to be expected in a mania of this sort, and refused to grant it any importance either favorable or unfavorable. Recognizing this prosaic attitude in his colleagues, Willett advised Mr. Ward to keep to himself the letter which arrived for Dr. Allen on the second of April from Rakus, Transylvania, in a handwriting so intensely and fundamentally like that of the Hutchinson cipher that both father and physician paused in awe before breaking the seal. This read as follows:

Castle Ferenczy

7 March 1928.

Dear C.:—

Hadd a Squad of 20 Militia up to talk about what the Country Folk say. Must digg deeper and have less Hearde. These Roumanians plague me damnably, being officious and particular where you cou'd buy a Magyar off with a Drinke and ffood. Last monthe M. got me ye Sarcophagus of ye Five Sphinxes from ye Acropolis where He whome I call'd up say'd it wou'd be, and I have hadde 3 Talkes with *What was therein inhum'd.* It will go to S. O. in Prague directly, and thence to you. It is stubborn but you know ye Way with Such. You shew Wisdom in having lesse about than Before; for there was no Neede to keep the Guards in Shape and eat'g off their Heads, and it made Much to be founde in Case of Trouble, as you too welle knowe. *You* can now move and worke elsewhere with no Kill'g Trouble if needful, tho' I hope no Thing will soon force you to so Bothersome a Course. I rejoice that you traffick not so much with *Those Outside;* for there was ever a Mortall Peril in it, and you are sensible what it did when you ask'd Protection of One not dispos'd to give it. You excel me in gett'g ye fformulae so *another* may saye them with Success, but Borellus fancy'd it wou'd be so if just ye right Wordes were hadd. Does ye Boy use 'em often? I regret that he growes squeamish, as I fear'd he wou'd when I hadde him here nigh 15 Monthes, but am sensible you knowe how to deal with him. You can't

saye him down with ye fformula, for that will Worke
only upon such as ye other fformula hath call'd up from
Saltes; but you still have strong Handes and Knife and
Pistol, and Graves are not harde to digg, nor Acids loth
to burne. O. sayes you have promis'd him B. F. I must
have him after. B. goes to you soone, and may he give
you what you wishe of that Darke Thing belowe
Memphis. Imploy care in what you calle up, and beware
of ye Boy. It will be ripe in a yeare's time to have up
ye Legions from Underneath, and then there are no
Boundes to what shal be oures. Have Confidence in
what I saye, for you knowe O. and I have hadd these
150 yeares more than you to consulte these Matters in.

Nephren-Ka nai Hadoth
Edw: H.

For J. Curwen, Esq.
Providence.

But if Willett and Mr. Ward refrained from shewing this letter
to the alienists, they did not refrain from acting upon it themselves. No amount of learned sophistry could controvert the fact
that the strangely bearded and spectacled Dr. Allen, of whom
Charles's frantic letter had spoken as such a monstrous menace,
was in close and sinister correspondence with two inexplicable
creatures whom Ward had visited in his travels and who plainly
claimed to be survivals or avatars of Curwen's old Salem
colleagues; that he was regarding himself as the reincarnation
of Joseph Curwen, and that he entertained—or was at least
advised to entertain—murderous designs against a "boy" who
could scarcely be other than Charles Ward. There was organized
horror afoot; and no matter who had started it, the missing Allen
was by this time at the bottom of it. Therefore, thanking heaven
that Charles was now safe in the hospital, Mr. Ward lost no time
in engaging detectives to learn all they could of the cryptic
bearded doctor; finding whence he had come and what Pawtuxet

knew of him, and if possible discovering his current whereabouts. Supplying the men with one of the bungalow keys which Charles yielded up, he urged them to explore Allen's vacant room which had been identified when the patient's belongings had been packed; obtaining what clues they could from any effects he might have left about. Mr. Ward talked with the detectives in his son's old library, and they felt a marked relief when they left it at last; for there seemed to hover about the place a vague aura of evil. Perhaps it was what they had heard of the infamous old wizard whose picture had once stared from the paneled overmantel, and perhaps it was something different and irrelevant; but in any case they all half sensed an intangible miasma which centered in that carven vestige of an older dwelling and which at times almost rose to the intensity of a material emanation.

V. A Nightmare and a Cataclysm

1

And now swiftly followed that hideous experience which has left its indelible mark of fear on the soul of Marinus Bicknell Willett, and has added a decade to the visible age of one whose youth was even then far behind. Dr. Willett had conferred at length with Mr. Ward, and had come to an agreement with him on several points which both felt the alienists would ridicule. There was, they conceded, a terrible movement alive in the world, whose direct connexion with a necromancy even older than the Salem witchcraft could not be doubted. That at least two living men—and one other of whom they dared not think—were in absolute possession of minds or personalities which had functioned as early as 1690 or before was likewise almost unassailably proved even in the face of all known natural laws. What these horrible creatures—and Charles Ward as well—were doing or trying to do seemed fairly clear from their letters and from every bit of light both old and new which had filtered in upon the case. They were robbing the tombs of all the ages, including those of the world's wisest and greatest men, in the hope of recovering from the bygone ashes some vestige of the consciousness and lore which had once animated and informed them.

A hideous traffick was going on among these nightmare ghouls, whereby illustrious bones were bartered with the calm calculativeness of schoolboys swapping books; and from what was extorted from this centuried dust there was anticipated a power and a wisdom beyond anything which the cosmos had ever seen concentrated in one man or group. They had found unholy ways to keep their brains alive, either in the same body or different bodies; and had evidently achieved a way of tapping the consciousness of the dead whom they gathered together. There had, it seems, been some truth in chimerical old Borellus when he wrote of preparing from even the most antique remains certain "Essential Saltes" from which the shade of a long-dead living thing might be raised up. There was a formula for evoking such a shade, and another for putting it down; and it had now been so perfected that it could be taught successfully. One must be careful about evocations, for the markers of old graves are not always accurate.

Willett and Mr. Ward shivered as they passed from conclusion to conclusion. Things—presences or voices of some sort—could be drawn down from unknown places as well as from the grave, and in this process also one must be careful. Joseph Curwen had indubitably evoked many forbidden things, and as for Charles—what might one think of him? What forces "outside the spheres" had reached him from Joseph Curwen's day and turned his mind on forgotten things? He had been led to find certain directions, and he had used them. He had talked with the man of horror in Prague and stayed long with the creature in the mountains of Transylvania. And he must have found the grave of Joseph Curwen at last. That newspaper item and what his mother had heard in the night were too significant to overlook. Then he had summoned something, and it must have come. That mighty voice aloft on Good Friday, and those *different* tones in the locked attic laboratory. What were they like, with their depth and hollowness? Was there not here some awful foreshadowing of the dreaded stranger Dr. Allen with his spectral bass? Yes, *that* was what Mr. Ward had felt with vague horror in his single talk with the man—if man it were—over the telephone!

What hellish consciousness or voice, what morbid shade or presence, had come to answer Charles Ward's secret rites behind that locked door? Those voices heard in argument—"must have it red for three months"—Good God! Was not that just before the vampirism broke out? The rifling of Ezra Weeden's ancient grave, and the cries later at Pawtuxet—whose mind had planned the vengeance and rediscovered the shunned seat of elder blasphemies? And then the bungalow and the bearded stranger, and the gossip, and the fear. The final madness of Charles neither father nor doctor could attempt to explain, but they did feel sure that the mind of Joseph Curwen had come to earth again and was following its ancient morbidities. Was daemoniac possession in truth a possibility? Allen had something to do with it, and the detectives must find out more about one whose existence menaced the young man's life. In the meantime, since the existence of some vast crypt beneath the bungalow seemed virtually beyond dispute, some effort must be made to find it. Willett and Mr. Ward, conscious of the skeptical attitude of the alienists, resolved during their final conference to undertake a joint secret exploration of unparalleled thoroughness; and agreed to meet at the bungalow on the following morning with valises and with certain tools and accessories suited to architectural search and underground exploration.

The morning of April 6th dawned clear, and both explorers were at the bungalow by ten o'clock. Mr. Ward had the key, and an entry and cursory survey were made. From the disordered condition of Dr. Allen's room it was obvious that the detectives had been there before, and the later searchers hoped that they had found some clue which might prove of value. Of course the main business lay in the cellar; so thither they descended without much delay, again making the circuit which each had vainly made before in the presence of the mad young owner. For a time everything seemed baffling, each inch of the earthen floor and stone walls having so solid and innocuous an aspect that the thought of a yawning aperture was scarcely to be entertained. Willett reflected that since the original cellar was dug without knowledge of any catacombs beneath, the beginning of the passage would represent the strictly modern delving of young Ward and his associates, where they had probed for the ancient vaults whose rumor could have reached them by no wholesome means.

The doctor tried to put himself in Charles's place to see how a delver would be likely to start, but could not gain much inspiration from this method. Then he decided on elimination as a policy, and went carefully over the whole subterranean surface both vertical and horizontal, trying to account for every inch separately. He was soon substantially narrowed down, and at last had nothing left but the small platform before the washtubs, which he had tried once before in vain. Now experimenting in every possible way, and exerting a double strength, he finally found that the top did indeed turn and slide horizontally on a corner pivot. Beneath it lay a trim concrete surface with an iron manhole, to which Mr. Ward at once rushed with excited zeal. The cover was not hard to lift, and the father had quite removed it when Willett noticed the queerness of his aspect. He was swaying and nodding dizzily, and in the gust of noxious air which swept up from the black pit beneath the doctor soon recognized ample cause.

In a moment Dr. Willett had his fainting companion on the floor above and was reviving him with cold water. Mr. Ward responded feebly, but it could be seen that the mephitic blast from the crypt had in some way gravely sickened him. Wishing to take no chances, Willett hastened out to Broad Street for a taxicab and had soon dispatched the sufferer home despite his weak-voiced protests; after which he produced an electric torch, covered his nostrils with a band of sterile gauze, and descended once more to peer into the new-found depths. The foul air had now slightly abated, and Willett was able to send a beam of light down the Stygian hole. For about ten feet, he saw, it was a sheer cylindrical drop with concrete walls and an iron ladder; after which the hole appeared to strike a flight of old stone steps which must originally have emerged to earth somewhat south-west of the present building.

2

Willett freely admits that for a moment the memory of the old Curwen legends kept him from climbing down alone into that malodorous gulf. He could not help thinking of what Luke Fenner had reported on that last monstrous night. Then duty asserted itself and he made the plunge, carrying a great valise for the removal of whatever papers might prove of supreme importance. Slowly, as befitted one of his years, he descended the ladder and reached the slimy steps below. This was ancient masonry, his torch told him; and upon the dripping walls he saw the unwholesome moss of centuries. Down, down, ran the steps; not spirally, but in three abrupt turns; and with such narrowness that two men could have passed only with difficulty. He had counted about thirty when a sound reached him very faintly; and after that he did not feel disposed to count any more.

It was a godless sound; one of those low-keyed, insidious outrages of Nature which are not meant to be. To call it a dull wail, a doom-dragged whine, or a hopeless howl of chorused anguish and stricken flesh without mind would be to miss its most quintessential loathsomeness and soul-sickening overtones. Was it for this that Ward had seemed to listen on that day he was removed? It was the most shocking thing that Willett had ever heard, and it continued from no determinate point as the

doctor reached the bottom of the steps and cast his torchlight
around on lofty corridor walls surmounted by Cyclopean vaulting
and pierced by numberless black archways. The hall in which
he stood was perhaps fourteen feet high to the middle of the
vaulting and ten or twelve feet broad. Its pavement was of large
chipped flagstones, and its walls and roof were of dressed
masonry. Its length he could not imagine, for it stretched ahead
indefinitely into the blackness. Of the archways, some had doors
of the old six-paneled colonial type, whilst others had none.

Overcoming the dread induced by the smell and the howling,
Willett began to explore these archways one by one; finding
beyond them rooms with groined stone ceilings, each of medium
size and apparently of bizarre uses. Most of them had fireplaces,
the upper courses of whose chimneys would have formed an
interesting study in engineering. Never before or since had he
seen such instruments or suggestions of instruments as here
loomed up on every hand through the burying dust and cobwebs
of a century and a half, in many cases evidently shattered as if
by the ancient raiders. For many of the chambers seemed wholly
untrodden by modern feet, and must have represented the earliest
and most obsolete phases of Joseph Curwen's experimentation.
Finally there came a room of obvious modernity, or at least of
recent occupancy. There were oil heaters, bookshelves and tables,
chairs and cabinets, and a desk piled high with papers of varying
antiquity and contemporaneousness. Candlesticks and oil lamps
stood about in several places; and finding a match-safe handy,
Willett lighted such as were ready for use.

In the fuller gleam it appeared that this apartment was nothing
less than the latest study or library of Charles Ward. Of the books
the doctor had seen many before, and a good part of the furniture had plainly come from the Prospect Street mansion. Here
and there was a piece well known to Willett, and the sense of
familiarity became so great that he half forgot the noisomeness
and the wailing, both of which were plainer here than they had
been at the foot of the steps. His first duty, as planned long ahead,

was to find and seize any papers which might seem of vital importance; especially those portentous documents found by Charles so long ago behind the picture in Olney Court. As he searched he perceived how stupendous a task the final unraveling would be; for file on file was stuffed with papers in curious hands and bearing curious designs, so that months or even years might be needed for a thorough deciphering and editing. Once he found large packets of letters with Prague and Rakus postmarks, and in writing clearly recognizable as Orne's and Hutchinson's; all of which he took with him as part of the bundle to be removed in his valise.

At last, in a locked mahogany cabinet once gracing the Ward home, Willett found the batch of old Curwen papers; recognizing them from the reluctant glimpse Charles had granted him so many years ago. The youth had evidently kept them together very much as they had been when first he found them, since all the titles recalled by the workmen were present except the papers addressed to Orne and Hutchinson, and the cipher with its key. Willett placed the entire lot in his valise and continued his examination of the files. Since young Ward's immediate condition was the greatest matter at stake, the closest searching was done among the most obviously recent matter; and in this abundance of contemporary manuscript one very baffling oddity was noted. The oddity was the slight amount in Charles's normal writing, which indeed included nothing more recent than two months before. On the other hand, there were literally reams of symbols and formulae, historical notes and philosophical comment, in a crabbed penmanship absolutely identical with the ancient script of Joseph Curwen, though of undeniably modern dating. Plainly, a part of the latter-day program had been a sedulous imitation of the old wizard's writing, which Charles seemed to have carried to a marvelous state of perfection. Of any third hand which might have been Allen's there was not a trace. If he had indeed come to be the leader, he must have forced young Ward to act as his amanuensis.

In this new material one mystic formula, or rather pair of formulae, recurred so often that Willett had it by heart before he had half finished his quest. It consisted of two parallel columns, the left-hand one surmounted by the archaic symbol called "Dragon's Head" and used in almanacks to indicate the ascending node, and the right-hand one headed by a corresponding sign of "Dragon's Tail" or descending node. The appearance of the whole was something like this, and almost unconsciously the doctor realized that the second half was no more than the first written syllabically backward with the exception of the final monosyllables and of the odd name *Yog-Sothoth,* which he had come to recognize under various spellings from other things he had seen in connexion with this horrible matter. The formulae were as follows—*exactly* so, as Willett is abundantly able to testify—and the first one struck an odd note of uncomfortable latent memory in his brain, which he recognized later when reviewing the events of that horrible Good Friday of the previous year.

Y'AI 'NG'NGAH,
YOG-SOTHOTH
H'EE—L'GEB
F'AI THRODOG
UAAAH

OGTHROD AI'F
GEB'L—EE'H
YOG-SOTHOTH
'NGAH'NG AI'Y
ZHRO

So haunting were these formulae, and so frequently did he come upon them, that before the doctor knew it he was repeating them under his breath. Eventually, however, he felt he had secured all the papers he could digest to advantage for the present; hence resolved to examine no more till he could bring the skeptical alienists en masse for an ampler and more systematic raid. He had still to find the hidden laboratory, so leaving his valise in the lighted room he emerged again into the black noisome corridor whose vaulting echoed ceaselessly with that dull and hideous whine.

The next few rooms he tried were all abandoned, or filled only with crumbling boxes and ominous-looking leaden coffins; but impressed him deeply with the magnitude of Joseph Curwen's original operations. He thought of the slaves and seamen who had disappeared, of the graves which had been violated in every part of the world, and of what that final raiding party must have seen; and then he decided it was better not to think any more. Once a great stone staircase mounted at his right, and he deduced that this must have reached to one of the Curwen outbuildings—perhaps the famous stone edifice with the high slit-like windows—provided the steps he had descended had led from the steep-roofed farmhouse. Suddenly the walls seemed to fall away ahead, and the stench and the wailing grew stronger. Willett saw that he had come upon a vast open space, so great that his torchlight would not carry across it; and as he advanced he encountered occasional stout pillars supporting the arches of the roof.

After a time he reached a circle of pillars grouped like the monoliths of Stonehenge, with a large carved altar on a base of three steps in the center; and so curious were the carvings on that altar that he approached to study them with his electric light. But when he saw what they were he shrank away shuddering, and did not stop to investigate the dark stains which discolored the upper surface and had spread down the sides in occasional thin lines. Instead, he found the distant wall and traced it as it swept round in a gigantic circle perforated by occasional black doorways and indented by a myriad of shallow cells with iron gratings and wrist and ankle bonds on chains fastened to the stone of the concave rear masonry. These cells were empty, but still the horrible odor and the dismal moaning continued,

more insistent now than ever, and seemingly varied at times by
a sort of slippery thumping.

3

From that frightful smell and that uncanny noise Willett's attention could no longer be diverted. Both were plainer and more
hideous in the great pillared hall than anywhere else, and carried
a vague impression of being far below, even in this dark nether
world of subterrene mystery. Before trying any of the black
archways for steps leading further down, the doctor cast his
beam of light about the stone-flagged floor. It was very loosely
paved, and at irregular intervals there would occur a slab curiously pierced by small holes in no definite arrangement, while
at one point there lay a very long ladder carelessly flung down.
To this ladder, singularly enough, appeared to cling a particularly
large amount of the frightful odor which encompassed everything.
As he walked slowly about it suddenly occurred to Willett that
both the noise and the odor seemed strongest directly above
the oddly pierced slabs, as if they might be crude trap-doors
leading down to some still deeper region of horror. Kneeling by
one, he worked at it with his hands, and found that with extreme
difficulty he could budge it. At his touch the moaning beneath
ascended to a louder key, and only with vast trepidation did he
persevere in the lifting of the heavy stone. A stench unnamable
now rose up from below, and the doctor's head reeled dizzily
as he laid back the slab and turned his torch upon the exposed
square yard of gaping blackness.

If he had expected a flight of steps to some wide gulf of
ultimate abomination, Willett was destined to be disappointed;
for amidst that fetor and cracked whining he discerned only the
brick-faced top of a cylindrical well perhaps a yard and a half
in diameter and devoid of any ladder or other means of descent.
As the light shone down, the wailing changed suddenly to a

series of horrible yelps; in conjunction with which there came again that sound of blind, futile scrambling and slippery thumping. The explorer trembled, unwilling even to imagine what noxious thing might be lurking in that abyss, but in a moment mustered up the courage to peer over the rough-hewn brink; lying at full length and holding the torch downward at arm's length to see what might lie below. For a second he could distinguish nothing but the slimy, moss-grown brick walls sinking illimitably into that half-tangible miasma of murk and foulness and anguished frenzy; and then he saw that something dark was leaping clumsily and frantically up and down at the bottom of the narrow shaft, which must have been from twenty to twenty-five feet below the stone floor where he lay. The torch shook in his hand, but he looked again to see what manner of living creature might be immured there in the darkness of that unnatural well; left starving by young Ward through all the long month since the doctors had taken him away, and clearly only one of a vast number prisoned in the kindred wells whose pierced stone covers so thickly studded in the floor of the great vaulted cavern. Whatever the things were, they could not lie down in their cramped spaces; but must have crouched and whined and waited and feebly leaped all those hideous weeks since their master had abandoned them unheeded.

But Marinus Bicknell Willett was sorry that he looked again; for surgeon and veteran of the dissecting-room though he was, he has not been the same since. It is hard to explain just how a single sight of a tangible object with measureable dimensions could so shake and change a man; and we may only say that there is about certain outlines and entities a power of symbolism and suggestion which acts frightfully on a sensitive thinker's perspective and whispers terrible hints of obscure cosmic relationships and unnamable realities behind the protective illusions of common vision. In that second look Willett saw such an outline or entity, for during the next few instants he was undoubtedly as stark mad as any inmate of Dr. Waite's private hospital. He dropped the electric torch from a hand drained of muscular power or nervous co-ordination, nor heeded the sound of crunching teeth which told of its fate at the bottom of the pit. He screamed and screamed and screamed in a voice whose falsetto panic no acquaintance of his would ever have recognized; and though he could not rise to his feet he crawled and rolled desperately away over the damp pavement where dozens of Tartarean wells poured forth their exhausted whining and yelping to answer his own insane cries. He tore his hands on the rough, loose stones, and many times bruised his head against the frequent pillars, but still he kept on. Then at last he slowly came to himself in the utter blackness and stench, and stopped his ears against the droning wail into which the burst of yelping had subsided. He was drenched with perspiration and without means of producing a light; stricken and unnerved in the abysmal blackness and horror, and crushed with a memory he never could efface. Beneath him dozens of those things still lived, and from one of the shafts the cover was removed. He knew that what he had seen could never climb up the slippery walls, yet shuddered at the thought that some obscure foot-hold might exist.

What the thing was, he would never tell. It was like some of the carvings on the hellish altar, but it was alive. Nature had never made it in this form, for it was too palpably *unfinished.* The deficiencies were of the most surprising sort, and the abnormalities of proportion could not be described. Willett consents only to say that this type of thing must have represented entities which Ward called up from *imperfect salts,* and which he kept for servile or ritualistic purposes. If it had not had a certain significance, its image would not have been carved on that damnable stone. It was not the worst thing depicted on that stone—but Willett never opened the other pits. At the time, the first connected idea in his mind was an idle paragraph from some of the old Curwen data he had digested long before; a phrase used by Simon or Jedediah Orne in that portentous confiscated letter to the bygone sorcerer: "Certainely, there was

Noth'g butt ye liveliest Awfulness in that which H. rais'd upp from What he cou'd gather onlie a part of."

Then, horribly supplementing rather than displacing this image, there came a recollection of those ancient lingering rumors anent the burned, twisted thing found in the fields a week after the Curwen raid. Charles Ward had once told the doctor what old Slocum said of that object; that it was neither thoroughly human, nor wholly allied to any animal which Pawtuxet folk had ever seen or read about.

These words hummed in the doctor's mind as he rocked to and fro, squatting on the nitrous stone floor. He tried to drive them out, and repeated the Lord's Prayer to himself; eventually trailing off into a mnemonic hodge-podge like the modernistic *Waste Land* of Mr. T. S. Eliot and finally reverting to the oft-repeated dual formula he had lately found in Ward's underground library: *"Y'ai 'ng'ngah, Yog-Sothoth,"* and so on till the final underlined *"Zhro."* It seemed to soothe him, and he staggered to his feet after a time; lamenting bitterly his fright-lost torch and looking wildly about for any gleam of light in the clutching inkiness of the chilly air. Think he would not; but he strained his eyes in every direction for some faint glint or reflection of the bright illumination he had left in the library. After a while he thought he detected a suspicion of a glow infinitely far away, and toward this he crawled in agonized caution on hands and knees amidst the stench and howling, always feeling ahead lest he collide with the numerous great pillars or stumble into the abominable pit he had uncovered.

Once his shaking fingers touched something which he knew must be the steps leading to the hellish altar, and from this spot he recoiled in loathing. At another time he encountered the pierced slab he had removed, and here his caution became almost pitiful. But he did not come upon the dread aperture after all, nor did anything issue from that aperture to detain him. What had been down there made no sound nor stir. Evidently its crunching of the fallen electric torch had not been good for it.

Each time Willett's fingers felt a perforated slab he trembled. His passage over it would sometimes increase the groaning below, but generally it would produce no effect at all, since he moved very noiselessly. Several times during his progress the glow ahead diminished perceptibly, and he realized that the various candles and lamps he had left must be expiring one by one. The thought of being lost in utter darkness without matches amidst this underground world of nightmare labyrinths impelled him to rise to his feet and run, which he could safely do now that he had passed the open pit; for he knew that once the light failed, his only hope of rescue and survival would lie in whatever relief party Mr. Ward might send after missing him for a sufficient period. Presently, however, he emerged from the open space into the narrower corridor and definitely located the glow as coming from a door on his right. In a moment he had reached it and was standing once more in young Ward's secret library, trembling with relief, and watching the sputterings of that last lamp which had brought him to safety.

4

In another moment he was hastily filling the burned-out lamps from an oil supply he had previously noticed, and when the room was bright again he looked about to see if he might find a lantern for further exploration. For racked though he was with horror, his sense of grim purpose was still uppermost; and he was firmly determined to leave no stone unturned in his search for the hideous facts behind Charles Ward's bizarre madness. Failing to find a lantern, he chose the smallest of the lamps to carry; also filling his pockets with candles and matches, and taking with him a gallon can of oil, which he proposed to keep for reserve use in whatever hidden laboratory he might uncover beyond the terrible open space with its unclean altar and nameless covered wells. To traverse that space again would require his utmost fortitude, but he knew it must be done. Fortunately neither the frightful altar nor the opened shaft was near the vast cell-indented wall which bounded the cavern area, and whose black mysterious archways would form the next goals of a logical search.

So Willett went back to that great pillared hall of stench and anguished howling; turning down his lamp to avoid any distant glimpse of the hellish altar, or of the uncovered pit with the pierced stone slab beside it. Most of the black doorways led merely to small chambers, some vacant and some evidently used as storerooms; and in several of the latter he saw some very curious accumulations of various objects. One was packed with rotting and dust-draped bales of spare clothing, and the explorer thrilled when he saw that it was unmistakably the clothing of a century and a half before. In another room he found numerous odds and ends of modern clothing, as if gradual provisions were being made to equip a large body of men. But what he disliked most of all were the huge copper vats which occasionally appeared; these, and the sinister incrustations upon them. He liked them even less than the weirdly figured leaden bowls whose rims retained such obnoxious deposits and around which clung repellent odors perceptible above even the general noisomeness of the crypt. When he had completed about half the entire circuit of the wall he found another corridor like that from which he had come, and out of which many doors opened. This he proceeded to investigate; and after entering three rooms of medium size and of no significant contents, he came at last to a large oblong apartment whose business-like tanks and tables, furnaces and modern instruments, occasional books and endless shelves of jars and bottles proclaimed it indeed the long-sought laboratory of Charles Ward—and no doubt of old Joseph Curwen before him.

After lighting the three lamps which he found filled and ready, Dr. Willett examined the place and all its appurtenances with the keenest interest; noting from the relative quantities of various reagents on the shelves that young Ward's dominant concern must have been with some branch of organic chemistry. On the whole, little could be learned from the scientific ensemble, which included a gruesome-looking dissecting table; so that the room was really rather a disappointment. Among the books was a tattered old copy of Borellus in black-letter, and it was weirdly interesting to note that Ward had underlined the same passage whose marking had so perturbed good Mr. Merritt at Curwen's farmhouse more than a century and a half before. That older copy, of course, must have perished along with the rest of Curwen's occult library in the final raid. Three archways opened off the laboratory, and these the doctor proceeded to sample in turn. From his cursory survey he saw that two led merely to small storerooms; but these he canvassed with care, remarking the piles of coffins in various stages of damage and shuddering violently at two or three of the few coffin-plates he could decipher. There was much clothing also stored in these rooms, and several new and tightly nailed boxes which he did not stop to investigate. Most interesting of all, perhaps, were some odd bits which he judged to be fragments of old Joseph Curwen's laboratory appliances. These had suffered damage at the hands of the raiders, but were still partly recognizable as the chemical paraphernalia of the Georgian period.

The third archway led to a very sizeable chamber entirely lined with shelves and having in the center a table bearing two lamps. These lamps Willett lighted, and in their brilliant glow studied the endless shelving which surrounded him. Some of the upper levels were wholly vacant, but most of the space was filled with small odd-looking leaden jars of two general types; one tall and without handles like a Grecian lekythos or oil-jug, and the other with a single handle and proportioned like a Phaleron jug. All had metal stoppers, and were covered with peculiar-looking symbols molded in low relief. In a moment the doctor noticed that these jugs were classified with great rigidity; all the lekythoi being on one side of the room with a large wooden sign reading "Custodes" above them, and all the Phalerons on the other, correspondingly labeled with a sign reading "Materia." Each of the jars or jugs, except some on the upper shelves that turned out to be vacant, bore a cardboard tag with a number apparently referring to a catalog; and Willett resolved to look for the latter presently. For the moment, however, he was more interested in the nature of the array as a whole; and experimentally opened several of the lekythoi and Phalerons at random with a view to a rough generalization. The result was invariable. Both types of jar contained a small quantity of a single kind of substance; a fine dusty powder of very light weight and of many shades of dull, neutral color. To the colors which formed the only point of variation there was no apparent method of disposal; and no distinction between what occurred in the lekythoi and what occurred in the Phalerons. A bluish-gray powder might be by the side of a pinkish-white one, and any one in a Phaleron might have its exact counterpart in a lekythos. The most individual feature about the powders was their non-adhesiveness. Willett would pour one into his hand, and upon returning it to its jug would find that no residue whatever remained on its palm.

The meaning of the two signs puzzled him, and he wondered why this battery of chemicals was separated so radically from those in glass jars on the shelves of the laboratory proper. "Custodes," "Materia"; that was the Latin for "Guards" and "Materials," respectively—and then there came a flash of memory as to where he had seen that word "Guards" before in connexion with this dreadful mystery. It was, of course, in the recent letter to Dr. Allen purporting to be from old Edward Hutchinson; and the phrase had read: "There was no Neede to keep the Guards in Shape and eat'g off their Heads, and it made Much to be founde in Case of Trouble, as you too welle knowe." What did this signify? But wait—was there not still *another* reference to "guards" in this matter which he had failed wholly to recall when reading the Hutchinson letter? Back in the old non-secretive days Ward had told him of the Eleazar Smith diary recording the spying of Smith and Weeden on the Curwen farm, and in that dreadful chronicle there had been a mention of conversations overheard before the old wizard betook himself wholly beneath the earth. There had been, Smith and Weeden insisted, terrible colloquies wherein figured Curwen, certain captives of his, *and the guards of those captives.* Those guards, according to Hutchinson or his avatar, had "eaten their heads off," so that now Dr. Allen did not keep them *in shape.* And if not *in shape,* how save as the "salts" to which it appears this wizard band was engaged in reducing as many human bodies or skeletons as they could?

So *that* was what these lekythoi contained; the monstrous fruit of unhallowed rites and deeds, presumably won or cowed to such submission as to help, when called up by some hellish incantation, in the defense of their blasphemous master or the questioning of those who were not so willing? Willett shuddered at the thought of what he had been pouring in and out of his hands, and for a moment felt an impulse to flee in panic from that cavern of hideous shelves with their silent and perhaps watching sentinels. Then he thought of the "Materia"—in the myriad Phaleron jugs on the other side of the room. Salts too— and if not the salts of "guards," then the salts of what? God! Could it be possible that here lay the mortal relics of half the titan thinkers of all the ages; snatched by supreme ghouls from crypts where the world thought them safe, and subject to the beck and call of madmen who sought to drain their knowledge for some still wilder end whose ultimate effect would concern, as poor Charles had hinted in his frantic note, "all civilization, all natural law, perhaps even the fate of the solar system and the universe"? And Marinus Bicknell Willett had sifted their dust through his hands!

Then he noticed a small door at the farther end of the room, and calmed himself enough to approach it and examine the crude sign chiseled above. It was only a symbol, but it filled him with vague spiritual dread; for a morbid, dreaming friend of his had once drawn it on paper and told him a few of the things it means in the dark abyss of sleep. It was the sign of Koth, that dreamers see fixed above the archway of a certain black tower standing alone in twilight—and Willett did not like what his friend Randolph Carter had said of its powers. But a moment later he forgot the sign as he recognized a new acrid odor in the stench-filled air. This was a chemical rather than animal smell, and came clearly from the room beyond the door. And it was, unmistakably, the same odor which had saturated Charles Ward's clothing on the day the doctors had taken him away. So it was here that the youth had been interrupted by the final summons? He was wiser than old Joseph Curwen, for he had not resisted. Willett, boldly determined to penetrate every wonder and nightmare this nether realm might contain, seized the small lamp and crossed the threshold. A wave of nameless fright rolled out to meet him, but he yielded to no whim and deferred to no intuition. There was nothing alive here to harm him, and he would not be stayed in his piercing of the eldritch cloud which engulfed his patient.

The room beyond the door was of medium size, and had no furniture save a table, a single chair, and two groups of curious machines with clamps and wheels, which Willett recognized after a moment as medieval instruments of torture. On one side of the door stood a rack of savage whips, above which were some shelves bearing empty rows of shallow pedestaled cups of lead shaped like Grecian kylikes. On the other side was the table; with a powerful Argand lamp, a pad and pencil, and two of the stoppered lekythoi from the shelves outside set down at irregular places as if temporarily or in haste. Willett lighted the lamp and looked carefully at the pad, to see what notes young Ward might have been jotting down when interrupted; but found nothing more intelligible than the following disjointed fragments in that crabbed Curwen chirography, which shed no light on the case as a whole:

B. dy'd not. Escap'd into walls and founde Place
below.
Saw olde V. saye ye Sabaoth and learnt ye Way.
Rais'd *Yog-Sothoth* thrice and was ye nexte Day
deliver'd.
F. soughte to wipe out all know'g howe to raise
Those from Outside.

As the strong Argand blaze lit up the entire chamber the doctor
saw that the wall opposite the door, between the two groups of
torturing appliances in the corners, was covered with pegs from
which hung a set of shapeless-looking robes of a rather dismal
yellowish-white. But far more interesting were the two vacant
walls, both of which were thickly covered with mystic symbols
and formulae roughly chiseled in the smooth dressed stone. The
damp floor also bore marks of carving; and with but little difficulty Willett deciphered a huge pentagram in the center, with a
plain circle about three feet wide half way between this and
each corner. In one of these four circles, near where a yellowish
robe had been flung carelessly down, there stood a shallow kylix
of the sort found on the shelves above the whip-rack; and just
outside the periphery was one of the Phaleron jugs from the
shelves in the other room, its tag numbered 118. This was unstop-
pered, and proved upon inspection to be empty; but the explorer
saw with a shiver that the kylix was not. Within its shallow area,
and saved from scattering only by the absence of wind in this
sequestered cavern, lay a small amount of a dry, dull-greenish
efflorescent powder which must have belonged in the jug; and
Willett almost reeled at the implications that came sweeping
over him as he correlated little by little the several elements and
antecedents of the scene. The whips and the instruments of
torture, the dust or salts from the jug of "Materia," the two lekythoi
from the "Custodes" shelf, the robes, the formulae on the walls,
the notes on the pad, the hints from letters and legends, and the
thousand glimpses, doubts, and suppositions which had come

to torment the friends and parents of Charles Ward—all these engulfed the doctor in a tidal wave of horror as he looked at that dry greenish powder outspread in the pedestaled leaden kylix on the floor.

With an effort, however, Willett pulled himself together and began studying the formulae chiseled on the walls. From the stained and incrusted letters it was obvious that they were carved in Joseph Curwen's time, and their text was such as to be vaguely familiar to one who had read much Curwen material or delved extensively into the history of magic. One the doctor clearly recognized as what Mrs. Ward heard her son chanting on that ominous Good Friday a year before, and what an authority had told him was a very terrible invocation addressed to secret gods outside the normal spheres. It was not spelled here exactly as Mrs. Ward had set it down from memory, nor yet as the authority had shewn it to him in the forbidden pages of "Eliphas Levi"; but its identity was unmistakable, and such words as *Sabaoth, Metraton, Almousin,* and *Zariatnatmik* sent a shudder of fright through the searcher who had seen and felt so much of cosmic abomination just around the corner.

This was on the left-hand wall as one entered the room. The right-hand wall was no less thickly inscribed, and Willett felt a start of recognition as he came upon the pair of formulae so frequently occurring in the recent notes in the library. They were, roughly speaking, the same; with the ancient symbols of "Dragon's Head" and "Dragon's Tail" heading them as in Ward's scribblings. But the spelling differed quite widely from that of the modern versions, as if old Curwen had had a different way of recording sound, or as if later study had evolved more powerful and perfected variants of the invocations in question. The doctor tried to reconcile the chiseled version with the one which still ran persistently in his head, and found it hard to do. Where the script he had memorized began *"Y'ai 'ng'ngah, Yog-Sothoth,"* this epigraph started out as *"Aye, engengah, Yogge-Sothotha";* which to his mind would seriously interfere with the syllabification of the second word.

Ground as the later text was into his consciousness, the discrepancy disturbed him; and he found himself chanting the first of the formulae aloud in an effort to square the sound he conceived with the letters he found carved. Weird and menacing in that abyss of antique blasphemy rang his voice; its accents keyed to a droning sing-song either through the spell of the past and the unknown, or through the hellish example of that dull, godless wail from the pits whose inhuman cadences rose and fell rhythmically in the distance through the stench and the darkness.

> *Y'AI 'NG'NGAH,*
> *YOG-SOTHOTH*
> *H'EE—L'GEB*
> *F'AI THRODOG*
> *UAAAH!*

But what was this cold wind which had sprung into life at the very outset of the chant? The lamps were sputtering woefully, and the gloom grew so dense that the letters on the wall nearly faded from sight. There was smoke, too, and an acrid odor which quite drowned out the stench from the far-away wells; an odor like that he had smelled before, yet infinitely stronger and more pungent. He turned from the inscriptions to face the room with its bizarre contents, and saw that the kylix on the floor, in which the ominous efflorescent powder had lain, was giving forth a cloud of thick, greenish-black vapor of surprising volume and opacity. That powder—Great God! it had come from the shelf of "Materia"—what was it doing now, and what had started it? The formula he had been chanting—the first of the pair—Dragon's Head, *ascending node*—Blessed Saviour, could it be . . .

The doctor reeled, and through his head raced wildly disjointed scraps from all he had seen, heard, and read of the frightful case of Joseph Curwen and Charles Dexter Ward. "I say to you againe, doe not call up Any that you can not put downe

... Have ye Wordes for laying at all times readie, and stopp not to be sure when there is any Doubte of *Whom* you have ... Three Talkes with *What was therein inhum'd* ..." *Mercy of Heaven, what is that shape behind the parting smoke?*

5

M arinus Bicknell Willett has no hope that any part of his tale will be believed except by certain sympathetic friends, hence he has made no attempt to tell it beyond his most intimate circle. Only a few outsiders have ever heard it repeated, and of these the majority laugh and remark that the doctor surely is getting old. He has been advised to take a long vacation and to shun future cases dealing with mental disturbance. But Mr. Ward knows that the veteran physician speaks only a horrible truth. Did not he himself see the noisome aperture in the bungalow cellar? Did not Willett send him home overcome and ill at eleven o'clock that portentous morning? Did he not telephone the doctor in vain that evening, and again the next day, and had he not driven to the bungalow itself on that following noon, finding his friend unconscious but unharmed on one of the beds upstairs? Willett had been breathing stertorously, and opened his eyes slowly when Mr. Ward gave him some brandy fetched from the car. Then he shuddered and screamed, crying out, *"That beard ... those eyes ... God, who are you?"* A very strange thing to say to a trim, blue-eyed, clean-shaven gentleman whom he had known from the latter's boyhood.

In the bright noon sunlight the bungalow was unchanged since the previous morning. Willett's clothing bore no disarrangement beyond certain smudges and worn places at the knees, and only a faint acrid odor reminded Mr. Ward of what he had smelled on his son that day he was taken to the hospital. The doctor's flashlight was missing, but his valise was safely there, as empty as when he had brought it. Before indulging in any explanations, and obviously with great moral effort, Willett staggered dizzily down to the cellar and tried the fateful platform before the tubs. It was unyielding. Crossing to where he had left his yet unused tool satchel the day before, he obtained a chisel and began to pry up the stubborn planks one by one. Underneath the smooth concrete was still visible, but of any opening or perforation there was no longer a trace. Nothing yawned this time to sicken the mystified father who had followed the doctor downstairs; only the smooth concrete underneath the planks—no noisome well, no world of subterrene horrors, no secret library, no Curwen papers, no nightmare pits of stench and howling, no laboratory or shelves or chiseled formulae, no ... Dr. Willett turned pale, and clutched at the younger man. "Yesterday," he asked softly, "did you see it here ... and smell it?" And when Mr. Ward, himself transfixed with dread and wonder, found strength to nod an affirmative, the physician gave a sound half a sigh and half a gasp, and nodded in turn. "Then I will tell you," he said.

So for an hour, in the sunniest room they could find upstairs, the physician whispered his frightful tale to the wondering father. There was nothing to relate beyond the looming up of that form when the greenish-black vapor from the kylix parted, and Willett was too tired to ask himself what had really occurred. There were futile, bewildered head-shakings from both men, and once Mr. Ward ventured a hushed suggestion, "Do you suppose it would be of any use to dig?" The doctor was silent, for it seemed hardly fitting for any human brain to answer when powers of unknown spheres had so vitally encroached on this side of the Great Abyss. Again Mr. Ward asked, "But where did it go? It brought you here, you know, and it sealed up the hole somehow." And Willett again let silence answer for him.

But after all, this was not the final phase of the matter. Reaching for his handkerchief before rising to leave, Dr. Willett's fingers closed upon a piece of paper in his pocket which had not been there before, and which was companioned by the candles and matches he had seized in the vanished vault. It was a common

sheet, torn obviously from the cheap pad in that fabulous room
of horror somewhere underground, and the writing upon it was
that of an ordinary lead pencil—doubtless the one which had
lain beside the pad. It was folded very carelessly, and beyond the
faint acrid scent of the cryptic chamber bore no print or mark
of any world but this. But in the text itself it did indeed reek
with wonder; for here was no script of any wholesome age, but
the labored strokes of medieval darkness, scarcely legible to the
laymen who now strained over it, yet having combinations of
symbols which seemed vaguely familiar. The briefly scrawled
message was this, and its mystery lent purpose to the shaken
pair, who forthwith walked steadily out to the Ward car and gave
orders to be driven first to a quiet dining place and then to the
John Hay Library on the hill.

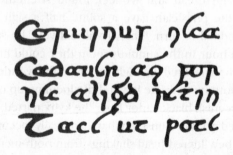

At the library it was easy to find good manuals of paleography,
and over these the two men puzzled till the lights of evening
shone out from the great chandelier. In the end they found what
was needed. The letters were indeed no fantastic invention, but
the normal script of a very dark period. They were the pointed
Saxon minuscules of the eighth or ninth century A.D., and brought
with them memories of an uncouth time when under a fresh
Christian veneer ancient faiths and ancient rites stirred stealthily,
and the pale moon of Britain looked sometimes on strange deeds
in the Roman ruins of Caerleon and Hexham, and by the towers
along Hadrian's crumbling wall. The words were in such Latin

as a barbarous age might remember—"*Corvinus necandus est. Cadaver aq(ua) forti dissolvendum, nec aliq(ui)d retinendum. Tace ut potes.*"—which may roughly be translated, "Curwen must be killed. The body must be dissolved in aqua fortis, nor must anything be retained. Keep silence as best you are able."

Willett and Mr. Ward were mute and baffled. They had met the unknown, and found that they lacked emotions to respond to it as they vaguely believed they ought. With Willett, especially, the capacity for receiving fresh impressions of awe was well-nigh exhausted; and both men sat still and helpless till the closing of the library forced them to leave. Then they drove listlessly to the Ward mansion in Prospect Street, and talked to no purpose into the night. The doctor rested toward morning, but did not go home. And he was still there Sunday noon when a telephone message came from the detectives who had been assigned to look up Dr. Allen.

Mr. Ward, who was pacing nervously about in a dressing-gown, answered the call in person; and told the men to come up early the next day when he heard their report was almost ready. Both Willett and he were glad that this phase of the matter was taking form, for whatever the origin of the strange minuscule message, it seemed certain that the "Curwen" who must be destroyed could be no other than the bearded and spectacled stranger. Charles had feared this man, and had said in the frantic note that he must be killed and dissolved in acid. Allen, moreover, had been receiving letters from the strange wizards in Europe under the name of Curwen, and palpably regarded himself as an avatar of the bygone necromancer. And now from a fresh and unknown source had come a message saying that "Curwen" must be killed and dissolved in acid. The linkage was too unmistakable to be factitious; and besides, was not Allen planning to murder young Ward upon the advice of the creature called Hutchinson? Of course, the letter they had seen had never reached the bearded stranger; but from its text they could see that Allen had already formed plans for dealing with the youth if he grew too "squeamish." Without doubt, Allen must be apprehended; and even if the most drastic directions were not carried out, he must be placed where he could inflict no harm upon Charles Ward.

That afternoon, hoping against hope to extract some gleam of information anent the inmost mysteries from the only available one capable of giving it, the father and the doctor went down the bay and called on young Charles at the hospital. Simply and gravely Willett told him all he had found, and noticed how pale he turned as each description made certain the truth of the discovery. The physician employed as much dramatic effect as he could, and watched for a wincing on Charles's part when he approached the matter of the covered pits and the nameless hybrids within. But Ward did not wince. Willett paused, and his voice grew indignant as he spoke of how the things were starving. He taxed the youth with shocking inhumanity, and shivered when only a sardonic laugh came in reply. For Charles, having dropped as useless his pretence that the crypt did not exist, seemed to see some ghastly jest in this affair; and chuckled hoarsely at something which amused him. Then he whispered, in accents doubly terrible because of the cracked voice he used, "Damn 'em, they *do* eat, but they *don't need to!* That's the rare part! A month, you say, without food? Lud, Sir, you be modest! D'ye know, that was the joke on poor old Whipple with his virtuous bluster! Kill everything off, would he? Why, damme, he was half-deaf with the noise from Outside and never saw or heard aught from the wells! He never dreamed they were there at all! Devil take ye, *those cursed things have been howling down there ever since Curwen was done for a hundred and fifty-seven years gone!*"

But no more than this could Willett get from the youth. Horrified, yet almost convinced against his will, he went on with his tale in the hope that some incident might startle his auditor out of the mad composure he maintained. Looking at the youth's face, the doctor could not but feel a kind of terror at the changes which recent months had wrought. Truly, the boy had drawn down nameless horrors from the skies. When the room with the formulae and the greenish dust was mentioned, Charles shewed his first sign of animation. A quizzical look overspread his face as he heard what Willett had read on the pad, and he ventured the mild statement that those notes were old ones, of no possible significance to anyone not deeply initiated in the history of magic. "But," he added, "had you but known the words to bring up that which I had out in the cup, you had not been here to tell me this. 'Twas Number 118, and I conceive you would have shook had you looked it up in my list in t'other room. 'Twas never raised by me, but I meant to have it up that day you came to invite me hither."

Then Willett told of the formula he had spoken and of the greenish-black smoke which had arisen; and as he did so he saw true fear dawn for the first time on Charles Ward's face. "It *came*, and you be here alive?" As Ward croaked the words his voice seemed almost to burst free of its trammels and sink to cavernous abysses of uncanny resonance. Willett, gifted with a flash of inspiration, believed he saw the situation, and wove into his reply a caution from a letter he remembered. "No. 118, you say? But don't forget that *stones are all changed now in nine grounds out of ten. You are never sure till you question!*" And then, without warning, he drew forth the minuscule message and flashed it before the patient's eyes. He could have wished no stronger result, for Charles Ward fainted forthwith.

All this conversation, of course, had been conducted with the greatest secrecy lest the resident alienists accuse the father and the physician of encouraging a madman in his delusions. Unaided, too, Dr. Willett and Mr. Ward picked up the stricken youth and placed him on the couch. In reviving, the patient mumbled many times of some word which he must get to Orne and Hutchinson at once; so when his consciousness seemed fully back the doctor told him that of those strange creatures at least one was his bitter enemy, and had given Dr. Allen advice for his assassination. This revelation produced no visible effect, and before it was made the visitors could see that their host had already the look of a hunted man. After that he would converse no more, so Willett and the father departed presently; leaving behind a caution against the bearded Allen, to which the youth only replied that this individual was very safely taken care of, and could do no one any harm even if he wished. This was said with an almost evil chuckle very painful to hear. They did not worry about any communications Charles might indite to that monstrous pair in Europe, since they knew that the hospital authorities seized all outgoing mail for censorship and would pass no wild or outré-looking missive.

There is, however, a curious sequel to the matter of Orne and Hutchinson, if such indeed the exiled wizards were. Moved by some vague presentiment amidst the horrors of that period, Willett arranged with an international press-cutting bureau for accounts of notable current crimes and accidents in Prague and in eastern Transylvania; and after six months believed that he had found two very significant things amongst the multifarious items he received and had translated. One was the total wrecking of a house by night in the oldest quarter of Prague, and the disappearance of the evil old man called Josef Nadek, who had dwelt in it alone ever since anyone could remember. The other was a titan explosion in the Transylvanian mountains east of Rakus, and the utter extirpation with all its inmates of the ill-regarded Castle Ferenczy, whose master was so badly spoken of by peasants and soldiery alike that he would shortly have been summoned to Bucharest for serious questioning had not this incident cut off a career already so long as to antedate all common memory. Willett maintains that the hand which wrote those minuscules was able to wield stronger weapons as well; and that while Curwen was left to him to dispose of, the writer felt able to find and deal with Orne and Hutchinson itself. Of what their fate may have been the doctor strives sedulously not to think.

6

The following morning Dr. Willett hastened to the Ward home to be present when the detectives arrived. Allen's destruction or imprisonment—or Curwen's, if one might regard the tacit claim to reincarnation as valid—he felt must be accomplished at any cost, and he communicated this conviction to Mr. Ward as they sat waiting for the men to come. They were downstairs this time, for the upper parts of the house were beginning to be shunned because of a peculiar nauseousness which hung indefinitely about; a nauseousness which the older servants connected with some curse left by the vanished Curwen portrait.

At nine o'clock the three detectives presented themselves and immediately delivered all that they had to say. They had not, regrettably enough, located the Brava Tony Gomes as they had wished, nor had they found the least trace of Dr. Allen's source or present whereabouts; but they had managed to unearth a considerable number of local impressions and facts concerning the reticent stranger. Allen had struck Pawtuxet people as a vaguely unnatural being, and there was an universal belief that his thick sandy beard was either dyed or false—a belief conclusively upheld by the finding of such a false beard, together with a pair of dark glasses, in his room at the fateful bungalow. His voice, Mr. Ward could well testify from his one telephone conversation, had a depth and hollowness that could not be forgotten; and his glance seemed malign even through his smoked and horn-rimmed glasses. One shopkeeper, in the course of negotiations, had seen a specimen of his handwriting and declared it was very queer and crabbed; this being confirmed by penciled notes of no clear meaning found in his room and identified by the merchant. In connexion with the vampirism rumors of the preceding summer, a majority of the gossips believed that Allen rather than Ward was the actual vampire. Statements were also obtained from the officials who had visited the bungalow after the unpleasant incident of the motor truck robbery. They had felt less of the sinister in Dr. Allen, but had recognized him as the dominant figure in the queer shadowy cottage. The place had been too dark for them to observe him clearly, but they would know him again if they saw him. His beard had looked odd, and they thought he had some slight scar above his dark spectacled right eye. As for the detectives' search of Allen's room, it yielded nothing definite save the beard and glasses, and several penciled notes in a crabbed writing which Willett at once saw was identical with that shared by the old Curwen manuscripts and by the voluminous recent notes of young Ward found in the vanished catacombs of horror.

Dr. Willett and Mr. Ward caught something of a profound, subtle, and insidious cosmic fear from this data as it was gradually unfolded, and almost trembled in following up the vague, mad thought which had simultaneously reached their minds. The false beard and glasses—the crabbed Curwen penmanship—the old portrait and its tiny scar—*and the altered youth in the hospital with such a scar*—that deep, hollow voice on the telephone—was it not of this that Mr. Ward was reminded when his son barked forth those pitiable tones to which he now claimed to be reduced? Who had ever seen Charles and Allen together? Yes, the officials had once, but who later on? Was it not when Allen left that Charles suddenly lost his growing fright and began to live wholly at the bungalow? Curwen—Allen—Ward—in what blasphemous and abominable fusion had two ages and two persons become involved? That damnable resemblance of the picture to Charles—had it not used to stare and stare, and follow the boy around the room with its eyes? Why, too, did both Allen and Charles copy Joseph Curwen's handwriting, even when alone and off guard? And then the frightful work of those people—the lost crypt of horrors that had aged the doctor overnight; the starved monsters in the noisome pits; the awful formula which had yielded such nameless results; the message in minuscules found in Willett's pocket; the papers and the letters and all the talk of graves and "salts" and discoveries—whither did everything lead? In the end Mr. Ward did the most sensible thing. Steeling himself against any realization of why he did it, he gave the detectives an article to be shewn to such Pawtuxet shopkeepers as had seen the portentous Dr. Allen. That article was a photograph of his luckless son, on which he now carefully drew in ink the pair of heavy glasses and the black pointed beard which the men had brought from Allen's room.

For two hours he waited with the doctor in the oppressive house where fear and miasma were slowly gathering as the empty panel in the upstairs library leered and leered and leered. Then the men returned. Yes. *The altered photograph was a very passable likeness of Dr. Allen.* Mr. Ward turned pale, and Willett wiped a suddenly dampened brow with his handkerchief. Allen—Ward—Curwen—it was becoming too hideous for coherent thought. What had the boy called out of the void, and what had it done to him? What, really, had happened from first to last? Who was this Allen who sought to kill Charles as too "squeamish," and why had his destined victim said in the postscript to that frantic letter that he must be so completely obliterated in acid? Why, too, had the minuscule message, of whose origin no one dared think, said that "Curwen" must be likewise obliterated? What was the *change,* and when had the final stage occurred? That day when his frantic note was received—he had been nervous all the morning, then there was an alteration. He had slipped out unseen and swaggered boldly in past the men hired to guard him. That was the time, when he was out. But no—had he not cried out in terror as he entered his study—this very room? What had he found there? Or wait—*what had found him?* That simulacrum which brushed boldly in without having been seen to go—was that an alien shadow and a horror forcing itself upon a trembling figure which had never gone out at all? Had not the butler spoken of queer noises?

Willett rang for the man and asked him some low-toned questions. It had, surely enough, been a bad business. There had been noises—a cry, a gasp, a choking, and a sort of clattering or creaking or thumping, or all of these. And Mr. Charles was not the same when he stalked out without a word. The butler shivered as he spoke, and sniffed at the heavy air that blew down from some open window upstairs. Terror had settled definitely upon the house, and only the business-like detectives failed to imbibe a full measure of it. Even they were restless, for this case had held vague elements in the background which pleased them not at all. Dr. Willett was thinking deeply and rapidly, and his thoughts were terrible ones. Now and then he would almost break into muttering as he ran over in his head a new, appalling, and increasingly conclusive chain of nightmare happenings.

Then Mr. Ward made a sign that the conference was over, and everyone save him and the doctor left the room. It was noon now, but shadows as of coming night seemed to engulf the phantom-haunted mansion. Willett began talking very seriously to his host, and urged that he leave a great deal of the future investigation to him. There would be, he predicted, certain obnoxious elements which a friend could bear better than a relative. As family physician he must have a free hand, and the first thing he required was a period alone and undisturbed in the abandoned library upstairs, where the ancient overmantel had gathered about itself an aura of noisome horror more intense than when Joseph Curwen's features themselves glanced slyly down from the painted panel.

Mr. Ward, dazed by the flood of grotesque morbidities and unthinkably maddening suggestions that poured in upon him from every side, could only acquiesce; and half an hour later the doctor was locked in the shunned room with the paneling from Olney Court. The father, listening outside, heard fumbling sounds of moving and rummaging as the moments passed; and finally a wrench and a creak, as if a tight cupboard door were being opened. Then there was a muffled cry, a kind of snorting choke, and a hasty slamming of whatever had been opened. Almost at once the key rattled and Willett appeared in the hall, haggard and ghastly, and demanding wood for the real fireplace on the south wall of the room. The furnace was not enough, he said;

and the electric log had little practical use. Longing yet not daring to ask questions, Mr. Ward gave the requisite orders and a man brought some stout pine logs, shuddering as he entered the tainted air of the library to place them in the grate. Willett meanwhile had gone up to the dismantled laboratory and brought down a few odds and ends not included in the moving of the July before. They were in a covered basket, and Mr. Ward never saw what they were.

Then the doctor locked himself in the library once more, and by the clouds of smoke which rolled down past the windows from the chimney it was known that he had lighted the fire. Later, after a great rustling of newspapers, that odd wrench and creaking were heard again; followed by a thumping which none of the eavesdroppers liked. Thereafter two suppressed cries of Willett's were heard, and hard upon these came a swishing rustle of indefinable hatefulness. Finally the smoke that the wind beat down from the chimney grew very dark and acrid, and everyone wished that the weather had spared them this choking and venomous inundation of peculiar fumes. Mr. Ward's head reeled, and the servants all clustered together in a knot to watch the horrible black smoke swoop down. After an age of waiting the vapors seemed to lighten, and half-formless sounds of scraping, sweeping, and other minor operations were heard behind the bolted door. And at last, after the slamming of some cupboard within, Willett made his appearance—sad, pale, and haggard, and bearing the cloth-draped basket he had taken from the upstairs laboratory. He had left the window open, and into that once accursed room was pouring a wealth of pure, wholesome air to mix with a queer new smell of disinfectants. The ancient overmantel still lingered; but it seemed robbed of malignity now, and rose as calm and stately in its white paneling as if it had never borne the picture of Joseph Curwen. Night was coming on, yet this time its shadows held no latent fright, but only a gentle melancholy. Of what he had done the doctor would never speak. To Mr. Ward he said, "I can answer no questions, but I will

say that there are different kinds of magic. I have made a great
purgation, and those in this house will sleep the better for it."

7

That Dr. Willett's "purgation" had been an ordeal almost as
nerve-racking in its way as his hideous wandering in the
vanished crypt is shewn by the fact that the elderly physician
gave out completely as soon as he reached home that evening.
For three days he rested constantly in his room, though servants
later muttered something about having heard him after midnight
on Wednesday, when the outer door softly opened and closed
with phenomenal softness. Servants' imaginations, fortunately, are
limited, else comment might have been excited by an item in
Thursday's *Evening Bulletin* which ran as follows:

NORTH END GHOULS ACTIVE AGAIN

After a lull of ten months since the dastardly vandalism
in the Weeden lot at the North Burial Ground, a
nocturnal prowler was glimpsed early this morning in
the same cemetery by Robert Hart, the night watchman.
Happening to glance for a moment from his shelter
at about 2 a.m., Hart observed the glow of a lantern
or pocket torch not far to the northwest, and upon
opening the door detected the figure of a man with
a trowel very plainly silhouetted against a nearby electric light. At once starting in pursuit, he saw the figure
dart hurriedly toward the main entrance, gaining the
street and losing himself among the shadows before
approach or capture was possible.

Like the first of the ghouls active during the past
year, this intruder had done no real damage before
detection. A vacant part of the Ward lot shewed signs

of a little superficial digging, but nothing even nearly the size of a grave had been attempted, and no previous grave had been disturbed.

Hart, who cannot describe the prowler except as a small man probably having a full beard, inclines to the view that all three of the digging incidents have a common source; but police from the Second Station think otherwise on account of the savage nature of the second incident, where an ancient coffin was removed and its headstone violently shattered.

The first of the incidents, in which it is thought an attempt to bury something was frustrated, occurred a year ago last March, and has been attributed to bootleggers seeking a cache. It is possible, says Sergt. Riley, that this third affair is of similar nature. Officers at the Second Station are taking especial pains to capture the gang of miscreants responsible for these repeated outrages.

All day Thursday Dr. Willett rested as if recuperating from something past or nerving himself for something to come. In the evening he wrote a note to Mr. Ward, which was delivered the next morning and which caused the half-dazed parent to ponder long and deeply. Mr. Ward had not been able to go down to business since the shock of Monday with its baffling reports and its sinister "purgation," but he found something calming about the doctor's letter in spite of the despair it seemed to promise and the fresh mysteries it seemed to evoke.

10 Barnes St.,
Providence, R.I.,
April 12, 1928.

Dear Theodore:—I feel that I must say a word to you before doing what I am going to do tomorrow. It will conclude the terrible business we have been going through (for I feel that no spade is ever likely to reach that monstrous place we know of), but I'm afraid it won't set your mind at rest unless I expressly assure you how very conclusive it is.

You have known me ever since you were a small boy, so I think you will not distrust me when I hint that some matters are best left undecided and unexplored. It is better that you attempt no further speculation as to Charles's case, and almost imperative that you tell his mother nothing more than she already suspects. When I call on you tomorrow Charles will have escaped. That is all which need remain in anyone's mind. He was mad, and he escaped. You can tell his mother gently and gradually about the mad part when you stop sending the typed notes in his name. I'd advise you to join her in Atlantic City and take a rest yourself. God knows you need one after this shock, as I do myself. I am going South for a while to calm down and brace up.

So don't ask me any questions when I call. It may be that something will go wrong, but I'll tell you if it does. I don't think it will. There will be nothing more to worry about, for Charles will be very, very safe. He is now—safer than you dream. You need hold no fears about Allen, and who or what he is. He forms as much a part of the past as Joseph Curwen's picture, and when I ring your doorbell you may feel certain that there is no such person. And what wrote that minuscule message will never trouble you or yours.

But you must steel yourself to melancholy, and prepare your wife to do the same. I must tell you frankly that Charles's escape will not mean his restoration to you. He has been afflicted with a peculiar disease, as you must realize from the subtle physical as well as mental changes in him, and you must not hope to see him again. Have only this consolation—that he was never a fiend or even truly a madman, but only an eager, studious, and curious boy whose love of mystery and of the past was his undoing. He stumbled on things no mortal ought ever to know, and reached back through the years as no one ever should reach; and something came out of those years to engulf him.

And now comes the matter in which I must ask you to trust me most of all. For there will be, indeed, no uncertainty about Charles's fate. In about a year, say, you can if you wish devise a suitable account of the end; for the boy will be no more. You can put up a stone in your lot at the North Burial Ground exactly ten feet west of your father's and facing the same way, and that will mark the true resting-place of your son. Nor need you fear that it will mark any abnormality or changeling. The ashes in that grave will be those of your own unaltered bone and sinew—of the real Charles Dexter Ward whose mind you watched from infancy—the real Charles with the olive-mark on his hip and without the black witch-mark on his chest or the pit on his forehead. The Charles who never did actual evil, and who will have paid with his life for his "squeamishness."

That is all. Charles will have escaped, and a year from now you can put up his stone. Do not question me tomorrow. And believe that the honor of your ancient family remains untainted now, as it has been at all times in the past.

With profoundest sympathy, and exhortations to fortitude, calmness, and resignation, I am ever

Sincerely your friend,
Marinus B. Willett

So on the morning of Friday, April 13, 1928, Marinus Bicknell Willett visited the room of Charles Dexter Ward at Dr. Waite's private hospital on Conanicut Island. The youth, though making no attempt to evade his caller, was in a sullen mood; and seemed disinclined to open the conversation which Willett obviously desired. The doctor's discovery of the crypt and his monstrous experience therein had of course created a new source of embarrassment, so that both hesitated perceptibly after the interchange of a few strained formalities. Then a new element of constraint crept in, as Ward seemed to read behind the doctor's mask-like face a terrible purpose which had never been there before. The patient quailed, conscious that since the last visit there had been a change whereby the solicitous family physician had given place to the ruthless and implacable avenger.

Ward actually turned pale, and the doctor was the first to speak. "More," he said, "has been found out, and I must warn you fairly that a reckoning is due."

"Digging again, and coming upon more poor starving pets?" was the ironic reply. It was evident that the youth meant to shew bravado to the last.

"No," Willett slowly rejoined, "this time I did not have to dig. We have had men looking up Dr. Allen, and they found the false beard and spectacles in the bungalow."

"Excellent," commented the disquieted host in an effort to be wittily insulting, "and I trust they proved more becoming than the beard and glasses you now have on!"

"They would become you very well," came the even and studied response, *"as indeed they seem to have done."*

As Willett said this, it almost seemed as though a cloud passed over the sun; though there was no change in the shadows on the floor. Then Ward ventured:

"And is this what asks so hotly for a reckoning? Suppose a man does find it now and then useful to be twofold?"

"No," said Willett gravely, "again you are wrong. It is no business of mine if any man seeks duality; *provided he has any right to exist at all, and provided he does not destroy what called him out of space."*

Ward now started violently. "Well, Sir, what *have* ye found, and what d'ye want with me?"

The doctor let a little time elapse before replying, as if choosing his words for an effective answer.

"I have found," he finally intoned, "something in a cupboard behind an ancient overmantel where a picture once was, and I have burned it and buried the ashes where the grave of Charles Dexter Ward ought to be."

The madman choked and sprang from the chair in which he had been sitting:

"Damn ye, who did ye tell—and who'll believe it was he after these full two months, with me alive? What d'ye mean to do?"

Willett, though a small man, actually took on a kind of judicial majesty as he calmed the patient with a gesture.

"I have told no one. This is no common case—it is a madness out of time and a horror from beyond the spheres which no police or lawyers or courts or alienists could ever fathom or grapple with. Thank God some chance has left inside me the spark of imagination, that I might not go astray in thinking out this thing. *You cannot deceive me, Joseph Curwen, for I know that your accursed magic is true!*

"I know how you wove the spell that brooded outside the years and fastened on your double and descendant; I know how you drew him into the past and got him to raise you up from your detestable grave; I know how he kept you hidden in his laboratory while you studied modern things and roved abroad as a vampire by night, and how you later shewed yourself in beard and glasses that no one might wonder at your godless likeness to him; I know what you resolved to do when he balked at your monstrous rifling of the world's tombs, *and at what you planned afterward,* and I know how you did it.

"You left off your beard and glasses and fooled the guards around the house. They thought it was he who went in, and they thought it was he who came out when you had strangled and hidden him. But you hadn't reckoned on the different contents of two minds. You were a fool, Curwen, to fancy that a mere visual identity would be enough. Why didn't you think of the speech and the voice and the handwriting? It hasn't worked, you see, after all. You know better than I who or what wrote that message in minuscules, but I will warn you it was not written in vain. There are abominations and blasphemies which must be stamped out, and I believe that the writer of those words will attend to Orne and Hutchinson. One of those creatures wrote you once, 'do not call up any that you can not put down.' You were undone once before, perhaps in that very way, and it may be that your own evil magic will undo you all again. Curwen, a man can't tamper with Nature beyond certain limits, and every horror you have woven will rise up and wipe you out."

But here the doctor was cut short by a convulsive cry from the creature before him. Hopelessly at bay, weaponless, and knowing that any show of physical violence would bring a score of attendants to the doctor's rescue, Joseph Curwen had recourse to his one ancient ally, and began a series of cabbalistic motions with his forefingers as his deep, hollow voice, now unconcealed by feigned hoarseness, bellowed out the opening words of a terrible formula.

"*PER ADONAI ELOIM, ADONAI JEHOVA, ADONAI SABAOTH, METRATON* . . ."

But Willett was too quick for him. Even as the dogs in the yard outside began to howl, and even as a chill wind sprang suddenly up from the bay, the doctor commenced the solemn and measured intonation of that which he had meant all along to recite. An eye for an eye—magic for magic—let the outcome shew how well the lesson of the abyss had been learned! So in a clear voice Marinus Bicknell Willett began the *second* of that pair of formulae whose first had raised the writer of those minuscules—the cryptic invocation whose heading was the Dragon's Tail, sign of the *descending node*—

OGTHROD AI'F
GEB'L—EE'H
YOG-SOTHOTH
'NGAH'NG AI'Y
ZHRO!

At the very first word from Willett's mouth the previously commenced formula of the patient stopped short. Unable to speak, the monster made wild motions with his arms until they too were arrested. When the awful name of *Yog-Sothoth* was uttered, the hideous change began. It was not merely a *dissolution,* but rather a *transformation* or *recapitulation;* and Willett shut his eyes lest he faint before the rest of the incantation could be pronounced.

But he did not faint, and that man of unholy centuries and forbidden secrets never troubled the world again. The madness out of time had subsided, and the case of Charles Dexter Ward was closed. Opening his eyes before staggering out of that room of horror, Dr. Willett saw that what he had kept in memory had not been kept amiss. There had, as he had predicted, been no need for acids. For like his accursed picture a year before, Joseph Curwen now lay scattered on the floor as a thin coating of fine bluish-gray dust.